Blood Reunited

Amber Belldene

OMNIFIC PUBLISHING
LOS ANGELES

Omnific Publishing
1901 Avenue of the Stars, 2nd floor
Los Angeles, CA 90067
www.omnificpublishing.com

First Omnific eBook edition, January 2014
First Omnific trade paperback edition, January 2014

Library of Congress Cataloguing-in-Publication Data

Belldene, Amber.
    Blood Reunited / Amber Belldene – 1st ed.
    ISBN: 978-1-623420-95-6
    1. Romance — Fiction. 2. Paranormal — Romance.
    3. Vampires — Romance. 4. Vampire Hunter — Romance. I. Title

10 9 8 7 6 5 4 3 2 1

Cover Design by Micha Stone and Amy Brokaw
Interior Book Design by Coreen Montagna

Printed in the United States of America

For Emily,
our weekly chats and your constant encouragement
give me the courage to face the challenges in all my vocations.
I truly could not have become a novelist without you.

CHAPTER 1

Bel jerked awake when his plane touched down. *Home sweet home.* He snorted at his own sarcasm. Did he even have a home? London, maybe. But it sure wasn't his father's house.

He'd slept through the entire flight from LA, a much needed refresher after his thirty-hour stint in the lab. But the work had been well worth it. Inside his jacket pocket, his fingers curved around a vial of victory — a protein called *hemoaurum*, which would cure all the vampires.

Bel Maras: Mercenary, Vampire Biologist, Hero.

He didn't mind the sound of that. He chuckled to himself as his private plane taxied down the single runway of the Sonoma County airport. With the vampire wasting disease cured, he could return to his real research, to the question that had driven him into science in the first place: how had he come to exist? He was the only known offspring of a human woman and a male vampire — a halfling, though he loathed the term.

The jet came to a complete stop, jarring him out of his thoughts. He phoned Andre, but his father didn't answer. Neither did Kos. So Bel tried option C.

"This is Pedro."

"Hiya. It's Bel. Just landed. How's the big guy?"

"You mean since his life's work just burned to the ground? He could be worse."

Andre had devoted himself to his vineyards the way Bel did to his research. Bel stared out at the grassy fields beyond the airport as a sympathetic tremor tightened his haunches and curled his toes. He didn't always see eye to eye with his father, but losing centuries of work straight-up sucked.

"Where is he now?"

"Holed up in the dining room with Kos and Lena."

"She's all right, then?"

"Yeah. Shaken, but all right."

Good thing. His brother had it bad for the human, and losing her might have wrecked poor Kos, which was surely why Andre had traded his vines for her safety.

"And Kos?"

"Wigged out and treating her like she's made of glass."

Bel laughed. "Sounds about right. I'll rent a car. Be there inside an hour. Cheers."

"Cheerio and tootle-loo, motherfucker."

Bel sighed. His new brother did love to provoke him. "Pedro. Make fun of my accent again, and I'll have Omar rip your tongue out, let it regrow, and do it again until you swear to stop your terrible impressions. *Comprende?*"

"Righty-ho."

The line went dead before Bel could utter more idle threats.

When he turned into the drive of the estate, the acrid odor of concentrated petrol and burned vegetation seeped in through the air conditioner vents. Hunters and their blasted napalm. The blackened hills rose up behind the house, their century-old vines incinerated.

He parked right next to the line of still-green shrubbery demarcating the invisible shield, powerful enough to deflect fire and major artillery, yet it didn't even glimmer in the sunlight. If he ever succeeded in unlocking the mysteries of his existence, he would make time to study the powerful magic generating the force field.

The estate's devastation was a scene right out of the apocalypse and he could almost feel sorry for his dear old dad. But as he left the car and slammed the door behind him, the clench of pity gave way to an entirely foreign sensation — his gut lit up with a warm buzz. He looked up, unsettled by the bizarre feeling. The house shone bright white against the ash-covered hillsides. Things had been tense between Bel and his father since his mother's suicide nearly two centuries ago. He'd never been comfortable at the Kaštel Estate, but this weird feeling was way more than his usual low-grade irritation with Andre.

His body thrummed with energy and a wave of unspecified desire washed over him, making him hungry and stirring his cock. Had he skipped breakfast? He couldn't remember.

The other, lower hunger…well, it was constant. He'd skipped satisfying that appetite for years, ever since Lexi had left.

With his hand on the brass handle of the front door, a sharp pain shot from his jawbone to the crown of his skull. He massaged his gums through his scratchy upper lip. Son of a bitch, that hurt. A toothache? Vampires didn't need to go to the dentist, not even a halfling. He'd survived nearly two hundred years without feeling this particularly excruciating pain and that was nowhere near long enough. What the hell was going on?

Inside, a murmur of voices came from the dining room. Kos spoke, and then Andre. Lena said something quietly and then a woman's voice rang out, loud and grating, in stilted English.

"There is cost."

Like the sound of nails on a chalkboard, hearing her voice tightened all the skin on his body. He shuddered. She sounded like a mail-order bride right off the boat from some Eastern Bloc country—possibly even their Croatian homeland. But all the vampires they knew had left Croatia long ago and were in hiding, lost to one another. Why would a human woman from the old country be at Andre's house?

He crossed the threshold into the room and caught a glimpse of her.

Oh, fuck. *Her.* After one hundred and fifty years.

Uta.

His throat dried out, and some deep instinct told him only her blood would quench the thirst.

Only, he didn't drink blood. As a halfling, he had the perk of a potentially unending life, with none of the downsides. He got to walk in the sun, drink bourbon, and eat steak, which he liked rare—but not hot, wet-blood-down-the-throat *rare*. Yet now, staring at Uta, he could have swallowed mouthfuls of the stuff.

She held her fine oval face high—long, narrow nose and a firm mouth. Had she always looked so captivating? He didn't recall this regal, sublime beauty.

He hadn't forgotten his hate, though, not for one day in the century and a half since he'd seen her last. His godmother, his best friend. The way she'd abandoned him when he most needed her—it was unforgettable, and unforgivable. His wrath burned in the back of his too-dry throat, as bitter as the ash and napalm in the air.

Yet some powerful force fastened his gaze firmly onto her.

Her gaze pierced him, her pupils filling her irises, making them black and glassy; her breathing was shallow; her fangs long. The strange force affecting him appeared to have control of her too.

What the hell was happening to them? No. There was no *them*. Never. Only a her and a him.

Her pink tongue darted out to rest on her lower lip and his cock twitched again.

She gritted her teeth and all the tendons in her neck flexed. Very slowly, as if she were straining against invisible chains, she turned her head away from him. Their stare broke with a snap, and he regained some control. He had nowhere to look but around the room.

His family circled the huge dining table, which had been cracked down the middle and bound up with thick jute rope like a big, angry vampire had pounded on it—which was entirely likely, but the story would have to wait. Both his brother, Kos, and Andre stared at him, their jaws dangling. Could they see the sensations roiling through him?

"That is price," Uta rasped.

Price of what? He'd clearly walked in on some important conversation and he was completely lost. But his mouth was too dry to speak and his knees wobbled. He took a chair, not one at the table but a closer one, pushed against the wall near the door.

Andre came to kneel beside him, resignation weighing down his features.

"Son, I am sorry. I did not know. But still, Mila wanted another child, and I have been thankful for you every day, even for all those years when we did not speak."

Shite. Andre had hardly ever said Bel's mother's name since her suicide. What did she have to do with any of this?

"I don't understand." He barely managed to croak out the phrase.

Uta's brown eyes glittered with a fiery intensity. He stared into them and a strange sensation slithered through his intestines, echoing the emotion in her gaze.

Kos cleared his throat and straightened his spine. "Auntie Uta was explaining to us how Lena and I could have a baby."

Oh, just that. A baby.

The word crashed into Bel's head like a hammer. His brain began to throb, pressing against his skull, a painful warning that his head might soon explode.

A baby with a vampire father and a human mother. A baby like him.

Just his luck. At the precise moment his life-long question might finally be answered, his body decided to undergo an atomic freak-out over seeing Uta again. What was wrong with him? He'd never wanted to fuck his anger out on someone before.

And he sure wasn't going to now—not when answers were in reach.

He gripped the seat and firmed up his backbone.

Kos stood up and raked his hands through his hair. "*Krist*, Bel, you look like a wrung-out rag."

"Nice to see you too," Bel bit out, trying to keep hold of his confused fury.

"This isn't good." Kos spoke directly to Andre.

Bel's throat seized up, causing a fit of coughs before he could ask. *What, damn it! What isn't good?*

"No. It is in fact quite bad." Andre examined Bel, peering into his eyes and then trying to part his lips with his fingers. Bel swatted him away.

Andre shook his head ominously. "He is not going to like it one bit."

"What?" Bel tried to shout, but it was the barest whisper. No one paid him any mind.

Zoey leaned over the table, all polished businesswoman. "Are you bonded?"

Bloody hell. Bonded? He shot up out of his chair. "No way. Not possible!"

"Yes," Uta said, her voice ravaged by whatever was happening to them. She had locked him in her gaze again and it did not waver, holding him prisoner, preventing him from lunging at her to silence her nonsense.

"Bel too?" Zoey asked.

"Yes."

"No," he growled, even as he wondered. Bonded? Could that possibly be the sense of homecoming that had lured him inside?

"But he's human." Kos pushed his chair back from the broken table and stood.

"Half." Uta sat up straighter, crossing one infinitely long leg over the other and glaring at Bel. "So, whatever he feel, only half as bad as what I feel."

He snorted. She wanted to throw down the gauntlet? He stood and all the years of his anger surfaced in a hot wave, searing his face.

"What the fuck are you talking about?" He clutched the edge of the table to resist lunging at her.

She rose to her full height and, damn, she was tall. He hadn't met a woman who stood eye to eye with him since he'd stopped growing, and he hadn't seen her since long before that. She hissed like a trapped cat, lithe and fierce, but afraid. In his own gut, a sharp stab of fight-or-flight reflex left him paralyzed in that third option — freeze.

"Sit, now," Andre boomed from beside him. "I know it is an effort for both of you, but at least pretend you are adults."

The order grated against Bel like steel wool, but he tried to comply. Rage would get him nowhere. He breathed calm into his veins and lowered himself into his chair. She mirrored the action.

"Start from the beginning." Bel barked the command, but she didn't respond.

Andre rubbed his eyes with his thumb and forefinger. "When your mother wanted a child with me, she asked Uta to be your godmother, and to help her conceive." He glanced at Uta, the muscles in his jaw contracting. "Uta resisted Mila for a long time and she warned her there might be unforeseen consequences. But Mila had a way of wearing a person down and eventually Uta gave in. I told them I did not want to know their secret magic, but I would do my part."

"It wasn't really magic, though," Kos said. "It might even make sense, scientifically speaking, if we knew more about vampire blood."

Uta blew out a dismissive breath. "Science! It just one more foolish human religion."

"What the fuck did they do?" Bel spat out the words, curiosity and fury tearing at him.

"Mila drank a regime of Uta's blood." Zoey covered Lena's hand with her own. "To help her body get ready for conception. It made her eggs stronger."

The scientist part of Bel's brain clicked into gear. Yeah. A woman's immune system might attack a half-vampire embryo as something foreign unless it was acclimated to vampire blood the way some pregnant women had to suppress their over-active immune systems with interferon.

"And then, her vampire-charged ovum was fertilized with Andre's blood," Kos said.

Like a ton of bricks in the face, the word hit Bel hard. "Blood?" he whispered.

"Some things are mystery," Uta said. "You young ones think you can know everything." She crossed her arms and huffed.

Bel angled his head, glaring at Andre. "Half of my DNA comes from your blood and not sperm?"

His father nodded.

"Damn it. That makes me your clone."

"Half a clone," Andre qualified.

Kos snorted. "No wonder you are so much alike."

The motion of Uta's tongue grabbed Bel's attention as she licked her lips. "Because Mila drank my blood, connection is forming between you and me before you are born."

"Why are you talking like that? Your English is appalling."

She flicked her hand. "Why bother? It just one more language is coming and going. Too many to remember."

"Because you sound like an idiot."

"Fuck you."

Of course, she would be able to swear fluently, even if she couldn't conjugate a verb. Problem was, images of fucking her sprang fully formed into his mind, of stripping her bare and pulling her onto his lap. Chances were her feet would touch the floor—good leverage.

A deep crimson blush bloomed on her alabaster skin as if she knew what he'd been thinking. Impossible. The red clashed with her mane of auburn hair, turning her altogether too ruddy.

"How do we break the bond?" he asked.

Andre whistled ominously, and Bel's stomach sank.

"We do not." Uta crossed her arms and her legs again, her blush now faded. "To break, one of us must die."

"I vote you," he said. No one laughed. Bel interlaced his fingers and leaned back, resting his head in his hands. For a long time, silence filled the room.

He stared at the ceiling, struggling to control his breaths as he remembered her unforgivable betrayal. Memories of a boyhood spent traipsing behind her around the island of Šolta came back in splotches.

"How long have you known?"

"Since you are born."

"What?" Andre bellowed. "Did you know it would happen? What the hell were you thinking?"

She laughed bitterly. "I am not knowing. Only after Bel is born, am I realizing the godmother must be having mate. If I am bonding with mate already, when Mila drank my blood, Bel is free."

"Really?" Lena's hopeful tone pawed at Bel's chest like a kitten batting a toy.

"So, if Lena drank my blood—" Zoey leaned closer to Uta "—the baby would not ever feel the way you and Bel feel right now?"

Uta nodded, blinking her pink-rimmed eyes.

"You would be insane to consider it." Andre closed his mouth to grind his molars.

Instinctively, Bel mimicked the motion, alleviating some of the ache in his gums.

Kos sighed at his mate like a lovesick puppy at a kitten. "Lena?"

She nodded. "I want to."

"No. It is too risky. I do not want—" Andre's thick black brows drew together and he took hold of Bel's hand, prying his fingers open and holding up the narrow glass tube. "Is this…?"

Bel nodded absently.

"The *hemoaurum? Davo*, son, I am so proud of you. A replacement for Blood Vine! Now the fire doesn't matter." He stood, holding the vial up to the light of the window.

For a moment, Andre's unfamiliar pride short-circuited every other thought in Bel's mind.

Then Uta stood and brushed at her clothes—if the shredded and bloody tatters of a suit could be considered clothes. "It not work."

Bel leaned forward, fists clenching. "Why not?"

"Some things are mystery." She shrugged.

Andre ignored her, addressing his question to Bel. "Have you tested it?"

"Not yet, but I engineered the protein to be chemically identical to the *hemoaurum* in Hunter blood and Blood Vine."

"You young ones are thinking you can know everything." Uta shook her head in an infuriating display of pity.

"I'll begin clinical trials right away."

"Why you are bothering? I am saying it not work."

Bel's fingers twitched with the need to wring her neck and he shot out of his chair.

Andre pushed him back. "Don't listen to her. You are the scientist. I trust you."

Bel tipped his head in a bow to Andre before turning back to her. "Well, this has been fun. Let's do it again in another hundred and seventy years. And in the meantime, have a nice life."

Uta clicked her tongue. "If I am helping it, we are not seeing each other ever again."

He exhaled with relief, but a hollow pit opened up in his gut and goose bumps rose up on every millimeter of his body, like even his skin strained toward her.

She blurred to him vampire-fast, narrowing her eyes and running one shiny red fingernail up the length of his hard-on. "Are you longing for me, Bel?" She spoke in a false whisper, loud enough even Lena could hear.

He refused to reply, but it didn't matter. Her answer pressed through his jeans.

"Good. Now you are knowing how I feel. Ten years since your Lexi is long time. I am having no relief since you are born. Welcome to my nightmare."

He stood, frozen, grasping to make sense of her words. How did she know so much about him?

She stepped back and strode to the door, calling over her shoulder. "I go home. Andre, your duties with Yousticia beginning immediately. You are expecting call from Loki." And then she was gone.

Bel closed his eyes and slumped into his chair, aching like every part of his body had been for a ride on a different roller coaster. He'd never felt so tired, and the fatigue mired his thoughts. Yet one thing was clear. In just a few words she'd explained the mystery he'd obsessed over for a century, and the explanation had done nothing to fill up the hollow inside him because the emptiness wasn't a gap in his knowledge after all — it was the lack of Uta herself, a vacancy that gnawed at him from the inside. That had been eating him alive from the day she'd rejected him, and he hadn't even known why.

A chair scraped on the floor and he opened his eyes. Everyone stared at him, their faces masks of horrified pity. Well, didn't that just make it a thousand times worse? He rose on wobbly knees and hobbled to the bar. The sharp smell of bourbon cleared his head, and he poured a whole highball of the nectar.

Steadier, he carried the glass back to the table, welcomed by the same wincing expressions. "Shite. Don't look at me like that."

Andre inhaled like he was preparing for a speech. "Bel, this is—"

Kos exploded in a fit of giggles. "Ten years?"

Oh hell no, Bel so did not want to talk about his sex life. He held up his palms, hoping to silence them. But Kos cast him a sidelong glance, winking.

When Bel grasped his brother's meaning, his bunched up shoulders relaxed, and he smiled, grateful for the distraction of brotherly ribbing.

Andre chuckled. He must have caught on to Kos's strategy. "Indeed, son, that is rather impressive. Even I never made it that long." He pressed his lips together in an obvious attempt to suppress a smile. Bel's hand clenched into a fist, wanting to punch Andre even if they were trying to make him feel better.

Zoey surprised him by jumping into the fray. "No wonder you think the whole vampires-not-being-able-to-masturbate thing is a fate worse than death."

Ouch. A low blow. She fit right into his family. He raised his glass to her. "Damn straight, Zoey. Which is why Uta is screwed, and I will be fine."

CHAPTER 2

The boat bounced over each wave, its hull slamming down again and again onto the choppy water like a thoughtless lover. Rotten, windy night for a cruise on the North Sea.

But the sky was clear, and this far from the light-saturated coast the stars shone brightly, taunting Uta. She refused to look. Stargazing belonged to another time, to the blink-brief years of her friendship with a young Bel, when they had stared at the night sky and talked of the greatest, and the smallest, things. Since she'd had to send him away, each point of light was a needle stabbing into her heart.

Runny sheep shit. Maudlin self-pity was the least attractive trait a creature could possess. Time for the much-needed distraction of battle.

An icy gust blew off the water and Uta hugged herself, shivering.

"Perhaps you should dress like a soldier," Oblak said in their native Croatian, "and not like a paramour on a lunch date."

She shot her arm out and smacked his temple with the back of her fingers. "I did not ask your opinion."

He chuckled as the shore came into view. From the hauntingly beautiful windswept dunes, plume after plume of smoke billowed, white under a bright sliver of moon in a clear sky. To the east, the lighthouse still stood—for the moment.

At dawn Caspar had reported the arrival of Hunters on his sparsely populated island. Over the course of the day, the enemy had demolished all the boats in the harbor and incinerated every house on the beach. Fortunately, the dwellings were summer cottages, left vacant with the arrival of fall so that only Caspar's vampire household remained. In all her years on the Justicia, Uta had never seen Hunters wreak such wanton destruction, acting without any regard for what the civil authorities would make of the violence. It did not bode well for the trajectory of Bennett's escalating war. Twenty vampire households had been destroyed or rescued by Uta's evac unit in the thirty days since she'd seen Bel at Andre's estate.

She had convened her unit on the mainland and waited for sunset while the household hid in Caspar's private keep, built into a cavern far below the base of the lighthouse. If they survived the day, they would ascend a secret staircase into the dunes and Uta's soldiers could collect them.

"I expect by now the sons of bitches know where Caspar is hiding," Oblak said.

"Yes." She hefted the satchel of c4, plus a detonator he had wired for her, and turned to face the other vampires. "Remember my instructions. I will wait for your signal before I blow the roaches up."

Five solemn faces nodded, exhausted by the endless stream of rescues they'd undertaken in the last month. She could not begrudge them their fatigue, a mirror of her own, but it was a liability in battle.

"Perk up, you melancholy goats," she commanded. "You are the heroes in this quagmire of a war. Tonight we save lives."

They rolled their eyes and grumbled, but the mood lightened. She gave them an exaggerated salute and turned, bending her knees and launching into the freezing air.

The wind stung her eyes and numbed her fingers as she flew circles over the island. Her hair came loose from its tie and blew about her like sea grass. Shoving it back with her forearm, she scanned the ground for Hunters scurrying in the night, but nothing moved on the grassy dunes.

Four trucks were scattered like dice in the sandy lot surrounding the lighthouse. The tower itself looked identical to drawings she had examined—a sheer, white, straight-sided exterior. The lantern was encased within large, thick stormproof panes. From the catwalk, one of the panes would open to give her access to the interior.

By all appearances, her plan was foolproof. They very nearly always were.

She alighted on the steel handholds of the catwalk and pressed her palms onto the glass to open it. It shook once, the tremble accompanied by a loud bang. After a short pause, a bang sounded again and after another pause of the same duration came a third powerful slam. That time, the entire edifice shuddered and groaned. The Hunters were battering at the door into Caspar's keep. How medieval. He had said it was a thick door.

Offshore, two yellow rubber dinghies cut rapid lines across the rough sea. When they beached, the vampires stormed over the dark dunes. Uta's keen eyes could barely discern the shadows of the householders moving toward them.

Or were those Hunters ambushing her soldiers? Sheep shit. Had she led her unit into slaughter? Would they even smell the scent of their enemies over the smoke blowing across the island and onto the sea?

One of the black-clad figures raised an arm, and a moment later a flare arced into the sky—the signal.

All was well.

She released a breath and then, from the narrow catwalk, she stepped inside the lighthouse and considered the rotating lamp, its glaring beacon flashing through the panels of the lens. She had planned to make a dramatic entrance by hurling it down at the Hunters, but thick heat filled the glass room like a sauna. The lens itself would be scorching. She spit on her hands and reached for it anyway. The damn thing seared her fingertips and she fanned them in the cool air as they healed. There had to be a less excruciating way to get the Hunters' attention.

She turned back to the storm pane she had come through. A sheet of glass taller than her and four feet wide would draw their notice if she dropped it on them. She yanked it off the hinges and used the pointy toe of her Ferragamo to raise the trapdoor, which opened onto stairs circling the interior wall. She peered down the wide-open center of the column. Forty feet below, the Hunters operated the battering ram in sync.

It required some finesse to angle the glass pane through the trap door without shouting a single curse, but once it was free she did not need to hold her tongue.

"You seem to have forgotten to mail my invitation to the party." She spoke in Croatian, although these Hunters were likely local, from Denmark or Sweden, perhaps.

They looked up all at once. Astonishment twisted into hatred on their faces. Men, young and middle-aged, on the Hunt and full of genocidal blood lust.

Their fervency repulsed her and she heaved the storm pane down with precision, aiming for two Hunters on the opposite side of the tower. It severed both their heads at once before it shattered against a pile of driftwood. They were probably planning to set the whole place ablaze with that kindling.

The remaining Hunters — ten or so — dropped the ram and reached for their machine guns. Uta tensed. She hated those things. The only firearm that could disable a vampire, their bullets stung like a motherfucking hornet. Her body tugged at her to shrink back from view but she stood firm and called out in Danish.

"Come and get me."

One of the Hunters fired upward and she gave in to instinct, plastering herself against the wall. Footsteps pounded on the wooden stairs and echoed deafeningly in the confined space. She counted to five, pulled the explosive device from its case, and tossed it down into the well of the lighthouse.

One. Two. Three.

It was time to go. Oblak had predicted the barrel of the lighthouse would turn into a cannon and shoot the Hunters and all the debris into the sky. She had a mind to watch that from the air. But the bomb ticking away at the bottom of the tower beckoned to her.

So what if ten more Hunters would soon be dead? One more household was relegated to exile. Nothing had been accomplished, and she would have to do it all again tomorrow. And worse, since seeing Bel at Kaštel, the ceaseless cycle of violence was no longer distraction enough to keep her longing for him at bay.

A familiar urge, nearly as old as Bel himself, gripped her and she folded at the waist. She could dive right down as if it were a plunge into the warm waters of the Adriatic. Surely the blast would spark the driftwood and set the wooden stairwell aflame. She could throw herself into the blaze and her suffering would be over in seconds.

But it would hurt Bel so badly he would wish he had died. Loki would know it was not an accident, and he would never forgive her. He would probably sorely punish Oblak, too. She stood and took one backward step toward the lamp room, resolved to keep fighting, for now.

The sound of the blast caught her off guard, but before it hit her head on, she dropped from the ledge and rode the wave of hot air upward. Mere feet from the vent cap of the lighthouse she somer-saulted backward and her shoes slammed against its surface just as it was blown off the building. She rocketed through the night sky, crouching feet first inside the airborne cap, which landed with a thud nose-down in the sand. Dusting off her slacks, she arose from the unexpected conveyance like Botticelli's Venus from her seashell. Uta the barn cat, always landing on her feet.

Oblak blurred to her side. "What the hell happened? You had plenty of time to get out."

"I got distracted."

He snorted. "Loki told me about your death wish, but I didn't believe him."

"Do not be foolish. I was simply curious what an explosion such as that would feel like."

"And?"

"Better than surfing a very large wave."

He shook his head, turning without another word and ambling toward one of the dinghies. She followed. They had just enough time to make it to Loki's before dawn.

CHAPTER 3

After a shower and a change of clothes, she kicked her feet up on Loki's couch. Her thoughts slogged through her brain and her belly growled, but she could not be bothered to get up and search out a meal, so she simply stared out the window. Over a white blanket of snow, daylight arrived very early in Norway, which made it an absurd place for a vampire to live. She despised its cold, its isolation, its damn stupid-sounding language. The sky reflected pink on the still water of his little fjord. His house was oddly quiet and she jittered with post-battle adrenaline. Only the sound of her nickel-plated knitting needles could soothe her frenetic mind.

She reached for her needles and tried not to think about diving into an explosion, tried not to think about Bel.

Click, click, click.

One thing to recommend Norway was the sheep — she never ran out of yarn.

She straightened the swath of navy blue blanket she'd already knitted, and her fire-engine red toenails peeked out from underneath it. A fleck of missing polish marred her right middle toe. She jabbed her needle into the couch cushion. Damn it, she'd just had that pedicure. Human cosmetics never withstood her duties.

Click, click, click.

The next time she glanced up, Loki was perched cross-legged in a chair, his ageless face in repose.

Her tongue tangled, struggling to call up words from the recesses of her mind. She had been speaking Croatian so often with her unit that the strange vowels of Norwegian, with all its fjords and Bjorks, filled her mouth like swallows of blood and flubbed her syllables. Still, she spoke it much better than English.

"News?" she asked.

"Yes." His word hung heavy in the air.

She didn't look up. *Click, click, click.* Just a few more rows and one more blanket would be complete.

"But before I tell you, you must feed. Oblak said you were injured."

She listened for an accusation, but heard none. "No." The intimacy of feeding grated on her since seeing Bel last month. He hated her, would never freely want her, and Uta found it unbearable to be so near to anyone else.

Loki flashed to her side so fast even *her* ancient eyes could not track him. "It has been too long." He cupped her face, forcing her to make eye contact. The prehistoric little male, perhaps a full foot shorter than her and impossibly boyish, employed a fatherly tone.

"Uta, I need you strong." He snapped his fingers and Nils, the finest piece of male flesh Loki employed, appeared in a doorway.

His face was all sharp Scandinavian lines, the planes of his chest shown off by a handsome sweater. Had she made that? It was impractical to keep track of these things. But the raglan looked good, *he* looked good, and her stomach growled at the musky evergreen scent radiating from him.

"Fine. I will eat."

With a buoyant step, he crossed to the couch and raised his eyebrows in invitation. She'd fed from him many times before, but not since her reunion with Bel — not since her body had been awakened to desires she'd buried for decades, which made this a bad idea.

"I can't."

"You must, Uta." Loki flashed to Nils and pierced the human's finger with a fang, tempting her with the iron scent.

When the human tilted his neck submissively, she was too hungry to resist. Straddling his hips, she perched herself on his lap and licked a long line up a secondary artery, its salty pulse calling to her tongue through his skin. She sank her fangs into him, the gush of blood sending delicious heat down her throat.

Experienced servants like Nils knew how to control their response to the bliss of a vampire bite. But Uta was old. Very old. And her bite was off-the-charts powerful on the bite-pleasure scale. So it took all of two seconds for the human's cock to harden, pressing against her pubic bone—against flesh that instantly flushed and tingled in a painful taunt. She could push his erection into her *pička* and grind on top of him for hours, and she'd never find relief. Only her bonded mate, only Bel, could satisfy her.

And since that wasn't going to happen, it was better to feel nothing at all.

She sucked down one more desperate swallow of blood before licking Nils's wounds closed. Pulling away, she examined his face. She'd hardly taken any blood, but a vampire must always ensure the health of the household. His eyes had glazed and his cheeks glowed a lusty pink. She'd give anything, her very life, to see that look on Bel's face just once.

Nils's eyes widened ever so slightly as if he could read her desire on her face. "Uta, I would gladly serve all your needs."

She shook her head and he frowned—the second reaction just as slight as the first. A well trained householder, but he hadn't managed to hide his hurt. If she were a nice vampire, she'd tell him how truly gorgeous he was and how very much she wished he could give her what she needed.

"Out. I need to speak to Loki."

When the blood slave exited, Loki clucked, chiding her for misusing his human. Then he powered on a flat screen that hung over his mammoth stone hearth. She hopped to her feet and froze after only one step, paralyzed by the horrific images on the screen—charred human remains, some clearly the blackened skeletons of children. She gasped. A nearly two-thousand-year-long life gave Uta a paradoxical appreciation for the preciousness of childhood.

Hours ago she had resolved to live, only to face this. Nils's blood curdled in her stomach and she held herself motionless, using her vampire strength to suppress the urge to vomit.

Loki waited for her to compose herself before speaking. "Three vampire attacks on Hunter cells: Indonesia, Chile, British Columbia. The humans were completely wiped out—men, women and children."

She exhaled slowly. "They know." The secret Uta had long-protected must have leaked—either from Andre's household where the vampire Pedro had taken the Hunter Lucas Bennett as a lover, or from the cruel Ethan Bennett's own research. Regardless of the source of the rumor, if vampires were now slaughtering Hunters *en masse*, it could only be because they suspected the Hunters' blood would cure their wasting disease.

"It would seem they know something." Loki's gaze traveled over Uta.

Mangy sheep scrotum, that was bad news. Where had her knitting gone? "Are Sadavir and his aggressionists behind this attack? I will kill them." She stormed toward the door. "I will hunt the bloodsuckers down one by one and take their heads. I will deprive them of the honor of sun-walking."

Loki grabbed her arm and held it fast. "Uta."

Perhaps only creatures as ancient as him could convey such a plethora of emotions in the timbres of a single voice—grief and anger were the high and low tones, with harmonies of impatience and concern.

She shied, turning from him. How could she bury her emotions under anger if he spoke to her that way?

"It is not your fault," he continued. "It is Bennett's. He escalated this war. He brought about the death of thousands of vampires and householders."

"I should have protected the secret better." She walked up to the screen, staring into the empty eye-sockets of a tiny, blackened skull. "I should have scoured their artifacts and made certain no one ever discovered the secret."

"And exterminated every one of them? We would be no better than them."

"We are no better. These are revenge killings, Loki. There is no justice to these deaths, nor is there logic in killing the source of precious blood, if the secret I guard is correct."

"Perhaps they also took hostages. With everyone in the compounds dead, there is no way to confirm the existence of survivors."

Uta could not look away from the television. "It is all my fault."

Loki flipped off the screen and took her hand. "Child, I grow tired of your self-recriminations. You are not Atlas."

She yanked away her hand. "Atlas was a self-important prick."

"Pot. Kettle."

His patronizing smile baited her, but she couldn't muster up the energy to be annoyed.

"You must tell me everything, Uta."

"The cost of breaking my vow is high. I will only do so once, in front of the entire Justicia." She pressed her fingers to her lips, closed tight, and tried not to think of the consequences.

"All right. I already have plans to convene them. Pack your bags. We are going to the Kaštel Estate."

Kaštel. Where she would be forced to break her vow. And to see Bel—her greatest failure ever.

"Loki, please."

He pulled her into a sideways embrace, the only kind that worked across their height difference. "You will face him, child, and you will survive, just as you always have. As our kind always has."

"Always has to end sometime."

"Nonsense," Loki said. Of the many tones in his round, melodious voice, not one rang with conviction.

CHAPTER 4

In Lucas's empty gut, hot coffee sloshed and mixed with too much stomach acid. He reached for one of Lena's scones on a tray in the center of the dining room table, finally mended after Andre had split it in a heartbroken rage. Outside the wall of windows, green grass had begun to sprout over the ashen hillsides like a promise, though every few feet, the promise was broken by the skeletal black vines straining skyward. New life might come, but it would not be the life his vampire friends needed.

The scone crumbled in his hand.

Zoey aimed the projector at the wall so everyone could see the photos Loki had sent to the newest member of the vampire Justicia, Andre Maras.

The vampire's ruggedly handsome face pulled into a grimace. "In all my years, vampires have never retaliated like this."

The old guy never really looked old, but since the fire, a cloud of defeat surrounded him, slumping his shoulders and adding years. Secretly Lucas preferred the change — dejected Andre was slightly less scary.

"It's not a retaliation. It's a feeding frenzy." Pedro stood behind Lucas's chair, resting his elbows on the seat back in a way that grounded Lucas.

"He's right." Zoey scrolled the screen so the report came into view. "The women, and the children…" Her voice had lost its professional air, trailing off on a gasp.

Kos stood alone, without Lena. Good thing, too, since she had baby fever. She didn't need to see the photos.

None of them did.

As far as breakfast scenes went, it was the most surreal of Lucas's life. Vampires had learned about the magic in his blood. Now they were slaughtering his people. He shivered. No—Hunters weren't his people anymore, maybe they never had been. The vampires sat discussing his worst fears over scones, which they didn't actually eat. And these once-frightening creatures, who had accepted him, sat grieving for the lives of their enemies.

What the hell was wrong with them?

"Snap out of it, you pussies," Lucas said. "This is no worse than the slaughter of household women and children that Hunters have been perpetrating for centuries. Or, if you're a lucky vampire, you get the slow death of the wasting disease instead."

No one replied, and everyone's eyes traced chaotic lines around the room in what had to be an attempt not to look at one another. The two other humans, Leo and Vania, reached for scones, and Lucas pitied the vampires they didn't have the distraction. Pedro pulled out the seat next to him. Its legs grated against the floor, setting Lucas's teeth on edge.

The big clock's pendulum swung. *Tick, tock.* Deafening even to his human ears. Each tock ratcheted up the tension in the room.

Pedro began to tap his finger in time with the clock. *Tick, tock. Tick, tock. Tick, tock.* Finally, he slapped his palm onto the table. "*Madre de Dios,* someone leaked the information." With a promise of protection, his warm hand settled on Lucas's thigh.

"Who would have done that?" Kos looked around the room. "Surely none of us."

Andre shook his head. "No one here has anything to gain."

"Could it have been someone on the Justicia?" Zoey asked.

"As far as I know, Uta has not shared her suspicions with them," Andre answered.

Kos rubbed both his hands over his head, smoothing back his short blond hair. "*Krist,* Hunters were bloodthirsty before they felt defensive. This will only amplify their violence. Soon, the human governments will be drawn in and then we are all at risk."

Lucas leaned his forehead into the heels of his hand, his eyes fixated on the scar of the giant crack running the length of the table. "It had to be Ethan." His words came out a whisper, meant only for the oak beneath his face.

"What?" several voices chimed at the same time.

He sat back, crossing his arms. "It's his type of move. He's the only one who benefits from an all-out war. All along, he's incited fear, and gained power from it. And of course, the Hunters would never suspect him."

"But how could he spread a rumor to vampires?" Kos asked. "Most of us don't even know how to contact each other."

"I don't know." Lucas hugged his ribs tight.

Pedro pointed at the wall, where the images had been. "Which was the first attack?"

"Chile was twenty-two hours ago. British Columbia eighteen." Zoey turned the projector on, and the final image reappeared. "And Indonesia, eleven hours ago."

Pedro didn't respond to the data, and Lucas wondered what he was thinking.

Zoey opened the briefing document and skimmed it. "Thirty-six hours ago, there were also two smaller attacks in Europe. They were simultaneous, and involved the cells positioned in former vampire enclaves." She rested her chin in her palm. "What does that mean?"

"Well, take Croatia, for instance," Kos said. "There is a small Hunter cell in Dalmatia whose purpose is to prevent the refugees from returning there. That's why the wasting disease is their best weapon. If vampires could return from exile, they would all be at their full strength."

"And they would have no need of Hunter blood." Andre's tone was bitter.

"Unless you count sunlight as a need," Kos retorted. They still weren't sure whether Hunter blood, or Blood Vine for that matter, would allow them to tolerate the sun; the conundrum was how to find out without getting fried to a crisp.

"So," Pedro called them back to focus, "there were two attacks on these Hunter outposts. How many died?"

It took Zoey a few seconds to find the information in the email. "All together, twenty-five."

Pedro reached down and scratched at his ankle. His memories of the torture Lucas's sadistic brother had inflicted on him seemed to surface occasionally as an itch and he'd repeated the unconscious gesture every time they talked about Ethan. Thankfully, since the two of them had become lovers, that itch seemed to be the only lasting damage from the trauma.

After another moment, Pedro straightened. "It had to be Ethan. He attacked them to set a precedent, then somehow spread a message to vampires encouraging them to do the same."

In silence that followed, the clock pendulum grated on Lucas—how could all these vampires with super-hearing stand that thing?

It had been Ethan. *Tick, tock, tick, tock.* Each click of the second hand drove certainty into Lucas's bones.

He glanced at his lover. Pedro combed his persistently fallen lock of black hair off his forehead, revealing his once-blue eyes, now turned golden from Lucas's own Hunter blood. Those yellow eyes, set off by all his bronze skin, were orders of magnitude sexier than they'd ever been in a Bennett, or any Hunter for that matter.

A Hunter-eyed vampire. Pedro would never be safe. None of them would be, as long as Ethan lived.

So Lucas had to kill his brother. Simple as that.

He stood. "I'll search online and try to find evidence that he's spreading the news about the Hunter blood. Leo, want to help?"

Lucas's fellow ex-Hunter Leo no longer looked like a kid. A month of training with Bel's crew of vampire mercenaries had turned his baby fat to muscle. The kid was fit, and cute in a boyishly handsome way that his carefully cultivated beard of stubble couldn't hide. And he had become an asset because of his insider knowledge of online Hunter networks. With Leo on their side they'd had ringside seats to Ethan's ascension as the Hunters' leader.

"Already on it," Leo answered. As usual, he had two laptops in front of him at the same time.

More thick silence followed Leo's words, but before the clock could tock again Pedro broke the spell. "Damn, it's stuffy in here. Where's Bel when you need him?"

"In San Francisco. He's monitoring his test subjects," Kos answered. "But if he were here, he'd say: 'Did any of you jerks die last night? Then cheer up, we've got work to do.'"

Zoey cleared her throat, and all eyes focused on her. "Nice try Kos, but this is what he would say." Zoey slid halfway out of her chair in a sullen slouch very reminiscent of Bel and crossed her arms.

"Those Hunter attacks are total bollocks. But the good news is, unlike you vampire fools, I can still wank. And that's a lot more fun than this meeting. So, I'm going upstairs to enjoy the only power I have that you don't. Later!"

She'd nailed his working class London accent and Lucas laughed so hard his side hurt. Andre turned the color of a tomato. Kos slapped his knee. Bel's lieutenant and resident fire-starter, Vania, snickered behind her hands, perhaps not wanting to seem too disloyal to her boss. And just like that, even without being in the room, Bel had lightened the mood.

CHAPTER 5

Bel's hands trembled as he set down the rack of vials on the stainless steel countertop. Over the pissed-off sound of The Ramones on his headphones, the tubes clattered.

Should he even bother running the tests? Clearly the treatment had failed — he'd failed.

The music fit his mood like a tailored suit, not that he'd ever worn one.

I hear you, Joey. Being sedated sounds perfect right about now.

He scanned the shelves, of half a mind to begin processing the blood, even though he knew it hadn't worked. The borrowed lab was small, but packed full of shiny new equipment. Only a letter from an old friend at Oxford and a very large check from Bel had opened up the prized workspace in the basement of the research hospital. He'd paid for it. He may as well get his money's worth. He reached for a flask. At least he could find out whether any of the *hemoaurum* he'd infused into the patients remained. Maybe it was just slow to work. The flask slid from his grip and clanged against the countertop; apparently it didn't believe that bit of fancy any more than Bel did.

Shite.

Andre was depending on him. All the vampires in the whole bloody world depended on him, but his test subjects fared no better now than they had two weeks ago. Federico, one of the frailest vampires, had even whispered his fear that his wife Liliana would die very soon. And she wasn't the only one so far gone — the wasting disease had decimated the entire test group, leaving them as weak and lethargic as the residents of a human nursing home.

He turned up the volume on his tunes and tried to silence his worries with Joey Ramone's shouts.

The door to the small lab swung open and bumped Bel into the counter, jostling the rack again. He caught the thing before all the tubes toppled, and reared around to shout at the intruder—but it wasn't one. It was Lexi, radiant and beaming, prettier even than she'd been a month ago in Los Angeles when he'd borrowed her lab's shiny new mass spectrometer.

His anger deflated and he grinned, pulling out the earbuds. "What are you doing here?"

Music blared from the little speakers and she grimaced. "I knew your clams had arrived and you would need to run the samples. Maybe this will be your big break—I couldn't resist coming to help."

She opened her arms to offer an embrace. He accepted it, relishing the feel of her, as tight and fit as ever. But no desire flared in his gut. Damn.

He called up the memory of her slim, muscular legs wrapping around him. Still nothing. Double damn.

He opened his eyes to find her waggling her fingers at him.

Oh. A rock, a big one.

"Guess what! I'm engaged."

Again, not a flare of jealousy over Lexi. *His* Lexi.

He wanted to punch the wall. But he couldn't let her see his fear, so instead he raised an eyebrow. "I distinctly remember you swearing never to do that." A decade ago, it had been part of her charm, and a month ago she had shrugged casually when he'd probed about her commitment to Mister-Rob-the-Douchebag. "What happened?"

"Bel, I'm thirty-five."

"So."

"You wouldn't understand. You're a man. And you haven't aged a day since we were in grad school."

That was true, and a subject to be avoided. He flashed his I've-seen-you-naked-and-remember-every-detail smile at her. "Flattery will get you everywhere, doll. And I promise not to say a word to Mister Dou—Uh, Mister Lexi about anywhere you want to go."

Her blush would have been very easy to misinterpret, if Bel had even an ounce of interest in misinterpreting. Triple damn.

"He prefers Mister Doctor Lexi." She squeezed Bel's wrist. "But enough about him. Can I see the clams?"

Shite. From one scam to another on the turn of a dime.

He inched to his left, trying to shield the vials of crimson blood from her view. No way could he fool her into thinking it was the gray-blue hemolymph of clams.

Over the years, he'd woven her an intricate lie about his research. Even though her questions kept him tap dancing, it was a hell of a lot easier to explain than the truth—he studied vampires, not mollusks.

"Actually, I extracted the lymph and dumped them into bio-waste already."

"Then I'm just in time. Where do we start?"

And just like that, he ran out of dance moves. The linoleum of the lab floor may as well have vanished. He floated in space with nothing to hold onto.

"Bel? What's wrong."

He stepped to the side, revealing the rack of blood. Her light brown brows pulled together in a puzzled frown, and he scratched the back of his head, hoping to hide his fidgeting fingers.

She leaned closer to the vials. "Is that human blood?"

"No."

"Well it's not clam blood."

The tiny lab closed in on him. His lies, his failure, this beautiful woman he'd once loved, and the female who'd bonded herself to him so he could never really love anyone else…His vision blackened at the corners of his eyes, and the flasks and beakers lining the walls began to spin.

"Bel. Bel! Sit down. Put your head between your knees."

He dropped his ass onto a lab stool and folded himself in half until his breaths came slower and his field of vision widened back to normal. When he looked up, Lexi's eyes brimmed with tears.

"What is it, doll?"

"You're sick. Your condition has finally become symptomatic, and, oh God—are you dying?"

His condition—part of the lie. When he'd lived with her all those years ago, he'd had to explain his obsessive research. He'd gone from their bed to the lab and back—never time for any fun that wasn't horizontal—out of desperation to understand his mysterious existence as a vampire halfling. The only one, as far as he knew.

Three human lifetimes of work spent to solve that mystery, when that hateful bitch Uta had known the answer all along. He wanted to wring her gorgeous white neck for everything she'd done to him.

A bitter laugh rose up in his throat, burning its way out like a strong acid. "No, Lex, I'm not dying." Although, he thought it would be nice if Uta were.

"Really? Promise?"

He nodded.

"Are you still searching for some kind of cure?"

A good bit of deductive reasoning, that, and it left him completely speechless.

"Are you having complications?"

Yes, one tall, red-headed, evil complication. "Nope. No symptoms, no complications, no need to worry about me."

"Then I honestly don't know why it bothers you. It's cool to be the only known of something. It's like having a vestigial tail."

Thank God, a retort sprang to mind. "That's your idea of cool? Lexi, my dear, you are much kinkier than I realized."

"Don't turn this into a joke." Narrowing her eyes and pursing her lips, she leaned forward to scrutinize him. She really had him under her microscope now.

He squirmed. "I've made progress on that research. I now know my condition isn't dangerous."

She pointed a finger into his chest. "You avoided my question."

"Technically, it wasn't a question." His voice was deceptively steady as he reached for a beaker and filled it with water from a tap.

"Fine, Alex Trebek. In the form of a question—why does it bother you so much to have a genetic anomaly?"

He gulped down the water, never taking his gaze off her. "It makes me feel lonely."

Her eyes swept over his face as she processed his words. She must have decided he was serious. "Because you're the only one?"

"Something like that." But more.

He forced himself to recall the beginning of his obsession. Uta had been not only his godmother, but his best friend, until she had dropped eleven-year-old Bel like he was made of the sun itself. His uniqueness had turned into a bone-deep loneliness that nothing ever eased for long. It had compelled him to research vampire biology in hopes of explaining his own existence. Only now it turned out he'd really just missed his psychopath mate all along. He pinched the bridge of his nose.

"I can't believe I used to think your tendency to sulk was sexy," Lexi chided.

He flashed her a well-practiced grin. "Don't beat yourself up over it. Women in their twenties always do, but by thirty, they see it for what it is: self-indulgence."

She laughed without knowing in just how many decades of twenty- and thirty- somethings he'd observed the phenomenon.

"But since you're all grown up now, I'll try to be less moody."

"I'm looking forward to seeing you try." She sidestepped around him. "So what the hell is this, if it's not human blood? Because my only working theories are you're a zombie or a vampire, and you've never tried to bite me, so I don't know which one." Her tone was light, but when she took his hand, something in her touch promised acceptance.

The little boy inside him screamed for him to tell her everything. He trusted her with his life—she would never hurt him or his family. Still, he couldn't manage the words. But he didn't laugh at her suggestions, and that seemed to be enough.

Her nostrils flared. "No." She shook her head, stepping back.

And that little boy began to panic. *Please don't leave me.*

But she stopped after that single step, gripped by curiosity, like the cool-headed scientist she was. "Really?"

He nodded.

Then her eyes lost their focus as she retreated inside her thoughts. "Andre. I've never seen him outside. Kos either. But you. I've walked in the sunlight with you a thousand times. We've—"

Yes, they'd walked home from the lab together for lunch and made love in their bed in the afternoon sun every day for years. "I'm half vampire. My mother was human, never wanted Andre to turn her."

Dear old mum had killed herself instead, and Bel had never forgiven her for it.

She took hold of his hand and examined the skin stretching over his tendons and knuckles. "And you want to be cured?"

Gently, he tugged his hand back. "No, doll, that can't happen, but the vampires need my help. My father needs my help." He waved at the rack of blood. "I need to get that protein into sick vampires, or they will die."

"Vampires," she murmured, raising her hand to his mouth.

He pressed his lips together to avoid her giving him an impromptu dental exam.

Thwarted, she tilted her head to look at the rack and smiled, rubbing her palms together in a familiar gesture. He used to tease she looked like a mad scientist when she did that, especially when she did it while wearing her lab coat.

"Can I help?"

Help? She may as well have sliced open his chest for a live dissection. The only woman he'd ever loved, who he'd kept at arm's length with all his secrets until she'd finally given up on him. And now, without a goddamn blink, she was eager to help him cure vampires.

"Lexi, my experiment failed. There's no sense in running the tests," he said, even as that little boy screamed, *Yes, stay, help!*

"Then we figure out why it failed, and what we need to do to make this cure."

She reached for a shelf overhead and grabbed a plastic cylinder. Her lean, gorgeous body stretched upward, and he sucked in a breath. So tempting, so familiar. But his cock could not even manage a twitch, hadn't since he'd seen Uta last month—unless of course he thought of her.

Maybe he just needed to get closer to Lexi. He gripped her hips, pressing the flat front of his jeans against the firm curve of her arse. Still no reaction. All the muscles encasing his ribs tensed, trapping the breath in his lungs. No hard-on? Not even for Lexi? This was bad.

"Lobel Tiberius Maras, back off." She enunciated each word with the calm, firm tone of an elementary teacher.

He forced out the air he'd been holding in with a hollow laugh. "Did I really tell you my middle name?"

"You were rather intoxicated." Her lips pulled to one side before curving into a hesitant smile. "What the hell were you thinking?"

He shrugged. "Sorry, I had to try."

Her anger faded with a giggle and a shake of her head. But not his.

His fury burned, bright and hot, at his mother, at Uta, and at the unjust rules of the universe that said she was the only female he could have anymore.

But Bel didn't like rules, never had, and he would find a way to break this one. No way would he let Uta steal his freedom. Only he would choose who he loved.

"Let's get to work." Lexi pulled him out of his mental tirade. "Tell me everything."

"I've isolated a protein that I believed had cured vampires of their wasting disease, but the version I engineered in the lab doesn't have any effect on the ailing vampires."

"Okay. What do you call it?"

"*Hemoaurum*."

"As in gold? Cool. I love metalloproteins."

Bel chuckled. Most women loved precious metals, not the proteins made of them.

"You're certain it's the cure? It could be a byproduct of some sort."

"I'm sure. I first found it in my father's wine…" He decided to leave off the part about the blood of his enemies. "It made Andre stronger—"

"Wine? Geez, Bel. This just keeps getting weirder."

Yeah, and she didn't know the half of it. He picked up a vial of the deficient vampire blood and held it up to the light. "I thought for sure I'd found it, Lex. A lot's riding on this."

"So there must be something else. A cofactor or a molecular chaperone of some sort that you haven't found." She rubbed her hands together again, grinning. "Feel like doing some biochemical sleuthing?"

All at once, hope flooded Bel. She'd always had a way of making him feel better. "Funny, I do."

"Then show me this wine."

He retrieved samples of Blood Vine and they began, working together with the easy companionability they'd had when they'd been lovers, but without any of the sparks.

The wine was complex, and it took a long time to isolate even a handful of the compounds and proteins, but after many hours, they had a dozen pure components. Tomorrow he would call the test subjects back and try again, administering each new sample to a different vampire in an infusion of *hemoaurum*.

"This has been fun." Lexi rinsed her hands and dried them with a paper towel. "I'm spending the afternoon with a friend from college. But I'll see you first thing tomorrow?"

"You don't have to."

"I want to. I can spare a few days away from home to help. It will be just like old times." She glanced down at his chest, and his stomach lurched. It would and wouldn't be like those times. She patted his arm and slung her purse over her shoulder. "We'll figure it out, Bel. We'll help your dad."

And then she was gone.

He wanted to help his dad, sure. Playing the hero would be damn satisfying. But this crisis was so much bigger than his family—it mattered to every vampire household his crew had ever rescued from Hunters, and all the ones that had burned alive because they'd waited too long to call for help, afraid of wasting away in exile.

CHAPTER 6

Gwen chewed her first bite of pancake, the sweetness of the maple syrup suffusing her with comfort. She hadn't made them from scratch, but they tasted good enough. Ethan hadn't said so, but he forked two more onto his plate then scooted his chair closer to the kitchen table. On the television, CNN ran breaking coverage of three seemingly random episodes of violence around the world.

Actually, Gwen didn't sit so much as hover over her chair—its caning irritated her spanked-raw ass. Balanced on her elbows and heels, her thighs burned with the effort of keeping her weight off her stinging skin. But Ethan wanted her to sit, wanted her to sting, so he wouldn't permit her to eat standing up. She obeyed as much as she could tolerate, submitting in some small way every single moment with him, each one a dark bliss.

The last month had been one long, dark, domestic pleasure—playing house with a devil.

Ethan's phone rang. "Bennett." He listened for a moment. "I see. And he's inside the laboratory now?" He looked at his watch. "Who is with you? Just Carmichael?" His mouth pinched in displeasure.

Gwen had sensed Ethan did not approve of that particular initiate.

"Call for reinforcements."

An insistent but garbled voice made its way to Gwen's ear.

"Fine. Move in now, but if you fumble this, you will put the Marasović household back on alert." Ethan glared at his pancake as it were the hated vampire himself. "Do not fail."

He cut a bite and speared it with his fork. "Bring the scientist to me, and I will teach you how to get information out of a prisoner. We must find a way through that infuriating shield." He set his telephone down with precision and raised the fork to his mouth.

Gwen wobbled and he turned quickly to look at her, noticing for the first time her bizarre posture.

"Sore?"

"Yes."

"Show me."

Gwen rose and turned, lowering her jeans and panties to just above her knees so Ethan could inspect his handiwork. She didn't expect the slap, but when his palm made contact, she went wet between her legs. He gave her another whack for good measure, then pushed his hand against her cunt.

"Do you know what I love about you, Gwen?"

She did, but she said, "No."

"I could do anything I want to you, and it would excite you."

"Yes." He had her number, and she depended on him entirely because of it.

"Bend over the table."

She started to step out of her jeans.

"Leave them right there, around your thighs."

She penguin-walked a few steps to the table and folded over. Bound by the fabric, she was unable to spread her legs. He slapped her again, this time an open-handed blow to the lips of her swollen sex.

She yelped. Once, she'd read there was a technique to spanking—the skillful delivery of a perfect ratio of pain and pleasure. Ethan did not practice this skill, but instead aimed for the blinding white-hot pain she craved.

"Where do you want me?" he asked. Giving her a choice was another one of his tricks. It created an expectation for him to break. As soon as she learned he would do the opposite of what she asked for, he disoriented her by occasionally heeding her request. Now the question just served to remind her that no matter what, he would do what he wanted and the only desires he permitted were his own. She'd taken the lesson to heart, so she didn't answer.

Without warning, he slammed into her wetness, thrusting hard once, twice. God, she loved the way he used her. But he must have been just getting himself wet because he pulled out and pushed right into her ass. She'd learned how to relax and open up to him fast and without foreplay. He had hurt her once, and the next day when he'd seen she was in pain, he frowned, pulling her into an awkward hug. That stiff embrace had underscored that it was her job to remedy the problem, because his being more gentle would not suit either of them.

He shoved his entire length into her. Oh God, he knew how to fuck her. Words dissolved in her brain, and there were only the animal sounds of her own grunts and his.

He spoke, and she struggled to surface from the dark cloud of her ecstasy to make sense of the sounds. "What?"

"Come."

And she did, just like that, at this command. He yanked back her hair and forced her to look at the television. The camera panned across images of burned bodies in Chile—a pile of charred skeletons, too small to be adults.

Still, he pounded into her.

Gwen sobbed. Her climax lost its momentum. Ethan ejaculated inside her, pounding her into the table without realizing she no longer met his thrusts. He didn't seem to notice her lack of response, which meant he was truly carried away by the success of his orchestrations—he'd provoked the vampires to attack his own people, to intensify the cycle of retaliation.

He pulled out and yanked her to standing by her hair. "You are my perfect whore, Gwen." His kiss was altogether tender, and it was the most frightening thing he had ever done to her. "Go get cleaned up." He spanked her again lightly. "Then we'll go into the office."

In the vanity mirror over the bathroom sink, Gwen washed her face and fixated on her own eyes, searching for something, anything she recognized. A vampire had made her this way, had made her crave pain, had killed her soul while her body writhed in pleasure under his bite. Now, Ethan was her dark prince, the only one who could satisfy her desires and help her avenge herself.

But he'd forced her to look at those burned-up babies, forced her to witness suffering in the throes of pleasure.

He was no prince. It was perfectly fine to hurt her—she was trash, defiled by a filthy animal. Hurting children, however, was unacceptable, even for the greater good. But if Ethan was no longer her prince, could she live without him?

Empty gray eyes stared back at her, devoid of answers.

He knocked on the door. "Come on, Gwen. I have a lot of work to do and I simply cannot wait for you to see what I have planned next."

Bel rinsed the columns he and Lexi had used and set them upside down to dry. A movement flickered in the corner of his eye. The door seemed to swing open half an inch, as if Lexi had failed to latch it. Or maybe she'd forgotten something and was coming back for it.

But the door didn't move again and he instinctively reached back under his sweatshirt to pat the handgun tucked into his waistband. There was nowhere to hide in the narrow lab. He ducked and pulled a cabinet open to shield himself just as the door swung open, crashing into the counter.

"Are you the mercenary Lobel Marasović?"

Hidden from view, Bel rolled his eyes.

"You didn't think you could get away with it, did you?"

The door clicked closed again.

"With what?"

"Shut up asshole, the attacks are all over the news."

Bel hadn't seen the news. "I haven't attacked anyone. I've been in the lab all night and all day."

"So it wasn't you," said a second voice. "But it sure as hell was vampires, and you are going to pay for it. First you, and soon every single motherfucking blood sucker we can find."

Bel had heard this crap so often it bored him. If Bel shot the fool, he wouldn't have to listen to it, but then he would never learn why they'd come after him.

"Stand up nice and slow. Hands in the air."

Bel rose steady and straight, like the mercury on a thermometer. The yellow-eyed youngsters wore scrubs. Probably initiates. No one would think they were anything but medical students, apart from their guns.

"We hear you are only half vampire, and Mr. Bennett says he's reasonably sure a gunshot will kill you. We can test that assumption, or you come with us. He would like to ask you some questions about that force field around your father's house."

Ah. So Bennett was looking for a way through the shield. All Bel needed to know.

"It's true." He assessed the slight tremor in the speaker's gun hand. The barrel wobbled enough to reassure Bel. However the other man's grip was relaxed and sure.

"What's that?" the steady one asked.

"A gunshot would kill me, but you would have to beat me to it." Bel drew his weapon with practiced speed and shot the steady one in the forehead. He crumpled to his knees before falling face first onto the linoleum floor.

The shaky one lowered his gun briefly, but lifted it again almost instantly. Bel shot him in the chest. Hunter blood began to pool around their bodies. Even with the silencer on, the shots would have been loud enough to draw attention. The one with the chest wound gurgled and twitched before his ribs fell with a final exhale.

Bel tugged off his sweatshirt and shoved his arms into the white sleeves of a lab coat. Even with his silencer screwed on, someone was bound to have heard him fire his weapon. He peered into the hallway, just as two security guards came around the corner.

"Hey, doc! Everything okay?" one asked.

"Copacetic."

"We had a report of gunshots," said the other guard.

Bel shook his head. "Damndest thing. Two little boys in hospital robes came racing through here with those plastic cap guns. Playing cops and robbers or the like. Skinny kids, one bald. You suppose they escaped from the cancer ward?"

The guards looked at each other, wide-eyed.

Bel feigned a laugh. "I wouldn't worry too much. They were having a bloody good time on their adventure."

The guards both chuckled. "Guess we better look for our escapees then. Thanks for your help, doctor."

"Glad to help. Seeing those boys play made my day." Bel waved before slipping back into his lab and locking the door behind him.

He dialed Lexi. She answered on the second ring. "Hey, what's up?"

"Oh, thank God." He exhaled.

"What's the matter?"

"Listen. Don't come back to the lab, no matter what. It's not safe. Stay with your friend."

"Are you okay?"

"I am now that I know you're all right."

"And the research?"

"Nothing is lost. I'll get started on phase two tomorrow. Just go home to Mister Doctor." *Where you'll be safe.*

"Okay."

Bel ended the call and took a deep breath. He would never forgive himself if Lexi became a casualty of this unending war.

He bent, staring into an unseeing pair of golden eyes. So young. These initiates were just kids, brainwashed into senseless hate. Bel shook off the regret. He had to clean up this mess, and sneak two new John Does into the morgue. Convenient corpse disposal was one advantage of having a lab in the basement of a research hospital that he hadn't bargained on.

First, he swept the Blood Vine component samples into his knapsack. Then, he knelt at the mini-fridge and gently laid a dozen bags of the *hemoaurum* on top of the plastic test tubes. Liquid gold, literally. Especially since it had taken two weeks for the bacteria he'd engineered to produce the stuff.

Next he needed gurneys, body bags—the pool of blood around the bodies grew wider—and a mop. Shite.

Once he'd gotten rid of the stiffs, he would make the ninety-minute drive back to Andre's and find out about the attacks the Hunters had mentioned. And then he would go back to work, trying to save the vampire world.

CHAPTER 7

Uta perched on Loki's couch and rested her elbows on her knees. Her needles moved so quickly they blurred beyond the focus of even her own super-sharp eyes.

Loki tinkered with the computer screen, preparing for a video conference with Kaštel.

Her needles clicked faster and faster. He cast a look over his shoulder and raised his gnomishly arched eyebrows. "Stressed, dear?"

Stress was an understatement, an emotion on a human scale. She was a hurricane of gusting torments, a downpour of emotions, and also the occasional squall of hope, which dared to taunt her with the idea Bel might forgive her, chose her, love her. Each feeling demanded to be vented somehow, so she would need more yarn. She inhaled, attempting to calm her internal storm. No luck.

She tossed aside her knitting and hopped up to pace while the bells and whistles of connecting via video chat fell into place. Fear jumbled her thoughts. Would Bel even be there, or off fiddling somewhere in his lab with that pretty little Lexi?

"Damned rutting ewe," she spat.

"Hello to you too, Uta." Zoey's head and shoulders appeared on the screen.

Damn it. "I am apologizing, Zoey. I am not speaking of you."

The other female waved her hand reassuringly before stepping out of view of the video camera. A handful of people came into view—Andre slumped in a chair, flanked by Kos and Bel. The brick walls of the cellar office provided their backdrop.

Side by side, the resemblance between father and youngest son astonished her—same short dark hair, but Bel had let his tight curls grow out longer; same green eyes, both glittering with intensity. She couldn't work up the nerve to look at him, so she examined her old friend instead.

Andre had lost much when Hunters burned his vineyards, and the doleful set of his mouth worried her. He might finally succumb to the despair that had nearly killed him after Mila's suicide. Zoey glided to him, and the tension in his jaw eased ever so slightly with the deep comfort of his mate's touch—a comfort Uta might never know.

She inhaled, summoning the courage to face Bel down before she flicked her gaze to him, like leaping off a cliff, or ripping off a bandage. More than two thousand years since she'd been human, but the memory of that particular sort of anticipation lingered.

At the eye contact, he flinched but regained his poise quickly. His hazel irises clouded with defiance, one of his many admirable traits. She recognized it from the adorably mulish days of his youth—even then he had always known his own mind. And later, she had witnessed from afar the tenacious determination he applied to his research.

But another, indecipherable emotion swirled with the stubbornness in his eyes and it twisted her stomach.

Alongside Andre, who was dressed in work clothes for laboring in vineyards that no longer existed, Bel occupied his clothes like an invading army. His black T-shirt had a large white logo for something she had never heard of, probably a band. His faded jeans hugged thick, muscular legs. Two nearly identical males, and yet Bel was the one she craved like blood itself. His Roman nose and dark brows dominated raw, masculine features. So much like the bulky Illyrian warriors of her youth, so ill-suited to life in a cramped laboratory, his oversized body taunted her. The lines of his muscles under his fitted clothes revealed he was everything she could admire in a male.

And at the same time he was the boy she had loved from the moment of his birth—not like a son, not like a nephew. The way she loved him was simply the way Uta loved Bel, with every beat of a heart that belonged to him, whether he wanted it to or not.

Since the moment he was born, she had wanted to hold him and promise never to let anything hurt him.

And she'd failed. The desolation in his eyes assured her of that.

One more defeat to add to her list.

He glanced away, his olive skin reddening slightly. And from half a world away she sensed his shame in the heat crawling up her neck.

"What is happening?" she demanded.

"Hunters attacked Bel in his laboratory."

Uta's heart raced, as it did every time he put himself in danger.

Loki stepped to her side. "Did they do harm to your research?"

"No. I managed to save everything. However, you should know I have not yet succeeded in curing the test subjects."

So tenacious. He had not given up hope, even though she had warned him of the futility of his work. She hid the pride she had no right to under an impatient tone. "I am trying to warn you."

"I believe there is a secondary factor required to make the protein effective. With my research partner I hav—"

"Partner?" Uta croaked.

Bel nodded. "Yes. Dr. Lexi Hall."

The urge to break something—or someone, rather—took hold of Uta. Short of that, she needed to knit. But before she could reach the needles she spotted another comfortingly sharp object, the fire poker, and tested its weight against one palm before leaning on it like a walking stick. Lexi had left him, and Uta could not bear it if the human woman had won him back. It was highly unlikely he could consummate a rekindled affair with the woman, but the thought of him even attempting it made Uta want to snap that little Lexi in half.

Cursing herself that she had not bothered to practice her English, Uta shrugged one shoulder as if she thought him a fool for trying. "Lexi is not being able to help. There are evidences you are not knowing about vampire blood. Your science is flaccid sheep dick."

Zoey snorted.

"My science is the only hope." He stood straighter. "Especially since your impotent Justicia flounders, unable to end this persecution."

He was not wrong on that count, which made it damn near impossible to have any hope it all.

"Enough." Loki nudged her aside and stepped into the center of the video camera's field. "I trust you all have seen the reports of the attacks?"

"Of course." Andre crossed his arms, a frown creasing lines in his brow. "It is…"

Andre stared into the camera, seemingly unable to finish the sentence. Uta understood—words failed her as well. Vampires had rejected aggression against the Hunters for millennia. The need to avoid the sun made it difficult to retaliate anyway, but Uta suspected the real reasons ran deeper—a collective trauma they carried in their blood, but only she among vampires knew the reasons in detail.

Now that technology allowed for safe travel in the daytime, some vampires championed aggression. But true to their traditions, Loki held to the official Justicia line hard and fast. They could not fight an enemy set on genocide without resorting to the same tactics—killing women and children and men like Lucas Bennett, caught up in a violent culture they despised. And so vampires must only defend themselves.

The logic was so deeply ingrained in Uta that, in the face of violence committed by her fellow vampires, she could not find a single word to utter in all the languages she knew.

Loki's world-weary sigh had to suffice. "Indeed."

"Do you hold the aggressionists responsible?" Andre asked.

"I do not know, but I plan to send my best field operatives to investigate at sundown."

Giddy relief surged through Uta. The mission was the perfect way to avoid Bel. "Send me. I am being merciless." She held the poker upright like a spear, the posture she'd assumed when she'd led her men into battle against the Romans, fighting for freedom before even Andre was born.

Loki gently pried the poker from her hands and placed it back in its stand. "You are always merciless, dear, but I need you with me. Oblak is taking command of your unit. Andre, I am convening an emergency meeting of the Justicia. We arrive at your estate tomorrow at sundown. Uta, you will assist Bel and his partner with everything you know about vampire blood. It is essential that he succeeds."

"No," Andre and Bel shouted at the same time. They glared at each other until Bel tilted his head, conceding to his father. Andre stood with his hands on his hips. "Not here. *Davo.* I do not want you lunatics in my home. You will make my household an even more tempting target for Hunters. They have already destroyed—"

Loki held up his palm. "With your shield, and Lobel's crew of mercenaries providing security, Kaštel is the most secure option." He might be small, but Loki was the oldest vampire in the world, and he did not take any guff from a youngster like Andre—not even one who was two millennia old.

Under different circumstances, Uta would have enjoyed seeing her old friend put in his place. Even now, she fought a smile from stealing control of her lips.

"What about your chateau?" he barked.

"I live on a glacier. The weather is much better in California."

Zoey laughed and Andre scowled at her. She stepped toward the camera. "You are all welcome. Only, I don't know how this works. Will you bring your own blood?"

"Thank you, and yes, dear. The Justicia always travels BYOB."

Uta hadn't considered that part. The last time she was at Kaštel, she'd snacked on a Hunter prisoner. Perhaps someone from her household apartment in Manhattan could meet her.

"Not to worry, Uta," Loki said, with an uncharacteristic solicitousness that put her on alert. "You can borrow Nils." He pointed his thumb over his shoulder to where the handsome blood slave had entered the room, carrying a stack of wood for the fireplace.

Bel paled, as Loki must have intended him to, and Uta's pulse tripped over itself.

Her vision narrowed as if the halfling were the only male on the earth. To her, he was. "Bel?" she whispered, but he strode away.

Jaw bulging with tension, Andre glanced between her and his son. "Fine. Tomorrow." Then he strode toward the video camera with his hand up, blocking the screen. "Turn the damn thing off." A moment later, the connection ended.

High pitched laughter burst from Loki, giving him the appearance of a jolly little Christmas elf.

With effort, Uta switched her brain from its clumsy English to the rolling vowels of Loki's preferred tongue. "I hate you. And you have much graver things to worry about than my love life."

He wagged a finger at her. "You do not hate me, and regardless of having been an impossible pain in my ass for two millennia, I am very fond of you. Tormenting you about your love life gives me a modicum of pleasure in the face of those worries." He stepped closer and stroked her hair. "And, child, I want you to be happy."

She leaned into his touch, desperate for the only affection ever bestowed on her. "The bond is not enough. He will not love me, and he will always resent what his mother and I did to him."

"Always is a very long time, Uta." Loki pulled a handkerchief from his pocket and reached up to dab at her face. "Now, now. I hate it when my warrior princess cries."

She couldn't help it. The only thing in life she feared was the pain Bel's absence caused her. "Loki, I cannot see him. I won't survive it. Surely you remember what happened the last time I was near him for too long?"

"I could hardly forget." He took her hand.

She yanked it back, crossed her arms, and flopped onto the couch, curling into a ball as she remembered.

Four decades ago, Bel had moved into a gloomy, abandoned warehouse, gathered together a handful of vampires, and amassed a notable arsenal. Each night Uta had perched on the slick, rotting tin roof and stared through a metal vent to watch the males train.

Apart from Bel's longevity, he possessed none of a vampire's special powers. He appeared extremely fit for a human, as strong as one of his size could be, but when he insisted on sparring with the vampires, Uta was forced to tamp down all her protective instincts and prepare to watch him take a beating. He held his own with surprising strength, though, and she relaxed a little on her rickety spot with newfound respect for her long lost mate. Until the young fool challenged the old one, Omar.

The ensuing match proved the most violent bout yet and with each blow Bel took, she dug the sharp corrugated metal edging of her spy hole into her fingertips and used the pain to scramble the insistent need to rescue him.

Omar pulled back for what would surely be a knockout strike, but Bel evaded it and landed a solid kick to the vampire's ribs.

"You pulled that punch," Bel shouted at the vampire after one particularly violent round.

"You're bloody right I did."

"Well, don't." Bel squared off and his fingers twitched at his sides. Under a threadbare sweatshirt, his bulky shoulders rose and fell with a menacing shrug.

From where Uta watched above, his sweat-dampened curls glistened in the glaring light of incandescent bulbs he had haphazardly strung from the rafters. Her own fingers twitched, itching to run through his thick hair. It would be so different to touch him now that he was a man — now that he stirred not only affection, but also desire. She shifted on her stiff legs and the rickety roof creaked loud enough for the other vampires to hear. Omar glanced up, but she ducked out of sight. After only a moment, she dared to peek down at them again.

"I like your courage, halfling." Omar grazed his knuckles against Bel's shoulder in a teasing punch. "But don't forget: the things that make you stronger are the ones that do not kill you."

Bel's handsome face split into a smile and he returned the playful blow. "Got me there."

"Besides, boss. You are the brains in this operation."

"What does that make me?" called out another male. The gathering devolved into masculine jokes and more sparring and Uta drank it in, recalling the easy company of her long-dead soldiers.

For weeks, she could not grasp the purpose of Bel's bizarre operation, so she watched and pondered. Finally, they departed one evening in a windowless van with Bel at the wheel. She flew above, following them across the channel into the French countryside. A band of smelly Hunters had surrounded a farmhouse, setting it aflame. Bel's crew descended upon them, keeping them at bay in order to evacuate the humans and vampires into their van.

An infant wailed inside the house — one of the most heartrending sounds on earth. Bel stormed in. Instinct took control of Uta and she bent her knees and launched herself into the air to rescue both him and the babe. But before she even reached full speed, he emerged, cradling the child to his muscular chest and shouting orders. Sweaty and smeared with ash, no creature alive had ever looked sexier.

Once the entire household was safe in the vehicle, a member of Bel's crew drove them away. Bel and the rest of his vampires laid waste to all the hostile humans.

The operation was remarkable. She called Loki and reported the activities. "The Justicia needs a unit like this. Think of the lives we could save."

"Form one, then, child. You have my support."

But she would have to leave Bel to do it. If she stayed, perhaps he would sense her, and come to her. "No. Find someone else."

Uta took up residence across the street. Bel, unaware of her watchful eye, spent days at the university and continued his research. By night he trained with more and more recruits, including a few human women who demonstrated supernatural powers. She envied the ability of the one called Vania to shoot fire from her palms, turning the brick walls of the warehouse black with soot.

The crew clearly regarded Bel with an endearingly irreverent devotion. Uta couldn't blame them, and as she had always known it would, the old affection inside her transformed into a deep love for the man he had become. Weeks passed and the ache inside her grew as acute as on the day she'd broken with him.

One night she flew through the London sky along the same path as the tube line he took home from his lab. He emerged from the station and she hid in a doorway as he walked by. Several paces past, he stopped and turned around, rubbing the back of his head. His scent, like the sea air of Šolta, reached her nose and flooded her with longing. He scanned the street, but his eyes never settled on where she stood, cloaked in the shadows. He shivered, pulling his jacket tight, and marched away in a hurry.

The next night, she overheard him coaxing the vampires out for a night on the town. "The Ramones are playing at the Roundhouse. It will be epic."

"Epically loud and sweaty," one said.

"I like more meat on my humans that those punk rock waifs," Omar agreed.

Bel went alone, and as usual, Uta followed.

She balanced on a third story windowsill, confirming the other vampires' assessment of the music and the scene. She expected him to be inside for a long time, but after only the second song, he exited with a woman in tow. The stupid sow was skinny and nearly as tall as Uta. Worse—she wore a short tangle of spiky hair—red.

May sweet Auntie Europa shrivel her ovaries into raisins.

Bel spun the woman and pressed her into the wall, kissing her. Uta's chest ruptured with a pain like the proverbial stake to the heart. She cried out. He threw a glance over his shoulder, but the woman laced her fingers in his hair and pulled him back to her mouth. Uta plummeted to the sidewalk, rolling her ankle as she landed awkwardly. The crunch of her joint sobered her enough to keep her from killing the woman. This was the result of what she had wanted for him all along—the freedom to love others, so that if he came for her, it would be a choice.

But seeing him exercise that freedom tore apart her insides and shredded her heart. She gasped for oxygen, but it simply seeped out of her lungs, leaving her breathless. She clutched at her burning chest. Surely such pain proved he would never choose her.

With great effort, she had launched herself into the sky and flown directly to Loki's chateau. The tendons of her ankle had knit back together quickly, but her heart had not healed. She'd lain down on a snow bank as the sun rose, its gentle caress rapidly turning into a searing burn that matched the fire in her heart. In the decades that followed, the desire to give up continued to tempt her.

And here in the present her suicidal tendencies were the only capital she could bargain with.

"Seeing him again will drive me straight into the sun."

Loki snorted. "I am not so easily manipulated, child."

Child? Patronizing old coot! "Go fuck yourself, Loki."

He scrawled something on a sheet of paper and passed it off to the busty blonde he favored. "No thanks, I have household servants to do that for me. But poor you, Uta—you can't fuck yourself and can't get your mate to do it either."

"I'll scratch your eyes out," she hissed.

"Don't bother. Last time you tried that I healed in less than one minute and you ruined your suit." He chuckled to himself as he straightened a stack of papers on his desk. Then he stood to his full five and a half feet, pinning her with his gaze. "I need you at Kaštel, Uta. All the vampires need you."

She sniffed and nodded. She would do her duty, as always, no matter how much it hurt.

CHAPTER 8

Bel stormed through the cellar, as if distance from the computer screen were distance from Uta herself. But it didn't work. She was inside him, and there was no escape.

Even in the musty damp of the cellar, his skin remained flushed from the sight of her and his humiliating, unwanted erection tented his pants. He closed his eyes, but her image lingered—her mane of auburn hair, her ivory skin. She was Aphrodite herself, with an unholy power over him. And with that poker in her hand, she was Diana too—a goddess of war and sex, all in one crass package. The heavy scent of wine barrels and damp cement cloyed his senses and the air become too thick to breathe. He raced up the stairs and emerged into the sunny foyer where he inhaled ragged breaths.

Dust motes glinted in the rays of light streaming through the windows. He'd been here before, in this exact pattern of light. The vision transported him back to that other, identical house of his childhood. To another day when he'd run from Uta. No, not quite. He'd run because Uta had sent him away, abandoned him when he needed her most. He'd run back to a house where his father lay mostly dead, wailing over the suicide of his wife, and where Kos fretted over Andre. No one had anything to spare for Bel, eleven and newly without his mother. And perhaps that was for the best, because if anyone had asked how he fared, he might have told the truth—that the loss of Uta's friendship was more devastating than Mila's death by far, something that still inspired a guilty lump in his throat.

Since that day, he'd never really been anything but alone, never belonged anywhere.

Someone knocked on the behemoth front door. Bel blinked, half surprised to find himself in California, not Šolta.

Goosebumps prickled over his skin. Hunters?

Whoever it was had to be unarmed since the shield was up. He cracked the door to find Lexi on the other side. He'd never been happier to see her, but bloody hell it wasn't safe for her to be out there alone.

He swung the door open wide and grabbed her wrist, pulling her inside and into his arms. Here was the one person who, at least sometimes, had penetrated his loneliness. Holding her svelte runner's body tight, he still hoped for a tremor of lust, a tingling in his cock.

Nothing.

"Um, Bel," she said into his chest. "Why are you squeezing me like a boa constrictor?"

"Just happy to see you. Though I distinctly remember telling you to go home."

"Since when do I take orders from you?" She tried for a light tone, but she didn't fool Bel. Swallowing, she continued. "After you called, I turned on the radio."

"Shite." He'd hoped to ease her into this crazy vampire world. That they were real, that he was half of one, that in exile they suffered from a terrible disease—it was enough for one day. But she'd already guessed there was more. "The radio?"

"Those people in Indonesia. Drained of their blood. Was that—"

He pulled her toward an uncomfortable looking old chair and nudged her to sit down. "It was, I'm afraid. So was the attack on the religious compound north of Vancouver, and the fire in Santiago that wiped out an entire neighborhood."

Her gaze darted around the foyer. "I thought you said the vampires were good, didn't kill people."

He knelt before her, holding her slim hands. "The people they killed weren't exactly good, Lex. They were Hunters bent on exterminating all the vampires."

"So it was some kind of self-defense? Those children…"

If only.

"No, it wasn't. A rumor was leaked to the vampires alleging that a Hunter's blood will cure their disease, and maybe allow their bodies to tolerate the sun." He swallowed, unsure how much to tell her.

"The sun?" She stared back with unblinking eyes.

Everything, then. He would tell her the whole story. "For weeks, the Hunters have been attacking vampires more ruthlessly, killing them and the humans in their households. Vampires are tense and afraid. Hunters raise their children to hate my kind, Lex. And the rumor clearly sparked the vampires' desperation."

My kind? The foreign sentiment caught him off guard and his chest tightened all over again. Lexi's eyes widened and he fixated on them—every speck and gradient of her irises familiar. How many times had he stared into them while making love to her? How many times had he driven them to tears by withdrawing into one of his bad moods?

But Uta had revealed all, and he had no more mysteries to brood over. Maybe he finally belonged to himself, finally could be what Lexi needed. If only he could get his dick to work. He certainly deserved her more than that preppy all-star douchebag of a fiancé.

Lexi brought her thumb to her mouth and nibbled at the nail. "If the blood can heal them, wouldn't they keep the Hunters alive?"

"It's very possible they took hostages. No one knows for sure. The violence itself was nothing but retribution."

"That's awful." She shook her head, thumb between her lips.

"It's why the *hemoaurum* is so important. If vampires no longer suffer from the wasting disease, they can live anywhere, they can flee Hunters at any time. It won't end the persecution, but it would take away the Hunters' most powerful weapon, and the vampires wouldn't be so desperate."

He chose not to mention his secondary hypothesis because he had no freaking idea how to test it, short of breeding a new species of vampire guinea pigs. Present in both Hunter blood and Blood Vine, *hemoaurum* might be the very thing that bestowed sun tolerance. But first they had to be sure they'd isolated the x-factor that would make it work.

"Then let's get to work." She patted her messenger bag. "I've been studying the shape of the protein, and I can see many potential active sites where a cofactor might interact. I'm certain we've already isolated the one we need."

"Woman, you are brilliant. Why did I ever let you go?"

When the familiar tears flooded her eyes, he kissed her. What else could he do?

Ten long years since his lips had touched hers. He begged the fire to ignite, for the spark to leap from his mouth right to his cock.

Instead, the cellar door crashed open and Andre emerged.

"*Davo,* Bel, stop that at once!" He rubbed his hands over his scalp like a man at a loss then dropped them and gave a little nod.

Lexi blushed, averting her eyes.

Inside, Bel shrank to the size of an embarrassed pre-adolescent.

"Alexandra," his father said. "How lovely to see you. Welcome to my home."

Bel's teeth ground. Andre always had politeness to spare for a beautiful woman and zero for his own son. Bel fisted his hands and rose to his full height, his shoulders bunching up nearly to his ears.

"Son, we need to talk."

"I'll get to work." Lexi stood and pointed at an open door. "This is the dining room, right? Can I plug my laptop in there?"

"Of course." Andre smiled, flashing all his white teeth. But the tension in his eyes left the expression cool.

Lexi stiffened, but marched into the dining room on a mission. That was his girl — single minded focus.

"I'm hungry. You want to talk? I'll be in the kitchen."

Andre growled, but Bel knew he would follow. Until two months ago, he'd refused to speak to his father for half a century, so Andre should be willing to take what he could get. Two, maybe three sets of footsteps sounded behind him on the stairs. Great — a family meeting.

Lena stood at the kitchen sink and jumped when he entered. Automatically, he glanced at her belly — flat — then at her pretty face. She smiled the very same half-assed smile Andre had flashed Lexi and Bel understood instantly that she was not pregnant — round one of vampire conception had failed.

The Maras household was a real barrel of laughs today.

He strode to the fridge.

"Are you hungry?" she asked him. "What are you in the mood for?"

Normally, Bel wasn't gracious about being waited on. He would gladly drink milk out of the carton and eat a handful of deli-sliced ham if she weren't watching. But he'd learned Lena took satisfaction from feeding others.

"I don't know. Got anything good?"

"I have homemade cherry pie."

Bel could imagine several scenarios where he would willingly die for a slice of her cherry pie, which sounded like an absolutely filthy thing to think about his sister-in-law. But seriously, her pie was that good.

"Yes, please, and a glass of milk."

"Sure." She always tried to feed him more, but he just didn't eat much — part of the whole halfling thing.

He managed a better smile that time, at the prospect of eating. When he turned toward the table, he found Andre, Kos and Pedro all standing in the doorway.

"What?"

"You kissed Alexandra." Andre crossed his arms over his chest.

Kos put his palm to his forehead. "Tell me you didn't."

"Kos, she's the only woman I've ever loved. I drove her away by hiding all this crazy vampire shite from her. But now she knows and she hasn't run screaming."

"*Davo.*" Andre's rigid posture softened and he swung his head mournfully.

Pedro leaned back and rested his elbows on the kitchen counter, striking a casual GQ pose. "Right on, Bel. That's cool. What does Lexi's husband think about you kissing her? Or did you buy her that bling?"

"*Krist.*"

Bel recoiled at Kos's curse, but the expression on his brother's face was pure compassion. Weeks ago, when Kos was pussying around about being in love with Lena, Bel had confessed the depth of his former feelings for Lexi.

"She's just engaged," Bel whispered, as if the trivial distinction mattered.

"Bel, I could not care less whether your Alexandra is married, but I care for you. You will all suffer less if you accept this simple truth — you have nothing to offer her — you belong to Uta now. I am surprised you could even stand to kiss Alexandra."

Bel's fingers travelled to his mouth of their own accord, that point of contact where, for once, Lexi's unfailing attraction had failed to turn him on. "I don't belong to anyone."

And sure as hell not to that cold, bloodthirsty bitch.

"Sit. We need to talk."

Twelve chair legs scraped along the tile floor as his father and brothers pulled out seats and Lena brought pie.

"What are we discussing? Hunter attacks? Vampire attacks? The coming apocalypse?" Bel tried to sound flippant as he tucked into the tart cherry perfection on his plate.

"Bel, Uta is coming here tomorrow. You need to be prepared for what might happen to you. To both of you." Andre's logical fatherly tone would have appealed to Bel if he'd been speaking to anyone else.

Pedro tilted his chair back and balanced it on two legs. "What's the problem? What will happen to Bel when she gets here?"

"That's a question for Bel — tell us what happened when you saw her before."

"It's not a big deal. So, my inner vampire will get a little worked up. I can handle it," Bel said. "Especially now that I know what to expect."

Kos's laugh was tinged with pity. "You don't understand how powerful a bond is."

"*Mierda!*" Pedro clapped Bel on the back. "Only you could wind up blood bonded to your own *madrina.*"

A mouthful of retorts sprung to mind — *only you would wind up a half-Hunter vampire, only you would fuck our archenemy's brother.* Those were below the belt, so he aimed for the gut. "What about you, baby bro? No sudden bonds to Bennett the younger?"

Pedro shot him a bird. "*Nada.*"

"Can you feel her, son?" Andre rubbed his hand over his sternum, as he often did when Zoey entered a room.

"A little."

"How the hell does that even work?" Pedro brought all four feet of his chair to the floor with a bang, and leaned over the table.

Bel opened his mouth to explain what he understood of the bond, but he had no real explanation. So he shut his trap and turned to Andre, who, for once, sat waiting deferentially for Bel to speak.

Instead, he shrugged. "I got nothing."

Andre interlaced his fingers on the table and leaned forward. "All I know is that it occurs because her blood is inside of him. They are connected in every cell."

Bel's mouth went dry. *In every cell.*

How had he forgotten that part? Too busy being pissed off, probably. At least the *hemoaurum* was an actual molecule he could look at under a microscope. This blood bond bollocks defied logic. A spiritual connection with physiological effects? But that's how it had been between Andre and Mila. And the broken bond had nearly killed Andre when Mila died.

Bloody hell — he was connected to Uta like *that*. If anything ever happened to her when she was out kicking Hunter ass for the Justicia, he would suffer what Andre had for all those decades that his body had fought for life. Unbidden, the image of her skin blackening under the sun sprang into Bel's mind.

The soft, worn collar of his T-shirt choked him.

He needed to be alone. The good news was, none of these chumps could follow him outside in the daylight. "I need some air."

"Bel —"

He dashed out the kitchen door before he heard the rest of Andre's sentence, thankful none of them abused their super power to keep him inside for their little intervention.

The spacious blue sky made room for him, and he drew in deep breaths. The afternoon sun warmed his skin, soaking into his dark shirt and jeans. Because the vines and trellises had all burned, he was able to cross over the hillsides in a crow's line. The air no longer smelled of fuel and ash, but the blackened earth left no doubt as to what had happened. A walk outside may have begun as a temporary escape from his family, but it was also a harsh reminder of his other problem — a population of diseased, desperate vampires who now believed Hunters were their panacea.

Was Lexi having any luck? He should go inside and ask for her help contacting the test subjects. He glanced back toward the house.

As much as he hated to admit it, Andre had been right to call him on that kiss. Even if he could get their spark going again, it would only hurt Lexi to learn of his bond to Uta. And he sure as hell wasn't ready to face Lex again.

In the opposite direction, a wooded copse stood in a shallow valley — a trickling spring where he had first met Zoey while she was making out with Andre. Bel chuckled to remember those two, disheveled and trying to play it casual.

Fortunately, the sweet little spot had escaped the Hunters' flame throwers and he slipped and scuffed down the steep path into the shadows of the small, scraggly trees.

Andre had reportedly found the spring because it smelled like their home on Šolta, and that scent alone had inspired him to buy the vineyards which eventually produced Blood Vine.

Bel had puzzled over just what the bloody hell his father had smelled to lead him to such a miraculous discovery. Trace amounts of gold or other *hemoaurum* precursors? A particular combination of plants that would only grow in soil like Šolta's?

Vampires and humans shared identically structured nervous systems, so the sense of smell was most closely associated with memory for both species. But Bel's perfectly average human sniffer could never have caught that scent.

Still, something about the small valley did remind him of Šolta. Not that the homeland mattered to him the way it did to a full-blooded vampire. Croatia had stopped being his home the moment Uta had dropped him. He wasn't the least bit sentimental about the place.

CHAPTER 9

The water gurgled, soothing away Bel's troubles. He didn't know
how long he'd been sitting there when quiet chirps caused him to
look up. The sun had sunk into twilight, and bats were stirring in
the trees and flying out over the vineyards to hunt.

Who would you spy on, if you were a bat?

Uta's voice rang out in melodic Croatian as if she were next to
him in the copse. He looked over his shoulder, searching, but it was
just a memory. Cherry-red toes peeking out of the sand, a perfectly
oval face in the moonlight, and the unspoken answer to her question.

You. I'd spy on you, in your bath.

The thought had shocked his younger self, and the naked picture
that had formed in his mind had filled him with shame—a fuzzy
image concocted by his eleven-year-old imagination, right out of
soft-core porn, with everything airbrushed and all the good bits
hidden by house plants and camera angles. Hard to believe he'd
once been so innocent.

His inner scientist spoke up. Any adolescent boy encountering a
goddess like Uta would find himself beset with indecipherable urges.
The remembered lump of shame in his throat dissolved.

And now one-hundred-and-seventy-eight-year-old Bel possessed
enough experience to fill in the details his boyhood imagination
had glossed over. Her small breasts would be high and capped with
long, upturned nipples like pink top hats. The plane of her abdomen
would be smooth and white, drawing his eyes down to a tangle of the
darkest red curls between her legs. The skin of her thighs would be

porcelain, and when he spread them her alabaster folds would open into the deep pinks and purples of her vulva. The flawless cheeks of her ass would be so small and temptingly round he could cup each one in a palm and hold her aloft to bury himself in her.

A twig snapped and so did the vision.

"Bel?" Andre asked. He must have come out looking for him as soon as it was fully dark.

He crossed his leg to hide his erection.

Andre gave him a once-over. "Feeling her?"

"Thinking of her."

"Likely more than just that." Andre leaned his back against a tree and crossed his arms. "You will begin to be privy to occasional thoughts, feelings, and images that flash through her mind if they evoke strong emotions from her. You have probably sensed her before without grasping the significance."

"And she can sense me too?" The idea shriveled up his erection like an ice bath.

"I assume so."

An unbreakable bond, a psychic connection. There was no escaping her. "I am completely and royally fucked, aren't I?"

"Do you think you could learn to love her?"

Andre still didn't understand how much Uta's rejection had hurt him. Bel tensed and his old anger surged. But the lines of regret deepened on Andre's face, and so Bel swallowed the past hurt and just told the truth.

"No. Love is something freely given, and she took my freedom."

Andre nodded. "I understand, son. But you are stuck with her forever."

"Andre, unless I can make a cure for the wasting disease, none of you has forever."

"What will you do about Lexi?"

"I suppose I have to send her home. But after that attack in my lab, I better set someone to watch over her."

Andre offered a hand and yanked Bel up to standing. His father rested a palm on Bel's shoulder, an unexpected comfort as they walked back to the house.

He found Lexi where he'd left her, in the dining room, alone and scribbling in a notebook.

"Hi." She stood, wearing a smile too shy for all they'd been through together.

Shite.

"Lex, listen…"

She closed her notebook, shaking her head. "Bel, don't bother with the blow off. I felt it."

"What?" He stiffened.

"That I'm not the one you want. It was in your kiss, like it always was. Only now I know enough to recognize it. I'll stick with Mister Doctor. He worships the hem of my dirty lab coat."

"As he should." Bel took her hand. "Doll, I didn't know it back then either. And I'm sorry. You can't imagine how much I wish it were you." He pressed a kiss onto her knuckles.

"Who is she?" Lexi dragged him to a chair and sat herself down alongside him.

"She's a heartless bitch, and if you stick around to help with this experiment, you'll meet her tomorrow."

"Really?" Lexi's eager grin bordered on predatory. "Then count me in. I've booked a room in town. Can you give me a ride?"

"There's plenty of room here."

"Actually, your stepmom says the vampire United Nations arrives tomorrow and there is a shortage."

Stepmom? Did she mean Zoey? Weird.

"Besides…" She stuffed her notebook into her bag. "No offense, but I think I will sleep easier in a vampire-free hotel."

"Lexi, I can't let you leave. I was attacked at the lab, and I can't guarantee your safety in a hotel. We'll find room for you."

She visibly bristled. "Are you saying I'm a prisoner here?"

"Shite, Lex, no. But you're protected. If you insist on going to a hotel, I'll just have to send someone to watch over you, and I can't guarantee he won't be a vampire."

CHAPTER 10

The sun had set long ago and all humans with good sense had tucked themselves into bed.

Pedro rested his shoulder against the doorframe, studying his human unobserved. Lucas worked at the dining room table with such intensity he didn't even look up to see Pedro arrive.

His man didn't look so good. Well, his man *always* looked good, but currently not as good as usual. His face had grown thin and dark circles shaded his eyes.

He looked…unappetizing. Pedro winced at the thought, which felt like a small betrayal.

Lucas slumped at the dining room table in front of a laptop. In contrast, Trys glowed with rosy health. She'd gained weight since the shield around the estate had condensed to a house-sized dome, no longer extending around the vineyards. When she wasn't eating chocolate to fuel her magical ability, she worked with the other ex-Hunter in residence, Leo, and Bel's tech geek Ani, to scour the Internet searching for chatter from Hunters and vampires alike. From that room, they had charted Ethan's ascent to power and reported it to the Justicia.

"Did you catch the son of a bitch red handed yet?" Pedro asked.

All the humans' heads shot up at once.

"Not yet, but I've got some leads," Leo replied. The kid had more than justified his place on the team. He'd gotten them into Ethan's email several times with his hacking skills. "The Hunter sites are full of all the outrage and self-righteousness you'd expect. More bluster than usual, but when we see any real plans taking shape, we forward it to the Justicia."

When the vampire council had tagged Andre as the tenth oldest vampire in the world, they hadn't known he had two Hunter insiders and a world class hacker in his household. But they were making good use of the new resources.

Pedro's gaze drifted to his lover. "Lucas, you missed dinner. Come eat something. Lena's lasagna smells good, even to me."

Lucas pursed his lips, refusal clearly spelled out on his face. But then his mouth opened and a "yes" came out. They'd had this discussion a dozen times. Lucas had to take care of himself both for his own sake and Pedro's. "Okay. Lasagna sounds good. You three all right if I call it a night?"

"We'll find you if anything happens. Get some grub and some rest." Leo patted Lucas between the shoulder blades.

Pedro growled at the kid for good measure. The gesture seemed harmless enough, but Pedro couldn't have the kid getting any ideas.

Lucas led the way downstairs, and remarkably, they had the kitchen to themselves. Pedro took a moment to appreciate that singular time of day after dinner when a kitchen was quiet and clean, warm and dimly lit, and smelling of food. For that instant, he missed being human. Then it passed and he settled in to watch Lucas eat.

A strand of cheese trailed from one big bite of the meaty pasta and Lucas's lips parted to receive the mouthful.

Pedro imagined kissing him, the decadent feel of his tongue when it slid hot and wet—damn. But if he started that shit, Lucas would never eat. "First time we've been alone since we saw the news this morning."

Lucas set his fork tines-down on his plate. "It's been a hell of a day."

"You look tired." Pedro didn't want to nag, but he couldn't shake his worry for Lucas.

"I am tired."

"How are you feeling?"

"How do you think?" Lucas snapped. "I'm disgusted by those attacks, although I know why they happened. In my gut, I know Ethan's been setting up dominoes. Yesterday, he knocked the first one over, and this is only the beginning."

"Shit, you never said—"

"What could I say? That I have a bad feeling? We've all had a bad feeling."

That was true. Pedro sat quiet, waiting to see if Lucas would say more. He didn't. "Are you scared?"

"Not for myself, if that's what you mean. I trust you and Andre. I guess I'm scared for all of us, and for the humans who get in the way."

Pedro watched his man eat. Eventually he asked, "How's the lasagna?"

"Damn good, as usual. If she becomes a vampire, do you think she'll still cook for us?"

"Yeah, I do. I don't think she can live without it." Pedro loved making wine, but it wasn't in his soul the way food was in Lena's.

"That's good news for you, because if she quit, I might have to whore myself out to the vampire with the best cook." Lucas smiled down at his empty plate, licking his fork clean.

Pedro hadn't seen him clear a plate all week. He laughed. "Then I'll make sure she doesn't. But since you mentioned whoring?"

"Upstairs?"

"Oh thank God." Relief poured out of Pedro. In spite of appearances, his man wasn't too tired for a little fun.

They held hands along the way to Lucas's room, across the hall from Ally and Susan, a long-time couple in Andre's household.

Lucas pushed the door open and tugged Pedro in after him. "You should move your things over here, you know, to the gay side of the house."

"Really?" Pedro closed the door and leaned against it. "It is crowded over in the master wing, with Andre and Zoey, and Lena and Kos. Hearing all that straight sex grosses me out."

Lucas reached over to smooth a lock of hair from Pedro's forehead. "If you think Andre and Zoey are having straight sex, you aren't listening closely enough."

"*Jesu Cristo*. I so do not want to picture that, whatever it means. And for the record, I'm not listening at all."

Lucas laughed. "I wonder if you feel that way about it because he's your *sire*, or whatever you call him." Lucas inflected the word to make it sound all solemn, as if vampires sires could control their offspring, or some other supernatural crap from the movies.

"Nah, I don't think so. He was like a father to me a long time before he turned me."

The lines on Lucas's fine face deepened, and Pedro pulled him into an embrace, whispering into his neck. "Hey, I just got lucky this time. My real father was only slightly better than yours."

"Slightly? That's how much you weigh genocidal hatred and sadism against your dad's run of the mill homophobia?"

Pedro stiffened until Lucas chuckled, letting him know he wasn't offended.

"Yeah, as far as fathers go, Andre is still a pain in the ass, but a lovable one."

"He's worried about Bel." Lucas's fingers played over Pedro's chest, sending notes of electric excitement all the way to his limbs.

Pedro caught his wrist to still the distracting caress. "Wouldn't you be? To find out your son was bonded to an old-as-hell praying mantis of a vampire. She's going to eat Bel alive."

Lucas stepped back and grinned. "Just because you don't want to be devoured by a six-feet-and-change mantis vampiress doesn't mean Bel doesn't want to."

Pedro lunged for Lucas, nuzzling his neck. "True. Some dudes get off on that femdom type."

Lucas tilted his head. "I don't think you're giving Bel enough credit. He can stand up to her—he is Andre's son after all."

"Yeah, which gives him major mommy issues."

"Hmm. Somehow, I'm not worried about him. She's a knockout, and she may be freakishly tall, but don't pretend you didn't notice her suit."

Pedro liked to keep his appreciation for clothes under the radar. He didn't want to be that kind of fag and Lucas knew it, so Pedro elbowed him playfully in the ribs.

Lucas grabbed him, tumbling them down onto the bed. "Hungry?"

Pedro was, but even after that plate of lasagna, Lucas didn't look like he could spare the red blood cells.

"Not for blood." Pedro waggled his eyebrows and leaned in for a kiss.

In the beginning, after Lucas had freed them from their blow job limbo, they had explored every facet of super-hot bitey sex. Pedro had bitten Lucas there, there, there…pretty much everywhere. Pedro'd always been in a hurry, afraid Lucas might change his mind. He had stripped their clothes off with vampire speed, destroying what few shirts Lucas possessed. But as he began to trust Lucas was his for keeps, he'd grown to enjoy taking his time undressing his lover.

Now he ran his palms around Lucas's neck, down his chest and splayed them around his waist. "You're losing weight."

"It's the stress. I'm fine."

"I worry about you." He unbuckled Lucas's pants.

"Yeah, well, I worry about us all."

When Pedro reached for him, Lucas wasn't even close to being hard. Pedro cupped him, gazing into the golden eyes that made them a matched set.

"A lot, I guess."

Lucas smiled. "Just give me a minute."

Pedro's own erection ebbed, but he kept undressing them both. He kissed Lucas's neck then whispered in his ear. "How about you take the world off your shoulders for a while, and let me treat you right?"

"How can I say no to that?" Lucas lay back on the bed, and Pedro climbed between his knees to suck Lucas into his mouth. True to his word, it only took Lucas a minute to get in the mood. Slow and steady, Pedro took him all the way.

After Lucas had grunted his orgasm, he looked a million times better. And he looked tasty again.

Pedro climbed up his lover's body and stroked feather light fingertips up his neck. Lucas's skin broke out in goose flesh, nipples hardening.

"Dinner still on the table?"

"Always, for you."

One particular inch of artery in Lucas's neck was Pedro's heaven, the skin soft and thin, the blood so full of potent Hunter mojo that Pedro soared, high on whatever mysterious chemistry existed between them. Pedro found that sweet spot and rocked them, chest to chest as he drew on Lucas's vein. All that skin on skin was ideal, because Lucas became so sensitive to touch. He was an oral kind of guy, so they'd played with candy and fingers, and curling up together in the shape of an infamous number.

But it turned out to be Pedro's lowly, innocent ear that took them both over the edge every time. After one wet swipe around its rim, conveniently just in reach of Lucas's tongue when Pedro fed at his neck, Lucas whispered, "I swear to God, I can feel how much you like that in your fangs. They tingle inside me."

Pedro believed him. Nothing about this crazy-ass vampire world could surprise him anymore. But with his fangs in his lover's neck, all he could do was squeeze Lucas's ribs tight.

When the bite worked its way into Lucas's muscles and he'd relaxed to his core, Pedro slipped inside him. He was hungry enough to keep pulling blood, but the shadows under Lucas's eyes warned him off, so he licked the wounds closed. Locking eyes with his man, he thrust into Lucas until the feeling that had been growing inside him for weeks finally spilled out as words he once thought he'd never say.

"I love you. I love you."

Lucas's eyes went wide. His lips, slack from pleasure, formed a sultry smile. "Me too. I love you too."

A rush of emotion flooded Pedro, a river of passion and lust and contentment—more than only one heart could hold.

Which could mean only one thing—

He'd bonded to his man.

His fragile, mortal, exhausted man.

He gathered Lucas close, wanting to squeeze with all his strength, but newly aware of Lucas's debilitating humanity. He could be taken from Pedro in one fell swoop—a bus, an illness, a goddamn Hunter. And then Pedro would unravel, heart and soul, suffering the death of Lucas inside his every cell.

There was only one thing to do to make sure Lucas stayed nice and safe, and he wouldn't like it one bit. He would have to become a vampire.

CHAPTER 11

The empty street outside Gwen's window reflected a sterile, urban gray light under the street lamps. The clock on her computer read nine p.m., but outside her door, the office still buzzed with workers. Her stomach grumbled for dinner, but Ethan would probably work even later. Her slacks stuck to her ass because she'd slathered an anesthetic cream on her raw skin. Maybe Ethan wanted her stinging all day, but she was out of sorts over his stunt with the television. No thank you, Sir, she didn't want to feel the burn of her submission until bedtime.

She went to look for him, to announce she was going to pick up a sandwich and go home.

"Have you seen Ethan?" she asked another yellow-eyed twenty-something. A month in the office, and she still wasn't used to those unusual irises in every face.

"In the conference room, I think," offered a helpful initiate, which seemed to mean something like intern. They all treated her with enormous respect because of her ability to interpret their artifacts. Ethan had intimated that otherwise, with her gray-blue eyes, she would not have been accepted, even as his girlfriend, or lieutenant, or love slave, or whatever she was.

What they didn't know was that after weeks of offering her body up on the altar that was Ethan, he had chosen to trust her. At work he gave the impression that she was not privy to his secrets, but in private she was his sole confidant. She alone knew that Ethan had, the day before, offered his own people up at that same altar. Their slaughter set a precedent, and exactly as he'd hoped, the vampires took the bait, perpetrating massacres on a far grander scale.

She strode down the hallway toward the conference room with an assurance she did not feel. Over the last month, Bennett Public Relations had transformed into global Hunter headquarters, all because of Gwen's translation of *The Book of the Day*, which had earned Ethan ever increasing prominence among his fellow Hunters.

"Good evening, Ms. Evans," two fresh faced, attractive young men called out to her in the hallway. The Hunters were secretive but also friendly and appealing, like she imagined missionaries for a cult might be. Or maybe Ethan had just recruited the cream of the crop. She got the feeling people in the office were often frustrated with the Hunters in the field.

The place was like a campaign office, full of intelligent young interns who worshipped their charismatic leader. The work never stopped. Some of the Hunters were managing Ethan's public image, some of them were investigating the whereabouts of vampires, and still others were overseeing operations against the hateful creatures. Gwen's job, for which she had her own staff of Hunters, was to research artifacts and reconstruct as much of their history as possible. She never saw what Ethan did with her research, but it clearly gave him a great deal of credibility with the interns and presumably with the Hunters around the world.

"Ah, hello Ms. Evans." Ethan's assistant Justine stood guard at the door to the conference room.

"Hello. I just wanted to tell Ethan I'm heading home for the night." The wall of the conference room was glass, and inside Gwen could see the same horrifying images she'd been fucked to that morning, still flashing on cable news. Lovely. Apparently nothing else cataclysmic had happened today to replace them in the twenty-four-hour news cycle.

Ethan spoke animatedly on the other side of the glass.

Justine pressed an intercom button, which beeped loudly. "Mr. Bennett, Ms. Evans is here to see you."

He came out, rather than inviting her in, as if mission-control were the holy of holies. That might just make him the ark, God's vessel on earth. He would like the comparison, but it twisted her gut.

"Going home?" He sounded almost friendly, not like a man who delighted in the slaughter of innocents and wanted to turn her into a monster like him.

"Yes. But first can I ask you a question?"

"Of course." He steered her down the hall where they could speak semi-privately. Her scalp tingled under the curious gazes of the onlooking interns. They were probably wondering what he was doing with someone like her. She could tell them *hurting me for fun while I have unceasing orgasms.* Blurting it out might earn her a punishment to look forward to.

"I was re-reading *The Book of the Day* and I found myself curious. Have any vampires been seen in the sun since the attacks?"

His eyes shone. "Not a one. I rather doubt they will have the nerve to try it."

"Do you believe Hunter blood will give them this power?"

He pressed all his fingertips together to form a steeple. "I hold it as possible, but unlikely. What do you think, based on your knowledge of the texts?"

"I am not sure what to believe. I've experienced so many things I thought impossible."

"My poor Gwen." He stroked her hair.

She stepped back. "I'm going to pick up dinner. Shall I get you something?"

"No, thank you. But before you go, there is something I want to tell you. I have good news. At midday, my men located the entrance to a tunnel a quarter mile from the estate. It must be the way through Marasović's shield. We are going in." The tendons in his neck flexed.

"You?" Her empty stomach twisted.

"If the opportunity arises, I want to be there to slay the vampire myself."

Strange that he had achieved success on a grand scale, but a single household still vexed him. Why did he care so much about Marasović? It must have to do with the woman Zoey. Justine had gossiped all about Ethan's former lover to Gwen, appalled that Zoey would have chosen life among vampires over allying with a powerful Hunter like Ethan. Did he want revenge, or did he want her back?

"I would like you to come." He smiled at Gwen with the same tenderness she'd seen after breakfast.

The monster liked her, a chilling turn of events. He slid his hand down her spine gently, and grabbed her ass, igniting her raw skin.

"We can find dinner on the way," he said.

She pressed into him, in spite of—no, because of the pain. The truth was, in spite of her uneasy response to him, she would do whatever he asked. "Of course. I look forward to witnessing your victory."

A group of the Hunters gathered down the hall, murmuring. One of them ushered a young woman through, her wrists handcuffed in front of her.

"Who is that?" Gwen asked.

"The bait."

The wasting vampire sat on a stool, his emaciated forearm turned up and resting on the long stainless steel table of the workroom at Kaštel. His thin skin had puckered into goose bumps, but short of curing him, Bel couldn't do a thing to make him warmer. The last drops of *hemoaurum* drained from the bag and into the clear plastic tube feeding into his vein. Bel pulled out the needle, and only the tiniest drop of blood oozed from the wound before it healed. Done—the final infusion.

Through the early morning hours of darkness, a dozen vampires had received the new, potentially therapeutic doses. He'd chosen the fittest of the test subjects to receive this last sample without any of the isolates they'd extracted from Blood Vine. The control dose, identical to the first round of treatment, would have no effect. Sloppy scientific method—but the best he could do under the circumstances. And if just one of them showed improvement, he would have a new direction to pursue.

He took the frail creature's elbow and steered him to the door. The healthiest of the group and still the male was essentially a sack of bones encased in loose, papery skin. The vampire's householder met Bel at the loading ramp and helped his employer into the car.

Bel should have offered the same optimistic words he had to all the others, but his tongue faltered on the lie. He ran it over his teeth instead. "Drive safe. Call me right away if you see any improvement. Otherwise, I'll monitor your progress in three days."

"Thank you, Dr. Maras," he said, in the Dalmatian dialect.

After Bel closed the door and they drove off, he whispered, "You can call me Bel."

The early morning smelled sweet and leafy, without a trace of burned chemicals in the air. Bel considered a walk, though his muscles ached with rare fatigue. He didn't require much sleep, but it had been nearly seventy-two hours since he'd caught any shut eye. The sky glittered with a million stars—a sight he never saw from London's bright streets. It was too gorgeous to abandon, and so he leaned against the outer wall of the workroom and gazed upward.

For a moment, déjà vu carried him away to the beach on Šolta. He could almost feel Uta by his side. An owl hooted, bringing him back to the present moment.

The same stars, but so many years later. Each one of those lights, shining from so far away. Each particle, sent from its star ages ago, before he had been bonded to Uta, before Hunters hated vampires, perhaps before there *were* Hunters and vampires. As a kid, the night sky had made his problems feel insignificant, but now, not even the glimmer of stars could make him forget the violent attacks on Hunters.

Slowly, the sun illuminated a band of blue sky along the horizon, and the stars began to fade. He pushed off the wall, intending to hit the sheets. His muscles had grown stiff in the cool morning air and he stretched his arms overhead, twisting to loosen the tension in his spine.

A knock sounded on the other side of the door, mere inches from his head. His heart leaped into his throat.

"Yeah?" he called out a reply.

"Boss, problem. A big one."

When Bel swung the door open, Omar danced back into the shadows.

"What is it?"

"We've got an army of Hunters in the tunnel."

Inside already? That meant they were right below him. "And the shield?"

"Holding them back like a clogged up toilet." They strode to the cellar door together.

"Omar, have you ever even seen a clogged up toilet?"

"No, but I grasp the concept." The big vampire spun with his hand on the knob, facing Bel. "Ethan Bennett is down there, boss, and he wants to negotiate."

Bel paused to let that news sink in. He took a mental roll call of the people he cared about—could Bennett have any of them? Lexi was here, and his family. Could the son of a bitch have Uta?

Did Bel care? Other than the pain worse than death part? His traitorous heart thumped out an answer he chose to ignore.

He met up with Andre and Kos in the cellar.

"Mind if I take this one?" Bel asked.

"Be my guest, son. Kos and I botched the last round of negotiations, to our great peril."

Kos's mouth pulled tight, and Bel knew his brother blamed himself for the destruction of their father's vineyards, although Andre did not.

"Ready?" Kos opened the door onto an astonishing scene.

Twenty feet into the tunnel, a few members of Bel's crew stood on this side of the shield. Everyone else would be above ground in case this was some kind of diversion.

Bennett occupied center stage on the opposite side, his palm pressed against the unbudging, transparent shield, testing. Six inches over his head, someone had sprayed paint on the shield to make it visible. Behind him, black-clad bodies filled the tunnel. Clogged toilet was bloody accurate.

"I wish I had been here when the first guy walked into it," Bel said.

Bennett looked up. "I confess we were caught off guard." His gaze swept over Bel. "You are not Marasović."

"I'm Lobel Maras."

Ethan's focus settled somewhere behind Bel; he must have seen Andre. His predatory smile sent ice down Bel's spine.

"What do you want, Bennett? Or should I even bother asking before we start throwing grenades at you from the other end of the tunnel?"

"I brought you a defector."

"Pardon?"

A young yellow-eyed woman was shoved forward between the Hunters. She almost fell face first into the shield, but Bennett caught her first. Good thing. She appeared to be unarmed, which meant she would have fallen straight through. Bel didn't have a clue how Trys generated the force field, only that it kept out artillery of all sorts, and people carrying weapons. An unarmed Hunter could march right through, but he would pose minimal risk to a household of vampires. And the chances of that happening were slim, since the vermin never went anywhere without guns holstered in every orifice. Still, the illusion of impermeability provided a great deal of security. The less Hunters knew about the shield, the better.

Bennett held her at arm's length. "This pure born Hunter has betrayed us by her love of vampires. She has come to join your household." He jostled the girl. "Beg."

Her face was bruised, and through her dirty blond hair, one swollen yellow eye was visible.

"Do you want to?" Bel asked.

She shook her head, her shoulders trembling with fear.

"Why did you bring her?"

"An act of mercy." Ethan's eyes flicked upward to the white marks on the shield. A nearly imperceptible gesture, but Bel didn't miss it.

"So we accept her and show you how to cross through the shield, or…"

"I kill her, right here in front of you, for being a traitor and parasite lover." He raised his voice, and from far back in the tunnel, cheers erupted. With a clean draw, he unholstered his weapon and aimed it at her head.

If Trys lowered the shield for even a second, these Hunters would storm down the tunnel with their machine guns blasting at every vampire. Maybe they could keep them out, but too many people would get hurt.

Bel locked eyes with the girl. Damn, she couldn't be older than twenty. She trembled violently, the poor thing, and she began talking. "Please don't hurt me. I'm so sorry." She sniffed and tried to raise her hand to her nose, but dropped it again when the handcuffs gave her trouble.

Ethan grabbed a fistful of her hair. "No talking." He ran the gun up the girl's hip and over her breast. "She is attractive enough. Surely you can take pity on her and enjoy her…*blood*."

The Hunters behind Ethan snickered like adolescents. Hell, most of them were only initiates, from what Bel could see.

"Do you drink blood, halfling?"

Bel had no intention of giving Ethan any information. "She's just a girl. How has she betrayed you?"

"Tell him."

She sniffed and gasped for breath. "My friend from the Hunter compound in Canada was taken hostage. By vampires. She emailed me, told me they invited all the women and children in her compound to their household, if they wanted to. I told her she was lucky. I wished I could leave my family to join the vampires."

"Whore," shouted one of the Hunters. More catcalls and boos followed. "Vampire trash."

"Quiet," Ethan ordered. "She is a fool to believe in vampire mercy, and a traitor to wish for it." Ethan backhanded her. Blood trickled from her lip.

Here she was, facing her own death at the hands of her people for wanting to escape them, and there wasn't a damn thing Bel could do about it.

"Tell him your name." Bennett pressed the barrel of the gun into her head.

"L-Lindsay, sir."

"Lindsay, I'm sorry. If I let you in here, I put everyone in the household at risk."

Was that right? Was he making the right choice? He wanted to look to Kos and Andre for reassurance, but she deserved his unwavering attention.

"Please," she cried. Snot and tears ran down her face.

Shite. Bel wanted to execute Ethan ten times over.

Andre and Kos stepped alongside Bel, their shoulders brushing his in silent support.

"Don't do this to me," she cried.

"If there was any way, sweetheart…"

Fuck Ethan. What a mastermind. He'd thoroughly tied Bel's hands. This particular torture would stay with him as long as anything the son of a bitch had done to Pedro.

Bel wanted to scream, to rail against the powerlessness of the situation, but he forced calm into his voice. "Leave her here, Bennett. We will see to her."

"Let her through the shield now, halfling, or I shoot her. In three… two…"

"I'm sorry Lindsay," Bel whispered.

"I know." She nodded, a gesture of forgiveness he would hold eternally dear.

"We'll see you in the homeland." Kos spoke the old benediction under his breath.

Bel wished it were true — that there were some kind of vampire Valhalla for martyrs on both sides. But there wasn't. There was only the waste of a young life.

The bullet went through her head and bounced off the shield. She fell sideways. Blood splattered, lower than the white paint, a red mist seeming to hover in space.

"More blood on your hands, vampires." Bennett raised his lip in disgust. "Retreat!"

He was quite a showman. Bel had to hand it to him.

The Hunters turned tail fast, a small one peeling out of the shadows at the back of the line to fall in step next to Ethan. They took their battery-powered lanterns with them and left the tunnel in darkness.

Bel spun to see the silhouettes of Vania and Omar side by side, illuminated by the dim light of the cellar. "Intercept them at the exit?"

"It's broad daylight above ground," Bel replied. "But you, me, and Arden could go. Pick as many of them off as we can. I'm sure Leo would like to come too."

Leo. He could have so easily been in this girl's shoes. Might have known her, even.

Bel shook his head. Without vampire speed, by the time the three arrived there the Hunters would be long gone. "Take Arden with you and clear the tunnel. Get the door fixed. And Vania, buy Trys the most expensive box of chocolates you can find."

"I'm on it." She smiled tightly, until her eyes traveled to the dead Hunter and she spun, leaving in a hurry.

"I will tend to the girl," Andre said, passing through the shield to kneel at her side.

"And me," Kos said.

Alone with his father and brother, Bel closed his eyes in relief. "Did I do the right thing?"

"You had no choice, Bel. Do not let Bennett trick you into believing otherwise."

No choice. Bel trembled with the fury of it.

"I am proud of you." Andre looked up from where he crouched next to the girl, smoothing her hair.

Words Bel craved, but all he could think was what a horrible world he lived in, when doing the right thing resulted in the murder of an innocent girl. And in a matter of hours, the other person who had stolen his choices would arrive. He kicked the brick wall of the cellar hard enough to jar his teeth.

Double shite.

CHAPTER 12

Uta's black rolling suitcases, five of them, leaned against one another in the underground garage of Loki's chalet. One of the householders carried out a stack of English grammar books. He handed the study materials to her and hefted one suitcase in each hand, lumbering toward Loki's Land Rover.

"Uta, I'm afraid you might have left something in the closet," Loki said. "Shall we run back and get it?"

She applied a coat of lipstick and flicked him off with the middle finger of her other hand.

"You're wearing that?" His eyebrows lifted in arch disapproval.

Uta dropped her lipstick into her pocket and looked down at her clothes then back up at him. What did he mean? It was her standard uniform—a designer suit and shoes, and underneath her jacket, a draping hand-knit shell in silk or angora or cashmere, depending on the season. He had to be teasing.

"Shut up. I look fabulous."

"Uta, child, typically I refrain from commenting on your…high beams, but if you want Bel to be peaceable, put on a bra."

She cupped her small breasts. So what if the fabric rubbed across her nipples, making them stick out? Yes, it was a little obscene. She liked it that way. "I do not own a bra. Vampire tits do not sag."

He pulled a white cardboard box from his pocket. "I anticipated you might say that. The women of my household have provided you with these instead."

"Band-Aids? Ridiculous. I heal instant—" Oh. For her nipples? "Loki, what is this sudden fascination with my breasts?"

"The bond between you and Bel is starting to flare as white-hot lust. I need you to work together, not fuck each other raw. And I hope an understanding will develop between you. But, unless I have misjudged him, the more Bel feels himself trapped by the bond and its sexual power, the more he will retreat from you. So put your titties away and act reasonable and professional."

"I am always reasonable and professional."

Titters and snorts sounded from the householders behind them.

She raised her voice, cursing them all in a foul string of old Norse expletives involving the genitals of livestock.

Loki's lips twisted into an S of wry amusement before he replied in the same ancient tongue. "I expect they comprehended about sixty percent of that."

"A sufficient amount. If they understood more, they might quit your employ so they no longer had to put up with your ill-mannered company." Uta was well aware most of them thought she was a monstrous pain in the ass. It was a matter of pride to her.

"So little faith in my prowess. I keep them far too satisfied to resign their positions." He clucked. "But now that I think of it, when I consider my predecessors in the post of eldest and chief, I am quite certain you have never experienced the pleasure of being plundered by the oldest vampire in the world."

Hell, she couldn't remember the last time she'd been plundered by anyone. And French was always the best language to admit when one had been bested.

"*Touché.*"

"How are you feeling? Nervous?"

"Vampires do not have nerves."

"That's ridiculous, Uta. Of course we do."

"Well, I am not nervous. And before you ask, I am not frightened either."

The look on his face confirmed she had anticipated the next question correctly.

"Loki, I crush the skulls of Hunters in my sleep. I am not afraid of Lobel Marasović."

"Uta, darling, you don't sleep."

"Do not quibble. You know what I mean."

Inside his custom Land Rover with the standard vampire-grade sunproof windows, she leaned her head against the magic glass. She should be thinking about the Justicia meeting, about how to stop vampires and Hunters from massacring each other and how to take down Ethan Bennett once and for all.

Instead all she could think of was last night, after she'd cast on her first row of stitches, when a bizarre sensation overtook her. Well, bizarre because it had been nearly two centuries since she'd felt it. At first, she'd thought she was dying—her heart raced for no reason, her blood heated, her skin tingled. What vampire sickness was this—sudden-onset wasting disease? Surely she would age a thousand years overnight from this feeling.

Then, a desiccated part of her, long dead, flooded with heat and moisture. *Oh. That sickness.* Images flashed before her eyes. Bel at her breast, holding her ass in his big hands, spreading her legs to taste her, just before he sunk his not-real fangs into her thigh.

Fangs? Her waking dream froze. They must have been *his* fantasies, resounding in her body and arousing her like she had not been in centuries, tingling and throbbing.

Thank the gods she hadn't been privy to his urges when they were about other women, and now the tantalizing images tempted her with the hope that he wanted Uta instead. Goddamn, it seemed like a million years since her body had wanted like that, and longer since her heart had soared with hope. With a starting point of explosive attraction, maybe he would eventually learn to love her too.

A loud crack against the car window disturbed her thoughts—Loki knocking to get her attention. She hissed at him. "What?"

Loki leaned too close to her face. "We are approaching the hangar. Shall we stop somewhere so you can take a cold shower before we board my plane?"

"I don't know what you mean." She flicked her fingers at him.

"Uta, you are panting and pungent."

She crossed her legs tightly and glanced at the human passengers in the vehicle. Surely they couldn't scent her arousal, but they'd heard Loki. Nils turned red, his nostrils flaring as he swiveled his face away from her.

Loki sent a message to her on a whisper, lowering his voice so that only her vampire ears could hear. "My sympathies. You are in quite a state."

Uta recrossed her legs, wincing. He was right. And she could have no relief apart from the object of her desire, could rub herself raw without attaining an ounce of satisfaction. In that way Bel had the advantage—he could masturbate. Well, she assumed he could, being a halfling. It wasn't exactly something they had discussed when he was a boy.

Loki's phone rang and he answered. On the other end, Ingrid, his assistant, launched into the news loud enough for Uta to hear. "Two more attacks on Hunter cells. A compound in suburban Mumbai was burned to the ground. We didn't know there were nearly eight hundred Hunters living there."

"Eight hundred Hunters dead?" Loki rubbed his eyelids with his thumb and forefingers.

"Maras's team of hackers has found a few websites where vampires are communicating. But they're too smart to plan on the sites; they only trade contact information. There was another attack in rural South Africa. Smaller, but no official numbers yet. And, Uta, brace yourself for this. Two households of Croatian refugees firebombed in retaliation last night. Houston and Miami."

Those households belonged to three of her oldest friends, and Andre's too: Emil and Naeda Bradić, and Sanjin Cvetko. The spark of hope Bel's lust had inspired shrank to a pinprick. If only she had somehow stopped the persecution of her friends, had been able to protect the secret she guarded. So many had died because of her failures. She eyed the door handle. She could be on the sunny street and out of Loki's reach in no time. Loki's gaze burned into her, not quite as hot as the sun. He arched an eyebrow.

She took a deep breath and resolved to face her problems, not run from them. "They must all be evacuated preemptively. Bennett will target the Šoltan refugees first, to spite Andre."

He shook his head. "If they have sired offspring in their new homes, they will resist evacuation."

He was right. No parent wanted their child to suffer the wasting disease, especially once they knew its costs. "Then they must be on the highest alert, prepared to leave at the first sign of attack."

"Ingrid, did you hear Uta's instructions? Good. Make it happen." Then he ended the call.

"I want evac units positioned at all their homes."

"We do not have enough soldiers, Uta. My five best units are hunting the aggressionists, and the rescue calls are coming every night."

He was right. She must not use her position to garner special treatment for her friends. Her conscience protested, but it always found something to complain about.

"So, darling, I know how you dislike being bested at anything. I suggest you bury yourself in those textbooks and learn to speak English better than Lobel himself. That should distract you until we arrive."

She threw her head back, slamming it into the car seat hard enough that the whole vehicle trembled. "Ugh. I hate studying."

One of the householders snickered. Good thing Uta could not tell which, because she felt positively murderous. "Loki, silence your minions. They irk me."

CHAPTER 13

Sometime after sunset, car doors slammed in the front drive. Lucas rounded the dining room table and slouched against the door frame. Across the foyer, Bel stood at the window alongside Andre.

Next to his father, the son was taut like a bowstring and vibrating with jittery energy. Poor guy. Ethan had put Bel in an impossible situation in that tunnel and Lucas had been replaying his own Hunter initiation in sympathy. At sixteen, his father had forced him to kill the handsome human consort of a vampire.

Maybe Bel had other skeletons in his closet, but the halfling would be living with the death of that young Huntress for a long time. Lucas wished he could offer him some comfort, but nothing less cliché than "time heals all wounds" came to mind. Vampires would know far better than he whether that aphorism held true.

Just then, Bel chuckled, jolting Lucas out of his despair. It was a welcome sound.

"Damn, that's a lot of them — nine vampires and their humans. They must have been crammed inside the vans like they were being hauled off in a paddy wagon."

In profile, Andre's sly smile barely raised the corner of his mouth. "It could not be more perfect. They will never invite themselves back."

Bel pulled his phone from his pocket and glanced at the screen. "Omar reports we are Hunter free for a mile in all directions."

"Good," Andre replied. "It is certainly preferable they do not know the Justicia is here."

Raised voices argued outside and Lucas shifted so he could see out the window. Two of Bel's vampires were patting down a black-haired visitor.

"*Davo.* That fool Sadavir is armed — he could not pass through the shield."

"You did warn them all," Lucas said.

"Shite." Bel staggered, reaching for the wall. "I'm going upstairs."

"You cannot run from her," Andre called out.

"Watch me." Bel jogged toward the stairs.

Lucas bit his lip, imagining a big green praying mantis eating the head off its mate.

Andre shook his head at Bel's back and then turned to crack the door. Lucas stiffened, bracing himself for any amount of hostility from the Justicia members.

A small man or, more likely, a male vampire, entered first and extended his hand to Andre. He glanced around the entryway, making his face visible to Lucas. This was Loki, the chief, even smaller than he appeared on video.

His eyes narrowed. "Lucas Bennett?"

"That's me."

Loki crossed the room at light speed and stood in front of Lucas, scrutinizing. Then he reached for Lucas's hand. Lucas jerked back.

"Let me look at your palm. It is an ancient custom of my people."

Lucas extended his arm. Loki traced the crevices and furrows with his index finger. He leaned close, sniffing. "It has been many years since I smelled a Hunter so close, and even longer since I touched one. Always in battle."

Lucas's heart tried to burst from his chest, but he would be damned if he let Loki see his fear. He inhaled deeply, forcing stillness through his body. "What can you see on my hand?"

Loki dropped it. "Not a thing. But I learned a great deal from the way you reacted."

Unsure of the impression he'd made, Lucas slid his fist into his pocket to hide the minor tremors shaking him. When he glanced up, nine vampires and more than that many humans filled the foyer. Everyone's attention seemed focused on Loki, and Andre who had come to stand next to them. Only one tall redhead looked around anxiously — Uta in search of her prey.

"Where are the mercenaries who work for Lobel?"

Andre gave Loki a sidelong glance, then addressed the gathering. "Bel's vampire crew is deployed on the perimeter of the estate, helping to secure your arrival. His human staff keep watch during the day, and several of them work with our Hunter ally Leo Carpoli on…" Andre frowned.

Lucas suppressed a smile. "Cyber security," he whispered, out of respect, even though half the room would hear him loud and clear.

"Yes. Cyber security."

Quiet chuckles behind Lucas told him the hackers had come to stand in the doorway.

"Some of you are acquainted with the oldest of Bel's warriors, Omar de Yaounde."

Lucas turned to follow the stares, finding Omar towering over Leo and Ani with his enormous hand raised. Shouts of greeting rang out.

"And now, if we may visit our rooms to refresh ourselves?" Loki asked.

"Of course." Andre swept his arm magnanimously. "Members of my household will direct you." The residents of Kaštel mingled through the crowd and pointed in all directions.

"May I speak to you?" Loki gripped Lucas's elbow. So, not a question, really.

They stepped out of the crowd into the empty parlor.

"I happen to have a set of theories that motivate me to work with you," Loki said.

Lucas leaned against the wet bar, his fingers curling around the countertop. "As do I."

"I suppose you would. I wonder to what extent we suspect the same things."

"I expect we will find out soon enough."

"Indeed." Loki strolled over to the panorama of windows overlooking the burned vineyards. His sigh echoed Lucas's lingering sadness at the destruction.

The little vampire tapped on the glass. "But make no mistake, Bennett. It is my duty to protect my kind from the Hunter threat." He spun on his heels. "If you betray us, I will drink down all your special blood and then take you apart, joint by joint."

"I'm certain you would have to fight Andre for the honor."

Loki cracked a cheeky smile. "You are not afraid of me?"

Lucas inhaled again, more easily than before. "Honestly? I am much more afraid of my brother."

CHAPTER 14

Bel took refuge in his room, but Andre was right, he couldn't run from Uta. A tempting sensation of homecoming teased his heart, demanding he search her out. It was a relief from the torment of picturing that Hunter girl, her unseeing eyes staring into the dark tunnel. But he didn't trust Uta's siren song, so he stayed put. She would find him eventually, and she would tell him what she knew about the wasting disease, and then he could be done with her.

A knock sounded on his door, and he jumped inches off the floor.

Without a bit of evidence, he knew it was Uta.

He frowned at his reflection in the mirror, noticing the scruff on his chin and his shaggy hair for the first time all day. His fingers caught in his curls and he shook them out.

No way. I'm not primping for her.

Uta opened his door before he reached it. She probably heard his heart racing. *Ba-boom. Ba-boom.*

Okay. It wasn't so bad. Not like he couldn't breathe, not like he fell at her feet and worshipped her. He just stared, and hungered.

It still surprised him she was tall enough to look him in the eye. Her expression remained neutral, mirroring his wariness.

He scanned every inch of her fair-skinned oval face, her narrow nose and the cleverest eyes he had ever seen. He sucked in a breath — she was beauty itself, an ideal imprinted in his every cell. The faces of the women he had been drawn to in his life flashed in his mind, all poor approximations of her. Ani's copper hair. That whore he had adored a hundred years ago in a London brothel. Even Lexi's lean form was just a shadow of Uta's lithe elegance.

He clenched his jaw, rage burning through his veins. He'd loved Lexi freely, not because it was biologically determined by some bullshit blood bond. But it turned out that his godmother was the cookie cutter for his perfect female all along.

Uta flinched at his anger before it could possibly have showed on his face. Then her eyes slanted downward and unexpected pity for her welled up inside him.

No. This was her fault. No pity.

He crossed his arms. "I don't know where to start."

She swallowed and the white skin of her throat rippled. "We will only speak of vampires, Hunters, blood, and your foolish…what do you call it?"

Strange. She didn't sound like a mail order bride anymore. Overnight, her English had taken anchor smack dab in the center of the Atlantic—half Manhattan, half Cambridge, with just a hint of the homeland in her consonants.

He cleared his throat. "*Hemoaurum*. And it's not foolish." Shite, he sounded like a twelve-year-old, even to his own ears.

"Yes, your *hemoaurum*. We will not discuss—" she paused, looking away from him "—anything else."

He didn't trust her and he squinted into her face, attempting to uncover what she was hiding. She colored, rose blooming on her cheeks and across her nose. Oh. That. Not a conspiracy or a secret plan. Just the shared knowledge of a mutual desire they'd telegraphed to each other over their bond. With the day's events he'd nearly forgotten his reverie out at Andre's spring.

He shifted his feet, unsure what to say next.

Her lips pursed. "Bel, I need to know. Last night, did you…"

He could imagine a million ends to that sentence, so he waited, but she didn't finish. "What? Did I what?"

She huffed. "Oh, fuck the biggest bull! This word was not in the English books I studied." Her pout was almost charming. "Did you…" Again she hesitated.

"Spit it out, Uta."

Instead, she gestured with a loose fist, back and forth.

He sputtered. "How is that any of your business?"

She didn't answer, only looked at her feet, apparently waiting for him to work it out himself. It didn't take long, once he recalled the state he'd been in last night. "Oh." He was beginning to hate that syllable; she dumbfounded him, perpetually.

"I had hoped that if you took care of your…business, I might find some relief. Across our bond."

"No, I did not. I had other things on my plate—vampire test subjects, a Hunter invasion." *The passive murder of an innocent.*

"Damned roaches," she snarled. Then her voice changed to pure sugar. "Perhaps you could try now?"

He wanted to scream at her that he was thoroughly not in the mood, but she batted her eyes almost demurely. It was so incongruous he had to laugh. "Come on, it can't be that bad for a woman."

"Do not be stupid. It is bad. Swollen. Aching. Throbbing. It is a terrible distraction. In a fight with Hunter, I could only think about my…*pićka.*"

Bel laughed harder. Apparently that English word wasn't in her textbooks either.

She narrowed her eyes at him. "I would slap you, but it would shatter your cheek."

He stopped laughing. If she decided to slap him, he'd likely end up with a concussion, possibly even a skull fracture. Maybe he'd been underestimating female arousal—it had usually seemed like women could take sex or leave it.

"We will discuss this no further. Only your experiment." She spoke with the slightly stilted formality of Andre like she'd skipped the lesson on contractions.

"Fine by me. I was thinking we could talk in the workroom."

Uta furrowed her brow and looked around as if about to say, why not here? Then her eyes landed on the bed and her lips pursed again. "A fine idea. I will follow you."

She didn't though. She apparently remembered where they were headed from her previous visit and she pushed past him and led the way. Behind her trailed an oddly familiar perfume he hadn't smelled in years. His brain searched through memories, trying to place the flowery scent as they descended the stairs.

In the cellar, she sniffed. "It still smells like Hunter. I take it the one called Derek remains here?"

"He's still a prisoner. No one wanted to kill him and we can't let him go."

She blew out a raspberry of air, clearly unimpressed by their show of mercy. "Are you keeping him for his blood?"

"No. Lucas has something else in mind."

When they arrived inside the large room, Uta strode to a worktable in the center of the room. She ran one long finger along its stainless steel surface and then hopped up, straddling a corner and tilting her hips forward. The position was suggestive, damn near obscene. Was she trying to provoke him?

She closed her eyes and released a slow, hissing sigh. Well damn. She must be cooling off her aching lady parts on the cold metal of the table. She stared at the wall behind him and sucked her lower lip. Goddamn, he burned for the heartless bitch.

She whimpered, and pity dragged him down again — pity for this ice queen who had broken his little boy heart. Despite two centuries of hatred, he felt the impulse to help. He could give her what she needed, what he needed too. Only, it was her damn fault they were in this situation. She had helped to create him and this unnatural bond. She had bound him only to her, taken away his freedom to love anyone else. If he had to suffer this unslakable desire, then at least she suffered too.

After a moment, Uta freed that lush red lip from her teeth. "I know something about Hunters, but it is a secret I have kept from the beginning."

He sighed, making sure she would hear his impatience in his tone. "The beginning of what?"

She huffed, as if the answer should be obvious. They were getting along great. On each other's nerves in two sentences flat.

"My life as a vampire."

He wanted to talk about his cure, not conduct an interview with a vampire *à là* Anne Rice, but damn, that was interesting. "You have a two-thousand-year-old secret?"

She glared at him. "Bel, keep up. You are not an idiot. No more stupid questions."

Déjà vu crashed over him again. She'd said those words to him often, just as impatiently, but full of affection. The air in his lungs turned to water. He swam in the nostalgia of the moment, barely keeping his head up.

"Maybe you overestimate my intelligence."

"No, you underestimate it. You always have."

It grated on him that she acted like she knew him. He wanted to wring her neck, especially since he couldn't really hurt her. Her jacket hung open, revealing the gentle curve of her breasts, big nipples erect through her top.

Uta's eyes flicked to him suddenly, and he was caught with his tongue dangling like a dog.

She held his gaze while she squirmed. If she had stood up and stripped her clothes off and splayed her legs open on that stainless steel table, he would have been helpless. Free will be damned. He would have dipped his head to her *pička* and tasted his fill of her soft skin for hours. He wanted those thighs clamped against the side of his head. The whole damn Justicia could have circled around them and conducted their meeting, and Bel would have just kept lapping at her.

And on some level she knew it.

But instead of stripping, she shifted on the table, uncrossing her legs and wriggling until she found a spot not yet warmed by her body on the surface of the table.

She could have him, but she didn't want him. Didn't want him any more now than she had when she abandoned him all those years ago. He was just a little boy she got stuck with, had accidentally bonded to. And at every moment she was still treating him like he was eleven. That humiliating realization deflated his hard-on in an instant.

CHAPTER 15

The languid desire that throbbed between Uta's legs grew fervent, tightening her chest and curling her fingers. Sweat beaded on her forehead and she wiped it off with the back of her hand.

Bel's jaw muscles clenched. His anger had flipped on like a switch and it only served to tighten the coil of arousal in her belly.

"Bel—"

"Don't. Just tell me the goddamn secret. But don't ever forget that you did this to me. I didn't choose to want you like this."

How could she forget? It haunted her every second.

"Not now. You need to know about the blood before the Justicia meets."

His dark brows formed a V and then lifted quickly in a display of curiosity. Always a scientist first, her Bel, and the expression reminded her so much of when he was a boy that her throat closed up and she coughed, trying to choke back her grief over what she had lost—something she'd never had a right to in the first place.

"Your protein does not work because it lacks *osjećaj*."

"*Osjećaj*—sentiment?" He leaned forward on the balls of his feet.

"Consider Blood Vine. Andre's passion, his love of the homeland, his nostalgia—the sentiments, as you say, permeate the wine and make it nourishing."

"But the wine has *hemoaurum* in it, like Hunter blood. That's what nourishes vampires."

"Pshaw! If a vampire made a cream puff with ties to the homeland, it would cure us too."

"You're bullshitting me. The *hemoaurum* has to matter."

"I know nothing of it, only the *osjećaj*. Sentiment feeds bonds." She crossed her legs and scratched at an imaginary spot on her knee so he wouldn't see what she wasn't saying. Sentiment fed all bonds, including those of mates. When she mastered her expression, she glanced back up. "And you cannot create that in a laboratory."

"*Osjećaj.*" He narrowed his eyes at her and his fingertips rasped over the stubble on his chin — such a masculine sound.

"Yes. Not just chemicals, but a state of sentimental connection instead of separation and exile."

"You're suggesting nostalgia for when Hunters and vampires lived together makes Hunter blood powerful?"

"I know it to be true."

"That's shite. I've seen the *hemoaurum* under the microscope — it is in Hunter blood, in Blood Vine, and in the blood of vampires when they drink from one or the other and are cured. That is scientific proof."

"And yet it does not work."

He scowled, shifting his focus to the ceiling, lost in thoughts she could almost sense in her own mind.

Such a scientist. He was already hypothesizing, when she had meant to deter him. This was a useless path, but she did not want to burst his hopes, only wanted to watch him stargazing, the memories of his youth rushing back at her like raindrops in a downpour.

She spoke without thought. "You always did look upward to think."

He froze. His hand rubbing on his chin, his breaths — everything stopped.

Too late for her to hold back now. "I assumed it was because we spent so many nights lying on the beach talking. But you had the habit even indoors."

Very slowly, he lowered his gaze to her and his eyes glittered with confusion over the thin line of his lips. "Were we really friends? I hardly remember a thing before you dropped me like a burning coal." His puzzled expression hinted at a boyish vulnerability, and it bit at her heart.

Had he really forgotten their attachment? She lay back and studied the corrugated steel of the roof. "We were true friends. I enjoyed your company more than anyone's."

She pressed both her palms to her chest, attempting to quell her pain enough to hone in on his feelings. Tightly controlled fury and hurt tickled at the edge of her awareness.

And then he spoke the inevitable question. "Why?"

She closed her eyes tight. "Bel, you know."

"The hell I do. I've never understood." A gentle thud sounded where he'd leaned against the table. "Why would you do that to me, right after Mother…" He swallowed a sob, the grief of a little boy abandoned at the very same time by the two women who loved him.

Maybe she could help him remember. She pushed herself up onto her elbows.

"Bel, lie back on the table and close your eyes."

He spun, backing away from her. "If hell has frozen over, I missed the memo."

"Please try. What can it hurt?" Both of them, a great deal. But she held his stare as if she believed the lie.

He remained in unmoving deliberation so she lay down again and focused on the ceiling. Twenty feet overhead, small spiders spun delicate webs that spanned the inches between the corrugation and the rafters. She envied them and she clenched her hands, missing her knitting needles. Where had she left them? Oh yes. In that horrid quilted tote bag Ingrid had given her that she hadn't had the heart to throw away.

Without a warning, Bel's weight settled onto the table with a creak, and he lay down, his head near hers, very much like they used to lie. After a few moments, his breathing became even.

She squeezed her eyes shut and prayed to the vast pantheon of Illyrian gods she had dismissed millennia ago. *Please let this work.*

She licked her lips. "What do you remember of your mother's death?"

CHAPTER 16

Bel fell into the long buried memory with surprising ease. Maybe it was Uta's familiar scent, luring him into the past. The last thing his mother had ever said to him leaped into his ear like it was only yesterday.

"Lobel Marasović, be home by nine o'clock. You are a growing boy, and you will keep normal human hours no matter how abnormal a vampire household is." Mila hadn't kept the bitterness from her tone. Whether it was over his friendship with Uta or one of her many other complaints against their family life, he didn't know.

He stepped out the front door and let it slam, racing off to meet Uta at the shore. They often walked there or in the hills in the dark hours before his curfew. Auntie Uta dressed as a man for their hikes — trousers and a cap with her dark red hair tucked up. That evening, for the first time, Bel noticed the shape of her long thighs, and how they curved into small, round cheeks. He couldn't take his eyes off her backside or stop wondering how it would feel to cup it in his hands.

They sat on the beach and watched bats come home from their hunting to fly back into the trees. "Why do you suppose people think vampires turn into bats?" he asked.

"I have heard some bats suck blood."

"That's right, vampire bats. I forgot about them," he admitted. "Too bad for you it's not true."

"Is it? I'm happy to fly in my own skin."

Her words were like an invitation to look at her skin — luminous in the moonlight and so fair she surely would have had freckles if she weren't a vampire, might have had before she was turned into one. How had he never noticed her beauty, with those dark, intelligent eyes?

"But being a bat would be almost as good as being a fly on a wall. Think of all the spying you could do."

His words earned him a laugh. "Indeed, that is an advantage I had not considered. Who would you spy on if you were a bat?" Boots off, Uta dug her bare feet into the sand and her toes peeked out.

His mother called Uta's tinted finger and toe nails garish. She was the only female on Šolta to have adopted the French fashion. Bel kind of liked the look of her cherry tipped toes in the sand.

Then he realized she had asked him a question. "What's that? Spy?" Yesterday his answer would have been simple—to watch Kos flirting with a girl or to overhear his parents arguing in order to better understand their troubles. But there, on the moonlit beach, the image of a slim Uta naked and slipping out of a bathtub entered his mind.

"The usual things," he squeaked, without looking at her.

"You must tell me. I'm certain you've thought of something naughty. I must know." Then she reached around him with her long arms and began to tickle him.

He froze. They always roughhoused and wrestled, but it would be different to roll around in the sand with her as that picture burned in his mind.

"Sorry to disappoint." He stood abruptly. "I haven't got any good ideas. And I know better than to tell you, anyway. You'll just steal them and go off spying while Mother forces me to sleep."

Uta stood and brushed sand of her trousers, laughing. "True, that is exactly what I would do."

The wrestling disaster averted, Bel's tension eased as they walked back toward the Marasović house. "What will you do tonight?"

"I believe your father is coming over to play cards. I won his grain silo from him, and he's asked for a rematch to win it back."

"Seems fair. He did give you the chance to win back your carriage."

"He did. The difference is, I am a much better loser than Andre. I always accept my defeat graciously."

The statement was so preposterous, Bel couldn't take another step until his laughter ebbed. "Sometimes I think you and Father would have been a happier couple than he and Mother."

Uta stopped in the middle of the road and Bel did the same, turning to look at her. A dove cooed nearby, until it was silenced by an unseasonably cool breeze. "Your parents love each other very much. And they are both very dear friends to me. But friendship is easier than marriage. When Andre gets on my nerves, I stay away. We didn't speak for eighty-seven years in the twelfth century."

"But you are very much alike."

"In some ways, but there is no spark of passion between us. We are like brothers."

"Brothers?"

"It's what Andre says. That I can take care of myself like a man, so I am not like a sister, but a brother. And he says I look like a boy."

"What does that mean?"

"You know…" She held her hands out in front of her, pantomiming a large pair of breasts. "And…" She did the same thing behind her, as if there were something wrong with that little round bottom.

Bel turned away, knowing she could see a blush in the dark. "Well, women shaped like that never go out hiking like we do. I think you're better off."

She didn't seem to notice his embarrassment. "You think so now, but maybe not when you're grown." She was talking to him like she always had, with no idea that his thoughts were becoming less and less boyish.

How would their friendship change when she realized he was growing up?

They had arrived at the dirt road leading up to his family's home. He stood there and asked, "Auntie, how old were you when you became a vampire?"

"Old enough to have grown as tall as a tree, but not to bear fruits…" Again she held out her hands as if her small breasts were lacking.

He laughed because she expected him to. Inside, a confusion of emotions roiled—he didn't want her to go home; he wanted to stay with her, to keep talking, to feel the warmth of her affection toward him. And he wanted other, new things too—to touch her face, stroke her thighs, he would even suck on one of her red-tipped toes if she would let him. This was all wrong. She was a grown woman, a powerful and ancient vampire far older even than his father. And she was his godmother, his aunt by sentiment if not by blood.

He swallowed the confusing emotions. "Good night, Auntie. Best of luck at cards."

"Good night, Bel. Sleep well. Perhaps one day, you'll be a vampire and have no need for sleep."

"Perhaps," he shouted over his shoulder as he hurried away from her.

The next morning, he woke up to find something unexpected—his very first hard-on. He was nearly twelve, so, according to the timeline Kos had laid out, this erection thingy was right on time. Nothing to worry about there. But one thing concerned him—his unsettling suspicion his newly hard cock was thanks to Uta.

She was all he could think about. He had a new toy and he wanted to play, to stroke it, to explore the sensations that were beckoning him. But if he did, his imagination would be full of Uta's body, her face, her silken red hair. It was wrong. If she knew about his new desires—

A bellow shook the house, rattling pictures on the wall and causing glass to shatter somewhere. *What on earth?* He stood and pulled on trousers. His erection responded appropriately to his concern—it deflated. *Good boy,* he told his cock. They were going to get along just fine.

At the end of the hall, the door to his parents' room stood ajar. Kos's hushed murmurs set the hair on Bel's neck upright. He inched toward them and swung the door wide.

Was Andre weeping? Bel sucked in a breath. How could anything on earth make his father cry?

"What happened?"

Kos whispered, trying to soothe him, but tears streamed down Bel's brother's face too.

Oh God. It couldn't be. Bel ran toward them where they stood in the doorway to the room that held his mother's copper bath. Blocking the doorway, Kos grabbed him and kept him out of the room.

"Bel, no. Don't look."

"What happened? Damn it, Kos, tell me what happened!" Cries followed on the heels of the words. Kos sobbed then, too, and Bel knew for sure, but he still asked. "Is she—"

"Yes."

In the bathroom—did she slip? Drown? A brain hemorrhage? "What happened? An accident?"

"No, Bel, not an accident."

Andre's whimpering cries were growing louder, becoming roars. He was angry?

Oh hell. "She did it to herself?"

"Yes." Kos gasped out the word.

Bel's world flipped over like a griddle cake. His mother was dead and the two men he looked up to were falling apart. Only one person could comfort him now.

"Bel, go downstairs and find all the servants you can. We will need help with Andre, and with…Mother."

Thank God—Kos was holding himself together after all. Bel followed his orders and Kos set the servants in motion. Soon, everything was out of their hands and Kos and Bel and Andre's task was simply to grieve.

All three of them preferred to be busy, but the servants would not allow them to help. Stir-crazy, they holed up in the parlor. Hour by hour, Andre looked worse. Bel resented the way his body showed his suffering. Why should it be worse for him? Wasn't losing a mother just as bad as losing a wife? Worse in fact, because surely Andre was to blame somehow for Mila's actions.

Bel's only distraction was Andre's fascinating physical reaction. Blood vessels had burst, turning the whites of his eyes red, and his skin was bruising.

Bel had to ask. "Exactly what is happening to you?"

"Mila's blood is a part of me. It has died."

"A part of you is dying? Will it kill you?" *Please God, don't take my father too.*

"No, I will just wish it would. For many years to come. For the rest of my life, perhaps."

That sounded bad, and Bel grew curious. How did vampires differ from humans? And where did he, a halfling, fit into the equation? He wanted to ask Andre, but his father grew unresponsive, and retreated into the bowels of the house. Kos filled the roles of father and mother remarkably well, keeping Bel company and restoring routines.

Within the shroud of sadness, it took Bel ten days to work up the courage to go see Uta. Not that he had stopped his shameful imaginings. They had kept him away for a week and a half, but he *could* put them out of his mind, had to if he wanted to see her. And he needed the comfort only she could give him.

The morning as he climbed the steep road to her house, birds sang and dew glistened on the grass. Nature conspired to assure him that one day his grief would end and the world would be all right.

She wore a black mourning dress, her dark eyes sad in her pale face. Heavy velvet curtains were drawn tight against the daylight, but a chandelier lit with perhaps fifty tapers illuminated the room. An eclectic mixture of ornate French and rustic Croatian furniture made the room comfortable, if not fashionable. Mila had criticized Uta's haphazard decor, but Bel found it more livable than the rooms his mother had over-decorated with uncomfortable couches and too much gilt.

When the servant announced him, Uta set down her book and slid over to make room. Bel sat down, and before he knew it she had gathered him into her arms. Tears burned in his eyes, and he felt no embarrassment at shedding them in her presence. Hers fell on his head, tracing hot trails along his scalp. For a long time they held each other and cried.

And then, he simply ran out of tears. In their place came the memory of the birds and the dew outside. All would be well.

"What took you so long to come see me?" She mopped her tears with a handkerchief.

Bel lied. "I didn't want to leave Father and Kos."

"How is Andre?"

"He suffers greatly, but I think he must deserve it."

"We must agree to disagree over that opinion, then." Her tone was sharp and he recoiled, wanting to argue. But she took his chin in her hand. "Have you been eating? You are very thin."

"I have no appetite."

"You will eat here; surely you feel hungry now that you are out of your house."

His hand went to his stomach which suddenly complained of its hollowness. "Yes, thank you. I could eat." Other people complained of Uta's domineering personality, but Bel didn't mind being pushed about by her a little. When it was important, he pushed back and she delighted in it.

The servant brought a cart stacked with cold chicken, boiled eggs, bread, cheese, and his favorite sour cherry preserves. Once he started, he made up for all his missed meals. A full belly improved his mood even more and he slouched next to Uta, his hands folded over his abdomen.

"Thank you, I do feel better," he said, stifling a yawn.

"These things go together. You must eat because you cannot sleep with an empty stomach. Lie down here." She patted her lap, gesturing for him to rest his head there.

That secret shame tickled in his chest, warning him. But far louder was the instinct that promised she could fill every urge Bel had. She had fed him, and held him; she was mother and she was that other thing he wanted but didn't understand. He obeyed.

She ran her fingers through his hair, massaging his scalp. He pictured the polished red finger nails moving through his dark curls and he dozed in her lap, safe and loved, curling onto his side and burying his face against her flat stomach. He kept his breathing perfectly even so she would think he slept and allow him to stay there. She stroked his head, and with her other hand, she rubbed up and down his arm. Without meaning to, he arched into her touch.

She stilled her hands. "Bel?"

"Hmm?"

"Bel, sit up." He obeyed, groggy, jostled out of his cocoon. "Look at me."

Why not? He opened his eyes.

When she sucked in her breath, he realized he had made a grave mistake. What did he know, after all, about what a woman could see in your eyes if you were feeling those strange urges?

"Fuck," she hissed. She had taught him the word. "Not now!" She covered her face.

The pain in her voice frightened him. "Uta, I'm sorry. Did I do something wrong?"

"Sweet Auntie Io, not now!" Her words were a strangled shout.

He took hold of her shoulders in a gesture so manly it surprised both of them. "What is it?" Unfamiliar emotions churned in her eyes. Panic tightened his chest. He didn't know what she was afraid of, but he was certain his new all-wrong feelings were to blame.

"You have to go."

"Uta, please," he cried, all illusions of being a man washed away with his tears. "Please, I need you."

"I know," she said, crying too. "I know. But you have to go."

"Don't make me. Let me stay here. With you, everything feels all right."

She crossed her arms and raised her chin. "Bel, no. You must go."

Like a dog who'd been kicked, he went back the next day. She wouldn't even come out, just sent down a note.

Bel, I can no longer see you.
Perhaps one day you will understand.
You must seek solace with your family.

With that note—an unforgivable cruelty—she had taken everything from him, and he hated her for it.

CHAPTER 17

Uta would have preferred to be flayed alive than to witness Bel remembering Mila's suicide and the days that followed. But it was necessary. So she lay, quiet and tense, on a cold metal tabletop. She shivered, hugging her arms tightly across her chest.

Finally, he stirred. She bolted upright too. He rubbed his eyes with his fists and when he opened them, the hatred still blazed there.

Her heart tumbled down almost to her diaphragm.

"What would have happened?" His voice rolled toward her, gravelly and thick.

Good—questions meant hope.

"You would have felt much as you do now—your desires, our connection."

He threw back his shoulders, lifting his powerful chest. "But I was a boy, so you had to send me and my inconvenient lust away."

"If I had not forbidden you from my side, you would have been overcome by needs you did not understand, and you would never have had a choice. You would never have wanted another woman, or loved Lexi." She clasped her hands in her lap, unable to look at him.

Every day, she had missed him. Since he had become a man, she had longed for him to come back, to finally understand why she had sent him away and choose her freely. She longed, but she rarely dared to hope.

"You should have told me," he whispered. "You took the choice into your own hands. Treated me like a child…"

He had been one, and he knew it, so she waited.

He hopped off the table and paced a small circle. "I may have cared for other women, but I never really had a choice and I didn't even know. I thought I'd failed at being what Lexi needed, when I never had a chance."

Tears prickled behind her eyes, but damn it, she was the ninth oldest vampire on earth—she could hold them in.

He halted and tilted his head. All the anger melted from his face. A single curl fell over his forehead and he swiped at it. "Fuck, what a mess you and Mila made."

"And Bel, I am truly sorry. Not just for myself. Please believe I have done what I thought best for you at every turn, until Loki forced me to come here last month. I would have stayed away until you came looking for me."

"Was it inevitable that I would have?" He took half a step toward her, and her heart climbed back into place.

"Yes. Eventually you would have felt the same ache of loneliness, loss of appetite, lethargy…frustration. Living apart from a bonded mate is not very different from the wasting disease."

He blinked. "Like the *osjećaj*, you mean? Damn, I wish I understood how that worked." The muscles under his face flickered with minuscule expressions, evidence of his ever-curious mind at work. Then his eyebrows came together over that fine patrician nose. "You suffered?"

Oh, if he saw even a glimpse of the sacrifices she had made for him. *"Yes,"* she breathed.

His gaze traveled to her mouth.

Her heart took off in a vampire-fast beat, like a hummingbird on stimulants. In an ancient Illyrian forest thousands of years earlier, her first kiss had inspired nowhere near the excitement she felt now.

And then he was on her, grabbing fistfuls of her hair and pulling her mouth to his. His tongue pried open her mouth and swept deep. He tasted like salty sea air. She opened wider, pressing her body into him. His hands slid up under her shirt, big paws splaying across her breasts, thumbs seeking out nipples.

Her body thrummed, gasping for breath. She'd never been more alive—

Bel. Touching her. *Finally.*

He took hold of her wrists and, standing between her legs, pressed her back onto the table. As his tongue took possession of her mouth, he rubbed his glorious erection against her aching *pićka*. Gods be damned, it had been too long.

She locked her legs around his waist and rolled him so that he leaned against the table, and she could grind against him from above.

He broke the kiss, shaking his head. "What the fuck?"

She stilled the roll of her hips. Come to think of it, she might have had to fly to orchestrate that little move. No wonder he was disoriented.

He pushed her away. "Fuck. I'm like a rag doll to you."

Not just disoriented. Angry. She wanted to grab hold of him, but his fury warned her off. She gave him a foot of space and clasped her hands behind her back.

"Sorry." She mouthed the unfamiliar word.

"No, worse, I'm like a little boy, wrapped around your finger." He backed away as if she might hurt him.

She stepped closer. "Bel, I truly am sorry. I—"

He held up his palms like a shield and their tenuous new trust shattered like a seashell underfoot. Her breaths came faster, panicked. She'd almost had him. Almost.

"Bel—" She extended her hand cautiously, as if he were a wild beast.

"Stay the hell away from me." He strode out of the workroom as fast as any human could.

Sheep bollocks. That could have gone better. She cupped her groin, hoping to quell the throb between her legs.

Should she follow him?

No. He would need some space, and she needed an icepack and a chance to think. She crossed the room at full speed and yanked open the door, colliding with Loki. She stumbled backward before she gained her footing. The tension around his mouth was not a good sign.

"What now?"

"Bad news."

"More attacks? Where?"

He reached out for her and tucked himself under her arm in the familiar sideways hug with which he offered reassurance. His refusal to answer frazzled the last of her nerves.

"Tell me."

"It's more Šoltan refugees. Their households are being destroyed in alphabetical order."

Another failure on the heels of Bel's rejection. Her knees liquefied.

Loki caught her. "Do not swoon like a useless female. We must make a plan. And Bel will not succeed without you."

She scrambled, the soles of her heels slipping before they found purchase on the concrete. She doubted his experiment could ever work, but she certainly wished him success.

Bel approached the door to Kos's office. Papers rustled on the other side. Good. His brother was in there.

He burst in. "What does it feel like?"

Zoey bent over the desk and Kos sat in his chair. Their heads were bent low, studying a set of papers. They must have been hyper focused on their task because both started, and glanced up at Bel.

"What does what feel like?" his brother asked.

Instead of answering, Bel stared at Zoey. "What are you doing?"

"Checking our spreadsheet of Blood Vine sales." Zoey turned her intense focus to Bel instead of the paper.

He tugged at his collar, wondering if she could inexplicably read his mind. No other vampires could do that.

"Why?" he asked.

"The wine sold very well for a newly launched brand. We're trying to estimate how much was purchased by vampires, versus unknowing humans."

"Are you hoping to find them?"

"No," Kos replied. "That would require each store's records, and they are safer in hiding anyway. But when we received the astonishing sales numbers, Zoey grew excited. Blood Vine in the hands of our old friends is a glimmer of hope." He handed her the stack of papers.

No evidence of hope softened the tight pull of her lips.

"Now, what does what feel like?" Kos asked.

Bel searched between the faces of the two vampires. "The bond. What does it feel like?"

Zoey's cheeks turned the color of a ripe strawberry and she angled toward the exit. "I'll let you all discuss this male to male."

"Is it so personal?" Bel asked, before she was even out of the door.

Kos pursed his lips. "You know it is. It cuts right to the core of one's body and soul. Hardly a casual conversation with our stepmother."

Bel thought of her as he did Pedro — just one more trash-talking member of the family, not his stepmother. But still, it was nice to have Kos all to himself. "Surely you can explain the sensations scientifically, without talking about all that warm fuzzy shite."

"And the hot and sweaty shite too?" Kos mocked his accent. "Hardly. Can you?" He straightened the blotter on his already impeccable desk and then put a pen back in a jar of writing implements. Neat son of a bitch. Bel couldn't see Kos's eyebrows, but he imagined at least one was arched to echo his brother's smug tone.

"No. But it's all new to me. I'll get some objectivity when it gets less intense."

"It grows *more* intense, but you will become accustomed to it." He jotted a note onto a neon square of paper.

"Kos, she sent me away when I became a man. It had nothing to do with Mother."

That got his brother's attention, and he looked up. "I'll be damned. She didn't want you to know." Kos's eyes roved over Bel's face. "That's quite a burden she bore for you."

Precisely what Bel hated to admit, even to himself. "She said she wanted me to have a choice, but I didn't really. It was her fault I couldn't love Lexi enough."

"Bel, it was the bond's fault. She didn't rope you to her on purpose."

A century-old habit of righteous anger did not soften on a dime. Kos's words glanced off Bel like a super-energized atom. "I will fight it, Kos. I don't want to love her."

Kos smiled in the particularly false, strained way that prevented his lopsided dimples from creasing. Bel hated that look, had ever since their mother had died and Kos had felt the need to reassure and protect him as Andre descended into the madness of his broken bond.

"What happened when you kissed Lexi?" Kos asked.

"I couldn't even manage a lusty thought about her."

Kos nodded, again with the un-smile. "You told me before that you loved her, would have done anything for her."

"I did."

"Why did she leave you?"

The answer had haunted him ever since Uta had reappeared. *Because I was empty inside, eaten alive with a hunger Lexi couldn't fill and it made me furious, at her and myself, so I withdrew.* But he said none of it, just shrugged.

Kos swallowed, the gulp audible. "When you were a boy you adored Uta. You were a child, bosom buddies with an ancient vampire. And she accepted your affection and returned it without condescension."

"Funny. A moment ago she tossed me around like a feather to put me where she wanted me."

Kos turned his palms up. "What, you're not into that?"

Glaring, Bel crossed his arms in reply.

Kos sobered and continued with his reminiscence. "It was so bizarre to see you two, walking along side by side, her twice as tall as you. I could not understand what drew you together—like a sexless bond. *Krist,* please tell me it was—"

"Shite, Kos, yes! The moment…I, um…came of age, she sent me away."

"It must have pained her greatly. Not just the separation, but having to hurt you."

The pity on Kos's face finally forced Bel to concede. He did know something about the misery of being forced to hurt an innocent. She had been imprisoned by the same accident of blood, and the acknowledgment flooded him with emotion. An unfamiliar sting pricked behind his eyes. Were those tears? He shook them off.

He would have to free them both from this oppressive bond. First *hemoaurum,* then he would engineer hemostatowhatever it was in her blood that drew him like an addict. Yoked to his enemy, just like the vampires to the Hunters. Surely if he could understand this mysterious *osjećaj,* everyone could be free.

CHAPTER 18

With clean, dry hands, Gwen used her thumb and forefinger to turn the pages of *The Book of the Day*, one after another, though by now she could recite its words by heart and knew the minute details of its gruesome images. The ancient codex was the most fascinating find of her academic career — the career she'd abandoned to assist Ethan, and to submit to him. Only half-seeing, her gaze ran over page after page in a ceaseless loop.

At first she'd thought the ancient text clear proof of vampires' evil. Golden-eyed and prehistoric Hunters, native to the mountains of Turkey, had fallen victim to the seductive power of vampires and their opiate-like bites. At least, that is what she'd thought when all she knew of vampires was Mason Kearney, her lover and abuser. But the story told by the early-medieval illuminated manuscript no longer seemed so simple. Now she knew Hunters too, knew of their genocidal hatred, and the absolute lack of scruples of Ethan's ambitions.

According to Hunter mythology, thousands of years older than the archaic book itself, the generation of young Hunters intermixed with vampires, fell in love, and bred. By doing so, they angered the sun god, Dela-Malkh, and their elders enforced his wrath by killing their own children to purify their race.

Myths had some basis in reality, and this one justified horrific violence — the Hunters' sacrifice of their own kind, just as Ethan had done to incite the vampires to attack Hunters, just as he had done with that poor girl this morning. She understood such sacrifice with a nearly religious reverence — and the logic of purifying violence both ordered her psyche and made sense of the world. She'd been a bad girl, after all. She'd let a vampire torture her until she'd liked it. Now she needed Ethan to do the same. He gave her pleasure; with him she wasn't alone. In the beginning, she'd hoped his violence would redeem her, make her lovable again, something other than a piece of vampire trash. Was that still possible?

She stared into the golden eyes of a victorious, blood-smeared Hunter on the page.

Ethan had made an offering of that girl. It had been frightening to watch — his calculation, his disregard for her life. But worse, his failure lodged cold dread inside of Gwen. So she searched the book for some other bit of knowledge she might offer him, anything to help him succeed.

She knew that in his chilling way, he had come to love her. And in the end, that was all that mattered. She closed the book, and her heart, to the questions of right and wrong, good and evil. None of it mattered — he was her lover and her god. All of a sudden, her need for him consumed her. Oh God, she had to see him.

She darted up from her desk and made it three steps out of her office before remembering the glass walls and gatekeepers that would keep her from him. She went back to her purse and found her phone to send him a text. *If you have a minute, can I speak to you in my office?*

No reply came, and emptiness gnawed at her.

She perched straight and still in her chair, trying to embrace the aching hunger in her heart as a masochistic pleasure.

When he appeared inside her office door, she sucked in a deep breath. He seemed to have recovered from his earlier disappointment, and he radiated satisfaction. Lord, he was beautiful.

Smiling, he flashed his even white teeth. "Lisjak."

"Pardon?"

"We are to L on the list of Šoltan refugees who bought Marasović's wine. Half have been exterminated."

Living, sentient creatures, systematically murdered. The words passed before her eyes like text on a page. She blinked them away and let his pride be her compass.

"I had forgotten about that list."

"It is only now complete. A particularly diligent initiate tracked down every sale from the list Derek Williams stole from the wine distributor."

"Congratulations."

His smile eased into repose. "You wanted to speak to me?"

"I just…well. I was thinking about this morning, and…" Her need for him opened up again like a deep crevice. She could barely stand to look up at him. "I suppose I missed you."

He crossed the small office in two long strides and pressed her against the desk. "What a pleasant surprise." Cradling her head in both hands, he kissed her with more gentleness than ever before.

When he finished, he pulled back. "Are you sorry you came with me to Kaštel?"

"No. I needed to see."

"Yes, I suppose you did. Still, I fear have been too rough with you," he whispered against her lips.

The words were ice in her veins. "No! I need—"

"Sshh. Do not worry. There will be as much pain as you need. But from now on, it will be more carefully administered, with precision. With needles and blades, not knuckles and fists."

She'd come to love the ache of her ribs after they'd been pummeled by those knuckles.

"Why?"

"Because I need you, Gwen. I need your body to last us both a good, long time."

Her body, her sacrifice—he wanted it on his altar. She gripped him, sniffling into his chest and wrapping her legs around his waist.

"My, my," he said. "What has gotten into you?"

"Maybe I've fallen in love with you. Or if not that, at least I can offer you my undivided loyalty."

He pulled back, frowning, and instantly she regretted her words. He hadn't even known her loyalty had been in question. Good submissives were always loyal. But just as quickly his eyes widened in understanding.

"Were you having a crisis of conscience about my methods?"

She swiped her tongue across her bottom lip. "Yes, to some extent. But then I remembered I have no conscience apart from yours. Because I belong to you."

He stared at her, his face absolutely without expression.

Her skin tingled all over. She might have believed it was vanishing, if such a thing were possible. Because surely, she was dissolving into him—and there, on the other side of this surrender, was the freedom of non-existence. She could taste it, a peace deeper even than the solace she'd found in pain.

His chest rose and fell in labored breaths, suggesting he sensed the power of her choice.

"Yes, Gwen. I need your loyalty, and I need your help."

"Anything."

"I'm sending you to the Kaštel Estate. You will be my Trojan horse."

CHAPTER 19

The high-pitched whirr of the milk steamer on Kaštel's resident espresso machine was the most annoying sound Pedro's young vampire ears had ever heard. *Note to self—no more coffee shops, ever.*

The steam jetted into the metal pitcher, frothing the milk under Lena's careful supervision.

"There. That's enough." She switched off the steam. "He doesn't like much foam."

Pedro nodded, storing the detail in the files of things that he wanted to know about Lucas. Not that it would matter for long, if this conversation went well.

Lena poured the milk into the waiting mug. She handed it to Pedro with a goofy-ass smile. "You know, there is an old saying among householders—a vampire makes a guy a latte, you know he's in love."

If only it were as simple as love, not as complicated as a blood bond to a human only recently recovered from his mortal hatred of vampires.

Pedro forced a smile. "Yeah, something like that."

Lena nodded, but kept quiet. She had that knack for knowing when not to talk that none of the rest of the Maras family possessed.

He made his way to the dining room, hoping like hell to find Lucas alone. And he did. The lanky ex-Hunter hunched over his laptop, his face awash with that eerie bluish electronic glow, his excellent cheekbones a bit too prominent. The toll all this stress was taking on him amped up Pedro's sense of urgency as if the need to ensure Lucas's immortality were a new vampire instinct. *Mierda,* how had Kos resisted turning Lena for all these weeks? A hungry animal inside Pedro demanded he do the deed here and now, on the dining room table.

Lucas didn't glance up until Pedro sat down and slid the mug toward him.

"Lena helped me make it just the way you like."

Lucas closed his computer and cocked his head. "What are you up to?"

"Hey, can't I just do something nice for my man?"

"Nice try, but you may as well come clean. You have guilty written all over your face."

Pedro wished the emotion was guilt, not anxious fear. He tapped his fingertips on the table, in line with the scar that bisected it. "So. About last night."

Lucas spluttered, spitting coffee all over before he erupted in full-blown guffaws. "I've always wanted someone to say that to me."

"Dude. Be serious. This is important."

Lucas wiped his mouth with the back of his hand and nodded. "What's up? Some vampire news?"

"*Sí,* but it's personal."

"Go on." A deep furrow appeared between Lucas's brows.

When had that worry been carved into his face?

Pedro took a deep breath. "Here goes. I need to turn you." His pulse accelerated, pounding in his chest like it used to on the dance floor of his favorite nightclubs. "Into a vampire, I mean. The sooner the better."

A red stain crept up Lucas's neck, coloring his face deep crimson. His eyelid twitched.

The room wasn't pin-drop silent, at least not now that Pedro was a vampire. It buzzed with distant conversations around the household, the gentle whistle of wind in the chimney, dishes clattering in the kitchen below, the frenzied beat of Lucas's heart, out of sync with Pedro's own. The frightened animal inside him panicked.

Splayed on both sides of his laptop, Lucas's long fingers started to curl under. He opened his mouth, but Pedro cut him off.

"Don't argue with me. This is nonnegotiable."

"What?" Lucas rose, and his chair pushed backward, scraping against the floor. "Nonnegotiable? This is my life. This is whether or not I drink blood, fall victim to a wasting disease, ever see the sun again. I don't want to be—"

"Like me." Pedro crossed his arms, shaking his head in furious disbelief. "I thought we were past this."

"Past what?"

"Your Hunter shit. Deep down, you still hate vampires." Pedro took an angry step forward.

"How can you say that?" Lucas turned away, toward the window where new green grass grew out of ash.

Pedro wanted to yank his shoulder to force Lucas to face him, but he gripped the back of the chair instead. "You like the biting and the fucking, and maybe you like me too—"

Lucas put his fingertips and thumb on the glass, shaking his head. "I said I love you last night. I've never said that to anyone before."

Pedro's rage fizzled, and he dropped back into the chair. He'd screwed that up pretty bad, wanted to bang his forehead on the table—*thunk, thunk.* Could he start over?

Then his skin tightened in warning. Someone had come into the room.

Andre closed the door behind him and leaned against it, looking between Pedro and Lucas only once. *El hijo de puta*—his sire's eyebrows lifted as if he were amused.

"Son. Perhaps this conversation would have proceeded more smoothly had you informed Lucas why you desire to turn him."

Lucas spun, his features forming a question.

And finally the right words appeared on Pedro's tongue. "About last night—I bonded to you."

Lucas pressed his lips together and his posture softened.

Encouraged, Pedro went on. "Now, even more than before, you are my life. Without your blood I might die."

"Shit. Why didn't you say so?" Lucas's sexy mouth was very nearly smiling.

"Indeed," Andre grumbled.

Pedro was too relieved to feel defensive.

Lucas sat down again. "But you need *my* blood. Can you feed from another Hunter if I turn?"

"This is the crucial question." Andre took a seat alongside Pedro. "But there is no time to address it now. Loki has called a meeting. All the vampires will be here in a moment. Perhaps they are already waiting outside, listening to your squabble."

Lucas rolled his eyes. "Great, now I have a starring role in *Days of Our Immortal Lives.*"

Pedro grinned at his man and mouthed an apology. *Sorry.*

The door swung open, and if anyone had been behind it, they'd have been squashed like a bug on a windshield. Dust flew up where the knob hit the plaster wall. Uta strode in with an ice pack and dropped it on a chair. Then she unceremoniously perched on top of it.

She shrugged shamelessly at Pedro.

Andre muttered under his breath. "*Davo.*"

Once, Pedro's cock had nearly exploded when he attempted to withhold sex from Lucas, forgetting he was the one who couldn't jerk off. If Uta was singing the same Stones tune about her lack of satisfaction, then that ice pack would cool her off for a total of ninety seconds before the heat of her desire turned it to slush. Tough as she was, she'd be no match for that. He actually felt sorry for the scary chick.

The Justicia members filed in, their householders behind them. Then the Maras household filled in the empty chairs — Kos, Lena, Zoey, Bel's security crew, and Andre's staff. They were packed in like sardines, and the room grew immediately warmer.

Just before Loki's assistant closed the door, a dark skinned vampire slipped in. He cast Lucas and Leo hateful looks. Pedro tensed.

Kos leaned down from where he stood to whisper. "Stay calm, he's a notorious Hunter hater. The leader of the aggressionist camp. But everyone else is copacetic, and we've got Lucas's back."

Bel slid in just behind the hater and he looked mighty pissed. Pedro would have expected his bro to be more smug about not putting out for Uta. Bel took a seat on the other side of Lucas from Pedro; it was the only empty chair, but it put him directly in her line of sight. While everyone focused their attention on Bel, waiting for him to settle, Uta's was conspicuously on Loki.

Lucas scratched out a note to Pedro, knowing a whisper would have been easily heard by more than a dozen sets of vampire ears: *This is going to be good.*

Then Loki spoke in his accented English. "We have much to discuss at this meeting, but I wish to begin with silence in honor of those fallen in the war."

The late-arriving vampire snorted, then fell silent with the others.

"To the homeland." Loki ended the silence with the traditional blessing.

"The homeland," everyone intoned.

On the same breath, the snorty one asserted, "I do not honor my enemies, Loki, and I resent your heavy handed moment of silence. As if being under a roof with them wasn't bad enough, this whole place reeks of Hunter."

Pedro finally placed his accent as Indian.

"Sadavir, your position is well known." Loki leaned one elbow on the table and angled himself ever so slightly away from the latecomer. "I trust no one mistook your silence for mercy. We will not debate it now. Several pieces of information are required before we decide on a course of action."

Sadavir shot out of his seat. "There is only one tenable course. We fight back."

Loki darted at him, hovering at eye level like a hornet, right in front of the pro-aggression mo-fo. "When I am dead and you are the oldest, you may give the orders. Right now, you will sit down."

When Sadavir complied, Loki alighted on the floor as lightly a butterfly, his tone once again turning gentle. "First, let me assure you every resource at my disposal is employed to defend households and hunt out the aggressors. Those we believe to be in special danger have been alerted." He strolled back to his chair and sat, folding his hands on the table. "The purpose of this meeting is to determine our strategy. We all know Sadavir's position, but I believe we have other options. A cure for the wasting disease has never been more critical. With it, vampires could flee their homes and go into hiding without the plague of exile. So, we will begin with Lobel Marasović. Bel, please report to us on your research."

Bel stood and, in spite of all the tension in the room, Pedro had to smile — the dude knew how to wear his jeans. His T-shirt hugged biceps and a broad chest, but hung loose around his narrow waist. The vampires were dressed to the nines, and Bel owned his skin better than most of them in their designer togs. Lucas must have thought the same thing, because a barely audible hum of appreciation sounded in his throat. Seconds later Kos coughed and Andre rolled his eyes. Two female Justicia members hid their smiles. Uta joined them, wiping the murder off her face when she realized it was Lucas who had made the sound.

He scribbled to Pedro. *Sorry. I like bad boys.*

If Bel noticed the commotion, it didn't faze him. "We recently discovered the special properties of Blood Vine and of Hunter blood. I found the unusual presence of gold in both sources. In the laboratory I was able to isolate a gold-based protein I call *hemoaurum*."

Everyone in the room knew the remarkable details, but the drama of it was still noted with murmurs.

"I was then able to engineer an exact copy of this protein."

"A protein?" asked a petite African female. *Nceba,* Pedro remembered. *One of the oldest vampires in the world.* Her voice was softly inviting and everyone leaned in. "Do you understand how it works?"

Bel started to answer the question, but the vampire's female assistant leaned in and the Justicia member whispered in a language involving those cool tongue-clicks. The blood servant's hands settled on the other female's shoulders and stroked her too-thin neck. They must be lovers. The female vampire's eyes fanned into crow's feet, and the slightest bit of silver dusted her temples—sure signs she was wasting away.

When the clicks ceased, Bel replied. "No. I do not yet understand the mechanism. And unfortunately, as of yesterday, the vampires receiving *hemoaurum* infusions show no physical improvements. My experiment failed."

Bodies stirred in their chair and the dining room resounded with the scuffle of minuscule movements. No one spoke. Pedro wanted to shout, or sing something, just to spare Bel the awkward moment.

Finally, Loki burst the un-silence. "And have you spoken to Uta as I commanded?"

Bel's eye flicked to Uta's. "Yes. She has informed me of a theory, but I—"

"Ah, yes. Uta's secret." Loki's eyes darkened. "Uta Ilirije."

She straightened her spine.

"You possess knowledge of the powers of Hunter blood?" Loki asked the question, but Pedro sensed he knew the answer already.

"I have sworn to keep this knowledge secret."

"And before us, you willingly break it?"

Huh? Loki's voice had gone all weird and formal.

"I do." She squirmed on her ice pack and it crunched like the breaking of a crust of snow. Then she rose with perfect grace.

The air thickened and everyone in the room shifted in their seats. Andre glowered, staring out the window at his ruined vineyards, so Pedro looked to Bel for a clue. But his gaze volleyed around the room, apparently equally confused.

Then Uta began her story.

CHAPTER 20

Thousands of years had physically conditioned Uta to hold this secret under her tongue. True, a giant, reeking sheep-orgy of events had transpired to reveal its gist, but there was still the matter of a vow. Her sire, Rize, had been a complicated male, but her reverence for him went beyond duty and it pained her to break his confidence. She was no conservative, hadn't kept the old customs in centuries, but a vow was a vow. A promise made to one's sire—well, the only thing stronger than that was a blood bond. There would be consequences, wet and messy ones. She licked her lips.

But Loki was right, it was time for the secret to come out. So she flexed her tongue, attempting to loosen it.

"My sire survived the first war between Hunters and vampires. And he told me of another survivor, a halfling child named Ayal. She still lives today, in the mountains of Eastern Turkey."

"A survivor? I don't believe it—she would be older than all of us." Sadavir glared at her as if he could intimidate her.

"I do not give one frigid fuck if you do, Sadie," she lashed out. What was wrong with the fool? Couldn't he tell she was on edge, horny, and about to break some shit?

"What is her secret, Uta?" Loki asked gently.

She took strength from his familiar smile and paused for drama. Simply because sticky chaos was about to rain down did not mean she could not enjoy being the center of attention. Spinning slowly, she made certain all eyes were on her.

"With Hunter blood, our ancestors enjoyed the light of day."

The collective gasp satisfied her flair.

"You insinuated this at our last meeting, and I did not believe you then." Sadavir crossed his legs, examining his fingernails. "How convenient that you now purport to have living proof in a mysterious, yet absent, halfling."

She inhaled through her nose, determined not to let him provoke her. "Apparently the other aggressionists do not share your doubts. We have reports of hostages taken from at least one compound attacked by vampires."

A room full of bodies shifted and she enjoyed owning all of their focus.

Andre leaned over the table, resting his weight on his elbows, and smirked. "Just tell us the whole damn thing already."

She cast him her best death glare, but he only chuckled—Andre was one vampire she'd never been able to intimidate. So she began.

"In the beginning, vampires lived like creatures of the night, like animals, predators. We had no civilization, and barely a language. We hunted by night and hid in the darkness of caves, or more often, human burial mounds. Few vampires even knew how to turn a human, and there was no desire to do so. More vampires only meant more competition for the hunt."

Bel's focus tugged at her—to be the object of his attention even just as a storyteller intoxicated her. She resisted the urge to speak only to him.

"Humans did not leave their hovels at night. Vampires stole into human villages and homes to hunt. One entire village fled, abandoning their homes for fear of murderous vampires. The vampires had to learn control, how to feed without killing the humans or driving them away. One day, a male vampire—they had no names then—found a girl alone. The legend said she was very beautiful, and like all her clan, she possessed yellow eyes."

Uta rolled her own eyes. Legends always said such things.

"In the face of a frightened, beautiful young woman, this vampire felt pity. He fed as gently as he was able, and for the first time, he did not kill his prey. According to my sire, this was the first time a vampire discovered the power of a bite over a human, and the communion transformed him."

"Wouldn't they have known from biting each other?" asked Joon Song, one of her favorite members of the Justicia.

"Maybe, maybe not. I do not know of their life in darkness—did they bond, did they make love? Could they do such things in their caves with no language? I have asked myself these questions many times."

"Indeed." Loki scratched his hairless, boyish chin. "And where did these poor creatures, our ancestors, come from in the first place?"

Sweet Auntie Europa, she'd had enough with their inanities. She squared off at him with her hands on her hips. "What do I look like, some kind of oracle? I never claimed to understand all the vampire mysteries. Adam, Eve, Lilith—they are all just stories. All I know is what Rize told me: this male vampire fell in love with her, and she accepted him. The woman was a widow and she bathed him, clothed him in her husband's garments, and taught him to speak her language. Over time, his fellows joined him, happily mixing with the humans and adopting their ways. Some of the humans became vampires, others bore children, or chose to remain human."

Sadavir leaned forward. "You expect me to believe all the vampires in the whole world went to this one Hunter hovel and acquired civilization?"

"Perhaps so, or perhaps it is only a myth. Perhaps some vampires are to this day still living in caves, hunting humans, and giving us a bad reputation."

Andre laughed and then Bel followed suit, the timbre of his chuckle a little richer than his father's—at least to her ears. She could possibly live on that sound alone.

"This was an idyllic time." She listened for a single breath. No one inhaled. She had them enthralled, a small consolation. "Then, out of the azure, the Hunter elders attacked—"

"The blue," Bel said.

"What?" She stared at him, not grasping his meaning until his self-satisfied expression revealed he'd corrected her idiom. She crossed her arms. Did he think she could learn thirteen tenses, memorize a dictionary, and internalize every asinine English expression in a single plane ride? She was only two thousand years old, for Io's sake. Even Loki could not do much better.

"*Davo*, Bel, let her finish."

Thanks to her seething irritation, it took a moment to find her place in the story. "With the advantage of surprise, they killed the halfling babes, the vampires, and Hunter mates. The remnant who escaped are our ancestors. Hunters pursued them to the ends of the earth. The survivors had been cast from paradise. Grieving and traumatized, they wanted no vampire to know the power of Hunter blood, so we would never mix again. I swore to my sire, Rize, I would keep the secret. But Pedro learned, and also Ethan Bennett, so now you must all know the story."

"Why did the elders attack them?" Loki asked.

Lucas stood up. "I've been considering that question since I recreated my family's record of these events."

Sadavir hissed. "You dare speak in the Justicia? After you have heard the cruelty your ancestors wrought against us?"

"Thought you didn't believe her story?" Bel leaned over the table with an air of casual menace only a man wearing denim could manage.

Was he defending her? He always had as a boy, when her swearing and impropriety had earned her insults. She might swoon, if it weren't so important to keep on her feet.

"Silence," Loki said. "Let the Hunter speak. He has proven his loyalty to Andre and that was no small task, I'm sure."

Lucas bowed his head to Loki before he began. "Hunter culture is inherently conservative. We remain isolated from society so that, at the fundamental level, little has changed since the period Uta describes. That influx of vampires would have meant a radical change in culture and power. The elders attacked the vampires and those who had mingled with them to restore the purity of their original culture."

She nodded. "My sire attributed their actions to just such a notion of purity. And because of it, he came to believe it is not possible for Hunters and vampires to live at peace. Rize insisted we must live without the sun because Hunters will always be waiting and plotting in secret, while their powerful blood lures us into a sense of security."

Pedro stood, shifting slightly to shield Lucas. "That's not true of all of them."

Sadavir shrugged. "Of course you would say that. He's seduced you with his special blood. Now tell me, have you walked in the sun?"

Pedro bristled, his barrel chest puffing. But then he flashed his charming smile and winked. "Too risky. I'm waiting for someone else to go first."

The room broke out in quiet laughter and Sadavir glowered.

"Enough," Loki said in the formal tone he used for official Justicia business. "Uta Ilirije, is your story at an end?"

"Yes."

"Are there more questions for her?" Loki asked.

"I understand our ancestors lived together and walked in the sun," said the African vampire, Nceba, "but what of the wasting disease? Did Hunter blood cure it?"

"You're missing the point." Bel hopped up, stealing the limelight. "There wouldn't have been a wasting disease. Before this slaughter, every single vampire lived in their homeland, without cause to leave."

Uta's chest rose with pride at his understanding, feeling for the moment like they were a team. "Yes, and Hunter blood satisfies our longing for the original homeland."

An astonished murmur rippled through the group. She did love to deliver zingers.

"Yes. Which is why I have to get back to my research." Bel made for the door.

"Not yet, Lobel," Loki said in a voice that prickled up Uta's spine. "Uta, your secret is told."

All the eyes of the Justicia flew to her, except Andre — loyal old friend — who tried to get Bel's attention. Bel, however, was fixated on her.

Uta searched out her blood supply. Nils had tucked himself into the corner. She sent a whisper in his direction. "Be ready."

He nodded once.

Oh gods of Illyria, this was humiliating. Not to mention that it was going to hurt like a sunburn, and make a monstrous mess. And she liked this suit. Damn the old ways and Rize for putting her in this position. She found the blade in her breast pocket and flipped it open.

CHAPTER 21

Bel itched to escape the room and think harder about *osjećaj* and nostalgia and Hunter blood, but Loki ordered him to stay. The vibe in the room went weird and Andre was nodding his head like he was having a seizure—what the hell?

Uta whipped out her shiny little switchblade. Fuck. Some ancient vampire code about telling secrets. He had to stop her. Sure, she could survive that blade but, through and through, his bonded body panicked.

She was so quick—he was years too late.

The slice happened at lightning speed, too fast to see.

Blood poured down her front, soaked into her top and splashed onto the table. Now hanging at her side, her fist clenched around the perfect pink tip of her tongue. Her eyes rolled back, and she swayed on her knees.

"You're all fucking crazy. Why would she do that?" Bel's shouts sounded distant to himself, as if someone else called out, but he didn't stop. He knelt, sliding his arms under her neck and her knees, still yelling. "Why would you let her? She was helping you."

"You know nothing of the customs, halfling," one of them said. Bel didn't care who.

A human tried to pull her away from Bel.

"Mine," Bel barked.

The man backed off.

Bel scooped her up and carried her into the hallway, where he laid her on the floor. Her own crimson blood covered her. Her lips were pressed tight and her eyeballs moved rapidly under closed lids. No more blood poured from her mouth, at least. Christ, what should he do? He had to help her.

Uta, please be okay.

He pushed auburn hair off her face with his bloody hand, the scarlet only one shade redder than her hair. Her skin had grayed.

Beside her, the human rolled back his cuffs. Stupid, this was no time to worry about blood on your clothes.

"I am Nils, her servant." The human pulled open her jaw.

"What are you doing?"

"She needs blood to heal faster. I'm going to feed her." Nils lined up her fangs with a thick blue vein in his wrist.

"Like hell you are," Bel said, pushing Nils back. He shoved his own arm into her mouth and punctured his skin on her razor sharp incisors. The moment she began to draw blood from him, his body shook with the pleasure. "Oh fuck."

Two voices laughed in response, Nils and—surprise, surprise—Andre.

Bel shuddered, his skin tingling directionally along the path of his blood flowing into her.

"First time?" Nils asked, amused.

Bel ignored him. Hard not to, given what her fangs were doing to him. He managed to lean against the wall, his arm still at an awkward angle, but the rest of his body relaxed. The heady iron odor of her blood mixed with that flowery scent that clung to her, making his brain cloudy.

Then he forced his neurons to fire in a singular direction so he could form a coherent thought. "Andre, what the hell did she do that for?"

Nobody kept the old customs anymore. Certainly not Andre, or anybody on Bel's crew. All that blood spilled—he gagged, couldn't look at her shirt. It was how he imagined Mila's bathtub suicide. The gags turned into heaves, and he tried not to wrench his wrist from Uta's mouth. Then she reached up to hold it, like a baby learning to hold its bottle, and the gentle grip on his arm tantalized him.

"Easy, Bel," Andre said in a surprisingly gentle tone. "You realize she will be fine? It is like a hard spanking. According to tradition, breaking a vow cannot go without punishment, even if done with good intentions."

"Fuck traditions."

"Honor is one of the few things that lives as long as we do, son."

Bel wanted to argue, but he was too blissed out. His skin burned, his nipples tingled. Uta lay silent, sucking his blood down fast.

"Is this how bites always feel?"

"She is your mate, Bel. This is what you long for."

Like a vampire longed for home, or Hunter blood…shite. There was another clue here, but Bel's mind was a sky full of pink and blue cotton candy clouds and he couldn't think straight.

He ran his tongue over his teeth, wanting to be naked. His cock was a rocket in his jeans. And then, oh yeah, her tongue flicked along the top of his wrist. Damn, she regenerated quickly. She mewled into his arm as she took pulls of his blood. He melted—from those sounds or her bite, he couldn't tell.

"Let's give them some privacy," Andre said.

Bel nodded, eyes squeezed shut. He would say thank you later.

"They're in the middle of the hallway," Nils pointed out.

"No matter, everyone else is in the dining room."

Bel hardly noticed they were gone. Could he come from her bite alone, or would he still need some manual stimulation? He didn't even want to orgasm if he could stay on that stairway to heaven forever, with her drinking him, licking him.

Then it was over. She broke the suction and pulled his arm out of her mouth.

Out popped her new perfect tongue to lick her lips. "Mmmm," she moaned, as if he were the most delicious thing she had ever tasted.

Then she opened her eyes. When she saw him, they went wide. "Sheep scat, Bel. You didn't—"

"Say shit, Uta. Scat's not profane enough a word to suit you." He could barely get the words past his clenched teeth.

"What the hell were you thinking?"

"Couldn't help it." He grimaced. "Instinct. You were hurt."

She sat up and tilted her head, smiling. "My bite has affected you?"

He wanted to fall into her dark eyes—they promised they knew him, wanted him. They promised him a home. "I'm buzzing like a bumblebee," he managed to say.

She leaned in, darting out her brand new pink tongue to kiss him. It tasted like his blood, a reminder of the fundamental difference between them. A reminder of her power over him.

"Uta, stop."

She did, eyes glazed. "Please, Bel. I don't want to stop." His fierce, ancient vampire pouted like a spoiled child.

He liked the sound of that please, and he couldn't help it—he chuckled. "Are you healed?"

"Yes."

"Show me."

She stuck out her tongue again, like a child on the playground.

Oh God, he wanted that up and down his shaft. "But first, your hand. Show me what's in your hand." Her eyes darted from her fist to her hand and back. "Show me."

She obeyed, and the two inch tip of her tongue, already shriveled past recognition, was revealed on her palm.

He gritted his teeth. "If you ever hurt yourself like that in front of me again, I'll kill you." He had been powerless over his instinct to help her, and *shite*—her bite. She'd taken away all his control.

She hid her fist behind his back. "Please kiss me."

"No. I'm like a fucking puppet—your blood is pulling all my strings. I don't want you."

She jerked back as if he'd slapped her and rose to her feet effortlessly. "Fine. But you do realize you've made things much worse?"

"What do you mean?"

"You are the only scientific expert on vampire blood in the whole world, yet you did not anticipate shoving your arm in my mouth would strengthen our bond? I believe in English you call that irony, yes?"

As she crossed the hall to the dining room, emotions collided inside him like two storm fronts. He couldn't separate her burning sense of rejection from his humiliating lust. Not just flashes of her thoughts and feelings, but her whole damn consciousness had taken up residence alongside his.

Fuck.

Maybe he could create a pill to cure him of their bond. An Uta pill made of her blood that would take the edge off his hunger for her. If he were really generous, he might make her a Bel pill too. Yeah, right. This bond was just like the wasting disease and it came down to the same damn *osjećaj*—some ephemeral sentiment he had no idea how to capture in his lab.

She opened the door to the dining room and the occupants gasped in chorus. She did look like she'd just barely escaped a serial killer.

"Listen, you herd of impotent goats, I say we adjourn. We can finalize our plans in the morning. Tonight, we play cards."

Loki huffed like a tiny drama queen whose authority had been usurped. "Uta—"

But Andre cut him off. "I second her proposal. We need a respite, and playing cards is the custom at my home. If you prefer to abstain in favor of other ways to rest your ever-waking minds, I will not take offense. However, Loki, I recall you have a fondness for cards."

"Indeed I do. It is also my habit in the night hours."

"I also believe you have an outstanding debt to me from Uta's last card party. A herd of prize Norwegian sheep, was it?"

"Andre, I really don't recall."

Resting against the wall, Bel's head hurt. He'd heard enough about livestock from these crusty old vampires to last a lifetime.

"This is no time for a card party," Sadavir said. "We're in the middle of a crisis."

Uta glared at him. "That is when you most need a party, you fool."

Bel couldn't disagree with her, even if he wanted nothing to do with her ever again.

He needed a glass of water, and then two of bourbon. Hopefully that would be enough to drown Uta's feelings, and some of his own.

"Eight o'clock," Andre said. "We'll play in the parlor next door."

Bel had no intention of partying. Or rather, he had every intention of enjoying a party in his room, alone with a bottle of bourbon—just as sweet as a woman, but the burn only lasted while it was in your mouth.

CHAPTER 22

As the Justicia and householders filed from the dining room, someone tugged at Lucas's sleeve.

"I have to show you something. You too, Andre." Leo held up his laptop like a will-work-for-food sign.

They crowded around him where he opened the computer and displayed a series of emails. "These were nearly impossible to find. They're from an alias I've traced to Ethan, and they confirm that he did hire people to attack the first Hunter cells."

"Loki," Andre said, raising his voice slightly. "You need to see this."

Loki stood at the other end of the table, talking to Sadavir. He came over directly, as did the other vampire. Lucas would have preferred the Hunter-hater stay away, but no luck.

Leo pointed at the screen. "I've found message boards where a vampire takes credit for the first attacks and reveals the secrets of Hunter blood, that it promises sun tolerance. But it's really Ethan and I can prove it."

"Bennett attacked his own people to incite violence against Hunters?" Sadavir asked. "That's a level of evil I wouldn't have expected, even from a Hunter."

"Ethan's not loyal to Hunters," Lucas replied. "He's only loyal to himself. This whole war is about his ego, a bullshit cause for him to garner power."

"Am I hearing a proposal in here somewhere?" Loki asked. The little guy was shrewd and he appeared interested, but that could just be the perpetually high arch of his eyebrows.

Lucas looked to Andre, who'd already made it clear he thought this plan was pure fantasy. Still, he nodded, granting permission for Lucas to share it.

"I want to take down the Hunters from the inside." Lucas waited for the rebuttal. None came.

Loki must be desperate.

"There's a bottom up and a top down approach." Lucas gestured with one hand high and one low. "We disseminate news of Ethan's betrayal, undermine his leadership. At the same time, we enlist vampires to kidnap but not harm Hunters. They feed from and essentially woo the Hunters. Subject them to that notorious vampire brainwashing, which turns out simply to be kindness, respect, and pleasure."

Loki's mouth hung open.

Okay, Lucas's plan was far out, but had they really never thought of sleeping with the enemy? In thousands of years?

"Preposterous," Sadavir finally spoke. "You heard Uta. Hunters can't be trusted. We must kill them before they destroy us all. When the last Hunter is dead, we can return to our homelands to heal and rebuild."

"Will the last Hunter be my friend Lucas, here?" Andre sidestepped closer, positioning himself between Lucas and the bully. "Because when you talk about exterminating them, you're talking like a Hunter."

Warm fuzzy feelings suffused Lucas. Andre had never called him a friend before, and he got a little taste of his famous fatherly affection. A guy could get used to that.

"Indeed," Loki said. "Wasn't it your wise countryman who said, 'Non-violence is the greatest force at the disposal of mankind. It is mightier than the mightiest weapon of destruction devised by the ingenuity of man'?"

"Don't quote that twit Gandhi to me. My whole household went on the salt march with him. I nearly starved."

"Yes, poor Sadavir. I'm sure in the entire country of India, you were unable to find a soul to feed you." Loki wore an impossibly bland expression, which made his sarcasm all the more amusing, at least to Lucas.

Sadavir seemed immune and simply crossed his arms. "Nevertheless, we're not mankind. The greatest force at our disposal is our great strength."

"See—" Lucas shook his head "—I beg to disagree. I've been living here for almost two months, and I'm pretty sure your greatest strength is that your bite feels like ecstasy, Viagra, and the best sex of your life every time."

Andre laughed.

As an afterthought, Lucas added, "And that you're mostly good."

Loki lifted his eyebrows into an even pointier arch than usual. "Lucas, I'm intrigued. How would you go about it?"

"I'd use Derek Williams. He's been captive here for a month, and I've tried to woo him to the vampire side."

"And?"

"Uta fed from him when she was here last month, and it was eye opening for him. Currently, he's neutral at best. But I think this news about Ethan will tip him over. And then if one of you vampires bites him, he'll understand the big picture better."

"A Hunter, to feed from?" Sadavir asked, with glaring interest in the advantageous prospect.

"To sip from, not to kill," Andre qualified.

"No offense, Sadavir," Lucas said. "But I think maybe your Xhosan colleague would better suit Derek's taste. And we do care if it he likes being bitten."

"Oh yes, Nceba would be perfect." Loki clapped his small hands together, then his face fell into sadness. "I fear she is wasting quickly. Perhaps his blood will help her."

"If we can convince Derek to switch sides, he can present himself as a challenger to Ethan's leadership. To lead the Hunters from hate to a new future." God, he sounded like a ridiculous Pollyanna. But again, no one refuted him. Perhaps they were all fools in hope together.

"I want to meet Derek," Loki announced. "I'll go get Nceba and you can take us both to him."

In that freaky-fast vampire way, Nceba and Loki were back at Lucas's side in a matter of seconds. The small group formed a procession, parading through the cellar to Derek's cell.

Lucas knocked before he unlocked the closet door.

The prisoner sat reading a novel on his bed, which occupied most of the cramped but hospitable room where Lucas himself had spent a few nights the month prior.

Derek sat up, clearly puzzled by the unexpected visitors.

Laptop in hand, Leo approached him. "I have proof that Ethan sacrificed two cells of Hunters, then impersonated vampires to encourage them to do the same."

Derek didn't speak, just took the computer from Leo. He read for a while, the light changing on his face as he opened and closed computer windows. Finally, he simply said, "Damn."

Lucas stepped directly in front of the Hunter. "Derek, we need you to help us take him down."

"No. I just want to be done with this. I want to walk away. Marasović, trust me that I'm done Hunting and let me go."

"Derek, this is Loki Falk, chief of the vampire council," Andre said.

"Chief?" Derek frowned.

"Yes, I am quite possibly the oldest living creature," Loki said, straightening his spine. "And this is Nceba Mandla."

Derek frowned at her. "What do you want?"

"Mr. Williams, Lucas tells me that your time here has persuaded you that we are not the incarnation of evil the Hunters believe us to be. Is that true?"

"Yes. It seems that, like humans, you must be judged individually."

"Very true. And what do you believe the cause of your people's mandate to exterminate us is?"

"Lucas says it's something in the past. That once Hunters and vampires lived together, until there was a war."

"That's right. And now there is another war. Leo, please show Mr. Williams the photos of the Hunter cells that have been attacked."

Leo brought up the images one by one. Indonesia, Mumbai, South Africa, Santiago, British Columbia. Derek reacted just the way someone who wasn't a sociopath named Ethan Bennett would—frozen in horror, shock on his face.

Lucas sat down next to the Hunter. "Ethan wanted this. He made this happen to foment rage against the vampires and consolidate his power."

Derek turned, meeting Lucas's gaze without any suspicion on his face.

Lucas turned up his palm. "We need you to help us bring him down. We need you to step up as an informed leader, proposing reconciliation."

"They'd crucify me."

"Not if you can prove their leader is a traitor."

"They'll never believe it. They'll say the evidence is fabricated."

"That's probably true," Loki said. "So, your options are to stay locked in this cell until the five thousand year war ends, or take a risk and try to save some lives—vampire, Hunter, human civilians."

Derek's eyes ping-ponged between Lucas and Loki, until Nceba stepped forward, capturing his attention.

"Mr. Williams, today I heard a story about a time when our people lived together in harmony. My sire hinted of this time to me, although I did not understand until today. I believe there may be a special affinity between Hunters and vampires that your ancestors drove a wedge into five thousand years ago. What if we could heal that wedge?"

Derek was mesmerized by her—hell, so was Lucas. Her gentle tone, warm and logical, could probably coax either of them into anything.

"How?" Derek whispered the word.

"Let me feed from you, and perhaps we can find out."

Damn. Lucas flushed and his collar grew tight. Was he anticipating Derek's pleasure, or did he actually have one straight bone in his body after all?

"Okay," Derek said. "But everybody leaves. No, wait. Lucas, you stay."

Surprised, Lucas studied the Hunter. Derek blinked rapidly and rings of sweat appeared at the underarms of his shirt. He was scared shitless, and Lucas couldn't blame him. Uta had fed from Derek once, a month back. The guy knew exactly how he was about to lose control to his enemy. Was he afraid she would drink him dry?

Sure, no skin off Lucas's back to referee. He nodded, and the others filed out of the room.

Derek perched on the bed cross-legged. "Tell me what to do."

"It will relax you most to lay down. Yes, like that. Now, turn on your side facing away from the wall."

Gracefully, the small woman climbed onto the bed and lay along Derek's body. She was petite, but both men knew she was also deadly powerful. "Ready?" she asked.

When Derek nodded, her fangs were in his neck before he could change his mind. All the air escaped from his body in one long exhalation as he relaxed into Nceba. Lucas's muscles relaxed sympathetically as he imagined Derek's bliss. This ancient bond, this symbiosis between Hunters and vampires, it was incredible—some mysterious, holy shit. It gave Lucas a purpose Hunting never had.

The thing between him and Pedro was good—they'd have been good if they were two normal guys. But the bond between them was way beyond normal. It mattered, the same way that first love between the vampire and the Hunter mattered so long ago. Hell, maybe they had a destiny to bring their kinds together again. But if he became a vampire—

"Mmghhh." Nceba made an animal sound very like a contended lioness.

The door opened quietly and Loki slipped in. "Oh my."

Neither Derek nor Nceba seemed to notice. She stroked along his spine with a slow motion. Derek threw his leg over hers, pulling her closer and rubbing against her. Okay, thrusting was probably a more accurate word. Derek was clearly at the height of his skin sensitivity. In a moment, he would be craving a kiss, or something to suck on.

Loki opened the door again and motioned for someone to enter. "I see I'm just in time."

It was Nceba's householder, the one she had seemed so close to during the Justicia meeting. For a moment, the sweet-faced and curvy woman just stared at the two on the bed. Then she smiled and climbed behind Derek. She angled up on her elbow and bent forward to kiss him as soon as his tongue appeared on his lips.

Deep in the back of the Hunter's throat, the sound of pure pleasure formed, but it was swallowed by the woman who kissed him.

"Lucas, I think Derek wouldn't mind if we gave him some privacy," Loki said.

They left together. Andre and Leo stood outside the room—an awkward pair.

"So…" Leo began, rocking on the balls of his feet. But he must have been trying to fill the silence because he didn't continue.

Minutes passed. The vampires were probably eavesdropping, but Lucas had nothing to occupy him and his eyelids drooped.

The now-familiar pain, which began days—or was it weeks—ago started up in his side, jerking him awake. Like a blade between his two lowest ribs, the damned stitch kept him winded and nauseous. It was probably a symptom of stress and that he wasn't taking good care of himself, and maybe of something more worrying, but he'd be damned if he had time to think about that at the moment.

He forced his attention from it to study the winery's vast workspace. Five enormous stainless steel vats lined the south and west walls and reached up to the high ceiling. A roller door for deliveries spanned half the east wall. Various pieces of machinery pressed against the fourth wall, flanking Derek's makeshift cell, and Lucas occupied himself with trying to guess their functions. That cylindrical thing had to be a press, and the long stainless steel trough would empty into a de-stemmer. Next to an industrial sink, coiled hoses hung in orderly rows. Was that how they got the wine out of the vats? His research into the Marasović family had turned Lucas into a wine connoisseur, but Pedro was the real expert, a first class vintner.

Finally, Loki spoke. "Lucas, I do like this plan. I will ask every member of the Justicia to reach out to the vampires they trust most. We will organize the friendly raids as soon as—"

The door to Derek's cell opened. Nceba appeared with Derek in hand, her eyes glinting gold. On closer inspection, they were simply chocolate colored, but the glimmer had drawn his attention to the fact that she looked fifteen years younger than she had when she went into the closet.

"Friends, Derek is returning to our room with us. We will give him the right to roam freely at Kaštel as a token of our trust in him. He will decide tomorrow if he is willing to lead a coup against your brother."

Lucas turned, curious to see how Andre would react to her giving orders. The old guy was pretty much a sucker for bossy chicks.

"Of course," he replied. "Derek, you are my guest." Only those who knew him well would have caught the faintest hint of sarcasm. Apparently Loki was among those who did, because he smiled, then hid it quickly by pressing his lips together.

"Thanks," Derek said, his voice hollow. His shoulders sloped and his eyes wavered. He was nearly unrecognizable from the Hunter Kos and Andre had captured a month ago. Everything about his appearance revealed Nceba's bite had stolen the last threads of his conviction. Lucas only hoped those two females and one pair of fangs would persuade Derek to do the right thing.

Once the threesome had gone ahead, Andre and Loki departed, leaving Lucas alone with Leo.

"There's something I need to ask you." Lucas tugged the kid into the closet and closed the door.

Leo glanced around the tiny cell, his guileless face revealing his surprise. "Yeah?"

They'd spent several days imprisoned there weeks ago, when Lucas had learned Leo was gay and primed to defect from the Hunters for all the same reasons Lucas had. He'd seemed like such a boy then, clever with computers, but a naïve virgin. The thing was, Leo had a lovable openness. As soon as he met real, live vampires, all his Hunter programming had collapsed. And somehow, he didn't seem so young anymore, although he had to be a virgin still. In the whirlwind of the last four weeks, who could have—

The kid snapped in front of his face. "Lucas, man, what's up?"

"Sorry, I…" Lucas's tongue stuck to the roof of his mouth. *Damn. Spit it out, cowboy.* "Pedro wants to turn me."

Leo nodded, seeming unsurprised. "And?"

"You know he has to feed from a Hunter, because I was his first blood."

"Yeah, I know." Then the kid's yellow eyes widened for a flash of a second, but he kept his face neutral. "Me, you mean?"

"If you're up for it."

Leo cracked a smile, making him a good bit more handsome. "Hell yes, I'll do it. More than happy to help out." He rubbed at his neck, grinning.

Lucas didn't like it. He wanted to yank the kid's hand away and strangle him for saying yes, for having good Hunter blood that might nourish Pedro when Lucas wouldn't be able to anymore. But he clasped his hands behind his back instead.

"Thanks, kid."

Irritation flickered over his face at the hated nickname, which was a minor consolation to Lucas. Then Leo's grin returned, even bigger now. "Are you guys…um…" He looked down at his toes. "Are you all, you know—open?"

Lucas's over-active imagination supplied him with an image of young Leo, cradled in Pedro's arms and lost to the bliss of his bite. It sent shudders down Lucas's torso, and he very nearly punched the kid.

"No, Leo. Don't even think about it."

Lucas crossed to the door. This thing between him and Pedro was raw, and real, and he did not want Pedro biting anyone else. Period. But Pedro was convinced something terrible would happen to Lucas if he didn't turn right away. And given his fatigue and nausea, Lucas knew he might be right.

CHAPTER 23

Bel sat at the antique desk in his room. His? Hell, when had it become his, not just a vacant one at his father's house?

Probably the day Uta had first arrived and explained that Andre wasn't the bad guy after all. That day, Bel had yanked off the sheets he'd used to shroud the all too familiar furniture, like this desk, identical to the one his mother had perched at to write her correspondence. Maybe Bel wasn't a full vampire, but Croatia still lingered in his heart — a haunting reminder of happy times, and devastating ones.

The fingers of his left hand curled around a tumbler of bourbon, freshly refilled.

Occasionally, an alien thought or emotion would course through him, distinct and clearly not his own. Uta had been right — he could feel her more acutely. In that infuriatingly mysterious way his blood communed with the part of him now inside her and he didn't like it one bit. Each time her frustration tensed his muscles, he had to push it away and force himself to refocus.

Short of showing his test subjects pretty pictures of their homeland, he'd had no epiphanies about how to satisfy a longing for the homeland, so he'd gone back to square one. With his right hand, he sketched angles and electrons — a molecular puzzle of bonds and receptors that might just fit together, hopefully proving Uta and her sentimental nonsense wrong.

He wasn't holding his breath, or — at the bottom of his third glass of bourbon — even bothering with his full mental faculties. He could go downstairs and ask for Lexi's help, but what would he tell her? *Sorry, doll, turns out this experiment is a waste of time. It all boils down to touchy-feely vampire shite.* She would lose all respect for him, if she even had any left.

A horn blared out front. His gaze jerked to the window—darkening in the last minutes of sunlight. The horn bleated again. Three long blasts. Then three more. Lexi's car stood in the center of the drive. What the hell? She was supposed to be safe in the house somewhere. Last he'd seen her, she was catching up on work at the extra desk in Kos's office.

He tore down the stairs and through a gathered crowd of vampires who couldn't venture out into the late day sun. They retreated from the light as he swung open the door, sprinting toward the car just as a second vehicle peeled out in the direction of the highway.

He halted at the sight of Lexi struggling in the passenger seat, her mouth covered in duct tape, her hair fallen over her eyes. Then a sign in the window came into focus. *A gift for Marasović is in the trunk.*

It would be a bomb. Lexi, locked inside a car bomb.

What would trigger it—her door, the trunk, a remote device? He scanned the surroundings for a Hunter spy. Fuck, he couldn't think, and he cursed the bourbon.

"They want us to get the message," Uta called out. "They will not have booby-trapped the trunk." She stood inside the door, too close to the edge of the light and he fought the urge to rush back and push her further inside.

"Do you know how to dismantle a bomb?" she asked.

He was already at the back of the car, feeling for a latch. "Depends on the bomb," he muttered.

There, the emblem was a button. At least the Hunters had thought to unlock the damn thing.

The device was a nest of wires tangling out of a double slice of c4. And just like in the stupid movies, the timer began to race, counting down from sixty seconds. His bourbon soaked brain had time to grate at the Hunters' lack of originality before it descended into panic. The back seat was down and a messy braid of wires stretched into the car. He didn't have to check to know they connected to Lexi and her door.

"Describe the device, Bel," Uta called.

Forty-five seconds. He ignored her. Lexi contorted her neck to see him, and the fear in her eyes shamed him. His hands trembled.

Focus. A manila envelope labeled Marasović lay next to the explosives. He frisbeed it toward the house, and went to work unraveling the wires. Goddamn it, a vampire could just fly the thing off into the open expanse of burned up vineyard, which is why the Hunters appeared right before sunset. More of Bennett's head games.

This was the part he hated — the reverse engineering of a bomb involved a lot of psychological guesses. This design itself was a mindfuck, or else they'd have locked the damn thing into a box and set it to go off when they wanted it to.

Thirty seconds. Lexi whimpered. His beautiful, brilliant Lexi. If she was going to die in this car, he sure as hell wasn't leaving her alone to do it.

"*Davo,* what the hell is all this?" Andre roared from inside the house.

A loud conversation transpired in about a dozen languages, but Bel paid it no mind.

Uta shouted again. "You pig-assed fool, tell me about the bomb."

"Pig-headed," he hissed into the trunk of the car and yanked one red wire. Nothing happened. He yanked a black one. The timer still raced down.

Fifteen seconds.

"How much c4 is it?" The pitch of her voice had risen slightly.

"Two blocks."

"No, Bel. I smell much more. A dozen at least. Those two are decoys. Get back in the house." Uta was nearly hysterical, no doubt considering her own suffering if he got incinerated. And it echoed inside him, amplifying his heart rate and tightening his throat.

Lexi sobbed.

"I'm not leaving her here," he said.

It happened all at once — the weight of someone crashed into him at high speed as the car flew into the air. Uta's flowery smell told him she had tackled him. With his cheek pressed into the cement, he searched for Lexi. Her legs protruded from under Kos's torso, which was wrapped in his thick gray coat, its hood pulled over his blond head.

Still aloft, the car exploded in a fireball over the vineyard as a dark, cloaked figure darted away from it.

"Infernal sunshine." Uta sprinted into the house with Kos on her heels. Andre literally flew through the door behind them.

Bel scrambled to his feet and hurried to Lexi. With a nod, she consented to him pulling the tape off her mouth.

"Are you okay?" he asked, embracing her.

She only nodded, leaning into his chest.

"Come inside. I'll cut this tape off your wrists."

Lucas strode out of the door. "What can I do?"

Bel nodded toward the ground. "Grab that envelope, would you?"

Inside, their rescuers were nowhere to be seen. But Uta's reassuringly seething anger over the bomb reached him from somewhere in the house. Good, if she was angry, she was alive.

When Bel's gaze landed on Zoey, she nodded, grimacing. "They are rather singed, but Loki assures me they will be all right. They're taking a cold shower."

"What?" Bel's stomach clenched at the image of Uta naked with his father and brother.

Loki chuckled. "I believe she means three, separate cold showers."

Pedro brandished a pocket knife and sawed the duct tape from Lexi's wrists. She'd regained her composure, although her mascara had run down her face. She never used to wear the stuff, and the raccoon eyes left her looking incredibly vulnerable.

"Who the hell let her out?" Bel shouted. He searched the room for someone to blame, but the truth was, she wasn't a prisoner. He hadn't told anyone to guard her. "Lexi, why did you leave?"

"I overheard Omar say Hunters attacked here last night, and I freaked. I thought I would be safer if I got out."

He inhaled. "Lexi. Trust me. This is the safest place you could possibly be."

Uta appeared at the upstairs balcony rubbing her hair with a familiar dark green towel. Maybe all the towels at Kaštel were green, but Bel had the sinking suspicion she'd used his shower. Wordlessly, she descended. Aside from rosier than usual cheeks, she seemed fine—no burns, not even a flaking sunburn. She extended her palm, and Lucas handed her the envelope.

Andre bellowed from above. "I believe that is addressed to me."

She scowled, but waited.

"Who's she?" Lexi whispered. Oops—he hadn't explained super hearing.

Uta stepped toward her, a haughty tilt to her head, which already stood at least half a foot higher than Lexi's. "I am Uta Ilirije, Bel's godmother."

He could have kissed her for not saying mate.

Lexi extended her hand. "I thought godmothers were always four-and-a-half feet tall with matronly bosoms, knitting needles, and magic wands." She smiled with the same warmth she'd always bestowed on Kos and Andre — a genuine affection for Bel's family.

Uta huffed, pinching her lips. "Magic wands only exist in fairy tales."

Lexi frowned, glancing at Bel. Only then did he realize he'd moved toward Uta like a bloody magnet. Their arms touched, as if his body had required tactile proof that she was all right.

"You're the one?" Lexi asked her.

Uta's eyes softened, and her regret hit Bel like a punch to the gut, telegraphing the truth right into his brain — she hadn't relished the way she'd come between Bel and Lexi without them knowing it. He licked his lips, searching for the name of the other bitter emotion he sensed in Uta — jealousy, carefully controlled.

His hand reached for hers of its own accord. "Yeah. She's the one."

Lexi offered her hand again, valiantly. "Good luck with him. He's a piece of work. And, as you saw out there with the bomb, he doesn't take instructions well."

Uta returned the handshake with a grin. "No. He never has."

He should have been irritated by their condescension, but instead, God help him, it was oddly comforting. Bollocks — he was really in trouble.

Andre ripped open the envelope with shaky hands. "*Davo.*" He passed it to Uta. "He's nearly through the alphabet."

"Yes. But, look again. He doesn't have everyone. At least half of them are missing."

"Small consolation," Andre said into Zoey's head, which she had tucked under his chin.

A pink tear trailed down her cheek. "I led them to the slaughter."

"Ssshh," he said, and nothing more.

What else could anyone say?

Uta cleared her throat. "Loki. We must redeploy the units. Split them up if need be. The refugees are sitting ducks."

"They've been encouraged to flee, Uta."

"Loki, please." Her lip trembled and she pressed the back of her hand to her mouth.

"All right. I will make the call."

Uta squeezed her eyes shut and then opened them to look around. "Now, you bleating goats, go get dressed. It is time for a party." Her heels clicked loudly across the hardwood floor of the foyer.

Bel wanted to go after her, to comfort her, to surrender to her pull — he put one boot on the floor to follow her footsteps and froze. So what if she'd just saved his life. So what if she was kind of funny and sweet when she wasn't being a total bitch. He was bigger than this goddamn blood bond, and he would not let her lead him around by his cock, or an invisible sentiment that might not even exist.

Lexi cleared her throat, trembling. "I guess I need to tell Mister Doctor we need to buy a new car."

"How about we wait on that for a while? It will only worry him." He took her elbow. "Right now, I want to tell you what I've learned about the wasting disease. I'm stuck all over again, and you always see the angle I overlooked." She raised her chin as he'd hoped she would, comforted by the promise of a problem to solve.

She was real. What they shared in the lab, and in the past — that was real. Uta, on the other hand, was smoke and mirrors and head games, and not to be trusted.

CHAPTER 24

Uta swung open the door of her room on a mission. Five minutes later, every outfit in all five of her suitcases was strewn across the yellow-painted room. What was wrong with her? It should be easy to decide. They all looked fabulous on her. Bel's emotions vibrated inside her like hornets in a jar—a complicated push and pull she knew all too well. It was enough to give her hope. Maybe he would come for her.

Finally, she chose a burgundy dress, the only shade of red that flattered her auburn hair. Then she surveyed the shoes she had dumped onto the floor. A pair of sparkling gold, open-toed Jimmy Choos called to her, even though she hadn't had time to get her pedicure fixed. She slipped them on anyway. As if anyone would be looking at her toes in this dress.

She paused, allowing herself one longing look at her knitting needles. They lay in a cockamamie X on the bed, a new sweater just barely cast on. In the old days on Šolta it had been a joy to spend her hours of waking rest lost in a card game, allowing her brain to process and unwind among the easy company of friends. Since then, she had changed, developing the need to rest alone with her yarn. But she held by her assertion that the Justicia needed a party. A bit of relaxation would make the decisions easier come morning. She licked her teeth so that her lips could manage a smile. There—party face applied, she blurred down the stairs.

In the parlor, Zoey gave her a thoroughly masculine once-over. She put her hands on her hips and laughed. "If you told me you wanted to torture Bel, I would have just given you a live wire."

"This old thing?"

Zoey snorted. "He doesn't stand a chance."

"Cards?" Uta sat down to a game of poker in play. "I hear you are something of a dolphin."

"I think you mean a shark," Zoey whispered.

Uta squeezed her eyes shut and pictured the tiny line drawing in the dictionary she'd studied. "Stupid dorsal fin."

Zoey's snicker wasn't quiet enough to escape Uta's notice. That was okay. If Zoey was a card shark, Uta was a sabertooth tiger—she'd teach the youngling to laugh at her.

Only it didn't work out that way, because she couldn't keep her eyes off the door. She missed plays, failed to notice tells. Good thing only livestock was at stake—no matter how many sheep she lost, Norway had more. And the somber atmosphere of anxious vampires made for low-stakes bets regardless.

Five hands of Texas Hold 'Em and still no Bel.

Zoey leaned in and whispered. "I can sense Andre yards away. I'm sure you'll know he's coming well before you see him."

"He's not coming. I can feel that he wants to, but he resolutely resists."

Zoey twisted her shoulders away from the others to face Uta full on and lowered her voice. "Well then, surely you're old enough to know what to do when a man ignores you."

"As a matter of fact, I do not. No man has ever ignored me before." Uta's lower lip jutted and she knew she sounded ridiculous, even if she told the truth.

Zoey laughed as if Uta were a child. "Then let me enlighten you. Ignore him right back. Make him wonder if you want him after all. Pretend every other male is more fascinating. And if all else fails, sit on their laps."

Music started playing, and Uta turned to see Kos at the stereo. Big band music blared—his attempt to turn the solemn gathering into an actual party. In the corner of her eye, she noticed bodies beginning to dance. She focused all her tension on her cards and wouldn't have been especially surprised if they'd ignited in flames from the heat of her effort.

Zoey leaned close. "What about Pimenov?"

Uta cringed.

The other female grew serious. "Fine. Take your pick. Just don't sit on Andre's lap, or I'll have to kill you."

"I wouldn't dream of it." Uta nodded solemnly, her face neutral in spite of the effort it required to suppress her chuckle at the laughable threat from the younger, weaker vampire.

"Did I hear you say cat fight?" Pimenov said.

"Take a walk in the sun, Pimenov," Uta said. The Russian had been hitting on her since she was a baby vampire. It was possibly the millionth time she had told him to buzz off.

"Actually, we were talking about mud wrestling," Zoey said.

What the hell was she doing?

He took Zoey's bait. "Mud wrestling? Tell me more."

"Sure. We were just going to play another hand. Join us?" the young vampire asked.

"Delighted." His mouth curved into a smug grin.

In a matter of minutes, Zoey had won all his poker chips and fleeced him of his Rolex while he continued to grin at the two of them like a dope. Her managing of Pimenov was diverting, and in spite of the ever present throb in Uta's *pićka*, she managed not to think about Bel.

When the hand was over, she glanced around to room to find Sadavir in a jovial mood too. Uta always forgot he'd been graced with a princely face, as handsome as any Bollywood star's, when he wasn't scowling.

At the moment, he was smiling broadly. "Uta, this was a fine idea. I can't remember the last time the Justicia joined together for recreation."

Her face spread into a smile at the unexpected compliment. "I told you so."

"Foxtrot?"

"I don't remember how. Will you lead?"

A hearty laugh burst from his mouth. "I will be truly shocked if you can suppress your instincts well enough to follow. But I shall gladly attempt it." He swept her up in his powerful arms and shuffled her around a patch of open space between card tables with impressive

grace. Her mind and her limbs surrendered to his masterful guidance. Her feet barely touched the floor, but when they did, each step
landed perfectly.

"You are a fine dancer." She peered into his face with a newfound
appreciation for the male. Who would have thought he had any
pastime other than despising Hunters?

A pleasant tingle tickled its way up her spine, alerting her that
Bel was nearby. She laughed—Zoey was correct—her inattention
to the problem had snared him, drawing him like she tugged on one
of those cowboy ropes with a loop at the end. She'd gotten what she
wanted, then, and her moment of delightful reprieve had come to
an end.

CHAPTER 25

Bel pushed up from his desk, his glass empty once again. How did it keep getting that way?

Lexi had been too shaken to brainstorm with him. She'd just stared off into space until he'd suggested she help him call the test subjects. None of them had observed a change. It had only been twenty-four hours—likely too early to see results, but he wasn't holding out much hope. Afterward, he'd tucked her in on the couch in Kos's office.

And now Bel was simply going to get another bottle of bourbon from the bar in the parlor.

He was not going to look for Uta and he was not at all curious why the tug of her longing had slackened. He'd grown used to the vast ocean of her desire pulling at him, begging him to dive right in. Then it stopped. And he sure as hell didn't want it back.

He took each step down the stairs at a leisurely pace. Why hurry? It was just a drink.

Was she all right? Maybe she was hurt. Or dead. Shite.

He tripped over his own feet and barely managed to grab the rail before he would have somersaulted all the way to the landing.

Righting himself, he shook off the tumble. He didn't care if she was dead.

Good riddance!

He rolled his eyes at his own lie, wishing he believed it. This is what she did to him, turned him into an irrational, unscientific child. He was going to need more bourbon.

Ragtime music shimmied from the room, not his favorite genre, but fun. She probably wasn't dead then, or they would have cut the swinging party vibe. Still trying to appear casual, he leaned against the doorframe and crossed his arms, scanning the gathering.

Sadavir glided Uta around in some retro dance steps, laughing as if he were a reasonably charming creature instead of a warmonger. The song ended. He promptly pulled her down onto his lap. The mean old vampire whispered something to Uta, and she threw her head back laughing with her fangs out.

Gorgeous, and fierce, and dead sexy in a red dress. Her knees pressed together and her ankles splayed akimbo—a girlish pose without even a hint of awkwardness to spoil her grace. And her dress was sex itself, slinky and swooping nearly to her navel. The line from her exposed throat, down her chest, onto her belly was an arrow pointing at her *pićka*, just like his cock. Just like his every neuron and nerve.

Slowly, like she knew exactly how much desire was coursing through him, she turned her head. Mouth open, eyes wide, she stared at him. Riveted, he couldn't have looked away if the Hunters were back and launching rockets at the estate. She was beauty itself, and he wanted to spread those long legs and know exactly what beauty tasted like.

Come get me.

For a split second the scientist in him wondered if she'd spoken the words, or sent them across the strengthened connection of their emotional wireless network. But the answer didn't really matter because their meaning registered as a command and he recoiled. He planted his feet in the doorway and glared, refusing to obey.

A minute passed. Two. Was everyone staring, or had no one noticed them? He honestly didn't know, and didn't care enough to check. She was the light at the end of his tunnel; she was all he saw. But he wouldn't take orders from her. Everything hinged on her ability to surrender control.

He jerked his head back, wordlessly commanding her instead. *Come with me.* Then he turned and crossed to the cellar door, while entreating God, Darwin and the universe to make her follow him. Heels clicked on the wood floor and he turned. When he saw her, he thanked his holy trinity of agnosticism.

At the threshold into the cellar, one gentle wave of longing splashed into him. Their connection had grown so much deeper that the force of it froze his boots in place. He had to know what this misery was about, and he opened himself up, raising his sternum in invitation to her feelings.

Haunting images of the Hunter attacks roared back at him, and then he saw himself—a boy, observed from a distance. The despair stole his breath. That was what she was hiding under all her bravado? Would he drown in the icy black sea?

"Bel."

She extended her hand to him. A thin strand of hope shot through him at that point of connection.

"It is all right," she said.

He didn't know what she meant.

Her delicate pink tongue ran across a fang and he shivered. "I am right behind you."

Again, her obedience proved irresistible. He held the door for her and she descended a few stairs into the bluish gloom of the cellar. At the bottom of the stairs, she stepped to the side and let him pass, her face neutral.

She'd waited. She'd chosen to follow. Who the hell was this, and what had she done with Uta?

He led the way toward the workroom and she trailed half a step behind, putting her hand on his shoulder as if she needed him to guide her in the irregular light of the compact fluorescent bulbs. She didn't, but it satisfied him to pretend.

They ascended a flight of stairs into the large workroom. Bel strode back to the same length of stainless steel table where he had kissed her earlier. He sensed her behind him and turned without warning to pick her up, placing her on the table.

"Right now, I want you. It doesn't mean anything."

"I understand." Her feet dangled, and the open toes of her glitter-gold shoes revealed her shiny red toenails.

Just like when he was a boy. He took off her shoes and held her feet in his hands. Somehow, she tugged at him without words, trying to force eye contact, but he would only look at her feet. An urge rose up in him that no other woman had stirred. Red tinted toenails peeking out of the sand on the Šoltan beach. Even then he'd wanted to suck one of her pretty toes into his mouth.

He shook off the urge. Hell no, he was not going to kiss her feet. There was a chip in the polish, the flawed reality to his airbrushed memory of her. All this sentimental bullshit and sex flowing between them was some heretofore unexplained biological phenomenon, predetermined by the laws of the universe. It wasn't about his true feelings. How could he possibly love someone like her?

He catalogued her offensive traits. Stubbornness. Brashness. Fierceness. Only they seemed like virtues to a mind twisted by their bond, unable to see clearly for want of her—desperate, ravenous want.

He pulled her knees toward him so the small curve of her sweet little ass was right at the edge of the table. Her perfume teased at his nose again, and finally he recognized it—the faintest trace of heady hyacinths blooming in springtime on Šolta. A rare longing for home took hold of his heart—but it was really Uta he wanted.

"How's your *pićka?*"

"It aches." Her lower lip pressed forward in a pout.

He pushed her shoulders backward, but she resisted. The illusion of her agreeableness unraveled in an instant, shooting tension up his spine and into his jaw. He ground his teeth.

"Bel." Her hands went to his belt. "Let me." And then she slid off the table onto her knees. The strain in his muscles melted at the sight of her kneeling before him. She unbuckled him and unzipped his fly. When she took his cock in her hand, he sucked in a loud breath. Her sharp hiss was even louder.

"I will be whatever you need to me to be, Bel. Anything for you." She didn't give him time to think about what that meant before she swallowed him whole.

It had been a while, but didn't these things usually start with a little licking and teasing?

Oh, shite.

The hot, wet suction of her mouth nearly pulled him right out of his skin. His circuit board was on overload. He squeezed his eyes shut to block out all extra stimuli, shuddering with the pleasure flowing from his extremities into her velvety heat.

The sensations took on a rhythm as she drew him in and out of her soft lips, and he settled into the pleasure. Had her mouth been made for him? No—it was the other way around. He had been made for her, like Eve from Adam's rib, Bel from Uta's blood, a God-given companion, a friend, and a perfect mate.

Could she be?

Her eyes opened, seizing hold of his gaze. Again, he couldn't have looked away from her had the world come to an end around them. Her dark brown eyelashes, and the faint pink capillaries on her eyelids, the fine golden hairs at the edges of her eyebrows, the tiny pores in her porcelain skin. The world had never been so crisp, so vibrant. He'd never seen so clearly before, hadn't really been alive, all these years apart from her.

His balls drew up, threatening to pour into her. But he didn't want to come in her mouth — he wanted to be inside her, to feel her pleasure around him.

"Uta, stop."

With her lips still wrapped him, she shook her head and gripped his hips firmly.

He stepped back, sliding his cock from her mouth. His erection bobbed free. "Not like this. Not the first time."

Her eyes widened then closed, and her body uncoiled as a sliver of a smile curved her lips.

Oh yes, she'd clearly heard his meaning. He pulled her up, crushing her swollen lips in a kiss. Her name clanged in his mind like a bell. *Uta.* His Uta wanted him after all. She sagged into him, opening her mouth to accept his tongue. He devoured her mouth, sliding his tongue across her teeth, and returning her sweet, teasing caress. Her fang nicked him, and she sucked on his tongue, moaning.

He lifted her onto the table again and bunched her skirt around her hips. No panties. He should have known. She couldn't have hidden them under that dress. He bent her knees and she settled her heels flat on the tabletop.

The exquisite folds of her sex, pink and dark, lay open before him. His heart pounded in his chest. His Uta, splayed before him like a feast.

"Are you going to look all night?"

He bristled.

She must have felt it. "I am sorry, Bel. I am trying." She pushed her hair off her forehead and her apologetic smile soothed him. "Do not hurry on my account."

Yes, he wouldn't; he'd show his control. He tucked his rigid cock against his abdomen and zipped up his jeans.

Then, behind his incisors, that tingling began. Damn, so many new hungers.

He surveyed her body, noticing a lush vein in the seam of her leg. His gums throbbed and his heart pounded. Under his nose, her finger appeared with a crimson drop of blood beaded atop it. On instinct, he drew it into his mouth, tasting her salty and metallic essence on his tongue. So hot. He groaned as it tingled against the roof of his mouth and instantly raised the temperature of his own blood.

All the while, he never took his eyes off her labia, which were beginning to glisten with the moisture of arousal. She stroked her hand up her thigh and across her vulva, taunting. Clearly, she wasn't one of those abashed women, shy about her private beauty, but loved to be looked at. He wanted to tease her and feel her writhe. His fingers twitched to slip inside her, to gauge wetness and to learn her body's pleasure.

"Bel, please."

Her plea was a salve on his old wound and it rendered him downright merciful. He leaned over and stroked her once with his tongue, tentatively tasting.

Hell. She was life itself, sweet and salt and softest flesh.

Then he began for real, pushing his tongue into her core. She lifted her ass off the table, meeting and accepting his thrusts. He licked her up and down while she squirmed and gasped, another sweet sound that stroked his ego.

To reward her, he sucked her bud into his mouth and filled her with his fingers.

She gasped and cried out. "*Volim te.* I love you."

His emotions poured out, tangling with hers—longing and satisfaction, anger and fear—blurring his edges. No matter. All he wanted was to dive into her. He explored inside her, finding the spot that made her groan. She rode his fingers so hard it took all his strength to meet her.

That should have been a warning.

With his tongue, he circled and teased and sucked some more. And then she was coming on his fingers, clenching him so hard his knuckles cracked even as his cock leaped again, begging for a chance at her. He brought her down with feather strokes of his tongue. With her fading orgasm, all his muscles went slack.

Intertwined, they slid down onto the cold cement floor. Their cheeks rubbed together and someone's tears slicked their skin. Wave after wave of frightening emotion crashed over him.

Was this happiness?

Could he really be whole?

This time, would she allow him to stay?

The questions came one after another in the voice of a child he barely recognized, but knew to be himself. In an instant, he became that little boy again, abandoned and alone. All these years later, it didn't really matter if she had her reasons.

He extricated himself from her arms and pushed onto his knees.

She sat up, clinging to him. "Bel?"

"I can't, Uta." He scrambled to his feet. "I can't put myself through that again."

She reached for him. "I promise I will not abandon you this time. Never again."

His longing threatened to swallow him, and he wanted to believe her, to run back into her arms. Instead, he backed away. "I need you to stay the hell away from me."

She stood, all bare long limbs, her nipples rocks, her skin rough with goosebumps. "Please Bel, try to trust me." She extended her arms in a plea.

Even unconscious and covered in blood she hadn't looked as vulnerable as she did now, but that wasn't his problem.

He spun, adjusted his angry erection and left, slamming every door on the way back to his room. When he got there, only an empty bottle of bourbon waited for him. He stormed into the parlor and found a fresh one—a surefire hard-on deflator. He poured himself a double and then rinsed the smell of her off him in an icy shower that did nothing to soften his cock.

Back at his desk, her emotions slithered toward him like tentacles across their bond. Longing, fear, desperation. And so he did what he'd always done to protect himself. He cracked open his laptop and began modeling the shape of the *hemoaurum* model, examining active sites where a cofactor might interact with the protein, rendering it active inside a vampire. He would find a way around this without Uta's *osjećaj*. If he could just get back to San Francisco, he could run each isolate through the mass spectrometer, and identify which ones might fit into the protein like a man fit into a woman.

Shite. It was hard not to think about his hard-on.

Each time the insidious, pointy tip of Uta's feelings prodded him, he squeezed his eyes shut and imagined himself in some impenetrable stronghold made of steel and held together by large rivets. And finally, it worked. Uta's emotions receded from his awareness, and he was left inside his air-tight mental bunker with an unwaning erection, a belly full of anger, and his research. Now this felt familiar. He plugged his headphones into the computer and let Johnny Rotten's rage about England's shitty future be his pissed-off soundtrack.

No future.

Not for him and Uta.

And not for the vampires, unless he found a cofactor for his *hemoaurum*.

CHAPTER 26

The sky turned dawn-pink outside the parlor's French doors as, one by one, the vampires trickled out of the party and back to their rooms to feed, or shower, or do whatever they got up to with their blood servants.

Pedro hadn't found a bit of rest. Cards didn't soothe him the way they did Andre and Kos. Months after turning, he still hadn't found a nighttime activity that suited him. Omar did crossword puzzles in French, but Pedro hated the things. He didn't know what Uta did, but she wasn't with Bel. He'd slipped into the parlor only long enough to nick a bottle of bourbon, and he'd smelled like he had been all up in some vampire but scowled like he hadn't enjoyed it for a second.

"I fold," Loki said.

"Me too. I'm going upstairs." Zoey laid down her cards and pushed away from the table.

"I call." Andre stared after her and when he turned back to the table, Pedro revealed his losing hand.

Pedro shoved all the chips at Andre and stood. "Loki, there's something I need to show you. I'll be right back."

Ever since Lucas had re-drawn a picture from an ancient Hunter book that showed a Hunter and a vampire marrying under an arbor of grape vines, Pedro spent his sleepless nights next to a slumbering Lucas, reading every academic article and encyclopedia he could find about wine. He'd pretty much given up finding anything, and studied because he didn't know how else to rest. So it was a surprise when what he'd been looking for turned up in his tattered copy of *Una Historia de Vino y la Cultivacion de la Uva*, written by his former wine making teacher in Argentina. Pedro dashed to his room and back quickly. He did love being fast.

When he put the book on the green felt card table, Andre said, "You finally found something?"

"I think so."

Loki cocked his elf-like head. Did his ears just twitch? Maybe not, but he sure seemed eager to listen.

"I've been wondering about the Blood Vine," Pedro began. "Why does it work like Hunter blood?"

"Yes, I've been pondering that little mystery myself." Loki rubbed his chin.

"Look." Pedro opened the fat tome to a page he'd dog-eared. He pointed to a thumbnail-sized picture of ripe grapes on the vine.

Loki and Andre leaned in, barely avoiding a skull collision. "It's Zinfandel," Andre said. "Like Blood Vine."

"No, it's a wild grape. It's native to the Eastern coast of the Black Sea, near the Caucasus Mountains."

"Near Turkey, where Uta's mysterious ancient lives?" Andre shook his head. "Son, it is merely a picture in a book. It means nothing."

"Look at the leaves," Pedro said.

Andre and Loki bent their heads together over the book, but said nothing.

How was it possible that Andre didn't notice?

Pedro pointed. "Look at the gold outline on the edge of the leaves."

"I see nothing," Andre said.

"What do you mean? It's distinct, like a metallic sheen."

"Pedro, you are hallucinating."

"Am I hallucinating it here too?" Pedro slid a close-up photo he'd taken before the fire onto the page.

"This is from Andre's vineyard?" Loki asked.

"Yes."

"Pedro, I don't see a thing."

"Nor do I," Loki said.

"Really, even when you compare it to this?" He had tucked the second leaf in the front half of the book. "It's from the Zin vines over at Rock Fall Winery."

"I don't see a thing," Andre said again.

Loki's mouth pressed into a grave line as he looked first at the leaves, then the picture. Pedro leaned forward, anticipating the little guy would see what Pedro saw and exclaim amazement. It didn't happen.

Instead the chief vampire said, "Bring in Leo and Lucas."

No way. No fucking way. Could it be?

Without giving voice to the thoughts racing through his mind, Pedro went to find his lover.

Lucas sat on the bed, slipping on his shoes. "What's up?"

"We need you to look at something."

"Okay." Reaching up to pull his sweater on, he bared his torso. He'd lost so much weight. Lean before, he was skinny now. One more reason to kill Ethan—all the stress he was causing Lucas.

They found Leo in the kitchen, holding a steaming cup of coffee and scouring the Internet. The three of them filed into the dining room and stood around the table where Loki and Andre waited.

"What did you tell them?" Andre asked.

"*Nada.*"

"Perfect." Loki clapped his hands together with apparent anticipation. "Lucas, can you see a difference between the two grape leaves?"

"Sure. This one has a gold rim."

"Leo?"

"Well, like he said, they look the same to me besides that gold edge."

"What about this one in the book?" Andre asked. "Which does it resemble?"

"It has a gold edge too," Leo said at the same time that Lucas touched the Blood Vine leaf.

"No. It can't be," Andre said. "Pedro, why didn't you notice the leaves looked different when you became a vampire?"

He closed his eyes and tried to remember what the world looked like before. His mouth went dry. "Give me a break. I felt like a microscope on Ritalin. Everything was blindingly bright and sharp. How could I have missed that little gold line? Yeah, right."

"It seems those golden eyes serve some purpose," Loki said. "And, Andre, your vines are apparently a part of Uta's story, and we must investigate further. Now, I would like a shower before the meeting." He stood up and departed with Andre at his side, leaving Pedro alone with the two ex-Hunters.

"Hey." Leo shifted his weight from side to side. "So when's the big day?"

"What day?" Pedro traced the outline of the Blood Vine leaf, his mind sprinting laps around all the new questions about wine and blood.

Next to him, Lucas framed the textbook between his hands, meticulously aligning its spine with the edge of the table. "He means, when are you going to turn me?"

"Oh."

"I'm happy to help." An eager grin spread across the kid's face.

Pedro wanted to ruffle his hair, pat him on the head and say good boy before sending him on his way. "Thanks kid. That means a lot to us."

"And Lucas already explained this is a hands-off kinda thing. Right?"

A lump clogged up Pedro's throat and he jerked his gaze to Lucas, who continued to fidget with the book.

"Yeah. Strictly blood. A blood bond pretty much makes me a one-man kinda vampire. Plus, my man's likely to get pretty jealous when he turns all predatory." Pedro laced his tone with laughter he did not feel.

Lucas sat up straight and his yellow eyes flashed with something ominous.

It only took a second for Pedro to form a plan. "Leo —" he steered the kid into a chair " — I think we need a test run. Make sure your blood will work before Lucas does the deed. You good with that?"

He frowned. "Uh, sure."

Lucas remained stoic, nodding.

Pedro came to stand behind Leo's chair and pressed gently on his shoulders. "Ready?"

"Go for it."

Pedro darted his tongue out to lick Leo's skin. His fangs dropped and he struck fast and clean — no foreplay and none of the problems he'd had trying to feed from non-Hunter humans. The kid groaned at the first pull and Pedro followed suit. Yeah, just as good as Lucas's sweet blood.

Lucas. Pedro's eyes popped open to find him watching, his impassive mask shattered. His mouth hung open and his eyes bulged. When he caught Pedro staring back, he shook his head and Pedro got the message loud and clear. He broke the bite and licked Leo, sealing the wounds.

"Kid, this isn't going to work."

Lucas recomposed his face and walked out without a word.

"Did I do something wrong?" Leo asked.

"No, Leo. It's not you."

This time, Pedro did pat him on the head before he slipped out, and caught up with Lucas. Taking his hand, they walked upstairs together in silence. All out of words, Pedro stripped Lucas of his clothes and took his off just as fast. They climbed into the shower, and their soapy bodies slipped together. Pedro tried to push his worries out of his head, and offer Lucas the reassurance he needed. Even skinny, Lucas was all he wanted, so he dropped to his knees before his golden-eyed man and went about showing Lucas just how much he loved him.

Chapter 27

The night was clear and cool with stars twinkling above. For once they did not mock Uta. Crickets chirped, owls hooted, the soil shifted quietly as earthworms and insects wriggled underground. The trickling of water came and went as she passed over places where it dripped through the soil into the aquifer. The air was thick with the scent of minerals in the loamy dirt, gassy cows in a distant field, the odor of car exhaust that lingered wherever humans lived. Her body thrummed, newly alive in sexual afterglow.

For long moments, her heart followed suit, rejoicing in the beauty of the night. She found herself singing old Croatian folksongs at full volume into the night sky.

And then she remembered.

At least for a moment, she had tasted what it might really be like between them.

But then he'd rejected her, and who could blame him? She hadn't earned that love. If anything she'd stolen his freedom. But she'd lost hers too — and the selfish man didn't have a shred of sympathy for her.

A rock jutted up from the soil, round and the size of a tennis ball. She drew back her foot and kicked the thing, dead in its center. Her eyes traced its path through the night sky and watched it land a quarter of a mile away, stirring up dust.

In many ways, he was still a petulant adolescent, refusing to grow up. Maybe what he needed was a slap in the face. Maybe, instead of hiding from him, as she had for decades, she should grab him by the lapels — figuratively, since he only wore T-shirts — and demand he give her a chance.

A narrow strip of light appeared on the horizon. How long could she wait it out? Or maybe this was her chance. She could simply sit here, watching the dawn until it burned all her problems away. But for the first time in more than a hundred years, she did not find the idea a relief. She wanted to be alive to smell the night and see the stars glinting like slivers of diamond in its sky. She wanted to be alive to prove her love to Bel, and attempt to earn his in return. No more freedom for him — he'd had his chance and it had not worked for him any better than it had her. She was done watching him from afar, drowning in her self-pity. It was time to show him what she was made of.

She flew to the kitchen and slipped inside.

"Uta!" Lena crossed the kitchen to embrace her.

Uta tensed. Besides Loki, no one hugged her, and he knew to restrict such affections to their private hours. But with some effort, she relaxed in the woman's arms.

After a moment, she stepped back and pressed her hand to Lena's belly. The girl's eyebrows flew up. "You can't…?"

"No. Not until there is a heartbeat. That will be next month, if it worked."

"Did it work the first time, for Mila?"

"Yes. And she said she had the very best sex of her life when she conceived Bel. Something about Andre's blood being very…hot."

Poor Lena blushed, far beyond pink. "Yes, it's…fun. You should try it." Then her mouth opened so big she might have fit her foot into it. "Oh, Uta, I'm sorry."

"Don't worry. I intend to get my chance." She patted her Lena's hand.

Uta hastened to her room. After a quick shower, she put on a slim cut pair of slacks. No jacket either. Why leave anything to his imagination? She would put her tiny tits and ass right in his selfish face — that was the extent of her plan. Over her shoulder, she looked at her backside and spanked the firm curve.

"My fickle Illyrian gods, I entreat you. Please give him to me."

In case they failed her yet again, it was time to ask Loki for help. *Pretty please.*

CHAPTER 28

In his imaginary Uta-proof box, Bel tried to pretend he wasn't hopelessly aroused. He hadn't been able to wank or drink his erection away. All that was left for him was work, a puzzle of epic proportions that left him banging his head against the wall. He let his left brain out to play, doodling angry crosshatches on a piece of notepaper.

Longing. Nostalgia. *Osjećaj*. He wrote the words and underscored them, twice.

What happened when a bond was satisfied? The blood bond, the bond to the homeland, whatever creepy symbiotic shit went on between Pedro and Lucas—any bond would do. That was the real question. He wasn't going to figure out the how any time soon, but the what…he could work with the what. He needed to observe a vampire go home—the before and after, with a battery of tests on both ends.

The door shook with a knock.

"Come in." Bel stood, wearing only his warm up pants since his hard-on wouldn't zip into his jeans.

Loki swung the door open and looked him over. The little vampire rolled his eyes. "I need you at the meeting this morning. And please do cover up that monstrosity. Otherwise, it will inevitably catch someone's eye and then Uta will shed blood."

Bel made of show of pulling on a T-shirt and zipping up a sweatshirt. Neither of them covered his monstrosity much at all.

Loki slapped his scalp. "Bloodshed may be unavoidable."

Bel winked, channeling a little of Uta's brashness into a who-gives-a-fuck smile. "Kind of you to notice, Loki."

"There is something else." Loki pulled a black plastic case from his pocket and popped it open to reveal a thick syringe.

Only large animal vets used such giant needles. Bel took an instinctive step back. "What the hell is that for?"

"Uta."

"Please tell me that is some kind of cure for our bond."

"No." Loki pursed his lips. "I had hoped you had guessed this tranquilizer may be a necessity, but I see I must explain."

Bel crossed his arms and leaned against the door. "You can't sedate a vampire."

"It is possible, with an extremely high dosage cocktail of opiates, ketamine, and atavan. Injected near the spine, it will paralyze her. Temporarily, of course."

"She does get on my nerves, man, but wouldn't it be easier just to avoid her?"

Amusement sparkled in the vampire's eyes for a flash, but then he grew grave. "I'm afraid this has another use. You may have to stop her."

"From what?"

Loki sighed like an old woman. "Uta takes her responsibilities very seriously. To her sire. And to our species. Even to you, Bel, as I gravely hope you are beginning to realize."

"So?"

"So she believes she has failed all of us, and that the continuing persecution of vampires is her fault."

"That's shite. It's the Hunters' fault, from the very beginning."

The little vampire closed his eyes and pinched the bridge of his nose. "Have you ever tried to talk reason into her? She may be only the ninth oldest, but she is possibly the stubbornest creature alive. She will not listen, and when she despairs..."

"Spit it out, Loki."

"Twice she has sun-walked. Both times, she came within seconds of her life."

Fireworks went off behind Bel's eyes, bursting flares of fiery red and electric blue fury. "She's attempted suicide?" Abandoning him was a small betrayal compared to this. "I'll fucking kill her."

Loki tapped the toes of one foot. "I must insist that you do not kill her, and instead that you make every effort to keep her alive. I am very fond of her. And of course there is your own self-interest to consider. I am sure you remember your father's suffering."

"I don't want this responsibility, Loki."

"Boy, we rarely chose the burdens that become our own." For the first time, the little creature actually sounded his age.

Bel regretted his childish whine. "It hardly matters. She'll be leaving soon."

"Regardless, you must keep it at the ready. And know this—it only works once. A second dose has no effect, not for the several weeks it takes for the drugs to break down in her system. So once you sedate her, you must secure her. In my experience, she awakens even more determined to end her life."

She had no right to kill herself. Didn't she know too many people depended on her?

"And one more thing." Loki touched Bel's elbow. "I know she is a royal pain in the ass, but I think you should give her a chance as your mate."

"I tried. I can't do it. I just can't make myself trust her."

Loki clucked disapprovingly. "For your own sake, try harder, Lobel. Now, let us go."

Everyone on the estate waited in the dining room for their fearless leader to arrive, even Lexi. She cast him a tentative smile. Bel stood behind the little boss-man, since there were no open chairs.

Uta looked his way and he expected her to gloat over his still evident desire. But her face twisted in empathy and he bolstered his defenses against their emotional connection.

Loki knocked on the table and two dozen laser beams of attention were directed at him. Bel had to hand it to him — the guy knew how to command a room. "I have a plan and with your approval, I will set it into motion. It is contingent on the Hunter Derek William's alliance."

The vampire named Nceba and her blood servant flanked Derek, leaning close. Something about the way the three stood made them seem like a family. Derek looked remarkably good; not just better for being free of his jail, but better than when he had been captured in the first place, maybe than he ever had. For all the ways Nceba looked younger, plumper, her honey-brown skin glowing with good health, Derek stood taller and held himself at ease. The word that sprung to Bel's mind was utterly unscientific—Derek looked whole.

Shite, what the hell did that even mean?

Bel hated the way his mind was leaping to conclusions, but Derek's transformation astonished him, made it all too easy to believe this blood connection was a two way street—a full-fledged symbiosis of some sort.

Derek stepped forward. "I will ally with you."

Loki bobbed his head. "Tell us why."

"Because my life and the lives of thousands of Hunters is based on a lie, told by someone who feared the magic between your kind and mine."

"Magic." Bel scoffed, but no one paid him any mind.

"The connection I experienced with Nceba is unlike anything I have ever known."

Sadavir narrowed his eyes. "A bit of pleasure is enough to defect?"

"No. A lifetime of hate imposed out of fear of that pleasure and its possibilities—that is reason enough to defect."

Sadavir turned toward Loki and gave a silent nod.

"Nceba has my allegiance," Derek continued. "And with her the Justicia. I will tell the Hunters everything I know about Ethan Bennett's betrayal and about vampires. I believe they may turn from him."

"Then it is decided." Loki smiled, his cheeks pink like a cheerful garden gnome. "We will not attack the Hunters with violence. We will attack them with bliss."

Loki gestured at Sadavir, who rose as gracefully as he had danced the night before. "I have endorsed this plan, and have already reached out to the vampires I trust most. They have agreed to kidnap Hunters, and show them their households are run freely and fairly. The vampires will feed upon the Hunters, and we can only hope they find the experience as enlightening as Mr. Williams." A few chuckles sounded. "I ask that each of you do the same. We must act fast and in great numbers."

"And at the same time," Loki said. "Derek will stand up in opposition to Ethan and propose a truce."

"I'll aim for a reconciliation," Derek corrected, "but settle for a truce."

Bel scratched his stubbly chin. Williams had big bollocks, if he was serious about negotiating an end to a five thousand year war.

Loki's eyes flashed with approval. "Lucas will coordinate both missions — the top down attack on Ethan and the friendly kidnapping of Hunters. Uta, you will go to Turkey to find the halfling Ayal and confirm the effects of Hunter blood. Do you know where to find her?"

Uta buffed her fingernails on an impossibly soft looking shirt. "It is not a problem. I know the ancient place names. Some minor research will be required to confirm their locations."

"I have a contact in Eastern Turkey," Trys said. She hadn't spoken in the Justicia meetings before and everyone turned to look at her. "She has an extensive historical library and knows the region well. If she doesn't have what you need, she will know who does."

Loki brought his palms together in a burst of applause. "Excellent. See to the arrangements. Bel, you will travel with Uta to pursue the cure."

A million objections screamed in his head like the blaring of a car alarm. He had to monitor his subjects, and continue his research, and stay the hell away from Uta. But he simply could not turn down the opportunity. Minutes ago he'd realized he needed to observe an exiled vampire returning home, essentially a before-and-after test, in order to finally understand the wasting disease.

The room's focus shifted to Bel like he was the disappointing main act after a killer opening band. Every face watching him looked to be expecting an argument.

He did enjoy defying expectations. "Sure thing, boss. But I will need to visit Croatia with Uta on the return trip."

Uta frowned, clearly puzzled.

He grinned. "Oh, and Uta, I will need to take some samples of your blood, to test your theories."

She opened her mouth to speak, but Loki cut her off. "Excellent. Lexi will remain in contact with your test subjects. Pedro Torres, you will travel with them to meet Ayal. You must find those grapevines from your book. Between you and Bel, I hope one of you will cure the wasting disease forever."

Pedro stood so fast his chair tipped over backward. "I can't travel without Lucas and he's needed here."

Andre rose. "Surely, Bel can search for these vines. Or me—"

"Of those who possess the necessary expertise in wine, only Pedro can see the peculiarly golden leaves."

"Loki, I only feed from Lucas. We cannot be apart." Panic tightened Pedro's whisper.

"You will take Leo." Pedro's bronze complexion went gray, but Loki moved on. "I hereby close this meeting of the Justicia."

The other nine members of the council stood and said as one, "To the homeland."

"Indeed, to the homeland." Loki smiled a peculiar smile, both knowing and hopeful. Like a contagion, his optimism spread around the room and both vampires and humans murmured with excitement. Bel took a deep breath. Soon he would observe how the nostalgic bond worked firsthand, and then surely he could find a way to replicate it.

Uta appeared at his side vampire-fast and began issuing commands. "We will take Loki's plane, leaving at sunset."

"My plane, Uta. It's bigger."

He stood tall and ignored the snickers and the muttered "Let's hope so" from Pedro.

"And we leave as soon as you pack up all five of your suitcases," Bel added.

Her long, slim middle finger thrust skyward. He spun and stormed out of the room.

CHAPTER 29

Lucas couldn't shake the sense of dread dragging him down; not a wet blanket, more like an entire body suit made of that lead cloth that shielded a patient from X-rays.

He'd vomited up his coffee, which could have just been more stress. But the blood streaking the brown bile suggested otherwise. If Pedro knew, he would insist on staying, and they couldn't risk that. Loki was right. Finding a cure was the most important thing, and if there were acres of Blood Vine growing somewhere in Turkey, Pedro needed to find it.

Dangling his legs from the high antique bed he now shared with Pedro, his toes barely touched the floor. Standing between his knees, Pedro squeezed him in a tight embrace. The pressure kicked up another wave of nausea and Lucas sucked in a breath.

"Please, *mi amor*, let me turn you. Andre and Kos will look out for you while I'm gone."

Lucas probably should let him, but he would lose days to the process of turning—critical days in Derek's coup against Ethan. And there was the other, less noble problem.

"I don't want to watch you feed from that kid for the rest of my immortal life. The moment you touched him I wanted to kill you both."

"We'll find a girl Hunter as soon as I get back. Someone non-threatening." Pedro stroked Lucas's spine.

Being sick didn't make him less jealous, not even a hair. "Great. That way I can watch you work out your mommy issues too."

Pedro stiffened and Lucas regretted provoking him, but fuck—the jealousy turned his angry stomach over and over.

"I'm sorry. I'm not saying never." He pressed his cheek into Pedro's chest. "I like the idea of forever with you. I'm just not ready yet. We have to take Ethan down first."

Pedro pulled back to look him in the eye. "If Hunters attack again—"

"That shield has withstood major firebombing. This is the safest place on earth from my brother."

"I don't want to leave you. What if I get ambushed by Hunters and never return?"

"Then you should know how grateful I am." He brushed his fingertips down Pedro's cheek. "You saved me from that life, helped me become someone I'm proud of."

Pedro stepped back and crossed his arms over his chest. "If you start saying goodbye, I am not leaving."

"No, not goodbye. Just thank you, for loving me in spite of impossible odds. If, God forbid, something did happen to me, I could die a happy man."

"*Jesu Cristo*, Lucas, I don't need this. I need shit talk and ass slapping. I need you to call me a pussy and tell me it's all gonna work out."

Inside, Lucas melted with compassion for his big strong vampire, but he couldn't let him off the hook yet. "Tell me you heard what I said."

Pedro's Adam's apple bobbed. "Yeah. I heard it."

Lucas held his gaze for one more second before he slapped his ass. "Now, big boy, go save the vampire world."

Pedro took his hand, and they walked downstairs and through the cellar to the workroom, where Bel's van waited.

Lucas shook Leo's hand, but the kid only held eye contact for a nanosecond. Lucas guessed he'd figured out what was at stake for them, and so Lucas clapped him on the shoulder.

"Take care of my man."

"Hey Lucas, I didn't mean to cause—"

"I know. And I'm serious. I'm counting on you to look out for him."

Leo stood taller. "I'll do my best."

From behind the young Hunter, Pedro cast Lucas a grateful look.

Bel extended his hand. "Good luck, man. I've got a good feeling about your plan. Its irony appeals to me. And that Derek has—"

"*Cojones.*"

Lucas smiled at his man. Yeah, Derek did, and he would need them.

And then Uta appeared, trailing suitcases. Bel turned without a word to her and climbed all the way into the back of the van. Uta stared after him with such forlorn longing that Lucas forgot his own worries. Well, well, well—look what lurked inside her spiky armor. She brushed away a lock of enviably thick auburn hair, and behind that gesture, she arranged her face like a mask and climbed into the van.

Pedro pulled Lucas into one last hug, whispering in his ear. "Promise me you will take care of yourself. I need you."

Lucas shivered, his lover's desperation resounding in his bones. "I promise."

Their lips met in the lightest of kisses, and then all the vampires were shut into the UV-proof vehicle. Lucas opened up the rolling door, flooding the workroom with morning light. The van drove off into the sunshine toward another dark hangar where they could board a sun-safe airplane.

When they were out of sight on the winding drive, Lucas closed the door. His stomach grumbled, and because he'd promised, he headed to the kitchen for breakfast.

Lena hummed out of tune—a song from the eighties that she wasn't old enough to remember. Everything about the fresh-faced youngster reminded Lucas he was aging and vampires didn't. Even if he weren't sick, how many years could he expect to last for Pedro as a human?

"Coffee?" she asked.

"No thanks. I've been hitting it too hard."

"I have scones, or I can scramble you some eggs," she offered.

"Maybe just some toast."

She tilted her head, looking too intently at him. Then she opened the fridge and took out a small container of yogurt. "This is good on a queasy stomach. Sourdough toast all right?"

"Great, thanks."

He sat down at the table, his fingers twitching for his laptop. But he forced himself to breathe through the anxiety.

Slow down; try to eat.

Outside, the sunlight caught on the dewy new grass, blanketing the blackened earth with a deceptively green sheen. It was so beautiful he could almost muster up a sense of hope. Then the toast sprung out of the toaster with a loud click and he jumped. Its slightly burned smell turned his gut and the nausea demanded all his attention, leaving no room for optimism.

CHAPTER 30

The sun glinted through oak trees lining the rural highway. Gwen used her hand as a visor, squinting at the landscape. The wine country vistas of gentle golden hills soothed her. How could anything bad happen in such an idyllic place?

"That is the drive to the estate," Ethan said. He pulled off the road and rolled to a stop in a wide patch of gravel where countless cars must have previously turned one hundred and eighty degrees.

Her stomach followed suit, spinning in what felt like a vertical three-sixty. She hiccupped.

"You can do this, Gwen. You are the bravest woman I have ever met."

She twisted in the seat to face him squarely. "Masochism requires a different kind of courage than vampire Hunting, Ethan."

"Nonsense. Your convictions will keep you focused." It was the moment for an embrace, or at least a pat on the knee, but he stared over the dashboard. "About Zoey."

Gwen's fists clenched around the straps of her backpack. "I understand. I will try to persuade her to leave with your offer of sanctuary. But if Marasović is anything like Mas —"

"I cannot predict what she will do. I have never been able to, in fact. But if you did not offer, I fear I might always regret it. It is, after all, my fault she is there in the first place."

Said the man who sent his own lambs to the slaughter to serve his greater aims.

Whatever this Zoey woman was to him, it wasn't a potential regret. Only hours ago, Gwen had surrendered her ego, felt her very self slip away in submission to him. And yet, here it was again, rearing up and demanding something—to be special, to be chosen, not to compete with another woman for his excruciating devotion. She couldn't belong to him, lose herself to him, if he wanted this Zoey instead.

"Of course you would, Ethan. I will do my best. If need be, I'll even tell her about what Mason did to me." Although Lena had probably confided her experience as Mason's prisoner to them already, she'd endured nothing compared to Gwen's six-month long torture. She'd required a medical leave of absence and ongoing psychiatric care until Ethan appeared, providing her with all the neuro-chemicals she needed by brute force: adrenaline, endorphins, and oxytocin in their perfect, divine ratio.

"Do I sense some misgivings about her?" He could read her every gesture and tone. Of course he would intuit her jealousy.

In reply, she forced a smile that probably looked more like a grimace.

He grazed a single knuckle down her cheek. "I will not lie to you—I have an attachment to Zoey. But it is nothing like what is between us, Gwen. Do you understand?"

"All I can know is my own…" The word felt wrong even though it was right. "My heart. It is yours to do with as you please."

His gaze roved over her face until it settled on her eyes. "All of my life I have hidden, but you saw past my deceptions, and still you gave yourself to me."

She needed this confession, needed it to carry with her on what easily could be a suicide mission, or the recruiting of another lover for him. But she shied from his vulnerability at the same time his revelation stroked the very ego she wanted him to destroy. Too many paradoxes—she needed him to be heartless, and to love her. She wanted him to adore her, and care nothing for her feelings or well-being.

In the face of contradictions like these, the wisest course was always to turn and run the other way. She put her hand on the door handle. "Off I go to ring the doorbell on the pit of vipers."

"Gwen." The intensity in his voice drew her gaze once more. "Please be careful. I know you can hold your own, but I want you, need you to come back to me."

"If that is what you want, then you know I will obey." She swung open the door and stepped onto the driveway, marching up to the shield of the Kaštel Estate. A line separating burned grass from lush landscaping indicated where the shield rose up from the ground. She stopped a few feet from it. What now?

The idea came to her with a snort, and she opened her mouth to shout. "I come in peace."

CHAPTER 31

Once Lucas mastered his stomach's rebellion, he spread the thinnest layer of butter he could manage onto his toast. A woman's voice came to him, shouting in the distance.

"Do you hear that?"

Lena nodded. Lucas stood so fast his ears rang. More slowly, he headed to the door.

She put down her dishtowel and followed him. When they reached the foyer, she peered out the window and gasped.

Kos blurred down the stairs. "Who's shouting?"

"Gwen," Lena whispered, pointing.

A wave of dread rolled over Lucas. "As in Ethan's girlfriend?"

Lena nodded.

"Ignore her," Kos said. Lucas whole heartedly agreed.

But Lena took a step toward the door. "What if she's running from him?"

Kos embraced Lena, stroking her hair. "Sweetheart, no. It's too dangerous. What if it's a trap?"

"Mason damaged her, Kos." Her words were a whimper. "Maybe she wants to change sides. And what if she knows something?"

Lucas strode to the window.

Gwen stood outside the shield, cupping her hands around her mouth to shout, "Help me!"

"Lena's right," he said, though he hated to admit it. Letting her in might be a necessary evil. "Gwen may know Ethan's next moves." Lucas swung open the door, the little woman offered up a sad smile from where she stood several yards away. If she was unarmed, she could just walk right through, but he wasn't going to tell her that.

"You must be Ethan's brother," she said.

"Andre, Loki—in the foyer," Kos shouted.

Lena squeezed in beside Lucas. "What are you doing here, Gwen?"

"This is the only place I'll be safe, and I knew you would understand."

"Let me see," Andre boomed from behind them, safely away from the sunset.

Lucas stepped aside to clear his line of sight.

"*Davo*, what the hell do I look like—a home for lost and injured Hunters?"

"Who is she?" Loki appeared with Zoey on his heels.

Zoey's face mirrored the revulsion Lucas felt. Only the two of them truly understood Ethan—well, and perhaps this Gwen. Seeing her was a bit like staring the most sick and pathetic part of his own psyche in the face. He had no objections to playing rough, had known some perfectly nice leather-types in his life, but Ethan's brand of sadism was enough to turn his stomach yet again. Good thing he had only eaten that one bite of toast.

He cleared the bile from his throat with a cough. "Her name is Gwen Evans, and she's Ethan's pet masochist. She says she wants sanctuary."

"Please," she cried. "I have nowhere else to go."

"She can fuck off," Zoey said, and her knuckles cracked as she formed two deceptively feminine fists.

"Indeed," Andre said.

"Wait." The words came from two sides of the room—Loki and Lena.

Oh hell. Lucas's heart pounded loud in his ears.

Loki propped his foot on the seat of a straight-backed chair and rested an elbow on his raised knee, leaning forward. "Maras, you now have a vacant cell in your workroom. What is the harm in keeping her there for interrogation?"

"Maybe she's telling the truth," Lena asked.

"*That* is the harm in keeping her." Andre rubbed the bridge of his nose. Then he turned toward Lena, and the muscles in his jaw softened. "*Ćerka*, you must realize the risk in allowing her to stay. At best, we increase his wrath toward us; at worst, she is a spy."

Lena nodded, and Lucas once again admired Andre's fatherliness. *Ćerka* must mean something like daughter, a relationship he and Lena had arrived at awkwardly, but now embraced with devotion.

"It's your home," she said, "and your decision."

Andre rolled his eyes—an oddly childish gesture. He shouted out the door. "Wait one minute while we lower the shield." He tapped his big, black-booted foot. Nice shoes, probably European, and from the looks of them longer and wider than Lucas's feet. Guess they wouldn't be sharing shoes.

"Do you suppose that is long enough?" Andre asked.

A ridiculous ruse, but necessary.

"*Krist*, just tell her to come in." Kos tugged at his short hair.

Lucas went to the door and waved her inside.

When she stepped over the threshold she glanced around. "Hello, Lena, Kosjenic."

Lena glanced at Kos.

"All clear," Andre bellowed, as if some mysterious shield operator would throw a switch and turn the thing back on.

Her eyes were so wide he could see white all the way around her irises, and she shook like a cold, wet Chihuahua. Lucas leaned in like all it would take to discover her trustworthiness was a closer look. When she met his gaze, the hair on the back of his neck stood up, as if Ethan's evil clung to her.

"What happened?" Lena asked.

Gwen's small chest rose with an inhalation and she rubbed the back of her hand against her nose. "I realized that if I didn't leave, he would kill me for the pleasure of watching me suffer, just like he killed that girl."

Lucas's ears buzzed and he tugged at them. Hell, that girl's murder would scare off the most devoted masochist. Maybe Gwen was telling the truth.

"Throw her in the cell, Kos," Andre ordered. "And Lena, child, please do not speak to her. Your compassion is—"

"Yes, I know. It can be a liability." Her lower lip swallowed up the top one.

Loki stood straight and the chair scraped against the hard wood floor. "She must be searched for communication devices."

Like a scene from one of Lucas's beloved soap operas, everyone stared at one another with insinuating glances.

Finally, Zoey huffed and marched at Gwen. "I guess somebody has to do it."

The human woman retreated, backing into the door.

Zoey froze, an icy smile stretching across her face. "You know who I am."

Gwen nodded. "But Ethan didn't tell me you are a—"

"Vampire?" Zoey dropped her fangs and hissed.

It would have been campy, if Gwen weren't clearly frightened half-dead. Her gulp was audible. "Yes."

"*Krist*. This just keeps getting better." Kos did not spare a kind look for Gwen as he pointed toward the hallway. "Come on, Zoey."

"Expect an interrogation, Ms. Evans," Loki said.

"I'd expect nothing less," she called out over her shoulder, with Kos and Zoey following close behind.

"And after I question her, my friend—" Loki sidled up to Andre "—I will return home and you can have your estate back."

"About damn time," Andre said gruffly, but with the hint of a smile. "But you could at least wait until sundown."

Lucas might have enjoyed their hyper-macho display, but he couldn't peel his eyes off of Gwen. He wanted to follow her and try to peer inside her soul. Was she another survivor of the Hunters' cruelty, or one more of Ethan's pawns?

CHAPTER 32

Uta winced as Bel retracted the needle, his little vial of her blood now full. He held it up to the reading light overhead before he dropped it into his pocket. Then he shone a pen light into her eyes.

"Ouch. Stop that." She swatted it away.

He took out his phone and reached across the armrest dividing their seats. "Fine. Stare into the lens." The phone made the artificial sound of a camera shutter. She blinked.

He took hold of her wrist and smoothed his thumb over the veins and arteries visible there. His touch awakened her desire, and her skin grew tingly. Breathless, she asked, "What is the point of this examination?"

"I need to establish a baseline before we arrive in Croatia, so I can observe how your homeland affects you." He flicked the inside of her elbow, seemingly unaffected by the contact. Adolescent mule. He had barricaded his emotions from her with impressive fortitude.

"How unfortunate for you that I cannot urinate in a cup."

His full, pink-brown lips trembled, betraying a repressed smile. "No need for that." He dropped her arm and stood. "All done. You should be pleased, Uta. I've taken your advice. I'm investigating the *osjećaj.*"

"You missed my point entirely. You cannot investigate an ephemeral sentiment; it exists beyond the grasp of science."

The muscles of his jaw flexed, making his face slightly squarer. "If that were true, it could not affect you."

"What of how it affects you?" She put her hand over his heart.

He lowered his head and when he spoke, his breath brushed over her knuckles. "I did not choose this."

"Neither did I. But it is, nevertheless, real. And there is no undoing these mysteries."

"It was your blood, Uta. It formed some sort of physiological connection. These bonds are not magic or mystical mumbo jumbo. They can be understood. And then maybe we can engineer freedom from them." With clinical detachment, he gripped her wrist and put it on the arm rest.

She wanted to scream at him and kiss him, but she just watched as he settled into the furthest seat from her on the small jet and opened his laptop. Soon she would renew her efforts to win him, but at the moment his peevish self-involvement rankled. Vampires were vampires, bound by passion, blood, and the past. They could not be freed from the conditions of their existence, just as humans could not be freed from their need for food or oxygen.

If she attempted to explain this to him, she would only succeed in scolding him like a child. Then he would puff up his beautiful chest in a show of male bluster, and she would want him and love him even as she ranted against his selfish, childish —

Was she so impossible to love?

She swallowed the lump of impatient words trying to crawl out of her throat. A tiny airplane cabin with an audience was the last place she wanted to air out the nuances of her emotions. She had no taste for public humiliation.

Twelve hours and four stops to refuel later, the plane landed, skidding to a stop and rolling into the protection of a hangar on the outskirts of Erzurum. Uta stood, stretching. A strange tingle began in the soles of her feet and traveled upward. She stooped to peer out the window, wiggling her toes with the prickly rush of blood to her extremities.

Pouty Bel stirred in his seat.

The curious sensation pulsed through her veins, soothing her frustration and melting it from her muscles. More at ease, she tempered her tone, managing to sound neutral. "What is this place?"

"It's an old airbase, out of use except for occasional private flights. Ani and Trys arranged for a special reception. There will be someone from customs along with our driver."

"Can I open the door?" Leo bounced on the balls of his feel like an eager toddler.

A chuckle escaped Uta's lips, to her own surprise. Something about Leo charmed her and after half a day of travel, the sweet tang of his potent blood clung to him, pungent. Her mouth watered and she nearly swooned from want, not hunger. Longing. She'd only fed from a Hunter once — Derek — and it had been an ecstasy. The tingle that crept through her veins intensified into a boiling heat, and she gasped.

"Do you feel that too?" Pedro asked.

"Feel what?" Bel asked.

"It's weird, like fingers of energy are reaching through my feet, up into my legs."

"Yes, I feel it." Uta rotated her ankles. It was a good description of the oddly pleasant pins and needles, enlivening her limbs.

Bel got in her face with the pen light again. "Is this what it feels like to be in Croatia?"

"No. Being home simply feels like being home. Why do you insist on looking at my eyes?"

"Just a data point. I'll take your blood soon. Yours too, Pedro."

And then all she could see was the underside of his scruffy chin, because he was staring upward, lost in thought.

She followed Bel down the short stairway of the plane. Shadows filled both ends of the dim hangar and sulfurous yellow light glared from the center of the arching roof. A mustached man in a white shirt leaned against a jeep with his knee bent and one foot on the wheel, smoking a cigarette. He wore a machine-gun slung over his shoulder. Uta cringed. She hated those infernal devices.

A middle-aged human woman in a flowing patterned skirt stood next to a second SUV. Inside it, a driver waited. The woman extended her arms and smiled, showing slightly crooked teeth. "Welcome to Erzurum. I am Damla."

Bel shook her hand. "Thanks for making the arrangements."

"It is a pleasure." She spoke English only slightly more thickly than Uta, with her new-and-improved English accent. "Hasan, do you need to inspect the aircraft?"

The man with the gun took a long look at the group, and Uta's heart ramped up. Stupid automatic weapons. She could take him, but unless she caught him off guard, she would lose a lot of blood in the process.

"No, you are free to go." The guard made an arch in the air with the point of his weapon and Damla handed him a thick fold of bills.

Turning back to Bel, she smiled. "Merely a formality."

He nodded. "You are sure this madrasa is suitable for my friends?"

"Oh yes. Young Trys explained all your needs. The underground apartment is entirely impervious to light." She bowed to Uta and Pedro. "I confess, I have always wanted to meet a vampire. In all my years here, I have never encountered one."

All her years? Uta snorted. Humans were so funny about age. But Damla met her gaze with an unfaltering stare—an unexpectedly old one. If she was the witch's friend, chances were good she also had magic.

Uta stepped toward her and raised her chin. "What are you?"

"Tsk, tsk. Surely that is a rude question, even among vampires."

Bel smirked. "Don't provoke Uta. She is surly."

"I am a witch." Damla's imperfect smile softened Uta. "And while my lifespan is small compared to yours, warrior queen of the Illyrians, I am older than your halfling here by a century, or so."

"Queen?" Leo whispered.

"Ssh. Not now." Pedro steered the young Hunter into the waiting vehicle.

How did she know that about Uta? Bel's people must have briefed her, which meant they trusted Damla, and that was enough to get Uta to climb into the SUV. "What is this madrasa you're taking us to?"

"Currently it is a museum and closed for renovations, but it was built in the thirteenth century as a monument to the ruling dynasty. Then it served as a seminary and mausoleum." Damla climbed into the passenger seat and turned.

"*Muy bien.* House the vampires with the dead people. We do get cold, you know."

"Ah. What do you call this type in English? A smart-aleck?"

"That's the polite term," Bel replied. A wide smile spread across his face—the first Uta had seen since he had bent his head between her legs and taken her to blessed relief. Seeing it again, the sweeping curve of his lush lips—she wanted to kiss it until the vacant sensation in her heart vanished.

Damla turned to Pedro, her eyes twinkling. "I think you will find the accommodations satisfactory. I have often found it necessary to hole up in secret, and the underground apartment is known only to me and my trusted friends. Somehow, it was erased from all the records." She winked.

"Somehow indeed," Uta agreed. After centuries of persecution, witches were wily by necessity, and Uta admired their subtlety the way a woman with straight hair admires another's curls. It was a trait she'd never possessed.

For such a late hour, the streets bustled with commuters. A woman carried a shopping basket, a bundle of leafy greens overflowing its rim. What would it be like to be her—to be on her way home to a family, to prepare a meal, to tuck children into a bed and lie down next to a husband? A satisfactory ordinariness, with no burdens bigger than your own simple life? Uta had never been ordinary, and even as a human she had borne the burdens of her people.

Nestled against the mountains, the city's buildings alternated in styles between historical and modern. It was a pleasant if unremarkable place, like so many old-world cities where Uta had evacuated vampires under siege by Hunters. Yet Uta had never traveled to eastern Turkey. To her knowledge, there were no vampires living there, which explained why Damla had never met one.

And perhaps why no one had ever described the extremely pleasant vibration zinging in her veins, a mellower version of the first prickly tingles she'd felt on the airplane. She sighed with the bliss of it. Bel's head whipped to look at her, his eyebrows raised. She plastered on a bland, agreeable smile—practice for when she would get him alone and seduce him with her sweetest, most charming self. His adorable, quizzical expression shot heat right between her legs.

Five minutes later, the driver slid the SUV into a parking place on the street, across a narrow lawn from the building Damla called the madrasa. Two spires ascended from the façade into the night sky, and on the backside a third, cone-roofed tower stood just as high. Impressive, if not inviting, the medieval stone building loomed large on a small city block.

Pedro grunted. "Home sweet home." Then he began to unload the bags.

Damla led them through a chain-link fence. Uta could not read Turkish, but guessed easily enough the neon orange signs indicated the museum was closed. Inside, surrounded by four walls of arches, the courtyard resembled a gothic cloister. The witch led them through a door in the corner. It seemed to open onto a flight of stairs leading up, but by some trick of light or illusion or just plain old magic, a smaller door appeared on the side of the stairs. It revealed a descending ramp, barely wide enough to pass. With his broad shoulders, Bel might have to walk sideways. The suitcases would be a pain in the ass, but not hers. Pedro could deal with them.

Second in line behind Damla, Uta reached the expansive apartment, which spanned the entire footprint of the Madrasa above. Dusty leather-bound books lined one wall—the sort of books any respectable witch would have on her shelf. Evenly spaced doors opened in the opposite wall. Presumably this had been a dormitory for the seminary at one time. A formidable oak table occupied the center of the room.

"Wow," Leo said.

Damla strode across the room and turned on a kettle. The weedy smell of dried plants itched in Uta's nostrils. Damn witches and their herbal teas and their—she scanned the room looking for the evidence—sweets! Tins of Turkish delight cluttered the table, as did boxes of cookies, and even half-eaten candy bars. Uta much preferred subsisting off of blood than noxious sugar, not that she'd ever tasted candy before.

Bel raised a box and shook it. Nothing rattled inside. "Please tell me you have some people food."

Damla cackled with apparent disregard for stereotypes. "Yes, yes. The larder is stocked."

"Good. Then let's feed the person so that he can feed the vampires." Pedro shoved Leo toward the pantry door.

"Do you want to see it now?" Damla asked.

Uta glanced around, trying to ascertain to whom the witch spoke. But she stared with hazel eyes directly at Uta. "See what?"

"But isn't that why you've come?"

CHAPTER 33

pparently this witch had a brain full of rusty nails. Or was it loose screws? "We've come to search for an ancient halfling. Didn't Ani tell you?"

"But I thought…" Even as she trailed off, her pitch rose in a question.

Goose bumps prickled on Uta's arms.

Bel raised his head from some scientific apparatus he was examining and furrowed his brows. "How do you know about Uta, Damla?"

"Because of the message from Rize, of course."

Uta found herself sitting in a chair, not sure how she had arrived there.

Bel gripped her elbow. "Who is Rize?"

"My sire." She leaned into Bel, allowing herself to rely on his strength and clear thinking.

"Let me show you." Damla stood, crossing to the bookshelves. She pulled three books down and set them aside, then repeated the motion until she'd fully exposed a large stone, engraved with sweeping Arabic calligraphy.

"What does it say?" Bel whispered.

Damla read it aloud. "For my beloved daughter Teuta, Warrior, Queen of the Illyrians."

He whistled.

"Why would he leave this message for me here?" Uta's mind processed the math quickly. She'd received news of his death in the year 1312, decades after this behemoth of a madrasa was built.

"This is not the message." Damla's tone had softened so much Uta was surprised her sentence didn't end with a diminutive like *child*, even though Uta was far, far older than the witch. At the mention of Rize, Uta did regress to childish emotions.

Damla worked her hands around the edge of the stone, her fingers catching on invisible holds. She wriggled out the block, which proved to be mere inches thick. Inside was a bundle wrapped in cloth. Damla handled it with obvious care before laying it in Uta's outstretched palms.

She unfolded the fabric to uncover a single sheet of vellum, covered in Rize's boxy, compact Latin. Blinking, she called up the long dead language of her conquerors. Her fingers trembled. She didn't want to crush the ancient document, or sweat on it. Another piece of parchment slipped from her grip and floated to the floor. Bel bent, catching the corner between his big fingers. As he stood, holding it out to her, an image in a familiar style came into focus—a relic depicting the mythic time, like a Hunter artifact, but from Rize's own codex. In it, a Hunter mother cradled a halfling child. Her vampire mate stood at her side in the iconic style of a Madonna and child, a holy family. Beautiful.

An acutely personal grief took hold of Uta. Ridiculous. She had not lost a family.

But all vampires had lost something in that war. Now they existed in a perpetual exile which she felt in her bones, without Croatia and without Bel.

Why had Rize left this for her? And here, of all places?

Tears blurred her vision, keeping the answer from her. "Can you read Latin, Bel?"

"Only scientific jargon. The empire was a bit before my time, you know."

She wiped her eyes on her sleeve, saline tinted pink ruining yet another fabulous jacket, and finally she was able to make sense of Rize's words.

If you are here, child, I can only assume the reason.

I too have begun to doubt my instructions to you.

After the massacre, when my mate was killed and I nearly died from our broken bond, my grief for her and our children, my horror at the scale of violence, I wanted to spare every vampire that fate.

I traveled west, and I met you. Do you remember that night I appeared in your tent and fought for the right into your bed?

You were so hard, your edges sharp and rough like a stone arrowhead. Only you fought an enemy with armor and swords. You, a ferocious freedom fighter, clinging to your land against a monstrous empire.

I showed you the power you could have, if you would only become like me, because I knew on first sight that the next generation of vampires must be like you — fearless and unsentimental.

Are you still, daughter?

I am not. In my old age, I have returned to my homeland. I was wasting away for want of it. The Hunters are here. I smell them and glimpse them on the street. I know they will find me eventually, and I no longer care. I must be here. I must remember. And Uta, child, I want you to remember too. I want you to keep the hope alive for a return to our paradise. For a new era of peace.

You have been a perfect friend and daughter to me. Perhaps not as cold as I first assumed. And if the longing draws you back, trust it. And fight for it. This place is your home as much as Illyria or Volta. It is home to all of us. Go, Uta. Go and feel the power of your true home. Meet Ayal. Recruit her to your cause.

I do not know when you will come. I have left this same message for you in a dozen places — churches, mosques, synagogues. Who knows what monuments will withstand human squabbles?

Uta, dearest, I see now I was wrong. It was not all of the Hunters who betrayed us. My wife was pure and true, as were so many others. It is wrong to hate them all for the actions of some, and so I hold out hope for a reconciliation, in your lifetime, if not in mine.

Your sire,

Rize

No. It was too much. She did not want this burden. It was the very opposite of the one he had given her before, and simply too much. Maybe her sharpest edges had been dulled, but she was no idealist. She set the parchment down on the table and splayed all ten of her fingers, inhaling deeply.

"Uta, what does it say?" Bel squatted to look into her face.

"It is a goodbye note. He knew he was wasting and he came back to his homeland to die at the hands of Hunters. The silly bastard went soft in the end."

Bel's eyes traced over her face, but his expression was unreadable and she still could not get a hold on his feelings. "There is a map here."

Go, Uta. Go and feel the power of your true home.

"Let me see."

Black lines zigzagged across the third and smallest piece of parchment above a placid lake, creating the type of map printed in the cover of a children's fairytale book.

"This is useless. We need GPS coordinates or the name of a town. Something concrete."

Damla leaned in. "That is Karagöl Lake, in Borçka Province, near the border with Georgia. The peaks are distinctive. My people believe it is a place of great power."

"Borçka." Yes. It was not the place she had planned to take them, but she had heard it spoken before, long ago, maybe even whispered to her in a dream—and it had been a very long time since she'd dreamed.

Feel the power of your true home.

Home. Was that what she'd felt in her bones since the plane landed? She shook her head fast, faster. "This is a bad idea. Loki should not have sent us."

Bel rested his hand on her shoulder and heat radiated through her, calming her a little.

"How far is Borçka from here?" he asked.

Damla's fingers drummed on the table. "Four hours or so. You may take the SUV, of course."

"Good. Is it sunproof?"

"No."

"Hhmm. I don't like that risk. If we got stuck…how are the roads?"

"Decent until the last ascent up to the lake. If you leave at sundown tomorrow, you will have no problems."

"No. We'll leave right away."

An objection echoed in the recesses of Uta's mind. No. She shouldn't go. This wasn't her fight. She didn't want to fight anymore—not with anyone besides Bel.

"We're leaving? We just got here," Leo whined from a bedroom door.

Damn. One look at the kid, and all Uta could think of was that icon of the family.

"Yeah, we did. And now we leave." Bel rewrapped the brittle sheets of vellum. "I want to finish this trip, report back to Loki and resume my research."

All the reasons for her not to go pressed against her lips, but she couldn't say them.

Rize's voice, so long gone, was loud in her ear. *Keep the hope alive for a return to our paradise.*

Her heart swelled in her chest, racing.

Fuck every sheep in the Turkish countryside, she would try. "Let us go."

CHAPTER 34

Gwen lay on the bed in the closet-turned-cell and breathed with practiced patience. Controlling her breath allowed her to tolerate nearly everything.

She'd been a fool not to expect the old fears to return, here among vampires. They raced through her veins and she began to sweat in the cool room. Any one of the creatures could do anything to her. They could swing open the door, bite her, and torture her—and she would like it, then hate herself for it.

Then her shallow breaths changed, her nipples hardened, and a weight settled on her pelvis. Fear transformed into arousal, as it always did because of the way Mason had crossed all her wires.

Did Marasović have the same sadistic streak as Mason and Ethan? Probably so, if Zoey was his slave now. She didn't act especially submissive, but then again, neither did Gwen in public. Was Zoey as strong as Gwen, was she as thoroughly addicted to pain? Something told Gwen she was not—a small consolation.

She slipped her hand between her legs—only because Ethan had given her permission to, while they were apart—and pictured him. The open-mouthed wonder on his face when she orgasmed under his cruel ministrations. His enjoyment made the sacrifice of her body worthwhile—eventually, it would simply subsume her, and she would be free.

Without inviting it, another image took shape, of herself pressed between the beautiful Kosjenic and Andre Marasović, fangs and cocks and hands battering her in a whirlwind of sweet torment while the whole household looked on, seeing her for the trash she was. She came with a cry. But as her pleasure unfurled, humming through her fingers and toes, her shame seared over her cheeks. She'd betrayed Ethan with the disgusting fantasy.

Her heart rate steadied and she wiped her slippery fingers on the sheets. If she stayed in this cell too long, her sick imagination would drive her insane.

She would have to persuade them to trust her and somehow get out. Ethan only needed Gwen to disable the shield, but so far she hadn't learned a thing about it. Did giant electromagnets somewhere generate the barrier, or was it magic, as some of the Hunters believed? Given what she'd seen since she'd met Mason, anything was possible.

A gentle knock on the door sounded, startling her off the bed. Polite jailers, these. Unfortunately, any vampire would know what she'd been doing — the smell of her fear and sex would hang in the air like catnip.

Please be Andre.

Seconds later, the smaller vampire appeared, looking just like one of Santa's elves in street clothes. He carried a tea tray aloft, balanced on the tips of his fingers and thumb. Upstairs, he'd been issuing orders, alongside Marasović. And now he was playing butler? Mason wouldn't have served her tea even if it would have somehow caused her pain.

"Hello, Ms. Evans. Care for something to drink?"

"Do I have a choice?"

He gave her an appraising glance. "You have many choices, child. More than you can accept, I suspect. And I certainly don't intend to pour tea down your throat."

Put that way, her insolence stung. "Thank you. I'd like a cup."

"With milk, no sugar?"

"Yes. How did you know?"

"It's a useless skill I've honed over a very long time, to be able to guess these things." He tilted his head and looked at her again. "I expect you take coffee with cream and sugar, prefer white wine, and rarely drink spirits, but if you did — " his sharply arched eyebrows lifted " — Scotch?"

A laugh escaped her. "Is there a beverage dossier on me somewhere?" But of course, there couldn't be. Mason had never known things like that about her. Oddly, Ethan had taken pains to learn her taste in food, but he wouldn't have shared them with the enemy.

The vampire poured the tea into a small bowl without a handle—an Asian tea set, although the scent and color of the tea revealed it to be a strongly brewed English Breakfast. Her mouth watered.

"I believe, Ms. Evans, that you are a historian by training?"

"Yes. Ancient languages of the British Isles are my specialty."

"I see, *kona, slægr eða fagr.*"

She spelled out the words in her mind letter by letter, finally recognizing them as Old Norse, the language of the Viking raiders of England. He'd called her a clever and beautiful woman.

"Thank you. Are you also a scholar of languages?"

"No, child, just a speaker."

"You mean—"

"Yes, for a time I spoke Old Norse, and before that the language which preceded it, brought by the first wave of Indo-European migrants. But I am a Laplander and my people have inhabited Norway since the creation of the world, so my mother tongue is Sami."

He had to be lying. "The Sami languages are nearly extinct."

"That is true. Only a few of us remember, now."

Remember? "You want me to believe you are more than a thousand years old?"

He smiled, and his eyes disappeared into slits, giving him a jolly, amused look. "Far more than that, child. I am the oldest one."

"One of what?"

He sat back. "How little Ethan has told you."

Was that true? Or was Ethan ignorant too?

"Whereas, I know quite a bit about you. About your abuse at the hands of Mason Kearney and how Uta Ilirije rescued you, brought you to her home, hired skilled therapists to treat your trauma."

She retreated, scooting backward on the bed. "I didn't know Uta was a vampire." That revelation had sent her into the streets of Manhattan barefoot and in her bathrobe at dawn. The police took her to a shelter, and eventually she'd crawled back into her life, numb to everything but her research until Ethan found her.

"I am very sorry for what Mason did to you, child."

A scream curled up from her stomach, lodging behind her sternum. With a masochist's self-control, she hid her revulsion. "Thank you."

"And Ethan Bennett is the same sort?" Loki's eyes penetrated her, peeling away clothes and skin and boring into her soul.

But she'd master her body's reaction to fear. She faked a quiver in her lower lip. "He is."

"You have become an addict and you will crave pain again. Why should we trust you?"

"I don't care if you do. Just keep me here, locked up and safe from him, and myself."

"So be it, child. I have asked Trys to visit you. If she has any magic to spare, she can heal your bruises."

Gwen shifted in her seat. "Magic?"

He blinked and bobbed his head with a single nod.

"How did you know I am bruised?"

"I can smell the clotted blood." He grimaced. "Extensive. And a cracked rib—white blood cells smell sweet."

Why should that surprise her? Mason's heightened senses had given the impression he could read her mind. He knew what she ate and could detect where she was in her menstrual cycle. She squashed down the unwelcome memories and passed a moment with the vampire in almost companionable silence.

"How old are you, really?" she blurted.

He blew out a breath through his nose. "Would you believe me if I said I had lost count?"

Something about his tone caught her attention. "Not for a second."

"Clever, indeed. I have never known a vampire who did. According to my parents I was born in the third month of summer in the year we now call two thousand one hundred and seventeen."

She immediately eliminated the possibility he came from the future, which meant he was four thousand, one hundred and thirty years old—quite literally prehistoric. She catalogued the eons he'd witnessed, a vast portion of human history.

His child-like face remained impassive, as if he sensed her awe, and without thinking, she stroked his cheek, supple like a young man's. He closed his eyelids, accepting the caress, and whispered, "Child, very few of us are like Mason Kearney. I take responsibility for his crimes; we should have stopped him."

Tears prickled in her eyes but she would not permit them to spill. His apology blew over her like a breeze on barbed wire. Nothing could change who she'd become under Mason's control, and therefore nothing would dissuade her from Ethan's mission.

"For some humans," the old vampire continued, "turning vampire is the best remedy for abuse—you would grow powerful, your body would heal, and over time, your heart as well."

Her stomach clenched, and she must have flinched, because he reached for her hand.

"There is time to decide."

"Thank you. I am honored by the suggestion." She barely managed not to spit the lie.

"Ms. Evans. I hope I have the honor of meeting you again under happier circumstances, but I must depart."

Caught off guard, her knotted gut fell into her pelvis. "You're leaving?"

"Yes, the entire Justicia leaves at nightfall."

He kissed her cheeks, and to her surprise, this time she didn't recoil.

Were Ethan's offenses in place yet? It would be such a tragedy for the little creature to die—a living, breathing trove of history.

Should she warn him?

"Be careful."

He flashed his impish smile over his shoulder. "I always am, child. That is how I have survived so long."

Lucas bent his head closer to Derek so he could get a better view of the screen.

"Do you know him?" The ex-Hunter moved the mouse over a name on the screen.

"Yes, a little," Lucas replied. "He's a good choice."

They had amassed a shortlist of the most moderate, reasonable Hunters in the United States. Amenable connections overseas would be more difficult to find, since the tribe resisted organization as if it were a plague—or at least they had until Ethan appeared and pretended to be the Messiah and Keeper of Hunter Mysteries.

Leo had wheedled his way in with the younger set, who had their own bizarre online Hunter world—Internet dating for burgeoning young sadists. A message from Derek containing the evidence against Ethan had gone out via those networks already. But, as always, the Hunter elders held all the power.

"I'll start making phone calls." Derek shut the laptop and pivoted to face Lucas. "But this is real, right? We haven't been brainwashed?"

"You know the saying about the person who wonders if they are crazy never being the crazy one?"

"I don't need a saying, Bennett, I need an answer."

Lucas sat up and put both hands on the table. "I can't begin to describe what I feel about Pedro, or what it's like between us, but I've never lost my ability to think clearly. I'm not brainwashed."

Derek leaned forward, his knees on his elbows. "My head feels crystal clear, too."

"I believe in this with everything I've got, Derek. I'd give my life for the smallest hope of ending this war, or hell, just the chance to save a few kids from growing up the way we did. Don't tell that to Pedro, though."

A deafening bang sounded, and a moment later, the house shook.

"*Davo!*" Andre's roar came from the north wing, the master bedroom.

Lucas walked as fast as the stitch in his side would let him. All the vampires beat him there.

The curtains on the windows had been flung wide, affording a perfect view of the highway, where a single car blazed.

"Who was in that car?" Lucas asked, but from the silence in the room, he already knew.

CHAPTER 35

Bel dozed in the back seat next to where Leo slept soundly. Uta and Pedro took turns at the wheel. Insomniac vampires sure came in handy on all-night drives. Since they'd left Ezurum, the SUV had climbed increasingly steep ascents into the mountains that rimmed the Black Sea.

Uta had been uncharacteristically silent since she read that letter from Rize. She was fighting something, and Bel had no clue what it was.

Pedro turned down the volume—of course he'd managed to find trancey Turkish dance music on the radio a thousand miles from any nightclubs. "So tell me, what that hell is this feeling in my veins?"

Bel came fully awake in an instant, but he remained still.

"I not know what you are meaning."

"Yeah, right, and you suddenly forgot English again, too."

Bel bit back a laugh—he wanted to keep on eavesdropping.

Uta didn't reply right away. But when she did, it was with her shiny new mid-Atlantic accent, not her mail order bride one. "I fed from Derek Williams last month, before Kos and I went out to save Lena."

"I heard."

"I felt something similar then."

"True. Feeding from a Hunter is like mainlining this juice. An intense flare that mellows out. What I've got now is this nice sweet buzz."

"It is the same for me. But you are young, you live where Andre turned you. Imagine how the buzz feels to me—I have been in exile for nearly two centuries. I feel more powerful than I have since I left, even though I go back occasionally to recharge."

She visited Croatia? Bel wanted to sit right up and extract a promise from her never to do that again. Hadn't her sire done the very same thing—returning to one's home was suicide. But that was probably why she did it, the selfish female.

Pedro's fingers fidgeted over the dashboard, twisting stereo and aircon knobs. "So this is where it all began. Where our ancestors crawled out of the caves."

Uta stretched her arms overhead, revealing the gentle curve of her breast. Bel's mouth watered.

"It must seem impossibly long ago to you," she said.

"Now that is an interesting question. Do you suppose it seems shorter or longer to you, since you lived it?"

She turned to look at Pedro and the lights from an oncoming car illuminated her glorious face. Goddamn, Bel wished she were just a woman. Hell, just a vampire, but not his bloody mate. What would have happened, if they'd met like that—fresh, without any attachments. Would he even have liked her?

She smiled wistfully at Pedro. "I've never thought of that, and I suppose there is no way to know."

Of course, Bel would have loved her—she was so perfectly beautiful and absurd and brilliant and brittle and kind and—but was that only because he was made this way, for her? He could never know. Nothing could turn back the clock and erase what she and Mila had done. No scientific test could tell him if he would have loved her freely. But he sure as hell loved her—

"Bel, it is time to stop pretending you are asleep," she said.

He laughed. "Not until Pedro turns off this shite music. Put on my iPod." He handed over the device.

She rubbed her eyes. "Perfect. The sun is very nearly up, and you want me to die listening to Joan Jett. Show some mercy."

That time Pedro chuckled.

Her words jolted Bel. He had never told her what kind of music he liked. She cast a glance over his shoulder, raising her auburn brows. But he had no retort.

She knew him. Bloody hell. She'd been watching him, loving him, from a distance for all these years. Suffering for him with the hope he might choose her. He reached for her, wrapping his hand around her bicep and grazing his knuckles against her breast.

"What is it?" she asked.

He had no words, but he held her gaze and dropped his emotional barricade, letting her feel the beginnings of acceptance settling in to his gut. Her mouth fell open before pulling into the sweetest smile he'd ever seen her wear. He leaned forward to kiss her lightly, just a brush of the lips. Not born of hunger, but choice.

He whispered into her ear. "Sing for us."

And so, as the SUV climbed the steep mountain Uta sang the Croatian folk songs of Bel's youth. They nearly lulled him back to sleep, and Leo continued to slumber.

Damla had routed out their trip after examining the satellite images online. She'd suggested they turn off the main road just before they entered the Karagöl Lake Nature Reserve, and take a dirt road approaching the lake from another direction. Uta's soprano suited the haunting beauty of the alpine landscape and the rustic architecture of the region — if it weren't for the occasional car or tractor, Bel could have believed they'd traveled back to the nineteenth century of his youth.

Surrounded by evergreens, one and two story houses spotted the hillsides. Higher up, homes sporting flat timber façades were built flush against the steep slant of the mountain. As they drew nearer to the lake, they passed several crumbling homes, their wooden siding in disarray, or their stilts leaning. But at the end of the road, one A-framed house jutted proudly from the mountainside.

Behind it, starlight shimmered on a placid lake and a jagged ridge loomed in the precise angles of Rize's map. Some things did not change in eight hundred years.

In the light of only a quarter moon, even Bel's human eyes took in three rows of brightly painted beehives lining the drive and a cone-shaped terra-cotta jar the size of a grown man leaned against the front steps. Trellised grape vines reached away from the house and vanished into the darkness.

Pedro crossed to the jar and flicked it with his finger. It rang like a bell.

"What is that thing?" Bel asked.

"It's a *qvevri,* for fermenting wine."

Though it rested on the muddy ground, the jar was spotless. In fact, the whole place possessed an air of tidiness. Excitement welled up his throat. Inside lived an ancient creature, even older than Uta, who knew the mysteries of Hunters and vampires, and who happened to be a halfling like him — the very first he'd ever met.

"The house is empty." Uta stood at the bottom of the steps, her conjecture apparently based on data from one of her super-sharp senses.

Bel's excitement turned to a lump he couldn't swallow. But Uta could be wrong. "Maybe she is sleeping."

"Perhaps." But the strain on her face showed her certainty.

CHAPTER 36

The lever of the front door gave way under Bel's hand — unlocked. Inside, the air hung slightly stale and thick with a sweet spice. At least nothing had died. Uta found a kerosene lamp and lit up the dark space, a kind gesture for his and Leo's benefit. Stairs led to a loft under the steep slope of the roof. The main room held only an iron stove, a kitchen, and a dining table. In the corner, a rocking chair perched beside a bookshelf, and another kerosene lamp sat beside it.

Set in the back wall, a small red door led into what could only be the mountainside. He opened it to find a hallway so dark and deep he couldn't guess its length. He lit the second lantern while Pedro and Leo climbed into the loft. Uta sat at the table and bent over the image of the Hunter-vampire family and the letter from Rize.

A stab of betrayal tightened Bel's gut. Finally, he'd chosen her, and still she kept something from him.

He stomped to the back door and entered a dark hallway. The passageway extended perhaps ten feet into the hillside, its floor simply carved from the stone. On each side, a door stood closed in a wood-paneled wall. If Ayal were like him, she could tolerate the sun, and yet, she'd taken precautions, digging out this safe place for vampires into the granite of the mountain.

Instinctively, he opened the door on the left. One more neat, small room, paneled in wood, its bed made. A note lay there on the lines of schoolroom paper. It was hand written in several languages, including English.

"Uta," he called out, even as he began to read.

I have gone. I heard in the village about the attacks, and I cannot wait here anymore. Perhaps it was foolish to stay so long, but this has been my home, and home is—well, if you know who I am, then you know what home is, but it will be mine no more. I do not know another like me, and it has been a lonely existence. I do not want to be alone anymore.

Uta took hold of the paper, yanking.

Bel didn't let go. "Stop. You'll rip it."

She obeyed, dropping her hands and stepping closer to read. It seemed to take her a quarter of a second to absorb the words. Then she kicked off her shoes and flopped on the bed, arms crossed over her mouthwatering little breasts.

"Rotten goat entrails. What do we do now?"

"Sun's coming up, so right now, you and Pedro hunker down in this bat cave. Then we make a plan."

Out in the hallway, Bel jostled the opposite door. It opened onto an identical room, but less personal—for Ayal's vampire guests that had never arrived. Pedro and Leo finished bringing in the suitcases just as dawn shone on the surface of the lake. Bel grabbed his bag.

He returned to Ayal's room to find Uta reclined on the bed with her eyes closed, so lovely in repose. Across the bond he'd allowed to open again, her frustration coiled tightly in his muscles. Underneath it, he sensed a hopelessness taking hold.

"Snap out of it, Uta. It's a minor setback." He pulled out his phlebotomy kit and found a new needle and vial. Then he searched for her vein. "We've lost our chance to interview a survivor, but we are still in the homeland. Pedro can search for his grapes. With this blood sample, I'll be able to test how being here changes it—I can observe the effects of your *osjećaj*."

She blew out an insulting little raspberry.

He ignored her. "Uta, this is a breakthrough."

Her phone rang and Bel's buzzed in his pocket seconds later. His screen read Kos.

Uta darted up. "It's Andre."

Both at the same time? That couldn't be good news. "You take it."

"No you. I will hear through your phone."

He nodded, already answering. "This is Bel."

"Is she with you?" Kos asked.

Bel locked eyes with her. "She is."

"It's Loki. They ambushed his car on the way to the airport."

She flashed to Bel's side. "Is he——"

"He's dead, Uta."

She opened her beautiful mouth and shrieked a frightening cry. Bel's heart nearly stopped in sympathy. He reached for her, but she slipped from his grip and he staggered forward. Shite, he couldn't let her get outside.

A freezing mist of dread fell over her from above.

"He's dead, Uta."

Dead.

Her best friend, her mentor, the only one who truly cared about her.

A cry tore from her throat, even as an unimaginable weight lifted from her shoulders. Her lungs filled with the relief. She didn't have to fight anymore——Loki wasn't there to make her. She could give up, could follow him wherever vampires went when they died.

She sprinted to the front of the house, ripping off her jacket to expose more skin. To get it over with as fast as possible. She was nearly at the door, reaching out her arms, just a little farther——bam! She rammed straight into Pedro's chest. She pushed, but the young vampire stood impossibly strong, catching her in a surprise choke hold.

The sobs came then. "Let me go." She writhed against his grip. "Please, Pedro, let me go." She didn't want to live in a world without Loki, in a world without hope, with only Hunters and hate and unending longing for Bel. She had fooled herself to think there could ever be anything else.

A needle pierced her low in the back and filled her muscles with a raging burn.

No. Not this again. Not another failure. She slid onto her knees and turned to face Bel.

"Please, Bel. Let me go."

Her voice echoed in her mind from a great distance and shadows crept into the corners of her eyes.

He shook his head.

"I beg you. I need it to be over. Drag me outside now. With the drugs, I will not even feel it. You will survive, and you will be free…"

His eyes widened in obvious understanding. She slid down the black tunnel into unconsciousness, comforted by the hope she might never wake up.

CHAPTER 37

Bel dropped onto his ass next to Uta's limp legs, finally able to breathe.

Pedro cradled her torso in a distant, awkward embrace as if he preferred not to touch her at all. He staggered into the shadows, away from the weak light creeping around the heavy curtains of the front windows.

"*Jesu Cristo*, what do we do with her now?"

"Hell if I know."

"You're not thinking of taking her outside?"

Actually, Bel was.

Goddamn it, how could he not, with the hurt he'd seen in her eyes, the emptiness, the longing? Echoes of his mother's misery bounced inside him, and a double wave of pity doused his anger at them both. He could almost bring himself to carry Uta into the daylight, no matter how it would rip him apart. But the world without her—it wasn't someplace he wanted to live. With Loki gone, the vampires would need her to kick ass, now more than ever. And, if he was honest with himself, he wasn't ready to give up on her, on them, quite yet.

"Not a chance," he lied. "We'll do everything we can to keep her alive. But Loki said she'll wake up even more determined to sun walk."

"*Esta madre* is too powerful to restrain." Pedro eased her to the floor and brushed his hands free of her cooties. "Too bad all that superstitious *mierda* about silver binding a vampire isn't true. I was surprised I could hold her off. She flew like a rocket to shield you from that car bomb."

Uta's limbs splayed like a lifeless marionette, deceptively vulnerable.

Pedro was right. Bel had no idea how to tie her down and keep her there. "I've seen Andre pick a car off the ground like a hawk with a field mouse. She could probably fly off with a whole locomotive in one hand."

Pedro's mouth quirked into a grin. "So, dude, I gotta ask. Do you think that's hot? 'Cause she kinda scares me."

Bel was not about to dissect the complicated anatomy of his feelings about Uta. "Bugger off, bro."

Pedro sat back on his heels and looked Bel over, his expression turning grave. "You can talk to me, you know. If you want." Pedro's golden eyes warmed with the invitation.

Had it only been two months since Bel had met him? He'd witnessed Pedro's turning, worked side by side with him to discover the mysteries of Blood Vine. They'd been on a hell of a ride in those eight weeks. Yeah, he could tell him.

"Sometimes I think it's hot. Sometimes she scares the shit out of me. And mostly, I just hate that I never had a choice. When I want her, when I enjoy being around her, I wonder if it's because I have to like her—you know—because she made me this way."

"Not on purpose, though. *Verdad?*"

"Yeah."

"Do you think we ever really have a choice? I mean, I liked Lucas all right when we met, but we wouldn't be what we are now if hadn't gotten addicted to his blood. Or Andre and Zoey, did they have a choice?"

"This is different."

"Sure, dude. If you say so."

Bel's molars came together, gnashing hard enough to grind down diamonds. It was a lot more fun to watch Pedro work his ninja psych-outs on Andre than to be on the receiving end.

"So, where should I put her?" the sneaky vampire asked. "In your room?"

"Our room?" Bel hissed through his clenched teeth.

"Dude. I said your room. Take it however you want."

Too tense to think of a snappy reply, Bel just opened doors to clear Pedro's path.

He set her on the coverlet with surprising care, like a father putting a child to bed instead of a grossed out vampire. "She weighs nothing, for someone so tall."

Asleep, she seemed delicate and lovely—a china doll. And calm, like she had been in the days of his childhood, lying on the beach and looking up at the stars by his side.

Leo scuffed to a halt in the doorway. "Is she asleep? I thought you guys didn't do that."

"We don't. She's out cold, sedated." Pedro withdrew from the bed, his tone a touch envious.

Bel raised her eyelid, she didn't stir and her pupils remained dilated from the paralyzing knock-out drugs. His palm curved to cup her face, a chance to touch her, unaware. Maybe it was creepy, but he didn't care. Her cheek filled his hand, soft and delicate, so fragile for such a ferocious creature.

Pedro cleared his throat, and Bel's cheeks flared with a rush of embarrassment.

"Um," Leo began. "You guys should check out the cellar. It's full of stuff for making wine, I think."

There was a cellar? Bel spun to face the kid. "Where?"

"This way—the door was hidden behind that carpet hanging at the end of the hall."

To be sure, Bel evaluated Uta's condition once more. Her chest rose and fell with the long breaths of someone under deep anesthesia. Surely she would remain asleep long enough for him to poke around downstairs.

Leo raised a kerosene lantern, and Bel followed the pair down stone stairs, carved into the granite mountain. Toward the front of the cellar, where the house protruded from the hillside, the floor turned to gravel, interrupted by several odd circles of stone.

"What the hell are those?"

"These are her *qvevri*, buried in the earth." Pedro knelt next to one of the rings.

The word sounded familiar. "Like the big jar we saw outside?"

"Exactly. This is the lip of the terra-cotta jug." Pedro ran his finger around the rim. "And it's been capped with a lid. She's aging her wine here. It's an ancient Georgian technique, one of the oldest ways of fermenting wine, but I've never heard of it being used…"

Pedro kept talking, but Bel didn't hear a work. Wine. Aged in the soil. This had to be important. Whatever power was in the earth might seep right into the wine. Power? Shite. When had he gone all new-agey? Probably the day he hired Trys to generate magical shields.

"Do you think this wine is special, like Blood Vine?" Leo reached for a jug, knocking down a tube and a stack of perforated tin cones.

They clattered on the hard floor and Bel flinched. Shite. Any unexpected sound could indicate Uta was making another run for it.

Pedro punched Bel's shoulder. "Go back to her. I'll crack open one of these babies and investigate." He pantomimed gulping from a cup with his pinky finger in the air.

The jugs pulled Bel, like they'd lodged little grappling hooks into his gray matter and yanked. It felt like a moment of wide open possibility like when he'd found gold in Blood Vine. Surely he was getting closer to the answers they needed. Would that wine cure the wasting disease? Was there *hemoaurum* in there? Did the soil of the homeland make it more powerful?

A crack sounded above and Bel jerked toward the stairwell, his halfling heart beating vampire fast. But it was only Pedro resting his knuckles against the low rafter where he'd knocked to make a point.

Message received. The wine could wait. Uta needed him now. Leo walked him upstairs with the lantern and closed the door behind him.

Bel took stock of the situation. Bonds at her slender wrists and ankles would never work. He could scare up some rope and wrap it around both her and the bed in a tight coil from her armpits to her ankles, and maybe it would hold. It was a big maybe.

When she awoke, he would have to get through to her fast, to convince her she had reasons to keep living. And he really only had one thing to offer. He took off his shoes and climbed onto the bed beside her, draping himself over her thin, muscular body, his only hope resting on the possibility his presence would bind her to life a little longer.

On second thought…

He knelt and unfastened his belt. Raising her arms over her head, he wrapped the leather band around her wrists in a figure eight and then hitched it to the headboard. If it bought him two seconds, it was better than nothing.

Then he settled himself on top of her again, chest to chest, hip to hip, burying his face in the thick curtain of hair pooling beneath her neck. Her hyacinth scent passed over him like a time warp, carrying him back to one of those many nights on the beach. Uta had stood in the moonlit surf, her breeches rolled up to her knees, her hair loose and wild in the breeze. She could reach into the sea and grasp a fish in her lightning fast fingers, though when she tossed it to him, he missed half the time. When one slippery gray mullet shot through his fingers and wriggled down his half open shirt, she'd laughed, pushing her red locks off her forehead. She was a goddess, the most beautiful thing he'd ever set eyes on.

Stunned, he had frozen. "Uta," he said. Then he closed his mouth, unable to find words for what he felt.

But rather than teasing, she stared back at him with a look that mirrored his own awe, and in the light of her love, his little boy self had been whole. "Me too, Bel." She flashed the unguarded smile she reserved just for him, before crouching to grab another flailing fish.

Maybe it didn't matter how such a thing came to be, only that it had been, once. And for the possibility of sharing it once again, he would offer himself to her, gladly.

For the last day and a half, he'd expended nearly all his effort tamping down his desire, and as soon as he flipped the switch, it flared bright and hot, his cock roaring to life. Damn, he had no chance of sleep with a hard-on that could drill through the mattress if it weren't pressed against her taut belly.

She exhaled, and her breath, her presence cocooned him.

Oh God yes. Who needed sleep?

Lucas sat on the sofa. A fire burned in the parlor's fireplace and its slithering flames mesmerized him.

"How could this have happened?" Andre spoke without emotion, like a robot with a Croatian accent. He poured himself a glass of Blood Vine and held it two hands.

"I checked the perimeter an hour ago." Vania's voice trembled. "And the satellite images again before he left. They came out of nowhere."

"He insisted on leaving early. I tried to stop him." Again, Andre's words held no inflection. He sounded worse than when his vineyards had burned.

"Still, the car—it was armored and sun shielded," Sadavir rasped. "He should have been—"

"R.P.G.," said Omar. "It goes off anywhere near the petrol tank, armor does you no good."

"Who else was in the car?" Lucas asked.

"His blood slave—the blond woman," Vania replied.

Andre crossed to the hearth and rested his forehead on the high mantle. Zoey went to his side and stroked up and down his spine. He took a long swallow, and when he spoke again, he sounded more like himself.

"Sadavir, are you next in line?"

Sadavir cleared his throat. "That is a matter of some debate." He searched the room until his gaze settled.

Lucas turned to find the vampire had locked eyes with Nceba, who stood arm in arm with Derek.

"Sadavir's parents were untouchables in rural India," she said. "They had no way of recording his birth date."

He stood stiffly, his hands clasped behind his back. "And Nceba's were goatherds in Southern Africa, also without the means of date keeping. We know we were born within the same year, but not the month or even season."

"Am I correct in believing there are official means for settling this dispute?" Andre slumped against the wall. "Or must you fight to the death?"

Nceba clasped hands with Derek and her female blood servant, shaking her head. "I do not aspire—"

"No, sister. I defer. Given what we have learned, and your alliance with young Williams here, you are best suited to lead us. You have my pledge." He took two long strides and knelt at her feet.

She blinked, running her hands through his hair. "Thank you, old friend."

As the Justicia and Derek made plans to depart, Lucas watched the fire, and for the first time, he believed his plan might actually work.

CHAPTER 38

On the bottom shelf, Pedro discovered Ayal's sampling kit—a lightweight crowbar, a ladle, a small tin cup, and a sieve. He knew a little about how Georgians made wine in *qvevris*, enough to know a sludgy mess of stems and skins filled the terra-cotta jug. In taste, it would likely be drier than California wines, more like the Spanish blends his father had made. But with all that roughage in the fermentation process, would it taste harsh or just full bodied?

Leo interrupted his thoughts. "So, he's locked himself in there with her. It seems like maybe we have a second alone."

Pedro ran the flat end around the rim of the *qvevri*. The lid held fast, sealed together with the beeswax lining the jar. He wedged the levered end, but couldn't bring himself to press down. What if he damaged it?

"Listen kid, I'm not hungry. Hand me the crowbar."

Leo's yellow eyes moved up and down Pedro's body. "You must be hungry by now. So what are you afraid of? It's got to be either that I'll get clingy, or I'll try to squeeze between you and Lucas."

Pedro closed his eyes and let his head sag forward. "Kid, it's not about you. It's just Lucas being crazy jealous, like a character in one of his *telenovelas*."

"Yeah, right. Thing is, Lucas isn't here, and you're hungry. So what's the problem?"

The pleading in his voice demanded Pedro look up at him.

"Leo, how many times have you been bitten? I count two — Kos last month, and me the other day. Did you see Derek and Nceba go all soul mate after one bite? This Hunter-vampire mojo freaks me out. If Lucas turns, we'll both end up sucking on other guys' necks. How is that not going to screw up our relationship?"

"That's it? That's what you're worried about?" Leo's tone flipped like a pancake, becoming authoritative.

Pedro bristled, gripping the rim of the *qvevri*. What did the kid know to start talking to Pedro like he was stupid?

"Have you ever been bit? I'm no pro, but you're a fang virgin, dude. Sure, it feels awesome, like sex feels awesome, but it doesn't make you love somebody."

"Since when do you know what sex feels like?"

Leo's face drained of color.

Oops. Pedro wasn't supposed to know that. Leo had shared only with Lucas.

"Hey, man, I'm sorry. That was uncalled for."

"Yeah, and it's not true anymore either." Leo raised his chin.

Pedro tucked his chin, surprised. "No?"

"Nope."

"*Mierda*, spill, kid. There are only so many people at Kaštel." He ticked off the candidates on his fingers. "Not Andre, not Kos. Which leaves Bel's crew. Not Henry, or Arden…"

"It's not my place to — "

"Omar? No way!" Pedro hopped to his feet and crossed the room to slap Leo's back.

His only answer was to turn the color of a wine-stained shirt.

Which of course made Pedro lay it on harder. "Damn boy. I'm impressed. That's one fine dude. How on earth did you guys end up fucking?"

Leo coughed. "We prefer to say dating."

Pedro snorted. "What, like going to the movies?"

"We have, actually. Twice."

Pedro tried to imagine the giant African vampire with skin like the blackest night holding hands with little Leo, munching popcorn the next seat over. "Leo, he is ten times your age." Pedro didn't say size, but…damn.

"He's older, actually. I've always liked older guys." The kid's mouth spread into a big-ass grin.

Okay, he'd underestimated Leo. Pedro knelt down, tracing his finger round and round the rim of the *qvevri*, thinking.

Finally, he understood the point of Leo's speech. The kid had been schooling him. Pedro attempted to recite the lesson. "So Omar's bitten you, he's…um…*dated* you. But you're casual. You're not all 'I want to adopt kids with you' in love with him."

"Yep." Leo's baby face spread into another smile.

"And so, if I fed from you, it might be hot, but it would not be earth shattering."

"Also yep. What's between you and Lucas is bigger than a magical Hunter-vampire bond, dude. And I'm not going to change it. When he first mentioned you needed me, I inquired about the, uh, benefits. But now I'm not interested. You two are like a pair of girls with your drama. Threesomes, sure. Love triangles, no thanks."

Girls? Ouch. Pedro raked his fingers through his hair. "Point taken."

"So now, are you going to eat?" Leo tilted his head, his pulse a regular flicker under the pale skin of his neck.

Pedro's mouth watered. But if the wine proved to be like Blood Vine, he wouldn't need a snack. "Soon, kid. Let's crack this baby open, first."

He levered the stone cap off, and it opened with a pop. The acidic, mineral scent of the wine knocked Pedro back onto his ass. Oh yeah — good stuff, real good. Even the fumes coming off it made Pedro's sinuses tingle. Not a sliver of worry that he'd wind up puking his guts out; this stuff was more than vampire-safe. It was golden. Literally.

"Hhmm." Pedro shivered.

"Smells good, huh?" Leo raised up the ladle like he'd won an Oscar.

Pedro took it, scooping up enough to fill the tin cup and running it through the coarse sieve. Plenty of sediment passed through — this wine was meant to be drunk with chunks, which typically didn't agree with a vampire.

"*Salud.*" Pedro gripped the cup in shaking hands.

Leo tapped his knuckles against it in a toast.

Drawing the cup nearer to his face, Pedro inhaled deeply. Its powerful aroma sent more twitches and shudders through him, like an addict jonesing for a hit. Pedro's brain swam inside his skull and he wobbled.

"Whoa, big guy, maybe you should sit down."

Pedro slid along the rough wooden wall, acquiring a few sharp splinters through his shirt on the way, but his skin was already expelling them. Steadier with the solid floor beneath him, he raised the cup to his lips again and let a trickle of the deep purple liquid flow into his mouth. On one level, it tasted unremarkable. The kind of wine folks made in their cellars—simple and richly tanic. Its acids might not mellow in a hundred years. However, on the sensitive level of his tongue, the soft skin of his palate and the insides of his cheeks, the wine coated his mouth like warm honey, not sweet, but sharply, intensely, potent. And hot, very hot.

He gazed upward and honed in on a knotty beam in the ceiling, focusing to steady himself. He took another sip, the beam vanished into darkness, and gravity went wonky.

Power rushed through him, his hunger sated in an instant.

Leo gripped his shoulders and righted him. "Whoa. Are you still with me? Your eyes rolled all the way up." He unlatched Pedro's fingers from around the cup.

"Yeah, I'm here."

"So I have a question for you. If the Hunters and the vampires were all peace, love, and understanding before the war, why did they start making their magic wine?"

CHAPTER 39

Uta's mind came awake in a bright flash of consciousness. Her body remained paralyzed, her limbs lifeless. Breaths required immense effort, as if a great weight lay atop her chest. Her nose filled with the rich salty smell of the Adriatic, a scent which somehow clung to Bel always.

She opened her eyes, dry and gummy from sedation, and raised her head off the pillow. A single candle flickered across the room. His big head lay heavy on her breast. His hot breath blew over her chest and his black curls nearly tickled her nose. She moved to run her fingers through them, but her hands were bound.

Bound? What a sheep-brained idea —

She could snap free in an instant, but instead she wriggled, testing her range of movement. Pulled overhead at an unnatural angle, her shoulders cried out with a stiff, but not entirely unpleasant ache.

Maybe these bonds weren't such a stupid plan after all.

He shifted in his sleep, emitting a low groan, and pulled her closer with both arms encircling her ribcage. She became aware of his thick leg thrown over hers, his pelvis cradling her right hip, and against her thigh his cock pressed, half erect.

No, not a stupid plan at all. She smiled down at the crown of his head with pride, understanding his intentions. His arms and legs held her, and his desire manacled her, but his willingness was the ultimate restraint. He offered himself as an incentive for her to live.

She'd begged him for freedom, and promised his own.

But he chose her instead.

Her arms stung with the need to embrace him. But the elegance of the position had too much potential. If he needed to be her equal, to trust she would not try to dominate him, she could play along with the bonds. She attempted to slide her heels on the bedspread. They responded sluggishly. The sedative's effects were wearing off.

Gently, she jutted her hip into that flat plane between his navel and his cock. "Bel," she whispered.

"Hhmm?" he grunted.

The raw, unguarded syllable pierced her heart. It had been so long since she'd lain alongside a male, and even longer since one had slept in her arms. She'd forgotten the way sleep turned them into big children.

"Bel, thank you."

The black fringe of his lashes fluttered. She expected him to pull away, either in confusion or maybe even revulsion at the choice he'd made to save her. Instead, he rolled fully atop her, pushing up on his palms so his face hovered inches above hers.

"I'm ready now, to try." His green eyes shone with emotions, and she sensed them across their bond so clearly she could taste them. Love and longing and fear and lingering reservations, but all offered to her in good faith, which made her intentions all the more cruel.

She would take what he was offering just the once. How could she refuse, after so long? But they were doomed to fail, just like everything she attempted. From the days she allowed the Romans to colonize her people, to Loki's death today, it was clear she could not be trusted to protect what belonged to her, and so she had to set Bel free.

His handsome black brow furrowed, warning her he sensed her ambivalence. So she boxed up her grief and slammed the lid.

"My love, I have waited so long for you." She lifted her head and pressed their lips together in a bruising kiss.

"Ah, ah," he scolded, backing off. "We will do this slow, and right."

His words, his command melted her—with him, for now, she did not have to be queen, warrior, protector. She would just be his. He pulled his shirt over his head without artifice, as if he didn't know what the sight of his body would do to her.

She bit her lip. Of all the males she'd seen in her thousands of years, he was the perfect specimen. The hulking rounds of his shoulders, tapering into thick biceps, the broad and powerful chest, dusted with dark hair. Olive skin, slightly fairer than his father's, as if he'd been born immune to sunlight. So much the image of Andre, and yet Bel was the only one she desired.

He unbuttoned his jeans and slid them off along with whatever he wore underneath, exposing his full, naked beauty to her. He stood fully erect, but frozen, seeming to wait for her. A niggle of his doubt slithered inside of her—a youthful self-consciousness. Though he'd enjoyed the attention of countless women, this glorious male feared she might find him wanting.

"Bel. You are perfect. The most desirable male I have ever seen. I knew you would be, and I have long feared the power you would have over me."

His chin lifted and his mouth spread into a rare, wide smile. He shook his head. "A female as old as you would know how to flatter."

"True. I know the words males like to hear, but all you must do is open yourself to my feelings, and you will know I speak the truth."

He rested his big hands on his lean hips, affecting a playful posture—hiding behind it, she knew—while he tested their connection. His splendid chest rose and fell, and she drank him in, the trail of black hair tempting her gaze from his chest to his erection, a proud, dusky thing, both thick and long. Her mouth watered at the memory of tasting it.

He groaned. "Shite, Uta, it's the same for me." He rubbed his palms over his head, one after the other, making his chest even wider as his muscles flexed. "But doesn't it bother you that you didn't choose me, or this?"

She had to tell him the truth. In the days that followed, these words might make him hate her even more, but she owed them to him, and maybe, in a thousand years, they would ring sweet in his ears.

"Everything about you pleases me, Bel. Your mind, your brave heart, your companionability. To me, every female who is not fighting to win you is a fool. Maybe it would have been otherwise, without this bond. We cannot know. But you are the one I want, and I cannot find a single flaw with you, even when you drive me insane with your stubbornness."

He laughed, even as his shoulders and chest lifted proudly.

Encouraged, she went on. "I would do anything, submit to anything that would give you pleasure. My body and my soul belong to you, since the day you were born."

His smile turned into a full blown leer.

"Now, heart of my heart, would you please take off my clothes?"

"I'll do it when I damn well please. And that just happens to be now."

CHAPTER 40

Bel trembled on shaky knees. What the hell was wrong with him? He'd been naked with plenty of women, and he'd never heard any complaints. But this was Uta, the woman he'd desired before he even knew what desire was. He couldn't shake the fear that everything depended on this moment. Either he would be enough for her to live for, or not.

"Would you please take off my clothes?" she asked so sweetly, fully into the spirit of this little ruse.

He'd never understood role playing in the bedroom, but her willingness to stay in those bonds told him plenty, and his heart, and his cock, swelled with hope.

"I'll do it when I damn well please." He imagined his grin looked as huge as it felt on his face. "And that just happens to be now."

"Thank the gods," she whispered.

He reached for her shirt—a soft wisp of a thing, woven, without buttons or any way to open it. He gripped its neck with both hands and tried to rip it. It didn't give at all. "Shite, what's this thing made of?"

"Silk, and cashmere, and a little angora. I don't think you'll be able to rip it. If you just untie me for a mom—"

"No. Stay where you are, I'll find some scissors."

"No," she cried. "Please don't leave me. I don't want to be alone, not even for a minute."

He was an arsehole for forgetting her grief. Of course she didn't want to be alone.

"I knitted this sweater, and—"

He crossed his arms, struck by the absurdity of that claim. His vampire warrior queen knitting? "Yeah, right."

Her eyes narrowed. "If you must know, I needed a distraction when I sent you away. I had an excess of nervous energy."

"Oh." He swallowed. Over and over, she proved herself more sensitive and passionate than the memories he'd allowed himself of her.

"If you find the end of the yarn that is woven into the hem, you can unravel it."

His cock twitched in rebellion. "Won't that take forever?"

"It will be a slow, sensual torture, with the yarn running through your hands and across my skin, baring me one row at a time." She wriggled, pressing her torso against his knuckles. "But I want this to last as long as is possible."

Her voice choked with emotion, and he wanted to reassure her—they had as long as they needed.

Forever, maybe.

And with all the desire he'd been tamping down, he'd surely be able to satisfy her, even if he was only a halfling.

He sure wasn't in the mood to play Mr. Patient this first go round. But the idea of slowly unraveling that shirt pleased her, and pleasing her must be his priority. He brought the candle to the side of the bed and spotted a row of thickened stitches at the bottom of the shirt. With this thumb and forefinger, he pinched and pulled until he managed to free the strand of yarn.

"The first row will be difficult," she warned, "but then it will unravel with ease."

Her words proved true, as the first row required he pull the slippery silken floss through each stitch. Sweat beaded on his forehead and he nearly gave up. He could have her pants off and be inside her in an instant.

"Keep going, it will be worth it." She twisted onto her side so he could reach the back.

So he did. When he reached the end of the stitches she had bound together the yarn simply tugged free, row after row. With each round, she arched her spine and he reached beneath her, caressing the soft skin at the small of her back. At each brush of his fingers, she sucked in her breath. With her arms over head, her back curving, her small breasts jutting, nipples erect through the delicate fabric, she gazed at him from under half-lidded eyes. It must have required great restraint for her to remain bound up like that.

It humbled him.

A pile of unraveled yarn grew on her stomach and then slid off onto the mattress. When the sweater came only to the bottom of her rib cage, she began to writhe.

The throbbing in his cock grew painful. "Uta, I can't—"

She released a loud breath. "Thank the gods. I've been waiting for you to say that for ages."

He laughed, shoving the rest of her shirt up to bare the perfect sweet mounds of her breasts. He extended the broadest part of his tongue, wanting to taste as much of her as possible. Beginning at one under its curve, he licked upward until he reached that rigid nipple and latched on, drawing from her as if he could drink in her pleasure. A piercing pain in his gums stopped him short, and he reared back.

"What is it?"

He ran his tongue over his lips. "Toothache."

"You hunger for my blood. Can you smell it?"

Maybe that hyacinth perfume she radiated? "Yes."

"I want you to have it. But every time we share blood, the bond grows. Is that what you want?"

Her tone had grown grave, like she was warning him. He couldn't think about more and the future—all he knew was he needed her blood now. "Yes."

Her throat rippled with a swallow. "Go to the kitchen and bring back a knife."

"But you—"

"Please Bel. When you come inside me, I want to be inside you too. I can stand for you to leave me alone a moment for that."

At the memory of the metallic tang of her blood, he could think of nothing more erotic than to taste it again, and surely no better way to bind her to him. "Will you bite me?" His hand went to his neck and her gaze followed.

"I would like to very much. Will you let me?"

For some reason, the word caught in his throat. "Yes," he managed to croak.

He strode to the kitchen naked. The afternoon sun shone hot through the front windows. He'd slept the morning away on top of her, the longest stint of sleep he could recall in years. He found a sharp paring knife in the top drawer next to the sink.

Returning to her, he gripped its well-worn wooden handle and sliced the rest of her shirt off. He did the same with her pants, until he'd bared her completely. She parted her legs, revealing her pretty *pićka,* slippery and smelling richly of female and her own flowery scent. The ache in his gums stabbed at him again.

He chose a spot under her collar bone, well away from major arteries and veins, and traced it with his thumb. He didn't need a gusher, just a taste.

"Cut wide and shallow and slip your finger into the wound," she instructed him. "Then replace it with your tongue, or it will heal too quickly."

"Ready?"

She nodded, her eyes trained on the blade. He inserted it under the bone just until the blood began to flow and then widened the gash enough to accommodate his tongue.

She groaned when he covered the wound with his mouth and tasted the salt and sweet of her, laced with that floral perfume. It took every ounce of self-control not to come.

Damn. Superhero vampire erections might actually outweigh the no masturbating problem. If you had a lifelong mate, that was.

He savored her, first squeezing both her small breasts in his hands, then dipping one splayed palm between her legs. She spread them wider, and he penetrated her with two fingers. She tilted her pelvis, rocking on him, and her tongue glided over his neck, lingering on his pulse. He angled his head to better expose the artery, a submission he didn't begrudge in the least, not with all the ones she'd made.

"Ready, my love?"

My love. She means me.

He grunted a yes against her chest.

She struck fast and her fangs were white hot pleasure inside him. Their magic worked on him in wave after wave of arousal, his skin burned, his tongue thrust deeper into the wound in her neck, and then his gut melted with need. He couldn't wait any longer to have her. His face still pressed into her chest, he pulled his fingers out of her wet heat, and raised his hips to position himself.

No, this was wrong. He had to look at her. He lifted his head, tugging his neck from her grip.

She whimpered.

"I need to see your face. I need proof that this is happening."

In reply, her tongue lapped at his skin, which tickled as it knit back together.

"Yes," she whispered.

Finally, they faced each other nose to nose. Apologies and declarations of love and lewd intentions swirled in his mind like the frenzied lyrics of a punk song. His lips parted to speak, but no words completed the journey to his tongue.

Damn it. Her bottomless brown eyes rendered him speechless.

"I know all of it, Bel. You do not need to speak." She smiled like a woman who had watched empires rise and fall, but saw the sun and moon set with him. Whether she had chosen it or not—she wanted him and it shone on her face.

His heart erupted with tenderness, and he kissed the tip of her nose. Then, his cock parted the hot silk of her *pićka*, and he slid home. Yes. That's what she was—had always been—his home.

Her chin lifted and she tried to throw back her head.

"Don't you dare look away from me, Uta."

Her breaths came irregularly, her lips pressed together, and she nodded her acquiescence. At least he wasn't the only one undone.

Then he began to move.

Her core clenched around him instantly—she was already coming. Just barely, he resisted spilling inside her and gentled his thrusts. When her spasms subsided, he pressed her harder, driving her into the bed with everything he had. She met his force, slamming herself onto him and making feminine groans each time he stroked her core. He reached between them to touch her clit, and she squeezed him with even more force. Damn, vampires were strong everywhere.

"Oh gods of Illyria, Bel, please do not stop."

"Never, Uta. Now that we've started, I will never stop."

He hadn't planned to say it, hadn't even been sure until the words spilled out. Tears shimmered over the surface of her eyes, and one pink bead trickled down her temple into her hair.

He knew exactly how she felt, could very nearly have cried with his own relief. Together at last. The emotions overwhelmed him, and tipped him over the edge. He closed his eyes as the pleasure washed over him, and he collapsed on top of her, reveling in the fullness of their reunion.

The belt tore from the head board with a soft rip. Then her arms circled his shoulders, her hands tangling his hair. She pressed her lips to his ear and whispered. "Thank you, my love. I cannot possibly tell you how grateful I am for this gift. Please believe me when I say it was the greatest moment of my life."

Silly old girl, getting all sentimental on him. Not that he wasn't indulging in a little mush himself.

He squeezed her tight and rolled her on top of him. "You don't say?" He smoothed her gorgeous hair off her damp forehead and smiled up at her, expecting an amused look in return.

But instead the corners of her mouth turned down, and a furrow appeared between her eyes.

"Forgive me, my love." She brushed a kiss across his lips, and disappeared in a blur of motion.

Uta gazed down at Bel's ruggedly masculine face—all angles and stubble and sullen beauty, his mouth pouting even when he teased. By all the gods, she wanted to stay with him, and laugh, and joke, and share pleasures with him forever.

But he couldn't possibly mean the promises he had uttered, still could not imagine what forever really meant. Clearly, he had given himself to her impulsively, an attempt at heroism he had not yet had time to second guess.

But he would.

She would fail at the task Rize had given her, fail to stop the violence, and Bel would leave her.

This way, he would finally be free. It was so much easier for them both.

"Forgive me, my love."

She could not trust her feet, so she flew, a straight shot down the hall, piercing the front door like a missile. She landed barefoot in cool grass, and just like the other times, the sun blanketed her bare skin, its first kiss pleasant and warm before the pain of searing flesh reached her brain.

However, it did not.

A cool breeze blew, tightening her skin into goose bumps. She stood in the clearing in front of the house, surrounded by evergreens. She stood in the sun for the first time in the millennia.

No. It could not be. She had only fed from a Hunter on that one instance, weeks ago.

As if in slow motion, Bel appeared in the doorway, his jaw set, his expression stony. Leo pushed in alongside him, looking Uta up and down.

She followed the path of his gaze, realizing she was completely naked.

"Well," he said, "this is awkward."

Indeed. Shamefully bare, and having failed even at killing herself.

"You are a coward," Bel spat. "Just like my mother."

"Your mother erred by allowing Andre to bond to her," Uta cried, pleading for him to understand. "With her suicide she spared them both an eternity of misery."

Bel exhaled through his nose. "And abandoned her little boy." Shaking his head, he turned back toward the house.

She had wounded him again, had thrown all he offered away for nothing, and she no longer had any escape. "Bel, wait!"

He did not, but he shouted over his shoulder. "If you want to be a hero like Mila, next time, make sure you succeed."

CHAPTER 41

Lucas lay on his too-empty bed, staring at his phone. No news from Pedro.

His man hadn't called him to say hi, to say I love you, to say, don't worry, I don't want to fuck pretty little Leo. And any second now, Lucas might jump right out of his tight, stir-crazy skin.

After Loki's death, a mournful hush had fallen over the estate. The initial reports had arrived from the first round of friendly kidnappings, but then his computer had gone quiet too. His plan was underway and he could only wait while, all around the world, several hundred Hunters were being subjected to some friendly fang.

He envied them. He hadn't been apart from Pedro this long since he'd come to Kaštel, and he missed the friendship and the fang. Loneliness gnawed at him, that and hunger. But nothing settled in his stomach right.

He needed a distraction from this misery, so he stomped through the cellar and when he reached the makeshift cell, he didn't knock. No need to extend politeness to his brother's punching bag girlfriend. She had to be responsible for the explosion that killed Loki, but Lucas couldn't guess how she'd gotten news of the Justicia's departure to the Hunters from inside the estate.

He slid the bolt and swung the door wide. She'd clearly heard him coming, and had backed herself against the far wall. Not a hint of fear showed on her impassive face and it enraged him, sending blood to pound in his ears. He would find out how she was communicating with Ethan, or convince one of these torture-reticent vampires to get it out of her.

Oh right, this bitch liked torture. They might have to give her what she wanted.

His heart pounded hard against his sternum. He closed the door and leaned against it, crossing his arms to quiet the hyperactive organ in his chest. "Loki's dead."

Her chin came up like a frightened rabbit. "How?"

"A rocket-propelled grenade blew up his car."

"Oh no." She deflated, sinking inches down the wall. "He was very kind, and so old. All that knowledge…"

"He was uncertain whether to trust you. I, however, am not. Your being here has Ethan written all over it. He loves Trojan horses. Zoey was his first."

Gwen pressed her tongue between her lips for a moment before she spoke. "Then why are you here?"

"Did you know about the bomb?"

"No."

He wanted to throttle her frail neck, but he fisted his hands and pressed against the door instead. "Liar. What else is Ethan planning? Does he know how the shield works?"

"He never shared things like that with me, just demanded I translate his precious codex." Her peevish tone nearly persuaded him, but not quite.

"I know you are communicating with him."

"How could I? Zoey searched me."

She made perfect sense, and it infuriated him even more. He broke out in a sweat, and trembled with anger. "You're on the wrong side, Gwen. Ethan is not the good guy."

She lowered her head. "I know that. But if you don't believe me, just leave me be. I'm fine here. I'm safe, as long as I'm away from him."

"No. You're not. No one is safe until this war ends. A war he escalated by stirring up all this violence. Did you see them, Gwen, the women and children he sacrificed to his cause?"

She closed her eyes and swallowed, by all appearances the first genuine response she'd showed.

"If that's how you feel, tell me what you know."

"I don't know anything." Tears shimmered in her eyes, another false emotion, a watery curtain to hide behind.

Perhaps he had to speak Ethan's language to get through to her — a disgusting last resort. He raised his hand to hit her.

A white hot pain pierced his gut and he doubled over. She stood against the wall, hands pressed flat, her mouth fallen open — just as surprised as he was. The pain knotted and twisted, like someone turned a giant corkscrew inside him. Then he toppled, and the world went black.

Gwen stared at the crumpled form of Lucas at her feet, then across the cement floor at the gray steel door, closed but unlocked.

His warm breath against her hand confirmed he was alive. How long would he be out? She gently shook his shoulder, but he didn't murmur or stir at all.

His unexpected faint provided her a way into the house. If she came across someone, she could claim to be searching for help. But hopefully she would find the shield instead. She glanced at the pillow on the bed. Would it buy her more time to smother him with it?

Maybe.

She reached for the pillow, hugging it to her chest and contemplating his face. In profile, he more strongly resembled Ethan — a square jaw set off with a long, straight nose. She didn't have the will to suffocate him.

She tossed down the pillow and hurried toward the door, but paused with her hand on its lever to slip off her shoes — anything to make her quieter in a house full of creatures with the keenest hearing.

In the cellar, she explored every dark, brick-walled passageway, peering between rows of barrels and racks of wine bottles. Her toes ached on the cold stones. She tiptoed toward a closed door at the end of a hall and pressed her ear to the door — nothing.

She made her way to the stairs, which opened onto the entryway of the house. A glance at the windows revealed a midday sun. Millimeter by millimeter, she closed the door to the cellar, wincing as the latch clicked into place. Still, all remained silent. No television, no voices, no dishes clanging in the kitchen. Then a faint tapping registered in her ears, the sound of fingers on a keyboard from a nearby room. Through its doorway, no people or vampires were visible, only a large table. She skirted the wall so that she could slink up to the side of the door and listen. Some minutes passed — she didn't know how many but they crawled, each heartbeat like the deafening tick of a clock.

"Had you met Loki before?" a woman's voiced asked as someone still tapped away.

"Many times. Sly old chap, but I…" The rumbling British voice trailed off into a heavy sigh. "I admired him."

Gwen itched at her sternum. She'd liked him as well, would have loved to ask him a dissertation's worth of questions.

A crinkling sound like the wrapper on a candy bar startled her.

"That was the last energy bar. Want me to fetch some more?" the male asked in a low voice.

"This will hold me over for now. And I'm sick of this health food Lena's put me on. I'm ready for chocolate ice cream again."

"Someone should tell her witches don't eat granola."

Gwen stiffened. A witch, just as Loki had said. The woman speaking must be the one he'd called Trys.

She giggled. "Believe me, I've tried, but Lena always makes such logical arguments about nutrition, and she's so sweet."

Their conversation lulled, and Gwen's mind rotated pieces of information like a puzzle, but they wouldn't form a whole.

The feet of a chair scraped against the floor. "I hate sitting here, safe and sound, but perfectly helpless," said the male.

"You're telling me. I haven't left the estate in months. But Bel would kill us if we let anything happen to his family, so I'm stuck."

"Sugar, we are all damn lucky you are here. Do I tell you enough what a good job you're doing?"

"Mmm. You can rub my shoulders all day, Omar, but don't try that Barry White stuff on me just because your piece of young ass is out of town."

He let out a good-natured belly laugh. "I'm just being a good friend."

Gwen's breastbone itched some more. She envied their easy rapport. Not since before Mason had she been able to joke around with men, to flirt, to relax. But was this Omar a man, or a vampire?

"Yeah right." Trys groaned in pleasure. "You've lured me into your bed with this friendly gesture one too many times. I won't be fooled again."

"Hey. You never complain." His baritone dripped with suggestion.

"Besides, it's awfully difficult to maintain the shield when I get, you know, orgasmic."

"Poor Trys. You are making a heroic sacrifice for all of us." His voice dropped even lower. "When this mission ends, I will reward you over, and over, and over again."

Once upon a time, Gwen might have found his promise arousing, but now it left her unaffected. She tessellated the data again—Trys maintained the shield, which required her concentration. Was it controlled by the computer?

An electronic bell dinged, probably signifying a message of some sort.

"Huh. Look at this," the witch said.

"Well, I'll be. Converts." Omar clicked his tongue. "Lucas's crazy-ass plan might just work."

Converts? Gwen sucked in a breath—too loud.

"What was that?" Omar asked, his deep voice penetrating the thunder of her blood in her eardrums.

She began inching toward the kitchen.

"I didn't hear anything," Trys replied.

"Well you wouldn't, would you?"

"We're all just jumpy, after—"

"Shhh."

Gwen slipped into the open door as his heavy feet thudded on the floor. She darted through the unlit and blessedly empty kitchen into a dark hallway. An open door led into a pantry of some sort.

She entered just as Omar called into the kitchen. "Lena?" After an eternal silence, he muttered, "Gods of my father, I am jumpy."

Gwen didn't dare move until his footsteps were a distant creak on the floor. She slunk into the darkest corner, wedging into a crevice between a shelf and the wall that wouldn't have fit a larger woman. And she thought some more.

Months—a witch—magical powers—orgasms—oh. Wow. The computer had nothing to do with it. Trys was somehow generating the shield herself, which meant if Gwen disabled her, Ethan could enter the estate.

She would have to risk calling him from the kitchen phone. Summoning up the self-control required to face Ethan, she swallowed her fear and crawled on her hands and knees through the kitchen. She examined the phone until she found its volume control and turned it as low as possible.

He answered after one ring. "Bennett."

"It's me," she whispered.

"Is it done?"

"Soon. Be ready." She wanted to tell him to keep his forces out of the vampires' sight and not to alert them, but such advice would overstep her purview. She had to trust him, and live or die with the consequences if he did otherwise.

"Good girl," he said, and the phone went dead.

She hung it in its base and then ran into the hall shouting at the top of her lungs. "Help! Help! It's Lucas. Something's wrong. He fainted!"

Feet pounded the floor from both directions as the entire household converged on the foyer.

"He's in my room, and I can't wake him up."

CHAPTER 42

Bel stormed into the house, pushing past Pedro.

"*Mierda,* Bel. I'm sorry. I knew she was a psycho bitch."

"Not helping."

"I'm thinking this is a good time to go catch some rays. Do a little grape vine detective work. Hey, I like that. Grape vine detectives. Maybe I can have my own reality T.V. show."

Bel ignored him. He beelined for the kitchen and began searching for anything alcoholic to consume. What had he been thinking, traveling halfway around the world with Uta sans bourbon? He should have commandeered one of her suitcases and brought a dozen bottles.

There was one dusty jug of raki, Turkey's national spirit, under the sink, next to the cleaning supplies. He poured a glass half full and filled the rest from the slightly sulfurous tap water, watching it turn cloudy. The anise overpowered any foul taste in the H_2O. He downed it all at once and poured another glass, this one to sip.

Outside, the booming sound of Pedro's laughter traveled over the surface of the lake and echoed off the mountainsides. The windows practically shook with his joy at the feel of the sun. Bel swallowed his bitterness and raised his glass in the direction of his brother's laughter.

Time to snoop around Ayal's house. This trip would be a waste unless he found something here. It tormented him to think of getting close enough to Uta to collect his before-and-after data now. Shite. Maybe he'd man up to the task with enough raki. He'd been stupid to trust her, but he couldn't let her ruin his chances at a breakthrough.

He found nothing noteworthy in the kitchen. Near her reading chair, a book shelf housed a collection of volumes in various European and Central Asian languages. Hell, there was even Japanese poetry. Apparently Ayal had not been wasting her five-thousand-year lifespan watching TV. Bel would have to give Pedro a nudge in the right direction.

His drink sloshed as he climbed the stairs to the loft — an art studio. Skylights in the A-frame bathed it with light. Oil paintings, sketches and sculptures occupied every surface. They demonstrated a range of styles — some pieces realistic, and others abstract. But it was the most primitive, expressionistic paintings that drew Bel from across the room. They weren't old by any means — the paint shone and the canvases stretched taut on their frames — but they were mythic.

Similar in composition to the illustrations Bel had already seen, some paintings depicted everyday life in the vampire paradise, and others showed its violent end. Yet these moved him in a way the others had not. In the tones of red, gold, and black, Bel saw that time through the eyes of a child drowning in awe, anger, and fear — a similar cocktail to the one keeping him afloat at the moment. If only she had stayed, Bel could have met her, another halfling, who had known the tyranny of blood bonds gone wrong even as a child.

Under one of the canvases, she had tucked a small bit of paper. This one was a highly detailed, precise line drawing. The horizontal line of the soil bisected the page. In the center of the page, a *qvevri* was buried underground. On both sides were the roots of what looked like trees, but proved to be people — or more likely vampires — rooted to the earth. One vampire had been chained to the unrooted humans in the picture. The other vampire was clothed only in vines.

Bel folded the paper and slid it into the pocket of his jeans.

Heavy footsteps slogged on the front deck and a moment later, the front door opened.

"We've got a match, Bel. Gold rimmed leaves."

Bel came down from the loft and bent over the table where Pedro had laid out a brown leaf next to a photo from Andre's vineyard. "Tell me what I'm looking at here."

Pedro smoothed the crinkly five-pointed leaf. "You're looking at Blood Vine, or a close relative."

"And the wine?"

Leo pulled up a chair at the table.

"Not as tasty," Pedro replied. "But a helluva lot stronger. I'd stake my honor on the fact it's a cure."

"Your honor? You sound like Andre."

"Did you hear me, bro? It's a win. We found another cure."

"Cool huh?" Leo chirped. "Now tell him my question."

Bel felt Uta without seeing or hearing her, and when he glanced up, she stood at the front door, a rosy glow on her cheeks. Somehow, with that kiss of sun on her face, she was even more beautiful, and he hated her for it.

He would never be able to think with all this fury pumping through him. He needed her to get the hell away from him, and he opened his mouth to bark out a command. But a sentiment tugged at him over their connection—gentle, the warmth of a wordless apology—not enough to inspire forgiveness, or heal what she'd broken, but an acknowledgment of his right to anger.

He sucked air down into the very bottom of his lungs, and on the exhale he found she'd given enough. He could now tolerate her presence.

"What's your question, kid?"

"Why did they make the wine in the first place? If vampires were so cozy with the Hunters, they didn't need a replacement for blood."

Uta came to stand at the table. "On Šolta we drank Andre's wine instead of blood—not entirely of course, but it freed us from relying so heavily on the household servants."

Bel's palm went to his back pocket and he slid his fingers inside, scraping his fingernails along the paper.

Pedro's phone rang, jolting Bel out of his irate trance. At least this time it wasn't all three phones buzzing at once.

Pedro slid his phone from his pocket. Andre's name appeared on the screen.

"What's up, big guy?"

"Brace yourself."

That could only mean one thing.

"Is he dead?" *Jesu Cristo*, wouldn't Pedro know, feel it? Wasn't that how a bond worked?

"No. But he is sick, Pedro. Very sick. I blame myself."

"What kind of sick?"

"It is cancer. I can smell it coming off his skin. But I did not notice because the Hunter scent was—"

"Cancer?" Fuck. Pedro must have smelled to too then, only he hadn't recognized it. "Let me talk to him."

Bel appeared at Pedro's elbow, and lowered him to sit on a stool.

"He is weak," Andre warned. "He was bleeding inside, and he collapsed."

Bel held his hands up in question.

Pedro pushed him out of the way and shouted at Andre. "*Hijo de puta*, put him on the line."

The phone was jostled for a few seconds before Lucas's voice rasped like dry leaves. "Hey."

"Let him turn you. Now."

"Hello to you too." A smile raised the pitch of his whisper.

It only made Pedro angrier, his chest tightening. "I cannot lose you. Do not be stubborn about this." His gaze darted to Leo. "We will solve the feeding problem somehow."

"I know. I know." *Gracias a Dios*, no hesitation colored his words. "But not Andre, okay? I want it to be you—I want you to turn me."

Pedro blew out a breath. He wanted that too. "I'll leave right away. We'll be there by sundown tomorrow. Give Andre the phone."

More thuds and crackles sounded as they passed the device.

Then Andre spoke. "Son, I am so sorry that I allowed this to happen." Typical—just like Uta, just like Bel—he took responsibility for the whole world.

Good. Pedro needed him to be responsible. "Shut up and listen. You do not leave his side. Any sign he is weakening, slipping, you turn him, no matter what he says."

"Of course. He belongs to my household, son. It is my duty."

No, he belonged to Pedro. But they could argue that point later. "There's something else."

Andre waited, silent.

Pedro wished like hell he wasn't delivering this news over the phone. "Uta walked in the sun—"

Andre roared. "*Davo*. Is she—"

"She's fine. Unharmed. *Puta* has a tan. Or she did five minutes ago."

"By the gods of my father. Are you saying—"

"She fed from Derek once, a month ago, and she can tolerate the sun."

"We can tell no one."

"*Nada.*"

"We cannot even risk being seen…" Andre had never sounded so forlorn.

"Big guy, you'll get your chance, I promise. Now, we've gotta get on the road. We're a long way from the plane."

"Journey safely," Andre said, as Pedro ended the call.

Leo and Bel both stared at him like they'd swallowed vinegar. "Don't give me that pity shit. Load up the car. We're gonna get there in time, and if we don't Andre's on it. Where's Uta?" He looked around.

"I have loaded the truck." She flew down the stairs carrying the gnarled stock of a vine. Dirt fell in clumps from its rootball. She jutted it toward Leo. "Carry this. I also want to return with one of these." She dropped to her knees next to the *qvevri*.

The one out front was taller than her and from this one's opening, Pedro guessed it would be the same size. He lunged for her. "Uta wait."

He was too late. She twisted the nearest jar, dislodging it from the soil, and corkscrewed the thing right out of the earth. More than six and a half feet tall, it easily weighed five hundred pounds. Not a locomotive, but still—impressive.

She reached her arm high and knocked on the top of the amphora. "How tight is the seal? Will it spill in the truck?"

"Not if you hold it up between your knees, sweetheart."

She hissed at him, and from some surprising place inside him, he found the ability to laugh. Yeah. He could laugh. Deep down, he knew Lucas would be okay. And his. Forever.

She hugged it to her torso and hefted it. "We will angle it upright with the suitcases in the cargo area and secure it with rope."

She glanced at Bel and rubbed one wrist and then the other. Was the crazy bitch wishing she'd stayed put? Probably. Pedro scratched his head. Did living forever make everyone bonkers or just her? Most days, Andre was pretty sane.

It didn't matter anyway. It was his fate, and now it was Lucas's too.

CHAPTER 43

Gwen pressed her spine to the wall outside of her cell while inside, Andre Marasović murmured to Lucas, who sounded dazed.

"That is quite a bruise developing on his abdomen." The vampire raised his voice, presumably speaking to the others.

"An internal bleed." That was the dark-skinned vampire, who sounded like a British Barry White. "Trys, can you try your thing on him?"

"Good chance I can stop the bleeding, but if you smell cancer on him—well, there's nothing I can do about that."

"Stabilize him, if you can," Andre said. "I will call Pedro."

They seemed to have forgotten about Gwen. On her bare toes, she sprinted to the other side of the workroom and ducked behind the long worktable. All she had to do was get the woman called Trys alone and…

And kill her.

Ethan hadn't exactly prepared Gwen for that possibility. Killing a woman, face to face, was very different than simply leaving a household of vampires vulnerable to their enemies. Gwen had no inclination to do violence, found the idea of causing harm repulsive. But she did like violence done to her. She would have to draw on her lust for her own harm.

At just over five feet, she stood inches shorter than the other woman. She would need a sharp weapon and the advantage of surprise.

She backtracked to the kitchen in search of a knife. She found a box-cutter in a drawer of miscellany, and then wedged herself into a cabinet in the dining room. Curled up on her side, she rested her hands on her head. Not exactly a feather mattress, but she'd found far worse hiding places at Mason's—a cleaning closet full of chemicals to mask her scent; a hot noisy, crevice behind the boiler to cover the sound of her breathing. He'd always found her, until she'd given up all hope of escape.

Now in the cozy cabinet, she just needed Trys to show up alone.

CHAPTER 44

Exactly how she had wound up underneath a giant terra-cotta jar of wine in the cargo area eluded Uta. None of the three males, supposedly superior at spatial organization, had managed to arrange the luggage more comfortably. Or perhaps they were punishing her.

Dazed under the singeing glory of the sun, she'd been shoved in the back and told to hold on to the amphora, tight. Since when did people tell her what to do?

A bitter burst of laughter erupted from her — since her whole world had been inverted, the moon no longer her sun.

Unsurprisingly, no one remarked on her hilarity.

She stared out the tinted window, blinking at the white ball of the light, dimmed to not-quite-blinding by the tinted film on the window. It might take her a hundred years to adjust to this new freedom.

Thank all the Illyrian gods for Pedro's little crisis, providing a distraction from her new state of aimlessness. Her longing for Bel had not changed, but she had no right to hope for him. In her veins, the buzzing power of the homeland waned as they drove from Ayal's mountain home. Her muscles turned the consistency of mushy human food — gruel, or custard, or that foul-smelling modern invention, Jell-O.

Bel sat in the back seat, catty-corner to her. Close, but across a wide gulf she had created by abandoning him once again. The muscles in his jaw bulged like smooth rocks, occasionally twitching. His lush lips pressed into a thin white line. He wasn't bothering to block her from his furious pain, and it wrung at her like she was a wet rag. When she had made the decision to die, she certainly had not planned to face him afterward.

Leo hunched over a GPS. Pedro sat straight-backed behind the wheel, intently focused on the road, and doubtlessly ruminating over the fate of his mate. They were no barrel full of apes, or orangutans, or whatever the stupid expression was. She closed her eyes and fixated on the punishment Bel's emotions wrought inside her.

"Uta?" Pedro asked, startling her.

She glanced at his eyes in the rearview mirror.

"How close do you think Ayal's house is to the actual place the Hunters and vampires lived together?"

Leo turned down the grating dance music.

Bel twisted to look at her. She wasn't certain whether she was glad for the eye contact, or if she preferred him shirking it.

She gazed up at the gray fabric lining the ceiling of the vehicle. "Perhaps between fifty to seventy-five kilometers? A good distance in the days of travel by foot."

"That's easily covered by horseback," Bel argued.

"True. And I do not know if the Hunters possessed horses, but Ayal fled the chaos as a child on foot. She likely escaped only because they believed her dead."

Leo whistled. "Poor girl."

"Indeed." Uta inhaled, her pity for the ancient halfling merging with the rest of her despair like puddles coalescing in a rainstorm. "She has been alone for a long time, knowing nothing of happy households or thriving enclaves. I hope she will find happiness now."

Leo turned and spoke over his shoulder. "Uta, how did you become a vampire?"

Pedro chuckled. "Kid, to vampires, that's a personal question. Like asking a lady her age, or her weight, only worse."

"Oh, sorry."

Uta frowned at Pedro's reflection. "How gentlemanly of you to correct him."

Amused creases formed at the edge of his golden eyes. "*De nada.* Truth is, I don't want to get covered in blood if you decide to rip his head off."

A smile tugged at her lips, but she fought it.

"But I don't understand," Leo said. "Why is it impolite to ask?"

Bel let out an exasperated breath. "Think, kid—it usually involves a lover, or a near death experience. It's like casually asking a stranger how he lost his virginity."

Uta studied Bel's profile—chiseled cheeks, strong chin. He had been so gawky—all nose and ears—when that human girl from a neighboring vineyard had deflowered him. Uta had heard of their flirtation. From a distance she had sometimes watched him go about his chores or with his friends in the evening—but only when it did not pierce her heart. She had witnessed him steal off with the girl, and because she was neither a pervert nor a masochist, had gone home. Across the thin thread of their bond, she had sensed a change in him after that night, a shadow of fear that everything in his life would be as unsatisfying as his first tumble in the grass with that girl. Uta had wept for days over the disaster she had made of their lives.

He jerked toward her all at once, coloring, his eyebrows knitting together. "What?"

"I did not say a thing." She shrugged.

He pulled one corner of his mouth to the side in a crooked frown, his fist pressing against his breastbone. "No, but you—"

Sweet Auntie Europa. Time to change the subject. "Leo, I would be delighted to tell you the story."

"Really?" The child's voice lifted in boyish delight.

If he became a vampire, he might preserve the same eternal youthfulness Loki had had. To her astonishment, the idea comforted her. Maybe she would offer to turn him, if—

She shook the inkling of optimism right out of her head and closed her eyes, descending into the memory of her ancient past.

"It began when my husband died."

Bel's head jerked, and the bench shifted against her side. Had that gotten his attention? It was only a small part of the story.

"Agron had been a minor king, and I ruled in his place, a regent for his son Pinnes. I led our armies into battle against the tribes of Serbia and Macedonia. And our ships captured many Roman vessels. We prospered—too much so. Our successes drew the attention of the Roman senate. They sent two diplomats to negotiate with me. I informed them it was the right of my people to conduct their ships however they chose and if they found piracy profitable, I was pleased for them. They had broken no Illyrian laws."

Bel snorted. "Of course you did."

She tamped down a surge of self-pity. He had accepted her, and she had rejected him. She had no right to expect understanding. All she could do was stare at the sneer on his face until he glanced away.

"Just get on with your story," he said.

"The envoy warned me that Rome did not like my laws, and had the capacity to impose its own. So I had his ship seized. He was killed in the fray."

Bel shook his head. "You provoked an empire out of pride."

"No. I exercised my sovereignty to defend the independence of my people. With a great iron hammer, Rome was imposing her version of peace on the region. We preferred to fight than surrender to be flattened. They arrived with twenty thousand troops, two hundred cavalry units and an entire fleet of two hundred ships."

She ran her palm along the rough curve of the amphora. Something about the rugged feel of the stoneware dragged her even deeper into the past, and she seethed at the memory.

"My sheep-brained governor Demetrius surrendered. He had coveted my role as regent, and the Romans made him a puppet ruler over half of Illyria. But my men fought for their freedom anyway, and most of them died, martyrs for their homeland."

Bel tilted his head and the movement caught her eye. She met his gaze.

"Perhaps it seems frivolous to you—a meaningless fight. But it was everything to us, our right to determine our own laws, and rule our own land."

"No, it doesn't. I just..." His focus wandered as his words trailed off.

She leaned closer, following his line of sight, and found they had left the mountains behind and entered the large, sparse valley that cradled Ezerum. Grassy golden fields and rocks of a similar color rendered the landscape nearly monochrome in the bright afternoon sun. If Pedro stopped the vehicle, she could stroll right across the land, a dot of red hair in a gray suit on a bland backdrop, could vanish like Ayal.

"Well, get on with it already," Pedro barked.

She jerked her head up, startled to see him watching her. She drummed her fingernails against the ceramic jug one, twice, before she found where she'd left off. "The Romans besieged me in Scodra, on what is now the Albanian coast. I pretended to surrender, agreeing to their terms and a large tribute. They retreated, but I defied them, so they pushed us north into Dalmatia. I lived on the battlefield with my men. I wanted to fight alongside them, but they would not let me. They guarded my honor as a chaste queen and mother to Pinnes."

Pedro laughed. "Chaste and maternal is how I always think of you."

Wistful, she shrugged. She had been those things once.

"Rize found me there, and stole into my tent one night where I dined with my officers. They raised their swords at him, but he lifted only his palms. He looked me in the eye and spoke in a coarse language roughly similar to ours, asking if I was Queen Teuta. I nodded, and from there I only understood a few of his words. Fight, fuck, food — that was the gist of it. He was rugged and dark and handsome, he radiated a mysterious power, and he promised a respite from the terrible monotony of our losing predicament, so I consented to provide all three."

Near her temple, Bel's hand squeaked where he compressed the leather seat-back in his big hand. The bond ruled them with a tyranny not unlike an oppressive empire and, even now, after she had trodden on his heart and set fire to his trust, he could not help but be jealous.

She wanted to stroke his ropy forearm and remind him that Rize had been dead for centuries. But if he jerked away from her touch, her instincts would demand she grab hold of him and she might not ever be able to let go.

"My men flanked me. One stepped forward to fight and Rize disarmed him in two clean moves. I demanded he stop before killing the man. One more general put up a fight and it ended similarly. And so I took Rize to my bed."

Bel's fingertips dug into the black leather, filling her aching heart with a senseless pleasure.

She licked her lips. "Before we had even undressed or laid down, his fangs speared me and took me beyond any pleasure old Agron had provided. Afterward, in the most basic words, Rize explained what he was — blood, night, fangs, strength. He wanted to make me like him, not out of love, but some need not to be alone."

"*Madre de Dios*, you were scary even as a human. No wonder he wanted to turn you."

She smiled to herself. "I was fierce, yes, and I agreed for all the usual reasons. After that, we attacked the Romans at night, and I fought alongside my men. They loved me even more for it, as if I risked as much as they did. I still cannot forgive myself for that deception."

Bel's hand relaxed and his arm slid down the back side of the bench. His eyes, however, did not leave the window.

After a long stretch on this straight highway, the GPS spoke. "In three kilometers, turn right."

They neared the airport. She would have to rush the remainder of her story.

"Night after night, we defeated the Romans, but they only sent more and more soldiers. Even with the combined strength of Rize and me, they decimated my army. My men refused to surrender, until finally, Rize helped me fake my death."

Leo whistled. "Man. Where did you go?" Leo asked, his voice unusually solemn.

"We settled on Šolta, close enough to where he turned me that I would thrive. He taught me the old ways, helped me establish a household and instructed me in my duty to care for them — another, smaller kingdom for me to govern. A few years later, he left me. Soon thereafter, Andre arrived and was turned against his will by those reckless ones bent on repopulating vampires. He ran feral until I tamed him."

Had Andre ever told Bel about his horrible, early days, left without guidance to survive all the changes? She could not guess, since Bel refused to look at her. She reached out for him over the bond, but sometime during her story, he had erected his emotional wall again.

"Your destination is on the left," said the automated voice of the GPS.

Finally he turned to her. "I think your friend there will need her own seat on the plane." He rapped his knuckles on the amphora, his words tripping out quickly with the joke, as if it escaped him without permission.

Uta hesitated before braving a smile. "Yes, I think she will."

Chapter 45

Bel followed Uta onto the plane. She nestled the *qvevri* against the front bulkhead like it was no heavier than a vase of flowers and then took a seat in the farthest back row. If she'd looked up even once to track his choice, he'd have sat next to the wine, but she didn't—she only stared out the porthole-shaped window, and he found himself next to her, needing to know more of her story.

She'd begun to flip through her Turkish fashion magazine again and didn't look up.

Across the aisle and up two rows, Pedro slumped in his chair, arms crossed over his stomach, his little white earbuds in his ears. Since he was out of sight, Leo must have chosen the seat by the wine.

Bel didn't speak until the engines started up and they began to taxi down the runway.

He didn't give her a warning, just turned to face her. "Did you love Rize?"

She tucked her chin. "Yes, of course. In every way—a father, a brother, a friend, a lover."

"I see." He stiffened, hating that he cared.

"You do not see anything. But you may ask me, if you truly want to understand."

"He left you, and so you created me."

She laughed, and he blushed, realizing the childishness of his assertion.

"That was not a question. And you already know I did not create this bond on purpose. But the moment you were born, I knew in my every cell that my love for you would be limitless compared to my affection for Rize. He was damaged—beyond repair, I thought—by the death of his family during the massacre."

"You thought?"

She twisted at the waist to face the window again, and Bel could not fathom her thoughts or read her expression from the sidelong angle. Finally she spoke, and her moist breath fogged the glass.

"The note he left me was astonishing."

"What did it say?"

The porcelain skin of her throat rippled with a swallow.

Instinctively, he swallowed too. "Please tell me."

"It said he had begun to hope for a reconciliation, and if he failed, he wanted me to accomplish it."

"Son of a bitch. After you cut out your tongue to keep your vow of silence?"

"It healed. We always heal, Bel. With enough time." She took his hand as if offering comfort to a child, frightened from a fall, but not injured. Then she spoke again into the window. "Just like Rize healed."

Inside his fortress of solitude, panic roiled up in him like a churning wave, the flotsam and jetsam of all that had happened bobbing up only to be dragged back down by the undertow.

"If you believe that, why the hell did you run from me?"

"You are not a wound that can heal. You are a thorn that I carry under my skin. It will pain me as long as we live." She turned away again. "I am tired of fighting. But it is not just you. It is also Loki, and the war, and Rize's imbecilic letter. My life is an endless battle."

Yes, and like the Romans, the Hunters kept coming, taking everything from her, even her will to live. Yet she managed to hold onto her brash pride, and he admired the hell out of her for it.

It is not just you.

Some part of him despised those words—the abandoned boy inside him that needed everything to be about him. He wanted to be enough of a reason to live, and she'd shown him unequivocally he was not.

And she was right. Love didn't fix everything. Not with him and Lexi, not with Andre and Mila, and not now either.

She wiped the cloud of her breath from the window. "If I am honest, I did not truly love him."

"No?"

"He was my master and he demanded obedience. We were not equals. In the end, he was only my sire, and it was best for me to strike out on my own."

"We aren't equals either, Uta."

A crease formed between her auburn eyebrows. "Of course we are. We are a part of each other."

"Uta, you are twenty times older and stronger than me."

Her gaze raked over his face, her frown only deepening when it landed on his tense mouth. "You think I want you to obey me? On all four thousand Illyrian gods, I could not respect you or desire you like that." Her slim fingers squeezed his hand. "Bel, since you were a boy, a very young boy, you opened your heart to me—but every time I ordered you about, you laughed in my face. And you still do. I loved you for it then and I still do."

But not enough to live for. He yanked his hand back, remembering her standing naked and shivering in the cold mountain air. "How does it feel? The sun?"

She pressed the pad of her index finger into the glass of the window. "Incredible, and with every ray, I wish it for Loki."

Not a celebration—just one more guilty burden.

He crossed his arms, shuddering with the effort it took to pull away. "You are an insufferable martyr, a coward under all your bravado."

She pouted, jutting her chin.

Still, he couldn't stop, wanted to hurt her as she had hurt him. "You always run. From your soldiers, your responsibilities and mistakes, from my childhood, and from my love."

"Yes," she gasped. Pink tears shimmered in her eyes and she wiped them with the back of her hand like a little girl. "I am. Now you see, when before you did not. Will you still offer your love to a coward?"

Oh hell. He did see. Finally. And he let out a long, slow breath.

No promises. No guarantees.

Only her brokenness, her despair, and under it all, her love.

He tipped his head close to her lips, which pulled into an O before he brushed his own across them. She exhaled a sweet breath and he licked her lower lip. She arched her back, raising her small breasts temptingly. His hand grabbed, squeezing. She opened her mouth and his tongue swept inside. Her animal groan vibrated down his spine and shot blood into his cock.

She flipped the arm separating their seats up and laced her hands into his hair, pulling his ear to her mouth. Her deft, slender tongue traced a wet line around the shell before she nibbled on the lobe with blunt teeth. Tingles crawled from his scalp down his shoulders and arms, and he pulled her onto his lap.

She whispered. "I have done many things in my life. But I am not yet a member of this club for people who have had sex on airplanes."

She was already fumbling between them for his belt, her tongue pressed between her lips in determination.

He pressed his forehead into hers and chuckled. "Yes."

He ached to be with her again like this, but he wouldn't make the same mistake as last time. This would change nothing. He glided his hands up under her shirt, and reveled at the feel of two hard nipples straining against his palms.

"Hell yes," he said, as her fangs grazed his neck.

"No!" Pedro stood, banging his head on the baggage compartment. "I can't turn this music up any louder, and I do not want to hear you two go at it again. Leo and I were traumatized enough the first time. I still have plaster in my hair."

Uta planted a kiss on Bel's neck before she slid across his lap, her pert ass rubbing friction between his cock and fly. He needed more, and he clutched at her hips, ignoring Pedro. But she slipped from his grasp and stepped up to the vampire, who stood a few inches shorter. She peered down at him, and lifted his chin to examine his face more closely. His golden eyes narrowed.

"I know you fear for Lucas. But I can see from looking at you he is all right. If he were worse, your eyes would be blood shot, your lips blue." Then she pulled him into a hug. Pedro's fists relaxed, and after a moment his hands came around her back. He surrendered to the embrace.

Bel adjusted his hard-on in his jeans. He wouldn't be joining the mile high club on this flight. No matter. He liked her priorities — taking care of Pedro was more important than a shag on an airplane.

The question was, would there ever be another chance, or was it all over once they got back?

CHAPTER 46

It seemed like hours, but Gwen had no idea how much time she'd actually spent wedged into the cabinet. All around her stood bottles of liquor and glassware. If she moved inches in the wrong direction, the stowaway in the bar cabinet would become the proverbial bull in a china shop.

She rehearsed scenarios in her mind. Would she jump out and lunge at Trys? Creep out of the cabinet and surprise her? She imagined unlikely headlines: *History Professor Slays Witch With Bare Hands.* Her eyelids grew heavy and as she slid into stage-one sleep, her plans grew into fantastical hallucinations.

She came awake with a start, to the sound of voices in the dining room.

She released a controlled breath, thanking the ancient Hunter deity Dela-Malkh that she hadn't betrayed her location with a snore or by kicking over a wineglass.

The witch gossiped with another woman about Andre's sons.

Finally, the woman said goodbye. "I'll leave you to your chocolates."

Trys mumbled a garbled farewell, presumably with her mouth full.

Gwen curled her hand around the neck of a bottle—a fifth of some unidentified liquor—and burst from the cabinet, banking everything on the advantage of surprise. The witch started, standing and backing away, arms forward and knees bent. Gwen brought the bottle down on her head with all her strength, and then crouched to break her fall before she crashed to the floor, bringing the whole household upon them.

After carefully lowering her, Gwen dragged her by the ankles until they were out of sight of the door where Gwen unsheathed the box cutter from her sock and held it to the witch's neck.

Her eyes fluttered. No time to hesitate.

Gwen sliced the blade deep across the woman's taut flesh. The blood gushed. He eyes flew open, her pupils narrowing in focus.

"Why?" she gargled, her throat full of the life draining out of her.

Gwen smiled down at her. "For love."

The woman's arms jerked. If she could touch the gash in her neck, she might be able to heal herself the way she'd stopped Lucas's bleeding. Gwen couldn't risk it. She held Trys's arms to the floor as the fight oozed from her in a stream of deep crimson liquid.

Another thing Gwen didn't know—were vampires like sharks? Would they smell all this blood and come in a hurry? She'd best not chance it. She closed Trys's eyelids the way people always did in the movies, and sprinted across the entryway to the front door. Across the highway, trucks were gathering in the grassy sloping field.

The Hunters had arrived.

She left the house, leaving the door open behind her, walked up the hill, and found the initiates bustling around efficiently, just as they did in the office. They all wore FBI caps and windbreakers. Ethan alone wore a dress shirt and a tie under a bulletproof vest emblazoned with the same yellow FBI letters. He stood under a tent talking with a group of men in suits, and when he saw her his broad smile radiated pleasure. Her stomach flew up into her throat as he turned back to the men.

Behind their sunglasses and ball caps, Gwen struggled to recognize the initiates she knew. Finally, she found Ethan's assistant.

"Who are those men?"

"Sheriff and fire chief. Their officers are on the way."

Gwen leaned in, whispering. "They think we're the FBI?"

Justine nodded, casting an admiring look at Ethan. "He's been putting this in place for weeks, impersonating an agent who has traced a human trafficking ring to the Kaštel Estate. Now the local authorities will provide no resistance."

Lucas would have preferred to walk. But he lost the argument, and so he determined to enjoy being cradled to Andre's chest like a child. It wasn't every day that a scrawny Hunter like himself got to cuddle up with such a fine specimen of raw vampire masculinity.

Andre smelled like soap and soil, as if he'd been out planting seedling grapevines minutes earlier. Lucas inhaled, reveling in the intimate knowledge of his strange new friend.

The vampire set him gingerly on the bed and patted his shoulder. "I am afraid it will be hours still until Pedro arrives. I will stay with you."

"There's no need for that." Lucas sat up.

"Do not bother arguing. Pedro demanded it."

"And what else?"

Andre's wry smile pulled up one corner of his mouth. "Ah yes, of course you guessed. In the event I think you are failing, I am to proceed without him."

Lucas's lips mimicked Andre's expression of their own accord. "He has you wrapped around his finger."

Andre chuckled. "He does have a way of getting precisely what he wants, but in this case, I required no persuasion. I take care of my own."

He did, it was why they all loved him, but it always had a cost. Last time it had been his vineyards. "I'm sorry. This is damned inconvenient of me."

"Yes. Next time would you mind scheduling your health crisis when we are not at war?"

Lucas sucked in a breath, chastised by the barb despite the affection behind it. Andre did have the liveliest green eyes, sparkling with amusement when they weren't shadowed with worry.

"But, *davo*, son. How long have you known you were sick? Things do not get this far without symptoms."

"Honestly, I thought it was stress, maybe an ulcer. Nothing like this." He settled his head onto the pillow, attending to the dull ache in his gut. After Trys had done her healing thing, the pain had all but vanished.

Andre glared, tipping his forehead toward Lucas. "What symptoms did you have?"

"Okay. There was some vomiting."

The vampire's gorgeous dark head came another hair closer to Lucas.

"Bloody vomit. But I figured I had time, or that I wouldn't need it."

"Once he turns you, Pedro is quite possibly going to kill you for keeping that from him."

Andre was probably right. Lucas closed his eyes, wriggling to get comfortable on the bed.

"Humans are so frivolous with their lives."

Lucas cracked open one eyelid. "No more frivolous than your sacrifice to save Lena. We agree—there are things at stake greater than our own wellbeing."

"Indeed." Andre rubbed the bridge of his nose.

A chill caressed Lucas's skin like icy feathers blowing across his face. It left him uneasy. He'd felt it before, but couldn't place the memory, only the foreboding. Andre shivered, though he seemed otherwise unaware.

"Where is Gwen?" Lucas asked.

"Gwen?"

Lucas's cancer riddled stomach sank. "Ethan's girlfriend. Whose cell I collapsed in."

"*Davo.* I know *who* she is. But I do not know *where* she is."

"Shit."

"Stay here."

"Yeah, right."

Andre's jaw bulged with tension, but he nodded. Then he bellowed at the top of his great big lungs. "Find Gwen!"

They took off down the servants' wing toward the central stairs. Instantly, the house buzzed with activity. Doors slammed, feet pounded, voices called out. The search was on. In no time, a shrieking scream sounded, reverberating off the high ceiling of the foyer. Lena appeared in the door to the dining room, just as Andre and Lucas stepped onto the balcony one floor above.

"Trys!" she cried. "She's dead. Oh my God! Trys is dead."

Lucas's dull mind raced to process the news. If she was dead, then the shield was down, they had to evacuate immediately. He opened his mouth to issue instructions, but Andre's came first and loudly.

"Into the cellar! The shield is down. Into the cellar."

Omar swooped into the dining room and emerged with Trys limp in his arms, his features wracked with grief. Dead — the witch was really dead.

How much time did they have? Lucas glanced out the window. Fire trucks and FBI vans lined the highway. The front drive crawled with Hunters. One knelt and hefted his cannon to his shoulder.

"Here they come!" Lucas cringed as the rocket flew toward the front of the house. "Run!" He took off down the stairs, but Andre gathered him up — this time flinging him over his shoulder.

Lucas barely had time to feel humiliated before the house shook with a thundering explosion. It wouldn't stand for long.

Kos stood at the door to the cellar counting everyone off.

"Zoey?" Andre said, setting Lucas upright on his feet.

"First in, she's comforting Lena."

"The humans?"

"All accounted for — I grabbed Ally and Susan as soon as you called for the search. Lexi, Vania, Ani and Arden just went down." Just then two more vampires from Bel's crew arrived at the door.

"Where's Henry?" Kos asked.

"Below," the bigger one replied. "He's guarding the tunnel door."

Once they all stepped into the cellar, Kos shepherded them down the stairs. Andre reached up to pull down a huge steel trap door. Lucas had never noticed the thing. Andre spun the retro wheel, like he was sealing off a submarine, or a radiation-proof bunker.

"Wow. I'm coming to stay with you in the event of the apocalypse." Lucas snorted at his own joke.

Everyone stared at him.

"Let us hope it does not come to that," Andre finally said.

More explosions sounded as they descended the stairs. Lucas pushed images of the beautiful house's destruction from his mind. Homes could be rebuilt, Andre had already done so once, but first they had to survive.

The entire household had gathered in his office, crammed into the brown leather armchairs, or propped against the wall. Omar bent over Trys where she lay on the oversized desk, and the rest of Bel's crew circled behind him. Lexi and Zoey tended to Lena, who shook with what looked like the first symptoms of shock.

"Is it too late to turn her?" Henry asked, wringing the hem of his denim work-shirt.

Omar caressed her face. "Yes."

"She had a do-not-turn form on file, and you know it," Vania scolded.

A few days ago, Lucas might have filed one of those himself.

"Stubborn witch," Henry muttered, not without affection.

Omar seethed. "I am going to kill that Hunter bitch when I get my hands on her." His anger hung thick in the air, and no one challenged his right to it. In the chaos of Lucas's collapse, they'd forgotten to mind her—a fatal mistake, which made his illness worse than just inconvenient.

"Will we be safe down here?" Zoey asked.

Andre reached a hand back to scratch his head, frowning. "The doors are Cold War-era. Henry, did you seal the one at this end of the tunnel?"

"Aye, aye captain. Locked up tight."

"They are by no means indestructible, but they were designed to withstand fire and radioactive fall-out. We have a high probability of surviving the day in here, and we can attempt an escape by night."

Kos looked to Lena. "I don't like the idea of fleeing—the humans will be too vulnerable."

Lena rubbed her belly, and the room fell silent.

Oh shit.

She must have realized everyone was staring. She glanced around the room, offering a heartbreaking smile. "Um. This wasn't how I planned to announce our good news." She choked back a sob.

"Oh my God!" Zoey said, embracing her. "But I thought—"

"I was wrong. Apparently, the regular schedule doesn't hold for halfling babies."

Andre's weak smile seemed just as forced. "That is true, as I recall. Bel arrived two months early, just shy of ten pounds."

"So you can understand why I prefer to hunker down," Kos said.

Vania stepped from Trys's side. "But surely the police will arrive, if they attack the house or set fire to it."

The words jostled Lucas's memory. "I'm afraid not. Across the street, they've set up camp. There are FBI vans, fire engines."

"What?" Andre snapped.

Lucas shook his head in agreement. "Goddamn Ethan. He must have infiltrated them."

"*Davo*. Hunters do not collaborate with human authorities. It goes against—"

"So does Ethan."

Kos encircled his wife's shoulders. "Lena and I stowed food stores down here, for the humans, just in case. And with the Blood Vine—"

"There is another possibility." Omar stood to his full height of nearly seven feet, the anger rolling off him like heat from desert sand. "I heard what Pedro told you, about Uta and the Hunter blood."

"What?" Lucas asked.

"Uta…" Andre rubbed his eyes with his thumb and forefinger. "She tested our hypothesis."

Even a human could have heard a flea hop in the silence, a thousand times more still than the one moments earlier. Then another explosion sounded above.

"She's alive?" Kos asked, finally, as if he hadn't heard the blast.

"She is. Unharmed. She fed from Derek Williams weeks ago and only that amount of blood saw her safe when she tried to sun walk."

Kos shifted on his feet. "I have fed from Leo."

"As have I," Omar said.

Lucas jerked his gaze to the giant, curious over that unexpected announcement.

In the meantime, it seemed everyone else had decided to stare at Lucas. Oh great. Here he was, the lone Hunter locked in the cellar—the secret weapon.

"No." Zoey stood, her hands on her hips. "Lucas is too weak, and Kos is going to be a father. We will not go on the offensive."

"I agree." Andre extended his hand toward her, and she crossed to him, reaching for it before he pulled her against him. "But if they breach the cellar…"

"We can fight in the sun," Vania said, turning up her palms to send up a harmless shower of sparks. "Arden, Ani, and I are not useless."

"Good. And if it comes to that, only I will feed from Lucas so I can join the fight." Andre raised his dark brows in a question.

Lucas consented with a nod.

Another, louder blast shook the ground, and it was followed by a series of crashes. Lucas imagined the walls of the house collapsing.

"Zoey, love, you will take the humans into the tunnel."

"I'm not leaving you—"

"Not if we can help it," Andre said. "Now, who will sit guard at the doors for the first shift?"

CHAPTER 47

Gwen waited, leaning against a car where Ethan would see her when he finished speaking to the officials. Finally, he shook their hands and strolled away, leaving behind two brawny looking Hunters in FBI hats. Presumably they would keep an eye on their new allies. He gestured for her to follow him behind another truck. He kissed her, pressing her against the door of the vehicle, hot enough to burn her skin from the blaze of the afternoon sun.

She surrendered to his mouth — no one had ever kissed her with such passion — his fingers digging into her hips, his tongue in her throat. She knew the kiss was her reward, a token of his pleasure in her success. He didn't even ask her about Zoey.

"I am glad you are safe," he mumbled into her hair.

"Me too. What happens now?"

He stepped back and cast a look over his shoulder at the men in the tent. His eyelid twitched and a bead of sweat trickled down his temple.

Like that, her moment of paradise vanished. "What's wrong?"

He swallowed, his Adam's apple bobbing. "Derek Williams claims to have proof I arranged the murder of Hunters and framed the vampires. He is amassing followers."

"As your rival?" A brick seemed to materialize in Gwen's belly, its sharp corners pressing into her stomach.

"As soon as I eliminate Marasović, I'll skin Williams alive in front of every Hunter I can gather."

Gwen's intestines clenched around the imaginary brick. Ethan did not make idle threats, although this one was not accompanied by the flush of his cheeks his sadistic propositions usually aroused.

"I have worked far too long to let one man destroy my plans," he growled, his eyes flicking away.

"Have I earned the right to ask what it is you intend?"

He smiled at her, every trace of worry wiped from his face. "You most certainly have. How could I ever have imagined Zoey could be my partner in this endeavor? Only you truly see me and have chosen my way, rather than clinging to some arbitrary notion of goodness."

She shifted several inches over, where the black metal of the van remained searing hot, and pressed her skin onto the burning surface. When the heat began to sting, she replied. "Yes."

He followed her movement, stepping with her. He traced his hands up her sides to cup her breasts. "I want them all at my mercy, Gwen. Every last Hunter as obedient as you are." Pinching her nipples between thumbs and forefingers, he twisted. She gasped at the sweet pain.

"I will earn their love with my victory over the vampires," he went on. "And once they have had a deep and satisfying taste of the violence they were reared for, they will be mine to command in all things."

"What things?" she asked on a breath, writhing and leaning toward him in spite of her instinct to pull away.

"It hardly matters." His feline eyes bored into her. He released his grip on her breasts and dug his thumbs directly into her already sensitive nipples. "The key is violence—the purest form of reality. Think of how the initiates enjoyed Lindsay's death. I hope to capture Maras's household alive because once my Hunters taste violence, they will know the only truth is power, and the only pleasure comes in taking it. Or, for a very few, like you, pleasure comes in giving up your power and your responsibility to make decisions. Which makes you very special to me."

Gwen's pulse thrummed with increasing need as pain stabbed into her breasts. Her sex throbbed, wet and hot. She wanted to wrap her legs around his waist and grind against him. But she had killed for him, had surrendered her humanity to aid him in this frightening plan, and she needed to grasp his logic. She was his to do with as he liked, a beast without morals, seeking the only form of gratification she desired—the pleasure of his annihilating abuse. And she had done it because the path of healing had been so much more painful and frightening. But she wouldn't wish her nearly soulless state on another living creature. And he planned to create an army of beasts like her, who hungered for violence and lived by the law of power—his power alone.

He dropped his hands to his side and studied her with a suspiciously neutral expression. Beneath it she saw his vulnerability. He had revealed himself fully to her, and of course he would need reassurance of her approval. His plan was sick, and wrong, and against the things she had once stood for. But now she stood for nothing and the revelation of his plan didn't upset her the way it should have—proof she was his first disciple.

"I am honored you want me by your side. What do you have in store for Marasović?"

"Reports say there is a locked vault leading into the basement. I am going there to oversee opening it."

He was leaving? She'd just returned to him. Fear squeezed her heart. "Can't you send someone else?"

"I want this finished—no mistakes." He brushed a lock of hair off her forehead. "Gwen, I am so close to my goal that I can taste it on your lips. You have ensured my success, and my defeat of Marasović will surely assuage any doubts Williams can stir." Focused on her mouth, his eyes shone feverishly bright.

She placed her palm on his chest. "Be careful."

"Not to worry, Gwen. Victory is at hand."

CHAPTER 48

No one waited for them at the airport. Where the hell was Bel's crew? Vania had promised to pick them up. He called her while Pedro called Lucas. Neither answered. He tried Andre. No luck.

Uta shielded her face from the glare of the afternoon sun, her eyes flicking back and forth between them as the phones rang ceaselessly. "We ought to leave our belongings here and rent a car. This way we can approach the estate in stealth."

Always thinking like a general, his Uta. He picked only one hard-sided case from the pile of luggage next to his plane, and it wasn't the chromatograph. Sometimes he didn't get to be the scientist, he had to be the mercenary.

Pedro drove as fast as he could without drawing attention. When they came to the turnoff for Kaštel, traffic piled up where a police car blocked the highway. An officer detoured people to the east or west.

"Is that the direction of the house?" Leo asked, pointing at an enormous black plume of smoke.

The car slowed to a stop, as if Pedro had simply forgotten to press the gas. "Yes."

"Shite. Are they all dead?" Bel asked, panic for his family reaching into his chest to squeeze his heart.

"No." Pedro shook his head. "I would feel it." He pressed the pedal to the floor and turned off the highway onto a county road. "This will take us to the back end of the estate, and we can take a dirt road in from there. It will give us an element of surprise."

Hell, that they were driving around at all in the middle of the day was an element of surprise.

Uta's arm snaked across the back seat, and she curved her palm over Bel's knee. A simple comfort. Like their kiss, their almost shag, it didn't have to mean anything—

At that moment, it meant everything. He wasn't alone.

If everyone he loved died in Kaštel, he wasn't alone.

"Surely the cops will have come?" Bel whispered.

"It's fire season." Pedro looked up from the road to scan the sky. "There should be helicopters carrying water from Lake Berryessa."

Pedro slowed the car, turning toward a steel gate. Before the car stopped, Uta was out the door, ripping the gate off its hinges. She hopped back in and Pedro gunned the engine, driving as fast as the little sedan could manage on the rocky, uneven road. Even if they'd wanted to speak, the gravel kicking around in the wheel wells would have made it hard to hear.

He came to a halt in a shallow ravine. "If we climb to the top of that hill, we'll have a view of the house."

Uta and Pedro raced to the top in a blur while Bel jogged behind, Leo on his heels.

At the crest, his lungs locked around smoky, oxygen-less air. There was no house anymore. Not really. Only a smoldering shell. The south wing still blazed bright, but only a few skeletal beams remained of the north wing. In the kitchen, molten piles of metal that had once been appliances steamed. Poor Andre—another home destroyed. Hunters swarmed over the property, presumably looking for remains—human or vampire.

"Are they dead?" Leo asked.

"I already said no," Pedro hissed.

"I know, it's just that—"

"Do not bicker." Uta swatted Leo's hand. "There must be some kind of underground—"

"Yes," Bel said. "The hatch door into the cellar would withstand a fire, even a hot one. But it must be getting pretty toasty down there about now."

"Is that the door there—where those men are gathered?" She peeled off her jacket and threw it on the ground.

He squinted. "Yes." The Hunters formed a semicircle in what would have been the front of the house. "What are they doing?"

"Cutting into the door with an acetylene torch," Pedro said.

"Time to swoop in to the rescue. Can you handle those men, Pedro, if I take out the rest of them?"

"Sure thing." He stood to his full height and bounced on the balls of his feet. For a split second, Bel wondered if he would fly. He was young, but he'd been drinking Hunter go-juice his whole vampire life, and he'd been to the homeland, which was apparently like the magical Land of Oz. But no, Pedro just sprinted down the hill like a roadrunner in a cartoon.

"Don't hurt the firemen," Leo shouted after him. "I like firemen."

"Leo," Bel called. "Go get my pistols out of the trunk. Can you shoot?"

"I'm better at long range."

Bel scanned the distance to the house; they were just in range of his PSG1. "Good. Grab the rifle. You take out anybody you can from here. I will back up Uta and Pedro with the handguns."

She snapped to attention, her face twisted in anger. "I would fuck a flock of sheep before I let you—"

In the heat of the sun, Bel went cold. "Let me?"

She took a deep breath, with exaggerated patience, raising her narrow chest like she might punch him. That would guarantee compliance—he'd be out like a light.

But she didn't hit him. "Think what will happen to me if you are injured. I am the greatest asset in this battle, Bel. Stronger than Andre, even. But you are my Achilles' heel. If you are hurt, I will be useless. I need you to stay put, and if they come after you, get in the car and flee. Protecting yourself is the best thing you can do for your family and your crew."

Her impeccable reasoning only infuriated him, but his pride was not worth risking his family. "Uta," he whispered.

She cocked her head.

"Don't get hurt. I'm fucked without you too."

She smiled, giving him a glimpse of her sexy fangs as she launched herself into the air like an arrow. There were times being bonded to a beautiful badass wasn't so bad.

Halfway down the hill, Pedro spotted the oil drums. A dozen of them.

They'd already burned the house to the ground. What the hell were they going to do with those?

O Madre de Dios. They had a hose.

Squinting, he glared at the man with the torch. Pedro couldn't be certain from the line of sight, but he seemed to be cutting a hole in the center of the door, not opening it up from the edge.

A hole in the door. A hose. A hell of a lot of gasoline.

Just like Papa had done with the rattlesnakes on their vineyards in Argentina. Fire in the hole.

All the men wore yellow suits, prepared for a massive burn. Igniting that much gasoline underground would surely blow the door, and maybe collapse the cellar.

Pedro flexed his palms, calling to mind the moves he'd rehearsed for years in his dojo, before he became a vampire. First he went for the men near the barrels. When he reached them, another instinct took over, guiding his hands in unrehearsed moves that came as second nature. He twisted off two of their heads like screw-caps. A spray of glorious, rich Hunter blood shot across his face and he licked his lips.

Well hello, boys. This could be fun.

The next time he snapped a neck, he made sure to aim the full stream of hot, potent lifeblood right into his mouth. Its power stoked an energetic, sun-heated fire inside him. He was invincible. They would win.

Above him, Uta buzzed through the sky toward a group of Hunters like a determined hummingbird.

The men huddled around the door didn't seem to hear a thing through their helmets and the whirring of the acetylene torch. Pedro picked off the two at the back.

"Almost finished now. It is a shame we have to burn them out," said a Hunter near the front. The familiar voice sent icy stabs of phantom pain up Pedro's legs. Ethan Bennett.

Just the man he was looking for.

Pedro laughed loud enough to turn the heads of the three remaining Hunters.

Behind the transparent plastic shield of the helmet, the look on Ethan's face was even more satisfying—his mouth fell open and he looked sunward. After a long moment, Ethan refocused on Pedro and shouted, "Seize him."

The unarmed Hunters turned, their mouths gaping nearly as wide as Ethan's. Face to face with a vampire, without their oversized arsenal of guns and explosives, they cowered like a bunch of chicken shits. Pedro scanned their faces, hoping to see if any of them were the ones that had beaten on him the day he'd been captured. But their faces, twisted in fear, did not resemble the ones populating his nightmare of a memory.

He delivered a roundhouse kick to the head of the one holding the torch, expecting to knock him over. Instead, he flattened the man's skull. Oops. And cool. The orange-blue flame sputtered out.

Ethan ran, darting toward the highway. Pedro let him run; he would just wear himself out.

With the success of his kick, Pedro couldn't resist grabbing the remaining two Hunters under their chins and crashing their heads together like a cartoon. He giggled.

Mierda, maybe he needed to work on some anger management. Or maybe killing Ethan would erase all his anger. Besides, these assholes were trying to kill everyone he loved.

Pedro's feet scuffed over the ash-covered foundation of the house—*Jesu Cristo,* even the wood floor of the foyer had incinerated, baring only the cement foundation. How long had the place been burning before he got there?

Please let everyone be safe in the cellar.

He scanned the horizon. No sign of Uta now.

Ethan's head popped up from behind the oil drums. One had toppled over. Pedro glanced down. He stood in a puddle of gasoline. The fire came all at once, from a flame thrower Ethan had picked up. He ignited the gasoline spreading all the way to Pedro's feet.

His pants caught fire and the burn was so much like the pain Ethan had inflicted on Pedro's extremities that he froze, trapped in the memory of his former helplessness. His flesh began to melt and sizzle, and he snapped out of the daze, leaping away from the flames.

And he never came down.

Gracias a Dios. He was flying. He spiraled over the ruins of the house, swatting at his burning khakis and allowing his skin to heal. Ethan gazed up at Pedro, his flame sputtered out, and the nozzle dangling limply at his side. The motherfucker looked even more surprised at this unexpected turn of events, which was pretty much exactly how Pedro felt. He was nowhere near the age of flight, but his little stint in the homeland and the infusion of Hunter blood had dialed up his power, big time.

His airborne maneuvers came naturally, and he descended like a graceful Tinkerbell right in front of his nemesis. Finally, they were face to face. Pedro finally had Ethan in his grasp, and the relief blazed through him almost as fast as the fire had.

"I bet this isn't how you expected it to end."

Ethan shook his head. "It is not over. It cannot be. I am going to win."

Pedro recoiled, glancing from side to side for the Hunter's re-inforcements. None came. The man's confidence was pure delusion.

"I have armies of Hunters at my beck and call." Ethan squared off his shoulders. "My power is limitless."

Pedro tilted his head. "Yeah, but it's just you and me here. And I'm like a bazillion times stronger than you."

"I do not lose." Ethan frowned at the charred earth.

"*Jesu Cristo,* man. Have you always been like this? No wonder Lucas hates you."

"He hates me because he had to live in my shadow. Now take me to Marasović."

"My thoughts exactly. He should be down in the cellar with Zoey and Lucas. When I take you down there, it will practically be a family reunion." Pedro jerked his head in the direction of the house. "Let's go."

Ethan bared his blunt human teeth.

Pedro shrugged. "It's your call, but you being taller, I expect your feet will drag."

The man's golden eyes, identical to Pedro's own, darted from side to side. Pedro sniffed, hoping for a whiff of urine or plain old fear. No luck. Ethan still didn't believe he'd lost, but he did begin to march toward the entrance into the bunker.

The house had nearly vanished, the hillsides were still black with only the barest hint of green grass sprouting. This paradise, Pedro's home for nearly fifteen years, had been obliterated. Walking alongside his nemesis across the scene of devastation, Pedro imagined himself in a Western — John Wayne marching the outlaw toward his reckoning.

Pedro stomped on the hatch, hoping the hole the Hunters cut had compromised it. No luck. And from the outside, no hinge-side or latch-side was visible. He would have to peel it back from the top. When he bent down to grip the edge of the door, Ethan grew twitchy in the corner of Pedro's vision. The Hunter shoved his hands in the pockets of his fireman's jacket and shifted his weight. Did the asshole have a gun?

Pedro blurred to the hose and back with a length of rubber tubing to bind up Ethan's wrists.

Surprised, Ethan fought against the restraint. "What the hell?"

That decided it. Pedro tore off another length of hose and gagged him. Then he went back to work on the door. Finally, he got a fingerhold. It took all his vampire strength to peel up a corner of the lip of the hatch. He fell back, winded.

Ethan exhaled through his nose.

Pedro narrowed his eyes. Not like Ethan's men had managed to open it either. "I'll wipe that smug look off your face. Or, better yet, peel your face right off. It is only my generous character that demands I take you down to them alive, but you don't have to be whole."

The door groaned, and a moment later the latches unlocked with a click. Pedro hopped off as it swung open, releasing air several degrees hotter than outside.

Kos stood on the step below, grinning. "I knew that was your voice."

Pedro called down into the darkness. "Honey, I'm home."

"Why didn't you just knock?" Kos's glance flickered to Ethan, and his smile flattened. "Damn. Get him down here."

Pedro shoved Ethan toward the door. He didn't resist. Did he have an ace in his pocket? Or was he drunk on some crazy delusions of grandeur?

"He's not rigged with explosives, is he?" Kos asked.

"Nope. I did the smell test. Besides, he's not the type to wear a suicide bomb—just to strap them to others."

Ethan marched in like he was on the way to his victory speech.

Kos held open the door to Andre's office. "When it got hot, we sent the humans into the tunnel. But don't worry, Bennett, we still have a welcoming committee for you."

Ethan marched in first with Pedro and Kos following.

Gray-faced, Lucas reclined in an armchair, his feet on the coffee table. *Mierda*—he'd lost more weight in the three days Pedro been gone. Pedro's chest clenched.

"Un-gag him," Lucas said.

Pedro loosened the knot. Ethan spat out the tubing. "You don't look good, brother."

Lucas simply raised his long, bony middle finger.

Across from him, Andre and Zoey leaned against the back of an armchair, their fingers intertwined. At the sight of them, Ethan blanched.

Zoey smiled, baring her fangs.

Ethan let out a breath. "Well, that is a disappointment."

Andre hissed.

"Surely we can discuss this," Ethan said. "Eliminating me has no real benefits. My Hunters are everywhere."

"Don't be stupid. Killing you will be very satisfying to all of us." Zoey turned to her mate. "Maybe I could rip his throat out—give him a little taste of the pleasure of a bite?"

"You won't win," Ethan said. "If you kill me, another leader will rise up. But if you leave me alive, we can negotiate a truce."

Andre ignored the Hunter. "He does not deserve the mercy, love."

"True." She crossed her arms and strode toward their enemy.

"You never did know your place." Fast, Ethan rushed at her head first. But far faster, she caught up a handful of his hair and bent his head back, stretching his neck long. He grunted, and Pedro chuckled.

"Good girl," Andre said. He snarled at Ethan. "Now, I will reach into his chest and pull his beating heart out for what he did to you, and to Lena, and to my vines."

"Don't be selfish. I want to help." Zoey shoved him.

Lucas's mouth quirked, but Pedro steamed. "You all are *loco*. He's mine. I'll show you the mercy you didn't show me, you sick prick. I'll cut your feet off nice and clean before I slice your throat."

"Maybe we should play rocks, paper, scissors for the pleasure of tearing him apart," Zoey said, licking her lips like a hungry tigress.

"No." Andre stood straight. "I am the head of this household, and this is my decision."

Zoey glowered. Pedro didn't know shit about women, but he knew Andre had made the wrong move. He'd just let them work it out, and take Ethan all for himself while they were busy discussing it.

A gurgle sounded just as Pedro turned to face him.

Ethan stood with the sharp end of something jutting from his chest. Behind him, Lucas sagged, but grinned triumphantly as his brother collapsed onto his knees and then fell forward, face first.

Jesús Cristo, where had he found the strength?

"Hope you don't mind me borrowing your sword, big guy." Lucas braced himself against the wall and nodded at an empty case where Andre had kept the antique. "I had to repay him for all the times he stabbed me in the back."

Andre frowned, but his expression quickly melted into a smile. "I suppose there is as much justice in that execution as any. And, in your condition, it was an impressive feat of strength."

"Power of hatred, or vengeance." Lucas shrugged. "Don't count on another one any time soon." He slid all the way to the floor.

"*Krist*." Kos wiped his brow, moving toward the door. "I'm going to find Lena and the others, to tell them he's dead."

When the door closed behind him, Pedro dashed to Lucas's side and squeezed his man tight, staring over at their enemy.

Ethan. Dead. Finally.

No one spoke, perhaps letting the reality sink in.

Eventually, Andre stirred. "What is the condition of my house?"

Pedro gulped. He hated being the messenger. "Pretty much gone."

Andre lifted his chin, more stoic. "That is as I expected. The fire burned hot for hours."

Zoey wrapped his arm around her shoulder. Inwardly, Pedro smiled at the way she played Andre's tune—pretending she needed comfort when really she offered it.

"What about the other Hunters?" Andre asked.

Pedro glanced at the ceiling. "Uta has them under control. This battle is over."

"But the war?" Andre stared at Ethan.

Yeah. The war. Ethan may be dead, but it wasn't necessarily an end to the violence. Pedro squeezed Lucas's hand, hoping like hell his plan was working.

Andre glanced up. "So, regarding the sun—Zoey and I must have a taste of Lucas."

Pedro tightened their embrace. "No way. He's too weak. Leo's just above gr—"

"There's always Ethan." Lucas toed his brother's shoulder. "That blood's got to be good and fresh for a few more minutes, right?"

"Eeeeww." A shudder shook Zoey's shoulders.

"I agree." Andre grimaced, rubbing the stubble of his chin. "That is truly repulsive."

Lucas huffed. "What do you mean? He's my brother. Our blood is practically the same."

Pedro gritted his teeth to hold back his laugh. Andre and Zoey hadn't guessed Lucas was pulling their legs. But as their revulsion took over their features, the giggle burst from his chest nevertheless.

Then Lucas laughed too. After exchanging glances, Andre and Zoey joined in.

"I'll go up and see if I can find Leo for you," Pedro said.

"No." Lucas made moves to stand. Pedro helped him up to where he could support himself with the back of a chair. "I want them to have my blood. It will bind us together, before you turn me."

"Lucas, that is unnecessary. We are already bound together in friendship and common purpose. And after two millennia, I can surely wait for Pedro to retrieve Leo."

Lucas unbuttoned his cuffs and rolled back his sleeves from his wrists. He held them out to Andre and Zoey. "Please?"

When the vampires knelt at his feet, and ever so gently pierced his skin with their fangs, a hot tear fell down Pedro's face.

Yeah. Lucas knew what he was doing.

After only a few sips, they both sealed up the wounds. Zoey reached for Andre to steady herself, but he wobbled too. Both trembled with the power of Lucas's blood.

She touched her lips. "Oh."

Andre wore a dazed smile as he leaned in to kiss her. They lip-locked like they were alone for the first time in weeks.

Yeah. Pedro knew the feeling, knew very well how Lucas's blood could intoxicate a vampire with its power. He also knew these two might start undressing without an urgent reminder of the situation. He coughed.

Andre pulled back hastily. "Where are Bel and Uta?"

Pedro waved away his worry. "She was subduing the rest of the Hunters. I'm sure she has everything under control."

CHAPTER 49

Uta flew low over the smoldering ruins of the house, careful not to be seen. The Hunters' fire helmets, with their narrow windows of vision, would help her stay out of sight.

Pedro darted toward the group of men. He yanked the head off one Hunter like a human decapitates a cooked prawn, only the Hunter bled more. She took stock of the entire area. They had placed their command center across the highway—an ideal position—just where she would have located it. Men wearing fire resistant suits used heavy tools to sift through the debris of the house. A row of official vehicles had parked along the highway—fire trucks, police cars and unmarked vans.

Would Bennett be safely tucked away with the authorities, playing the hero, or down on the ground trying to get to Andre?

He wasn't in the tent where a handful of law enforcement officials sat, peering through binoculars. They'd been fooled by Ethan and didn't deserve to die. She landed just out of their sight. A coiled orange extension cord lay under the bumper of a nearby van and she picked it up, spinning the heavy plug at the end.

"Listen to me, gentlemen. You have been deceived by Ethan Bennett. I regretfully inform you that you have chosen the wrong side."

One of them puffed up. "Who are you?"

"One of the good guys. I am going to lock you up, for your own safety, until this thing is finished."

They raised their voices in a murmur of dissent. She whipped the extension cord down on a folding table. It split in two right down its width and collapsed.

"Okay, okay," the pompous one agreed. "We'll come with you."

She herded them toward a van — the type full of surveillance equipment.

"We can't all fit in there," cried a vulpine man with large glasses.

"I promise you can. I am very strong."

No one else complained, even when she pushed them into the narrow confines, packed tighter than commuters on a Tokyo subway, which she had always despised — too damn much blood pumping and tempting her. She broke the handles off the inside of the van's door, then did the same on the outside, sealing them in. Still, the men didn't peep. Maybe they realized they were in over their heads.

Now to clear the grounds.

From the vantage of the Hunter command center, she took stock. Her eyes still unaccustomed to the sun, she blinked and squinted until she found Leo and Bel, perched on the hilltop across the shallow valley from where she stood. Good. For once Bel had listened to reason.

Pedro had vanished into the cellar, leaving a pile of Hunters behind. Also good. With Andre, Zoey, Kos, and Bel's whole crew downstairs, surely he had things under control.

She would clean up the stragglers who still searched the demolished house — oh, the lovely house. Just like Andre's on Šolta. Her poor old friend had lost so much.

And Loki had lost his life.

She squeezed her eyes shut in a silent prayer to Loki's ancient gods, and her own, and Andre's too. Maybe one of them would hear. *Please let this be the end.*

Two men in yellow fire suits gestured at one another on the north end of the ruins. She dove off the peak and flew close the ground. The men stood side by side, and as she alighted gracefully on her feet, they turned toward her. She snatched the protective helmets off their heads to look into their eyes — two golden sets stared back at her, wide. For these Hunters there could be no mercy. She took hold of both their throats, crushing their windpipes as she lifted them off the ground. It took a little longer to let them suffocate than to simply rip their heads off, but she had spared many outfits with this bloodless technique.

When first one then the other's legs stopped flailing, she dropped them.

She dispatched two more pairs of Hunters in the south wing.

A group of men in official-looking fire helmets used shovels and their feet to stamp out a grass fire bordering the highway. If they were not Hunters, it was probably best to use shock and awe. She flew toward them and circled several times until she was certain she had their attention. By the time she landed, they'd all lifted their goggles, revealing eyes in the ordinary range of blue and brown.

A few of them rubbed said eyes as if she were a hallucination. Another asked, "What the fuck?" All of their mouths hung open.

"Hello," she said. "I am going to kill all those yellow-eyed sheep-fuckers over there. I have locked your superiors inside a van. I advise you to climb back into your fire engines and drive back to your station. It will work out better for all of us."

"Ma'am," one soot-faced man asked, wiping his hand over his sweaty head. "What are you?"

She liked his respectful tone, and his handsome smile was nothing to complain about either. How to answer? She tilted her head, thinking, and Loki's voice whispered in her mind.

Tell them something amusing, child.

Was he speaking to her from the beyond, or simply alive inside her after so many years of friendship? She didn't know. But words came to her nonetheless, in his honor.

"I am a Valkyrie, come to carry the souls of fallen heroes to Valhalla."

"Cool," said another bright-eyed firefighter. "I've read about you in comic books. You're hot."

She grinned. "Thank you. Now, off to your station."

"We can't do that, ma'am. Not without orders. The fire is still burning."

She strode right up to him and looked down to meet his eye. "Young man, that is very honorable. But I will have this fire taken care of momentarily. Your duty is to tend to your commanding officers."

He stood at attention like a well-trained soldier, but did cast a glance over his shoulder at the other men before saying, "Yes, ma'am."

The comic book fan nodded eagerly, and gradually the others voiced their agreement. She shooed them away, a dozen docile beefcakes.

She brushed the palms of her hands. Almost finished. She launched herself upward, and immediately the staccato rhythm of a machine gun punctuated the air, echoing off all the hillsides.

Sheep shit. She hated those things even more than Japanese subways.

She hovered, using her hand as a visor from the blazing sun while she searched out the shooter. The first bullet hit her shin in a white blast of pain, and she took off blindly, away from the blast of the gun, but the echoes in the valley confused the sounds. The bullets came faster, arcing across her pelvis then another round splinted across her chest. By Zeus, each one hurt like an exploding star. The shock of the pain slowed her as she flew to safety. The sound of the bullets stilled and she searched for cover — anything to hide behind until she could heal. She flew behind a tree and the Hunter fired into the branches, the bullets cutting across her midsection. Her blood pulsed out of her in a hundred hot rivulets. He ceased firing once again, and she spied a boulder just on the edge of the nearest vineyard.

As she approached, the shooter stood up from behind it and took aim.

Her senses sharpened and her mind raced at the peak of its vampire capacity — each bullet's trajectory became clear — a straight line across her neck. At this range, it may very well take her head off.

There was just enough time to recall her prayer. *Please let this be the end.*

She had meant the war. For once, she hadn't been trying to end her own life. The desire to live gripped her, demanding she see the end of this ancient conflict, even as she knew she might die.

As the first bullet landed, she twisted, hoping for a last glimpse of Bel. But the rest came too fast, and she dropped, falling to earth in black, bottomless pain.

CHAPTER 50

As soon as Bel saw the shooter, he took off down the hill. He had to get to her. Anyway, if she was dead, it rendered his promise to stay out of danger moot.

"Leo," he shouted over his shoulder, "take him out."

"I'll do my best!"

Over their connection, he sensed something awful. Fear, from the fearless Uta. His heart ceased beating, paralyzed with dread. He looked up, and she began to fall.

Then her presence inside him flickered out, gone. In its stead, a dull ache began to throb.

Bel sprinted toward her. He hurdled over a fallen trellis and stumbled over the stumps of grapevines. Twice he tripped and rolled, scraping against rocks and sharp, burnt vines. The pain of her absence grew sharper, a burn in his skin and muscles.

Leo's shots kept the Hunter gunman under cover behind the boulder.

Finally, Bel reached her.

Shite. The bullets had perforated her neck. She lay in a muddy, crimson ocean of blood and she wasn't healing—she'd lost too much. Her skin had gone gray. Maybe if he fed her his own blood?

Trembling with the burning ache of her dying inside him, he pried open her mouth, but her fangs had retracted behind her teeth. Only the scent of blood would draw them out, but he had no knife to pierce his skin.

He couldn't give himself a chance to think about it. He bit into his forearm as hard as he could, breaking the skin and tearing into flesh.

Fuck!

Wincing from the pain of it, he raked his bloody flesh under her nose. Nothing. Nothing.

Then, far too slowly, her fangs slid from her palate. He forced his arm into her mouth, pressing her jaw to bite down. Could she even swallow with her neck sliced through?

Another round of machine gun fire started up.

Gears clicked into place in Bel's mind. A Hunter fired that gun.

Or, more importantly, a big bag of magic blood.

With his free hand out of sight of the Hunter, he waved at Leo, hoping the kid would get the idea: stop shooting, draw him out.

No luck.

Bel stopped waving and tried again, slicing a horizontal line through the air. *Cut it off.*

Finally, Leo ceased firing.

Nothing happened. Bel massaged the underside of Uta's chin, trying to coax a swallow. His blood wasn't doing shite.

The Hunter stayed put.

The last thing Bel wanted was to leave her, but if he had to go get that Hunter and rip his throat open with his own teeth—so be it.

He tried to loosen Uta's jaw so he could remove his arm. It had locked shut with impressive force, even though she still hadn't swallowed. His own blood filled her mouth seeping from the corners. *Swallow, damn it!* How could he help her if she couldn't drink it?

He glanced up to see the Hunter nearly on top of them.

Perfect. He drew his weapon and planted a bullet in the man's forehead. The Hunter crumpled. She would have been proud of that one. Bel set his gun aside.

Leo scrambled down the hill, sliding in an avalanche of dust and gravel. Bel fought again to unlatch her teeth from his forearm with only one hand.

"Nice shot."

"She won't swallow," Bel shouted, panic raising the pitch of his voice.

"Shit." Leo stared at her, frozen. "What do we do?"

Bel wished like hell he knew.

The kid turned to the Hunter.

Fearful impatience shook Bel to the bones. He could not lose her.

The kid bent down to grab the Hunter and began dragging him. "Remember that story…" He stumbled backward with a grunt then recovered. "About her getting skewered on a fencepost at Kos's house?"

No. But the kid clearly had an idea, and that was enough to get Bel's attention. "Tell me."

"The Hunter. Impaled on top of her." Leo spoke through his labored gasps. "Bled into her wounds. Kept her strong." He dropped the man's arms so the dead Hunter lay at Uta's side.

Bel sucked in a breath. "Tear that son of bitch open."

Leo's switch blade extended with a click. His hand shook, but he paused for only a second before slicing open one of the Hunter's wrists to bleed onto her gaping neck. He made three deep incisions, but only a trickle oozed out. The man's heart had stopped and his blood flowed too slowly.

Bel took hold of Leo's arm with his free hand. "Compress his chest, like CPR. Pump the blood out of him."

Leo pressed with his palms, clumsy and careful. Bel held the open, un-bleeding wound tight against Uta's neck.

"Damn it, Leo, harder!"

The kid straddled the man and pounded on his chest—not a technique that would resuscitate an unconscious human, but the brute force of it worked. The blood came faster, spurting and coating her torn-open wounds.

Bel didn't know what to look for. No one on his crew had ever been injured like this. He'd thought he'd seen every kind of vampire death. A clean decapitation, a fire, the sun, the wasting disease. Would hers be a new variation?

If so, the pain clawing at his gut and tearing through his muscles might kill him. His heart labored to beat.

Would she survive? Would she begin to breathe? Would her flesh knit back together?

Nothing happened. Distantly, he feared for Andre and Kos. But with the roar in his ears, the slow thud of his straining heart, the raw fear for Uta's survival—he couldn't sustain the focus on anything but her.

She was slipping away, and in turn, his world began to rock with the undulations of a slow-motion earthquake. He needed to puke. He closed his eyes and lay down.

Leo gasped, and Bel sat up.

Her eyes had opened. Rigor mortis?

"Uta?"

She blinked. He breathed. She'd fucking blinked.

"Are you—?"

She wriggled her jaw, clamping and digging into his flesh. He grunted, jerking from the pain. Then her tongue swiped over the ache, soothing and healing the place where he'd bitten himself. She released his arm from her mouth. Dried blood obscured his view of her wounds, but altogether more skin covered her muscles and veins, sinews and arteries.

Good enough. He pulled her into an embrace, his own equilibrium returning slowly with her in his arms. The smell of her blood, thick and potent, stirred him—not quite desire, just the promise of their bond, of an eternal connection.

Uta was alive, so the world was all right.

She whispered in his ear. "I told you to stay put."

He stiffened, then laughed. It may be all the thanks he got for saving her life. He'd take it.

But then she pulled back to look him in the eye. "Thank you."

With those words came the knowledge that she did see him as her equal. She'd meant it before, but he hadn't believed it.

"Fuck, I am glad you are alive."

"Hurt, did it?" She raised one eyebrow.

It had, worse than he ever could have believed, but that wasn't why.

His cheeks spread into a smile. "I've had splinters that hurt worse. But someone has to deal with my father now, and since you're an official member of the Justicia—"

Andre emerged from the hatchway, staring up at the bright blue sky. Behind him stood the ruins of his house atop the ashes of his vineyards. He turned in a slow circle, arms wide, his head thrown back, and let out a deep, loud laugh. Bel drank in his father's joy along with the sight of him in the sun.

Uta stood and yanked Bel up. She kept hold of his hand and they marched toward his father.

Zoey's dark head peeked out, and she exited slowly then ran to Andre, wrapping her arms around his waist. He lifted her up, spinning. Pedro appeared, supporting Lucas with one arm. Bel couldn't tell whose smile stretched bigger. Then came Kos and Omar, carrying a body between them.

Bel's stomach dropped—who could it be?

They put the man on the ground and circled around him as the rest of the household and crew stepped out of the cellar.

Bel leant over to examine the man's face. Ethan, dead. Good. "Who killed the son of a bitch?"

"Lucas." Pedro grinned.

Lucas's smile was somewhat more circumspect.

Leo joined the circle at Omar's side, and the vampire rested a hand on his shoulder.

A strange, quiet calm settled over the valley. Bel's nerves settled; it might all be okay. All the fire trucks and police vehicles had disappeared, but soon they would have to deal with a lot of dead Hunters.

Feet scuffed the earth and Bel looked up. Everyone tensed, on alert as Gwen approached from the direction of the road. She must have been at the Hunter's command center.

Uta's hand stiffened in his.

"She has a gun," Lena said.

She had Bel's gun, in fact, which he'd set aside to care for Uta when he'd thought the last Hunter was dead.

Damn it.

Kos stepped in front of Lena, and all the vampires followed suit, taking positions to shield the humans. Uta looked at him, and he shook his head. She stayed put.

"Is it him?" Gwen asked.

At the question, Uta stepped aside, tugging Bel with her so that Gwen could see the body.

Her gun came up so fast that Bel flinched. But she pointed into her own temple.

"No! Gwen, don't," Lena shouted.

Gwen looked to Uta, who might just be fast enough to pry that gun from her hand.

A wordless communication between the females stretched out for long seconds.

"I chose him over everything," Gwen finally said.

"But you have a different choice now," Lena insisted. "It can get better, Gwen."

"No." Gwen wrapped her free arm around her ribcage, shaking her head and staggering backward.

Uta dropped Bel's hand to hold up her palms. "Gwen—"

"Uta, you don't understand. You never did." And then she pulled the trigger.

Bel flinched, turning his head. He had seen quite enough blood and brains for the day.

Uta sagged.

A question formed on Bel's tongue—a question that meant everything. Could Uta have stopped her? Or did she let the woman make the choice she'd been prevented from making herself?

Was his mate glad to be alive, or not?

He took hold of her elbow, leaning close. "Did you let Gwen—"

A telephone rang. Bel jumped at the strangely surreal noise, sounding amidst the desolate scene. Everyone's faces were drawn tight as they patted their pockets.

"It's mine," Lucas said, and pressed the phone to his ear. "Bennett." He glanced at Andre. "It's Derek."

His expression gave no clue of what the Hunter said, and Bel envied the vampires who could hear both sides of the conversation.

Finally Lucas replied. "Yeah. The son of a bitch is dead. Leo's texting you a photo right now."

A few more seconds passed.

"A cease-fire?" Lucas shifted his eyes to Uta, and she nodded. "Done."

He slid the phone back into his pocket. "He says he has a bit more work to do before he's ready to negotiate a treaty, but he has an agreement from some key players on a truce."

"Please let this be the end," Uta whispered so reverently it sounded like a prayer.

"The end?" Andre asked. "Uta, old friend. We are standing in the sun. It is only the beginning."

He held out his arms to her, and she went to him laughing.

Bel glanced at Zoey, who winked back at him, smiling. One big happy family.

Vania inched her way up to him. "There's something we need to tell you."

The look on her face sent his heart right into his gut and he scanned the gathering for the members of his crew. Only one was missing. The realization hit him like a punch to the face. He stepped back, reeling.

"Trys?"

"Gwen killed her to take down the shield."

He'd never lost a member of his crew, and the death settled into his gut like a heavy stone.

Vania wiped at her eyes. "Me and the boys would like to take her body back to London."

"Of course." Bel pressed his hand against his mouth to hold back his grief. He trained his eyes on the charcoal and ash.

"Where do we go now?" Kos asked.

"I do not know about the rest of you all." Andre released Uta and stepped back. "But I would like to go home."

"Yes," Uta said. "You are all welcome to stay my house."

"Home?" Kos lifted Lena in a hug. "Sweetheart. Let's go home!"

Pedro cleared his throat. "I'm sorry to miss the party, but Lucas and I have some things to take care of, just the two of us. We are going to stay at my place for a while."

"Son?" Andre frowned.

"It's okay. Uta gave me some pointers on the plane."

Andre nodded, but Bel didn't miss the flash of grief that tightened his eyes.

"But," Pedro continued. "I wouldn't mind some detailed instructions." He offered Andre his hand, and the old guy clasped it, pulling him closer. Not long ago, Bel might have resented the easy intimacy between the males, but no more.

The stood in silence, as a new reality settled into Bel's bones.

It took him a long time to realize everyone was waiting on him to announce his plans, every face turned to him in expectation. All but one. Uta looked at her shoes.

London? Šolta? Hell. He wasn't ready to decide.

"I think I am going to hook up with Lexi and try to finish our experiments. Uta brought back some wine from Ayal's house, and I want to analyze it. You know, in case home doesn't work out for you all?"

Uta glanced up, her lips pursed. He couldn't read the expression on her blood-smeared features. Good. He didn't want to. He needed to figure stuff out for himself. Alone.

And that was how he felt, as soon as everyone began to sort out the dead bodies and make arrangements without him: alone.

CHAPTER 51

The redwood shingles had faded to a dull gray, and the porch needed a good sweeping. A layer of pollen and grime covered all the windows. It could have been worse, considering Pedro hadn't been home in two months.

The last time he'd approached the door, it had hung open, a Hunter ambush awaiting him inside. Pedro slid the key into the lock and froze, shivering.

Gray faced and stiff, Lucas took his hand and stepped into the dark, musty cottage first. "Cute."

Dust motes flew in the watery light filtering through the dirty windows.

Lucas flipped a switch. The room remained dim. He smiled. "It's got crappy light, but otherwise, I like gingerbread houses."

"Shut up." Pedro had loved this little house once, before he'd been attacked there.

Lucas ran his hand along the dark wood paneling beside the door. "I'm serious — I love this old Victorian style — the funky details. Every home needs more scallops and finials and fringe."

"Nice try. You're not that gay."

"Oh no, I am." Lucas leaned against the wall. He must have felt unsteady, but still he joked. "I just go in for the uber-modern style, not a flourish to mess up my feng-shui." He sat down, straightening a pillow on the couch. "I told you I wanted to be an architect, once upon a time?"

"No. You didn't." Pedro pressed his lips together and considered the aspiration. "You'll have time to be anything you want to be."

Lucas pulled his chin, leaning over to inspect Pedro's book shelf of techno CDs and Spanish paperbacks. "I guess I will, although for now it seems I'm needed to forge a peace between our warring tribes."

"You master-minded it. I think it would be fair to bow out now." Pedro grinned, hopeful. A quiet little life somewhere, until everything blew over — nothing sounded better.

Lucas glanced up and shook his head. "You know I couldn't. They're going to need me."

Yeah, they all needed him. A rush of pride welled up in Pedro — his man, the hero. And it was Pedro's job to make sure Lucas would be there, fit and ready to help.

"You remember what it was like when I turned, right?" Pedro tossed his keys into a bowl on the shelf.

Lucas clutched at his gut even as he stood to examine a pair of watercolor paintings of Pedro's family vineyards in Argentina. Pedro wanted to demand he sit down.

"I remember you being very pissy with me," Lucas said.

Pedro snorted. "That was totally your fault."

"It was Ethan's fault. You just took it out on me." Even in profile, Lucas's smile curved, subtle but evident. *Mierda,* it was anything but funny, yet somehow they had moved on and could joke about it.

"I'm sorry about Ethan."

Lucas stood straight and cocked his head. "Hell, I'm not."

"I never had a brother, besides Kos and Bel. But I'm pretty sure it's not supposed to be like that. So I'm sorry."

Lucas exhaled a burst of breath through his nose. "Not much in life turns out the way it's supposed to." He crossed the room, peering into the bedroom. Then he strode to the kitchen and swung wide the cabinets. His unabashed curiosity reminded Pedro of their lazy explorations the first times they'd had sex. He leaned against the doorjamb and watched his man, letting a cautious contentment settle over him.

Finally, Lucas looked up and grinned. "This will do for now."

"I'm so glad you approve." Pedro rolled his eyes. But really, he wasn't sure he wanted the house to *do,* wasn't sure the cottage could be his home again after what had happened here. There would be time to sort that out later, too.

He dropped into his favorite chair and kicked his feet up on the coffee table. "How do you feel?"

"I told you, I'm not sorry. I feel like a hero."

"I meant, are you tired? Hurting?"

Behind the kitchen counter Lucas stilled and crossed his arms. "The truth?"

"Uh, yeah."

"I'm about to keel over, but I'm not looking forward to getting this party started." He leaned forward and put his elbows on the counter, resting his chin in his hands. "I remember everything about when Andre turned you—you were supposed to be crazed with blood lust, only you weren't because of my blood. Then, you were miserable for days, with a headache, and a major case of overstimulation."

Pedro swallowed, trying to moisten his dry mouth. "I wish I could make it easier."

"Yeah, me too." Lucas rubbed his mouth. "You can do one thing for me—I want to feed from a girl."

"Already taken care of. Ally and Susan are on call. They're staying with a friend in Guerneville, and more than happy to oblige."

Lucas's Adam's apple bobbed, looking far too prominent in his thin neck. Soon vampire blood would heal him, return him to his natural strength, filling out his emaciated muscles. But first Pedro would have to almost kill him, draining him of blood. Andre had given him a ceremonial blade—the one he'd used to turn Kos decades ago. The sharp steel curved oddly, designed to remain in a vampire's skin and keep a wound open while his blood poured into his new offspring. Compared to the sexy business of feeding and fucking, this reproduction stuff was gory.

Lucas filled a glass of water from the tap and set it on the counter with a bang. "Are you scared?"

Should Pedro lie? Probably. But he couldn't, not after everything they'd been through. "Yep."

"Me too." Lucas drank a long swig of water. "Let's get it over with."

Pedro sent Susan a text, then took Lucas by the hand and led him to the bedroom.

Pedro knelt and reached for Lucas's fly. But Lucas covered Pedro's hands. "If you are going to suck my dick and then kill me, will you at least put it away before the girls show up?"

He looked up Lucas's long, lean body. "Sorry, I can't. That was the deal. Their blood for a good, long look at your dick."

Lucas's eyes went wide in the split second it took him to realize Pedro was joking. "Damn." He dropped onto the edge of the bed with his jeans around his knees. "And I'm signing up for forever with you and your jokes."

"Uh huh." Pedro swallowed Lucas's cock whole, teasing the tip with his tongue. Lucas groaned, hardening. In an instant, Pedro's own erection pressed against his zipper. Astonishing, given the strain of the task before him.

After a few moments of sucking and licking, Lucas bucked, grabbing at the bedspread. "Damn. This isn't what I want. Fuck me, Pedro. One more time."

Pedro needed it — needed to be inside him, needed the reassurance of Lucas's whole body against him, quaking with pleasure as he took him and his blood. He shucked off his clothes quickly and moved between Lucas's legs. He reached into the bedside table until he found a dusty bottle of lube and began a slow, gentle kiss as he worked his fingers inside Lucas.

"*Jesu Cristo*." His man felt so good, and he had never wanted anything so much as he wanted to possess Lucas, now and forever. Pedro sank his fangs into Lucas's neck at his carotid artery, just as Andre had instructed. The blood came faster than any other bite, and he nearly gagged trying to swallow it down.

"Please, Pedro. Now," Lucas mewled on a breath.

Pedro gripped his cock and slid all the way into his man. Home.

Lucas grunted, pushing back harder, before angling to receive another thrust.

"Jesus, I'm dying and it feels so good." His voice floated, reedy and weak.

The blood flowing into Pedro's mouth slowed, confirming Lucas's words. Pedro wished like hell he could offer some reassurance.

But Lucas did it instead, with a whisper. "I love you. I love you. Make me yours forever."

The words took Pedro over the edge and he pounded Lucas until he came with a soft splurt on his skinny stomach — an instinct of his nearly dead body, a cry of pleasure frighteningly absent. It was all Pedro could do not to cry.

When the blood finally stopped, Pedro sat up. The sight of Lucas, still and gray on the bed twisted his gut, and he nearly vomited all the blood filling his stomach. He remembered Zoey's turning, with Kos's prayers, and Lena's fussing — a room full of well wishers — and he longed for his family. He'd been a fool to try this alone.

Andre's words came back to him. *Your courage will waver, but you must take heart. Do not give up.*

Pedro sliced a diagonal incision across his wrist, wedging the sharp crescent under his skin. The narrow trough funneled blood in a clean stream. It spilled onto the bedspread before he got Lucas's mouth open.

It will take more of your blood than you expect, and time will crawl.

God, he wished Andre were there, his heavy hand resting on Pedro's shoulder.

Nothing happened.

He'd killed his lover, his savior, his best friend.

It wasn't going to work.

Lucas had been too sick to turn.

A gurgle sounded in Lucas's throat. His eyes popped open.

Pedro swallowed with relief. "Dude, you're not gonna believe this, but your peepers have turned gold."

Lucas gulped down a mouthful of blood. "God, no more jokes," he croaked, a trace of a smile on his bloody lips. "What now?"

"More of my blood, and then Ally's, as soon as she gets here."

"Cover me up, asshole."

Pedro laughed, cleaning up Lucas and covering the bloody sheets as well as he could, while a trickle of his blood continued to fall onto Lucas's tongue. He'd had more than enough, but it kept them both occupied until someone rapped on the door, only loud enough for a vampire to hear. He pulled out the blade and licked his wrist clean.

Just in case, he peered through the window. Susan waved, smiling. Ally chewed her lower lip.

"How is he?" she asked, when the door swung open.

"Hungry."

From there, everything proceeded perfectly. Fangs appeared, friendly lesbians were fed upon under Pedro's careful supervision, to prevent Lucas from harming them in his bloodlust.

When they left, Pedro darkened the room, and pulled Lucas up to lie back against his chest.

"All I can think about is blood — the way it smells, tastes — heaven."

"I was the same way, only all I could think about was your blood. It will pass." He stroked Lucas's hair with the lightest of touches, not wanting to irritate his sensitive skin. "Can you hear the river flowing?"

"Is that the river? I thought it was your blood, or mine."

"Focus on it. It will soothe you."

"Where will we go?" Lucas murmured, leaning in to Pedro's touch.

It was the question he'd been dreading, because he had no idea how Lucas would react. "If it's okay with you, there is a little house in Turkey available, with some vineyards attached."

"Turkey's not far from Croatia."

Pedro smiled into Lucas's hair. "No, it's not."

"I'm game then. I don't want to be too far from the old guy."

"Me either, man. Me either."

CHAPTER 52

Uta had not seen the Island of Šolta under the sun since hundreds of years before Jesus Christ had been born. That time she had stood on the stern of a pirate ship, not a ferry. Unchanged, Šolta's gentle hills rolled up out of the turquoise of the Adriatic, stealing her breath. The salty breeze caressed her face, reminding her of Bel's scent.

The boat approached the narrow harbor housing the tiny port village of Rogač. The island's ivory colored villas roofed with terra-cotta tiles were so picturesque that they adorned many postcards, but she was no tourist. For a moment she even felt like a queen again.

Andre stood a meter in front of her and he reached for Zoey's hand. Uta took pleasure in witnessing his homecoming, even if she envied him his mate. He hadn't been home once since they were driven away, but she had secreted herself back often enough to soothe her aching homesickness, and her wasting disease. Her old friend turned around to look at her, his eyes shimmering pink in the sunlight. He extended his hand, and she went to stand next to him, grateful for the big palm that settled onto her shoulder — heavy and strong like Bel's, but with none of the pull or heat that his held for her.

Nearby, Kos rubbed up and down Lena's back where she bent over the side of the boat, green with sickness even though no wind had stirred the ocean and the harbor's waters lay still and glittering much like Andre's eyes.

The boat pulled alongside the dock and the deckhand looped a rope around the mooring. Only the gentlest waves rocked the boat as they stepped off. Uta scanned the strip of parked cars for the one she had hired, but instead she caught the scent of Hunter on the breeze. Instantly on alert, she glimpsed an odd pair — a raven haired woman raised her hand in greeting, a handsome young blond man behind her. The female whispered on the wind, in the way only old vampires could.

Greetings. We are here to welcome you.

Uta reigned in her urge to run to them.

"Andre, can you see to the luggage? We will meet our driver near the lamppost."

Without waiting for a reply, she turned and strolled to the pair. The female extended a hand. "I am Carmen Pallatina."

Uta recognized the name of an ancient female from Northern Italy, her isolated household one of the few old-world estates to survive. Uta grasped her hand firmly. "What are you doing here?"

"Loki sent me to attempt persuasion on the Hunters patrolling your homeland. He wanted you to be free to return as soon as possible."

Uta could not hold back the tears. "You heard of his death?"

"Yes, sister, and I am sorry for our loss, and yours especially."

The blond man was not as young as Uta had first guessed — he was fit and handsome, and nearing fifty.

Pallatina faced the Hunter. "This is Petar Ferić. His family has been patrolling Šolta since your community was driven out."

This man descended from the Hunters who had tortured and executed her household, burned Andre's vineyards, and killed many of her friends that day. But these were the debts that must be put aside if a reconciliation was to be possible.

Perhaps sensing her unease, he did not offer his hand. He lifted his chin proudly and spoke in the Dalmatian dialect that she preferred. "My people are moderates."

Flying sheep. Was there such a thing as a moderate Hunter?

"We knew of your visits here, for example, and we made no moves against you, since you did not harm the humans of Šolta."

She recoiled at the idea she had been observed, but she snorted to cover her discomfort. "Harm is not an accurate word."

He raised his palms, casting a glance at Pallatina and blushing. "Please let me continue. We were not pleased by Ethan Bennett's violent aspirations. And when we received evidence he sacrificed Hunters to escalate the war, we voted to disassociate from the tribe. That same day, Carmen arrived. None of us had ever met a vampire face to face. It was…an education." There was that charming blush again, on his ruggedly handsome face. "I am an amateur historian, and I am intrigued by what she has told me about the Hunters and vampires living together." He rubbed at his neck. "There is a connection I cannot ignore."

Pallatina raised her eyes to the dock were the Maras vampires pulled a caravan of suitcases, mostly Uta's. All three glowered, while Lena walked empty handed, a green and sour twist to her mouth. It had been the same for Mila. Vampire-strong morning sickness.

"Is she all right?" Pallatina asked.

"She is pregnant," Uta replied, as Kos took Lena's elbow.

The Italian vampire's dark brow shot up. "With…?"

"Yes."

With a little cluck, Pallatina moved on. "We have readied your house with groceries for the human. Petar's clan is willing to feed you."

Had Uta heard that right? The offer was beyond generous.

"In exchange…" he began.

Of course there are strings, Uta thought.

"…we would like to know what you know of those prehistoric times."

"Thank you." Uta swallowed. She could comply with such a reasonable request. A true peace would require such conversations, one at a time across the whole world. "Please allow us to settle in today, and we will welcome you tomorrow."

"Certainly." He smiled, and Uta witnessed just how much warmth golden Hunter eyes could radiate.

Uta introduced the pair to the Maras family, and then they were off in the little van.

Lena didn't fare much better in the car than she had on the ferry, dry heaving on the bumpy roads. They wound north and west across the island toward Uta's villa until, finally, they were there.

She inserted the key into the door. Home.

The word clattered in the hollowness of her heart. Nowhere was home without Bel.

She let out a long, steady breath, steeling herself. For once, the air inside the house blew fresh, rather than hanging stale. Pallatina had left an unlikely vase of purple hyacinth on the table. Odd — the flowers were wildly out of season. A white notecard peeked from under the vase. Pretty, neat letters spelled out *Hyacinths — for rebirth* in both English and Croatian.

The jarring bustle of her guests behind her set her teeth on edge and she turned.

When had Andre's hair gotten so long? He looked more like Bel. Too much. How would she stand to see him? Gods of Illyria, why had she invited them all to stay with her — a band of homeless strays, another burden she didn't need.

"Stop it," Andre said.

"What?"

He raised his eyebrows, confirming he'd known her thoughts.

That was the trouble with old friends.

His chest lifted in a breath. He had his own demons to face. "Will you walk with me? I want to see my land."

She softened, compassion somehow swelling larger than her loneliness and irritation — for the moment.

"There is nothing there. The vineyards, the ruins of the house — it is all overgrown. The last time I looked, a palm tree grew straight out of the foyer."

"I need to see."

"Shouldn't you take Zoey?"

"First I want to see what I have to offer her."

Uta peered into his face. His lip quivered.

"Nice try. She's ordered you to interrogate me about Bel?"

"I planned to anyway, but she insisted I do it now. She senses you are suffering."

"I am fine." She shook her head, tears stinging her eyes.

"Good. You can tell me how fine you are all the way down the hill."

He and Zoey would just wear her down, like water torture, if she did not explain soon. She crossed to the door.

"You are going in that?" He looked her over, narrowing in on her heels.

She could have changed into jeans and walking boots—she had some in a closet upstairs. "Why not?"

"You will draw attention."

"I enjoy attention."

"How could I forget?"

They walked in silence until they reached the land that had been his estate. In front of the ruins, he dropped to his knees and dug his fingers into the earth. Uta could not bear to see his display of emotion if she hoped to keep her own locked up tight. She wandered to an outcropping overlooking the harbor, a favorite boat-watching place for her and Bel. The sun crawled down the sky. Her very first sunset since becoming a vampire ages ago.

Finally, Andre shuffled up behind her and lowered himself to sit cross-legged. She smiled. Bel had always dangled his legs.

"Do you love him?" Andre asked.

"It goes without saying."

"Actually, it does not. Love is not the same as the desperate need of the bond. I know that now in a way I did not with Mila."

"I do. I always have, and even more now."

"Does he know?"

"Yes."

"Does he love you?"

"Yes, but he does not trust me because I walked into the sun."

Andre sucked into a breath. "You rubbed salt into the one wound that cannot heal."

"If I had succeeded, it would have been salt in that wound. I failed, so now I am a large, sharp splinter inside his raw flesh."

"Do you want to be alive now?"

He had asked the crucial question, the one Gwen had asked with her stare when she held that gun to her head. Was Uta glad for all the times she had been stopped from suicide? Or would she rather be dead, free of her burdens and her bond? She had been paralyzed by the question, and it had swallowed up the split second in which she might have saved the woman.

But here she sat, in the sun, on Šolta, hyacinths on her table — the symbol of a fragile peace.

And even better, Bel loved her, even if he did not yet trust her. And that gave her a reason to hope.

"Yes. I want to be alive."

"Then you must go to him, and do your best to convince him."

She turned sidelong to see the face of her old friend, her lover's father, who surely should know the answer. "With Bel, it is better to wait until he comes to me, ready to be convinced."

Andre chuckled. "My experience has proven that could take a very long time."

"It very well might. But I will wait as long as he needs."

CHAPTER 53

Bel's eyes watered, straining to focus on the spreadsheet in front of him. The results confirmed that none of the cofactors rendered *hemoaurum* effective, even though Ayal's wine was chock full of the Hunter-protein, and so was the sample of Uta's blood he'd taken at Ayal's house.

All his test subjects had returned to their homelands to heal and rebuild, but they'd promised to send him blood samples so he could track their progress. Soon he would have more data, but probably no more answers.

"When was the last time you ate?" Lexi asked from her neighboring workstation. She'd ostensibly come up from LA to help him analyze the data, but he was beginning to suspect her mission was more of an intervention.

He pressed the heels of his hands into his eyes. "I don't know. Breakfast?"

"Today?"

He had to think about it. "Yesterday."

"It's time to give up, Bel."

"Not yet." He leaned closer to the screen.

"Vampires and Hunters are at peace, acres of Blood Vine vineyards have been found, you somehow even figured out *hemoaurum* would cure a rare human sun allergy. There's no need to continue."

"I just want to know how the bonds work."

"You're not being rational."

He sighed, hoping for a calm tone. But it came out more like a martyr's whine. "Of course I am. Blood bonds have physiological effects, therefore I should be able to trace their mechanisms. It's perfectly logical."

"That's the problem. With other things, like this far-fetched science around how you were conceived, or that witch who worked for you—"

The loss of Trys's death stabbed at him and he must have winced because Lexi stopped mid-sentence and backpedaled.

"I'm sorry to bring her up. But from what you've told me you never understood a bit of science about how she could heal, or, damn it Bel, create magical, selectively-permeable shields. Yet you never killed yourself trying to figure it out."

"It's totally different." The frustration seethed inside of him to the point of dizziness. He cradled his forehead in his hands to keep from falling over. His heart rate shot up nearly to tachycardia.

"Shite." He jumped off his chair. "Something's wrong with her."

"No, Bel. You're just starving and about to pass out from it." She pulled a granola bar from her drawer and shoved it across the desk. After a glance at his face, she grabbed a handful and tossed them at him.

He sat down and unwrapped one. It tasted like heaven, which proved her hunger-hypothesis. Otherwise oats tasting like they'd been glued to cardboard and sprinkled with cinnamon would have been like eating horse fodder. First the vertigo subsided, then his panic. Finally, his brain seemed to reboot. Back online, he returned his gaze to the laptop. Lexi stood and slammed the thing shut.

He barely got his fingers out in time. "Ouch."

"Stop being a baby. You're just desperate for some kind of explanation you can hide behind, because conceding to the mysteriousness of the whole thing gives her power over you."

"She already has power over me." He unwrapped another granola bar.

"And you have power over her. That's what it means to love someone, and I saw she loved you the moment I met her."

"I hate to burst your amateur psych bubble, doll, but she and I already crossed this terrain. Been there, analyzed it."

"Then what are you afraid of?"

That he wasn't enough. That the sun, and all the people that loved her, and life itself wasn't enough. And she would give up again. That she was sorry to be alive. It was the only explanation for why she'd let Gwen kill herself.

"Do you remember how my mother died?"

Her lower lip swallowed up the top one, such a cute frown. "Of course I do."

"That is what I am afraid of."

She blew out a breath. "Then you have to ask if she's still suicidal. Stop burying yourself in this futile experiment and find out the truth."

"I know. I'm just not ready. Let me hide a little longer."

Her eyes crinkled at the edges.

"Please?"

Her frown turned to a pitying smile. "Fair enough. Ass kicking over for now. I'm off to catch my flight. Promise me you'll get yourself some lunch."

"Sure thing."

But he didn't. Instead, he sat at his desk and tried to imagine asking Uta if she had any more plans to kill herself. Yeah, right. She would make him a gift of her middle fingers and grow herself two more.

A knock sounded at the door. Remembering the last time someone paid him an unexpected visit, he reached for the gun holstered safely at his side. "Come in."

The door inched open, and the hairs on his neck bristled. He stood so he could see around it before it came fully open.

A petite young woman with light brown hair waited, her hands dangling non-threateningly at her side. Set in her coppery, olive skin, her big yellow eyes struck him as especially cat-like. He gently played with the trigger.

"You are Lobel Maras?"

It was her voice that gave her away, almost like Loki's in its richness of tone, the layers of a thousand languages in every word.

"Ayal?"

She extended her hand and her smile made her appear painfully young, that same Loki-esque contradiction.

"What are you doing here?"

"I wanted to meet the other halfling."

He gestured at an empty chair. What did a guy say to a five-thousand-year-old woman? "I'm sorry you were alone for so long."

"Thank you." She perched on the seat. "In truth, I only regretted it near the end. And now I am not alone anymore. In fact, I visited your brother Pedro at his new home."

"Your home, you mean?"

"No, it belongs to him and Lucas now. It was time for me to leave." She leaned close, scrutinizing him. "But I did notice a drawing was missing from my studio."

Bel pulled it from his pocket, and laid it open on his desk.

"Have you guessed what it means yet?" She touched the edge closest to her with just the tips of her fingers.

He zeroed in on the vampire, chained to the humans. "I think it means that a bond is sometimes a prison."

"Yes. And what else?"

"They made the wine to be free of it."

"We made the wine so we had choices. Not to stay in our land. Not to take a bonded mate. Not to take partners in the intimacy of feeding. But still, almost always, vampires and Hunters alike chose their bonds."

They wanted the choice, but still they chose each other. Could it really be so easy?

"Did she send you?"

"Pedro sent me." Ayal handed him a business card before pushing back her chair. "I have an email address now. And I will leave you with one last thought: If I had been born bonded to a mate, I do not think I would have chosen to stay alone. Sometimes a bond is a prison, and sometimes, though it is imperfect, it is a blessing."

He already knew which one Uta was.

Five minutes in the airport reminded him why he preferred flying by private jet, but both of his were in London, and if he sent for them, the whole crew would know where he was headed.

Thirty-six hours later, the last ferry of the night pulled into Rogač. A crisp breeze blew off the water, warning that winter approached. At this time of night, with only a few street lamps on the dock, Šolta appeared nearly unchanged from the days of his youth.

Her presence tugged at him. Shite. If she felt it too, it would ruin his surprise. He strengthened his internal barriers, cutting off the emotional wire.

The route to her house took shape in his mind as clearly as if he'd walked it last week. But of course, there were no taxis in sleepy little Rogač. A young man waited for the only other passenger on the boat, a young woman. When she reached the end of the dock, he lifted her off her feet into an embrace, and pushed her up against a car for a kiss. Bel should have turned away, wanted to, but all he could think was that the kid had wheels.

"I'll pay you five hundred euros to drive me to the north end of the island."

Dazed, the man slid the woman down his body and turned. "Are you crazy? That's a ten minute drive."

"Yes, but it's a two hour walk, and I am exhausted."

He took a step closer, peering at Bel in the dark. "Andre?"

"I'm his son, Lobel."

"Oh."

"So. About that ride?"

He glanced at his girl, who nodded. "Sure thing, but don't bother with the cash. I'm happy to do you a favor."

Ten minutes later, he pulled up to her house. Just as Andre had built Kaštel in California, she had rebuilt an exact replica of the one he'd visited so often as a boy. Graceful stone walls extended up two stories. Upstairs, only one light burned in all the wood-framed windows.

"Is my father staying here?" Bel asked the driver.

"I'm not sure. They've made a lot of progress on his place already."

Something about that news buoyed Bel as he waved farewell to the friendly kid. His father was rebuilding, and the war was over.

He didn't knock, but he treaded lightly on the stairs—their polished pine catching just enough moonlight to illuminate his path.

Yellow light seeped from a door hanging slightly ajar at the end of the hall. If he remembered correctly, that was a small room with a bathtub.

"Kos, is that you? I thought you all were staying in the big house tonight."

His nerves thrummed, his blood buzzed, and his cock, which had been on an extended vacation since she'd left California, sprang to life.

Then she gasped, and warmth bloomed in his gut, radiating out into his limbs.

She knew it was him.

He needed to seize the final moments of surprise. He strode to the door and pushed it open, to find her exactly where he expected—submerged in an antique copper tub, her mass of auburn hair pinned into a messy knot with knitting needles. Candles lit the small room. Her red-painted toes curled around the faucet. Mounds of bubbles covered the surface of the water, but he didn't need to see to know the perfect lines of her body under the suds. Even his eleven-year-old self had known, somehow.

He staggered backward, sliding down the wall to sit on his arse.

His hazy boyhood fantasy returned—the youthful imaginings of an inexperienced child who had nevertheless known her body from years of roughhousing, from walking behind her pert little arse all over the island.

Her hands came out of the bubbles to grip the side of the tub. "Bel?" she whispered.

But it was too late. The bathtub triggered another memory—of his mother. Poor, miserable Mila, who hadn't really wanted to live for as long as Bel could remember. Dead, floating, blond hair spread across pink water. He'd never seen her like that, Kos had prevented him, but his imagination had concocted its own visuals nonetheless.

Oh hell. All his ghosts were in this steamy little room.

"Bel?" The water sloshed around her. Oh God, he would lose control if she stood up all wet and naked.

"Why did you let Gwen kill herself?"

"Oh." Uta's full lips parted.

That confirmed his worst fears. "Shite."

She shook her head. "No, Bel, it was not like that. I froze. I started thinking about all the times I had failed, and how I had let her down, and what she had to live for, and…" She pressed her lips together and closed her almond shaped eyes, then opened them to meet his stare. "I want to be alive. And I want to be with you."

Something caused her voice to waver, and the relief her words promised taunted him, just out of reach. "But?"

"This is not a fairytale. All I can tell you about is now. I cannot say you are all I will ever need and I cannot promise forever." Tears sparkled in her eyelashes, but she laughed. "Not much of a bargain, am I? All my luggage, and no guarantee of a happily ever after."

"Your baggage." His face tightened into a smile, he couldn't help it. "And I don't want to be your reason for living. That's just one more burden neither of us need."

She nodded, her mouth set in a grave line.

He tilted his head to stare at the ceiling and didn't look at her. "Will you try?"

She exhaled on a sigh. "With every ounce of strength I possess, I will fight to want to live, for your sake."

Loud and clear, he heard what she wasn't saying—she hadn't fought before. "Why now?"

"Because I gave you a choice, and you have finally chosen me." Her voice had gone low and husky.

This needing, this trying—it had to be enough.

She already knew it, but he wanted her to hear the words from his mouth. "Yes. I chose you."

"Then I am yours." And she stood up, the water pouring off her in one silken sheet—her sweet breasts, the flat plane of her belly, her long slender thighs, coming together in that vee of auburn curls.

He wobbled, finally getting to his feet and crossing to her in two strides. With the tip of his index finger, he tweaked her nipples, first one, then the other. "I choose these."

He trailed his hand down her to her core, dipping into her slit. "I choose this." The slippery moisture of her desire covered his finger, slicker than mere bathwater. He sucked it into his mouth. Her ragged breaths echoed on the tiles of the small room. Or were those his?

She smiled, beauty herself.

Yes. The breaths were definitely his. "Maybe I never had a choice about wanting your body."

A tiny crease appeared between her eyes. He smoothed it away and tapped her there. Behind her thick skull lay that lightning quick brain and a frontal lobe holding more personality that he'd have thought possible.

"But this, I choose of my own free will."

She grabbed hold of his wrist and pressed his hand to her heart.

"Yes," he said. "And this, I will love as long as you will let me."

"Show me," she whispered. Or were the words just a plea across their bond?

He unzipped his hoodie, yanked his shirt off, kicked off his boots.

When he reached for his fly, she covered his hands. "Let me."

Before he could agree, she knelt before him, undoing his jeans and sliding them down his legs. She reached for his erection, and the power that arced between them sent him staggering backward.

"Sheep teats. I am sorry, Bel. I swear, I do not mean to push you."

He chuckled. "I know."

One day, they would get past this awkwardness, but for the moment, he actually enjoyed it—the adorable push and pull of her demands and retreats, her vulnerable need and her shy remorse.

"It scared me at first, Uta. But I would be a fool not to be honored by your desire."

She flashed him a fangy smile. "Still, I can be very agreeable. I will give you anything you ask for. I can suck—"

"Not now, Uta."

"Bend me over the sink and take me—"

"No, Uta."

She pouted. "Then what?"

"Then…you take me." His pulse raced at a dangerous speed as he lowered himself onto a plush rug and lay back, resting his head in his palms. "I'm not afraid of you." His words caught in his throat, rasping out as a whisper. Okay, he was a little afraid, but mostly in a good way.

The smile vanished from her face and a look of solemn reverence came over her. Water still beading on her from the tub, she knelt astride his hips and pressed her palms into his chest, capturing his erection flush against her hot *pićka*.

Where their bodies touched, blood throbbed, his and hers together drumming an incessant beat and demanding he taste her. He lifted his head to her breast, his cock rubbing friction between them.

She raised up and sheathed him in her glorious heat, driving all thoughts from his head. He became only sensation — her curves of her face, the taste of her skin, the feel of her on his body, up and down his cock, the scent of hyacinth cloaking them both.

She rode him, sweating and slipping over his body, driving him closer and closer to release. He stiffened, and she stilled — calming his need to spill.

"I love you, Bel, and I will fight to give you forever."

She bent to his neck, preparing to feed with a lick. But he captured her hand. "I need to taste you too."

Under half lidded eyes, she smiled and sliced her wrist open on a fang. His mouthed closed over the slit, tasting the blissful salt of her blood, before she pierced his neck and took deep draws of his own. The effect of her bite seized him all at once — heightening every sense and melting him to the core. She rocked on him again, pressing her clit against his pelvic bone and grinding out her pleasure as she pulled on his vein. When she contracted around him, his orgasm roared through him, an explosion of pleasure in every cell.

And for the very first time in his life, he knew what it meant to be home.

CHAPTER 54

Four Years Later

Andre wiped the dust from his sunglasses and slid them back onto his face. His eyes still had not acclimated to the bright light of day, even after these years of sun tolerance.

Just one more graft. He cut a sliver from the vine, a popular Croatian varietal the former owner of the vineyard had been producing with moderate success. But Andre had no interest in *Plavac Mali*.

From a pouch on his hip he pulled a bud — a rusty red knot of new growth cut from an ancient vineyard in eastern Turkey — and slid it into the cleft of raw plant flesh he had exposed. With clear plastic tape, he wrapped the splice together, leaving a gap for the bud to grow through.

There. He had finished his share.

He surveyed the hillside.

Pedro strode toward him, raising his hand in greeting. Kos came from the other direction, curling the brim of his baseball cap in his hand. They had done a good night's work, all the way through the morning, even without Bel who insisted on spending his time in a small lab where he still worked to understand the mysterious mechanisms of blood bonds. But by this time of day he was surely lazing away in a shaded hammock drinking bourbon; he always begged off the hard labor with the excuse that he was only human.

So the three vampires had worked alone to splice Ayal's vines onto every knot of rootstock in the entire span of Andre's new property.

Pedro mopped his sweaty forehead. "I hope she thrives here. The climate is warmer than on my mountain."

"All we can do it wait and see." Andre did not fret over things like this now that he had come home. There would be time to cross and graft over and over again until he grew another perfect wine. In the meantime, they had as much of Pedro's wine as they could drink—good, rich stuff that gave even Andre a buzz.

He clapped his hands on both their shoulders as they ambled back to the house, enjoying Pedro's company. He and Lucas's frequent visits were not enough. Andre missed the days of everyone being under one another's feet, the sounds of fucking, and arguing, and make-up sex from all corners of the Kaštel Estate. Funny that he now felt nostalgia for the place of his exile, though it only tugged at his heart and not his body.

At the edge of the vineyard, they passed onto Andre's old estate. He'd begun to clear it, and prepare the earth for planting new vines.

Pedro knelt and let the soil fall through the sieve of his fingers. "How much land will it be all together?"

"About a third of what we had in California."

"Papa!" Young Mirko sprinted down the row, a tiny blond figure on the hillside.

Kos wrapped his hands around his waist and raised him overhead. "Mirko, you know I don't want you running so far from the house all alone."

"But *Kuma* Zoey said she heard you just over the hill."

Kos frowned at Andre. He just shrugged—Kos and Lena protected Mirko so much, so different from the way Mila and Andre had let Kos and Bel walk the length of Šolta four times in a day. But those had been idyllic times, and neither of the young boy's parents were entirely settled into the new safety of their lives in this time of peace.

Andre ruffled Mirko's hair. "Listen to your Papa. Soon you will be big enough to explore on your own, and now you have your pick of friends to wander with you."

The little boy's face, nearly identical to Kos except for the hints of Lena's fine mouth and jaw, grew solemn. "Yes, *Deda*. I just wanted to see Uncle Pedro."

So earnest, so much desire to be good — he was Kos all over again, yet with parents whose bond would last. Andre's chest grew tight with love for his family.

Kos hugged him before setting him down. "You are forgiven, son. Now run along and tell your mother we are returning."

The little boy took off, gangly arms wide as he ran over the uneven earth.

"Wait, Mirko," Andre called behind him. "Have the guests arrived?"

"Just a few," he shouted into the air, his high sweet voice carrying on the breeze.

He walked with Kos a few steps toward the house before he realized Pedro did not follow. He stood stiff, his face perplexed.

"What is it?" Andre asked.

Pedro's dark brows pulled down over his golden eyes. "Maybe we should get one of those."

Andre looked out at the sea for some yacht, but no boats spotted the turquoise-turning-blue Adriatic. What on earth did he want to acquire?

Kos laughed. "It's a big decision. You might want to think it over. Besides, I don't exactly see Lucas as Mr. Mom."

Realization dawned on Andre, and he studied Pedro's face, guessing at the spark that had lit up that surprising idea — to redeem Lucas's past with a new, happy family.

"Son, there are all kinds of families."

Pedro met his eye and smiled. "*Verdad.*"

On the back lawn, watered by some desalination contraption of Bel's devising, a table covered with a red-checked cloth held stacks of jars, arranged by Lena in careful lines. Lucas carried out a cask of Ayal's wine and set it next to them before saluting Andre.

A band tuned their instruments on the brick patio. Bel had one hand wrapped around Uta's waist, whispering in her ear and trying to shove a fiddle into her hand even as she pushed it away, laughing.

Andre's chest grew even tighter as he gazed at the pair — an excellent, deserving match. One more good thing to come from his broken past.

Lena came out of the kitchen door with Mirko balanced on her hip. The boy was nearly too big to be carried around in that manner. Lucky for him, his mother possessed a vampire's strength. Kos hugged them both, kissing Lena first on the cheek, then longer on the mouth.

Andre glanced away.

The music began and, all around him, old friends converged as if on cue, from the air, the fields and around the side of the house, greeting one another. Ayal the halfling lifted Mirko high into the air, exclaiming how much he had grown. Even Petar Ferić and his sons had joined the party.

Zoey stepped into Andre's side, tucking herself under his arm, where she belonged. He inhaled her sweet, familiar scent.

"I dreamed this," she said, looking up at him with her wide smile.

"This?"

"Yes, or very nearly—with Uta and Lena, and the music, and all your old friends wandering out of the vineyards. You were there too, and you told me it was the Night Harvest."

"Ah, yes." He recalled her mention of the dream before. "Only now we harvest and feast under the sun."

"And the moon."

"No." He bent to her ear. "When the moon rises, I am carrying you inside for our own private feast."

Four years since she had become his mate, and she still blushed.

"I love you," she whispered.

"And I you. Now, let us greet our guests." He clapped his hands together and the voices quieted, turning to face him. He had a short speech prepared, but it flew from his mind on the sun-warmed breeze. There were only three words that mattered anyway.

"Friends, welcome home."

The End

Acknowledgments

I remember very well telling my beloved beta reader Emily Mellott what I had in mind for Bel and Uta before the first book in the series was even finished. I had the premise in mind, but executing the character of Uta really challenged me as a writer. In addition to Emily, I am indebted to the insights of my writing friends Anne Francis, Ed Hoornaert, Jessica Gibbons, B.B., and especially to Samantha MacDouglas who finally helped me figure out how to show the readers what I already knew to be true about Uta. And of course, I'm so grateful to the team at Omnific for making this series possible and for loving my characters as much as I do! Traci Olsen, Katherine Teel, CJ Creel, and Elizabeth Harper—thanks for taking a chance on me and my vampires!

About the Author

Amber Belldene grew up on the Florida panhandle, swimming with alligators, climbing oak trees and diving for scallops…when she could pull herself away from a book. As a child, she hid her Nancy Drew novels inside the church bulletin and read mysteries during sermons — an irony that is not lost on her when she preaches these days.

With a B.A. in comparative religion and an M.A. in theology, Amber is a Christian minister and student of religion. She believes stories are the best way to explore human truths. Some people think it is strange for a minister to write romance, but it is perfectly natural to Amber. She believes the human desire for love is at the heart of every romance novel and God made people with that desire.

Amber is addicted to vampire stories, but loves to read all kinds of romance and literature. Her favorite books examine history and cultural origins, like Neal Stephenson's *Baroque Cycle*, Anita Diamant's *The Red Tent*, or Salman Rushdie's *The Satanic Verses*. And, yes, she was named after that Amber, of the classic romance novel *Forever Amber*.

From the wine country of Sonoma County to the foggy neighborhoods of San Francisco, all of Amber's fiction is set in Northern California, where she lives with her husband and two children.